"Fascinating history, interesting location, touching romance—Sarah Sundin packs it all in this page-turning story as she takes us *Through Waters Deep*. Readers are sure to enjoy living this stirring World War II era adventure with Sundin's characters."

—**Ann H. Gabhart**, author of *Love Comes Home* and *The Innocent*

"*Through Waters Deep* reeled me in from the start. Endearing characters combine with intrigue and mystery in a tale that begs to be read in record time. This thrilling splash into Sundin's new series is sure to keep readers hooked to the end."

—**Jocelyn Green**, award-winning author of the Heroines Behind the Lines Civil War series

"Open the cover to *Through Waters Deep* and step back to 1941 Boston in the days before the United States entered WWII. It's a story of sabotage, mystery, and sweet, heart-stopping romance. In this novel, Sarah Sundin demonstrates why she is a gifted novelist. The historical detail will transport lovers of historical fiction into the Naval Yards, a location ripe with sabotage and intrigue in the days leading to US entrance in the war. The characters are richly drawn and struggle with real-life issues. The supporting cast is fantastic and already has me longing to read the next installment. Bottom line—this book is perfect for lovers of WWII romances and mysteries that would give Nancy Drew a run for her money."

—**Cara Putman**, award-winning author of *Shadowed by Grace* and *Where Treetops Glisten*

★ WAVES *of* FREEDOM · 1 ★

THROUGH WATERS DEEP

A NOVEL

SARAH SUNDIN

Revell

a division of Baker Publishing Group
Grand Rapids, Michigan

Published by Revell
a division of Baker Publishing Group
P.O. Box 6287, Grand Rapids, MI 49516-6287
www.revellbooks.com

Printed in the United States of America

Library of Congress Cataloging-in-Publication Data
Sundin, Sarah.
    Through waters deep : a novel / Sarah Sundin.
        pages ; cm. — (Waves of freedom ; 1)
    ISBN 978-0-8007-2342-2 (softcover)
    1. Destroyers (Warships)—United States—History—20th century—Fiction.
  2. Criminal investigation—Fiction. 3. Sabotage—Fiction. I. Title.
  PS3619.U5626T48 2015
  813'.6—dc23   2015000435

This book is a work of fiction. Names, characters, places, and incidents are the product of the author's imagination or are used fictitiously.

Published in association with the Books & Such Literary Agency.

15   16   17   18   19   20   21   7   6   5   4   3   2   1

To our youngest son, Matthew,
my research buddy, bodyguard,
and enthusiastic reader.

1

On a platform by the bow of the USS *Ettinger*, Mary Stirling prepared supplies no one would notice unless they were missing.

While nautical pennants snapped in the sea breeze and the band played "Anchors Aweigh" for the ship-launching ceremony, Mary set down a box containing rags, a towel, a whisk broom, and a first aid kit. Then she nestled a bottle of champagne in a silver bucket.

Something crinkled. Odd.

Mary picked up the bottle in its decorative tin shield that prevented shattering. Yesterday, she'd tied red, white, and blue ribbon around the neck. Now the ribbon didn't lie flat, the bow was lopsided, and the foil around the cork seemed loose and wrinkled, as if someone had taken it off and replaced it.

Why? Scenarios zipped through her head, each more ludicrous than the one before. "Too much Nancy Drew in junior high," she muttered. And too many spy and saboteur stories in the press lately. With the United States clinging to

neutrality in the war in Europe, tensions between isolationists and interventionists had become sharper than the prow
of the *Ettinger*.

Mary stroked the sleek red hull of the new destroyer tow-
ering above her. "Into the wild Atlantic you go."

"That is a bad year."

Mary smiled at the French accent and faced her roommate
and co-worker at the Boston Navy Yard, Yvette Lafontaine.
"I doubt the *Ettinger* cares about the champagne's vintage."

"She should." Yvette narrowed her golden-brown eyes at
the ship, then lit up and grasped Mary's shoulders. "But you
look *très magnifique*."

Mary knew better than to argue. "Thank you for helping
me choose the hat. I love it." The shape flattered her face, and
the fawn color blended with her brown hair and the heavy
tweed coat she wore. It would also go well with her spring
coat—if winter ever ended.

Yvette fingered the puff of netting on the brim. "I still
prefer the red one."

"Not red."

"Sometimes a woman needs to . . . to accent, not match."
The glamorous brunette tapped Mary's nose. "You listen to
me. We French know fashion, wine, food, and love. Obviously we do not know war." Her voice lowered to a growl.

Mary puckered one corner of her mouth in sympathy.
Poor Yvette had been studying at Harvard when the Nazis
trampled her country in May and June of 1940. Almost a
year ago. Stranded in the States after graduation, Yvette took
a job at the Navy Yard.

"I'll see you at the apartment. I must find Henri and Solange." Yvette trotted down the steps.

"See you later." Mary spotted her boss, Barton Pennington, next to the platform. She leaned over the railing draped
with red, white, and blue bunting. "Mr. Pennington!"

He smiled up at her and folded his gloved hands over his broad belly. "Ah, Miss Stirling. All ready?"

"Yes, but . . ." She held up the champagne bottle. "The foil is loose and the ribbon is disturbed. It looks like someone tampered with it."

Mr. Pennington gave her the amused fatherly look he wore whenever she fussed over something trivial. "I'm sure it's nothing but rough handling."

"Very rough." She smoothed out the wrinkles and her worries and settled the bottle in its bucket.

"You've done a great job again. And look at all the people." Mr. Pennington gestured to the crowd. At least a hundred naval personnel and shipyard workers milled about.

Nausea seized Mary's belly. But why? None of the people looked at her. None of them had come to see her. She hadn't put herself on display. Yet logic and panic never listened to each other.

"I—I'm all done, Mr. Pennington." Mary gripped the banister and scurried down the stairs, each step quelling the nausea.

"I'll see you after the launching."

Mary waved over her shoulder and headed toward the back of the crowd to watch the ceremony. To one side, a cluster of shipyard workers praised President Roosevelt's newly signed Lend-Lease bill to send billions of dollars of aid to Britain. To the other side, another cluster of workers denounced the legislation as nothing but warmongering.

Although Mary certainly didn't want American boys to die in another European war, the images of bombed-out London wrenched her heart. The United States had to do something or Britain would fall.

A laugh filtered through the noise, a familiar male laugh, tickling at her memory.

Across a parting in the crowd, she saw two naval officers in navy blue overcoats and caps—"covers" in the naval jargon. One man had fair hair and one had dark.

The dark-haired officer had a friendly, open face, very much like Jim Avery from back home in Vermilion, Ohio. Except Jim was tall and scrawny, and this man was tall and . . . not scrawny.

Jim had attended the Naval Academy, and Mary hadn't seen him since high school. A lot could happen to a person in five years.

Mary inched closer, and with each step the officer looked more like Jim Avery, except he held himself straighter, with more assurance.

He laughed at something his friend said, and in a flash, Mary was sitting around a table at the soda fountain with her best friend Quintessa Beaumont, Quintessa's boyfriend Hugh Mackey, and Hugh's best friend, Jim. All of them enraptured by Quintessa's effervescence.

Jim's gaze drifted to her, and he gave her the mild smile men gave silver girls like Mary, without the spark reserved for golden girls like Quintessa.

Oh, why had she come over? How silly of her. She returned the mild smile and angled her path away.

But Jim peered at her and took a step in her direction. "Mary? Mary Stirling?"

He actually remembered her? "Jim Avery?"

With a grin, he strode forward and gripped her hand. "Well, I'll be. What are you doing in Boston?"

"I work here. Almost four years now." She gestured to the grand expanses of scaffolding. "I'm a secretary." No need to go into prideful detail.

"Isn't that swell?" In the icy sunshine, his eyes were clearly hazel.

Had Mary ever noticed that before? "I assume the Navy brought you to town?"

Jim beckoned to his companion. "Mary, this is my friend, Archer Vandenberg. Arch, this is Mary Stirling from Ohio. Arch and I went to the Academy together, and we've just been assigned to the *Atwood*."

"Oh yes." The Gleaves-class destroyer had been launched at the shipyard in December and had almost completed the fitting-out process before commissioning.

"A pleasure to meet you, Mary." Arch spoke with the measured tones of upper-crust New England, but the shine in his blue eyes said he didn't deem a Midwestern secretary beneath his acquaintance. "Four years in Boston, did you say?"

"Yes."

"Say . . ." Jim nudged his friend.

Arch crossed his arms and narrowed his eyes at Mary. "Yes, she'll do quite nicely."

She drew back. "Pardon?"

Jim laughed. "Never mind him. We were just talking about how we're new to town and wish we knew someone to show us around."

The thought of an excursion lifted her smile. "I could do that. I love exploring this city. So much history."

"Swell. I had visions of Jim and Gloria and I walking into the harbor while trying to navigate." Arch held up the launching program as if it were a map and squinted at it.

Jim dipped a partial bow. "And you'll save me from being the third wheel. Again."

What fun. Although Yvette was a dear friend, she socialized with French refugees, and Mary didn't speak French. "How about this Sunday? You could join me for church or meet me afterward."

"A real church with pews? That doesn't rock with the waves? Count us in." Jim pulled a pen from the breast pocket of his shirt. "Arch, you have something—"

"I have a notepad." Mary always did. She wrote down the church's address and sketched a map.

The band stopped playing. Mary passed Jim the slip of paper and turned to watch the ceremony under a bright blue sky. If only the temperature hadn't dipped to sixteen degrees, one detail Mary couldn't control.

The *Ettinger* filled her sight, sleek as an arrow, 348 feet in length and 36 feet across at the beam. Above her red hull, everything was painted gray. A string of colorful pennants swooped from her prow up to her mast and down to her stern.

Mary pressed up on her toes. What a joy to watch ceremonies as keels were laid down and ships were launched. Thank goodness her grandfather and Mr. Pennington had become fast friends in school.

The dignitaries climbed onto the platform. Then the band played the national anthem, while Mary pressed her hand over her heart and Jim and Arch stood at attention and saluted.

After the anthem, Mr. Pennington approached the microphone and thanked a list of people. He adjusted his glasses. "Today I realized I've been remiss. Never once at a launching have I thanked the person who works behind the scenes, making sure every little detail is in place, from the programs in your hands to the supplies at my feet."

Mary's breath rushed in and turned to bile. He wouldn't. No, he wouldn't. She eased behind Jim, behind the shield of his navy blue back.

"That person is my lovely secretary, Miss Mary Stirling. Miss Stirling, would you please join me on stage?"

No, no, no. She pressed her hand over her stomach, willing it to settle. Why hadn't she made some mistake, forgotten some detail, missed some deadline?

"Mary? What's the matter?" Jim looked over his shoulder at her, the visor of his cap hiding his expression.

"I can't. I just can't."

Silence. Then he nodded and faced the stage. His shoulders stretched even broader. "I haven't seen Mary, have you, Arch? Not a sign of her."

"Who? Never heard of the girl."

Mary took slow, even breaths, grateful for her inconspicuous hair and hat and coat, for Jim's height and protection and whatever miraculous physical fitness they taught at Annapolis.

"Miss Stirling?" Mr. Pennington called over the buzz of the crowd. "Well, she must be hard at work. Let's get on with the launching."

Mary peeked around Jim's shoulder as Mr. Pennington introduced Massachusetts state senator Ralston Fuller and his wife, Dorothy, the *Ettinger*'s sponsor. The mahogany fur on Mrs. Fuller's coat danced in the breeze.

Senator Fuller gave a speech, the chaplain intoned the "Prayer for Our Navy," and the commandant, Rear Adm. William Tarrant, presented the bottle of champagne to Mrs. Fuller.

She held the bottle aloft. "In the name of the United States, I christen thee *Ettinger*. May God bless her and all that sail in her." She smashed the bottle over the hull, and the crowd erupted in applause.

The destroyer slipped down the ways and into Boston Harbor, sending giant roaring wings of water arcing on each side.

Mary's delight flowed out in her sigh, forming white curlicues in the frosty air.

Up on the stage, Mrs. Fuller yelped, jumped back, and swatted at her coat.

Chuckles swept the crowd.

"Must have gotten champagne on that fancy fur coat," Jim said.

But everyone on stage stepped back, staring at the champagne spill. "Put out your cigarettes!" someone shouted.

The men flung down their cigarettes, stomped on them.

What was going on? Mary stepped out from behind Jim.

Senator Fuller dropped his cigar, and tiny orange flames flickered around it. Mrs. Fuller screamed. Mr. Pennington tossed down Mary's rags and smothered the flames.

A murmur started at the stage and rolled out through the audience. "Gasoline."

The word slammed into Mary's chest. "The bottle."

"The bottle?" Jim frowned at her.

"The champagne bottle. I knew something was wrong. The foil was loose. Thank goodness no one was hurt."

"You think someone . . ."

"Poured out the champagne and put in gasoline. Then replaced the cork and the foil."

"But who? Why?"

"I don't know, but I'm going to find out." She almost smiled at the intrigued look on Jim's face. "Excuse me, but I think the police will want to talk to me."

"I'll see you Sunday." Jim winked at her. "Unless you're in jail."

"I won't be." Her fingerprints on the bottle would be expected, and since she'd called Mr. Pennington's attention to the tampering, she wouldn't be considered a suspect.

As she worked her way through the crowd to the stage, her Nancy Drew theories seemed more and more plausible.

She'd discounted her instincts, but she was right. If only she'd pressed Mr. Pennington further and investigated more.

Who would do such a thing? And why?

Did a political rival want to harm Senator Fuller or his wife? Did someone hope to keep the *Ettinger* off the seas? Did someone want to discredit the Boston Navy Yard? Was it a saboteur?

A thrill tingled up her spine. Not only did she have an excursion to anticipate, but she had her very own mystery.

2

Boston
Sunday, March 23, 1941

Jim pressed his hand to the doorjamb and inhaled the smoky scent of old wood as he left Paul Revere's house. In 1775 the hero might have touched this same spot on the night he rode into history. He gazed up the muddy gray clapboard wall to the overhanging second story. "'Listen, my children, and you shall hear of the midnight ride of Paul Revere.' I can't believe I'm in his house."

"Not anymore, you aren't." Arch Vandenberg draped his arm over Gloria Washburn's shoulder and sent Jim a droll look. No matter how hard Arch tried to act middle class, he couldn't shed the upper-class affectation of boredom.

"Isn't Boston the most fascinating city?" Mary tipped back her head and turned in a circle, her spring coat rippling around her legs. Nice legs.

Nice legs wouldn't turn her into the bubbly blonde type of girl Jim preferred. Just as well. Since the *Atwood* would ship out soon, Jim didn't want the complication of a romance.

"I thought we'd see even more history this week." He gave

15

her his best attempt at an evil grin. "The hanging of a young secretary on Boston Common for sabotage."

She laughed and headed north up the hill, past a triangular plaza. "Thank goodness, no. They questioned me for about ten minutes and sent me on my way. According to the newspapers, the police are fixated on the senator. They think a political rival or his jealous lover wanted to harm him or his wife."

A note of doubt in her voice led him to quicken his step and catch up. "You don't agree?"

"I don't know." Light blue eyes narrowed. "The papers are drawn to the sensational, of course, but with all the division in the country right now, all the intrigue, I hope they look into it thoroughly. Hundreds of shipyard workers had access to that bottle."

The last person Jim wanted working on his ship was a man inflamed by politics. He hopped off the sidewalk and crossed the cobblestone road. The hearty smell of tomatoes and garlic from the Italian restaurants made his mouth water. A plate of spaghetti and meatballs sounded good, even with the lobster roll he'd had for lunch still cozied up in his stomach. Boston agreed with him.

"Jim," Arch called from behind. "I thought you said Mary was quiet."

"I did. I've heard more words from Mary Stirling's mouth today than all through high school."

She lowered her head and tucked brown hair behind her ear, revealing a smile. "I can talk when something interests me."

"You can sing too."

Her gaze jerked up to him. "Sing?"

If he knew her better, he'd give her a playful nudge. "We shared a hymnal this morning, remember? You sing well. You should join the choir."

"Heavens, no." Alarm flashed across her face, same as when her boss called her onto the platform at the launching the other day.

"Stage fright?"

Ripples crossed her forehead. "I don't like to call attention to myself. Besides, there are so many hams in this world. Let them have the stage."

"Looks like your choir actually needs more sopranos." His church in Ohio teemed with the songbirds.

"They sound lovely as is. Did you like the service? The sermon?"

"Very much." Jim stepped behind Mary to let an elderly lady pass. "Your pastor is a great speaker. Dr. Ock—?"

"Ockenga. Harold Ockenga. I visited Park Street Church when I first arrived in Boston. If I was going to live in a historic city, I might as well attend a historic church. But his preaching! Well, it's wonderful. Every week I'm both inspired and challenged. Isn't that a perfect combination?"

"Sure is." Jim smiled at her delighted expression. In high school, Mary had been the invisible sidekick. Although he'd known her for years, in a way, he didn't know her at all.

"And your family?" Mary turned left on another road, also lined with red brick buildings with white window frames. "How are they? I'm so fond of your mother. She was my favorite Sunday school teacher."

"She's still teaching those Bible stories, and Dad's still building sailboats on the shores of Lake Erie."

"And your brothers? They're in the Navy too, aren't they?" Mary turned right, onto a broader street.

"Ed and Charlie are still in high school, but my older brothers are Navy men. Dan's on a cruiser in the Atlantic, and Rob's based in San Diego." Jim twisted his gold Academy ring, thankful for his brothers' outstanding records and content to float in their wake.

"And the twins? How are they?"

Jim's fingers tightened, and he massaged the scar tissue on his palms. "Lillian's ready to graduate from pharmacy school in June. Ohio State. Nothing can stop her."

"No, it can't." Mary tilted her head in a thoughtful way and watched Jim's hands. "They were a year behind me in school, so I didn't know them well, but I always admired Lillian's tenacity, especially since . . ."

Since she only had one foot. Jim winced, tugged his jacket straight, and put on a smile. "She's a spitfire. She and Lucy might look identical, but—"

"But they couldn't be more different. I heard Lucy married."

"She did. Martin Freeman, right out of high school."

"I remember Martin. Everyone liked him." Mary spread her hands wide toward a park across the road. "Here we are."

Jim peered down a long walkway lined with trees. A statue of a man on horseback led the way to a brick church with a tall white steeple. He grinned. "Old North Church?"

"'One, if by land, and two, if by sea.'"

Jim whooped and jogged across the street. He'd always loved the story of Paul Revere, galloping at night, evading British patrols, alerting the people of Lexington before he was arrested on the road to Concord.

He came to a stop at the foot of the statue. Paul Revere, in his tricorn hat, shouting out his warning from his steed.

"The statue was dedicated last year," Mary said behind him.

"Then I'm glad I came this year."

"Jim Avery certainly enjoys his tourist attractions." Arch led Gloria to the statue. "You should have seen him in New York City."

The cool blonde let out a low laugh. "You're just jealous,

Arch. Deep inside, you want to run around like a little boy too."

"Only if I'm running after you, darling."

That must have been the right response, because Gloria nuzzled up to Arch's shoulder.

Jim leaned closer to Mary and spoke in a stage whisper. "I'm glad you're in town, so I don't have to be alone with this lovey-dovey nonsense."

He led Mary down the mall toward a fountain, leaving the lovebirds cooing to each other by the statue.

"The British are coming! The British are coming!" Raucous voices sounded up ahead. Three young men approached, laughing and jostling each other.

Jim stood taller and scooted closer to Mary.

"Those lousy Brits are still coming." One of the men spat to the side. "Coming to drag us into another war."

Jim and Arch had been warned that isolationist sentiments ran high in Boston, and that wearing civilian clothes might be wise. But Jim was too proud of the smart dress blues he'd longed to wear all his life.

"Say, what do we have here?" The burliest of the men locked gazes with Jim. "A tea-drinking Brit-lover, that's what."

Jim's breath stilled. Not only would it be wrong for an officer to have a confrontation with a local, but he didn't want to make any waves. Someone was sure to get hurt, especially since Jim and Arch had excelled at boxing at the Academy. The only good course was to sweep away on the current.

Jim put his hand on the small of Mary's back and guided her toward the church. "Excuse us, please. We're just taking a Sunday stroll."

The brute stepped right into his path, eye to eye with Jim, a grungy brown cap low on his thick forehead. "Why don't you stroll on over—"

"Ralph Tucker?" That was Mary. Speaking in a pleasant voice, as if she'd run into her oldest friend.

Tucker blinked and glanced at the brunette. "Miss—Miss Stirling?"

"I assure you the ensign had a good American cup of coffee with his lunch, strong and black."

Bushy eyebrows disappeared beneath that ratty cap. "Yes, miss. No offense meant."

"None taken." Jim gave him half a smile, half more than he deserved.

The men skedaddled in the other direction.

Jim pretended to wipe his forehead. "Well, Arch. Thank goodness we brought along Mary as our bodyguard."

"Speak for yourself." Arch's eyes glowed with blue fire. "I've always wanted to get into a good honest fight."

Jim motioned toward the three men who'd show him a good fight, all right. "Be my guest."

Gloria tugged on Arch's arm. "Don't be silly. I like your face as is, with two eyes and a nose and a mouth in their customary positions. Let's keep it that way."

"Besides, Jim needs to find a spot of tea."

A joke from Mary Stirling? He followed her toward the Old North Church. "Isn't it illegal to drink tea in Boston? Don't they throw you into the harbor for that?"

"Only during parties."

Jim smiled, nodded, and tucked his hands into his trouser pockets. She'd make a fine companion while he was based here.

He drew next to her. "So those three fine specimens of manhood—"

"Work at the Navy Yard."

"Please don't tell me they worked on the *Atwood*."

"They did."

Jim groaned. "Poor ship will fall apart at the seams."

Mary laughed. "Don't worry. The men are full of hot air, but they're excellent at their work. And they enjoy their paychecks. Have you been on board yet?"

"Tomorrow. Can't wait." His feet twitched, threatening to add an ungentlemanly skip to his step. "An assignment to a destroyer is the best thing for an officer."

"Oh? I'd think you'd want to be on one of the big ships—a battleship or a cruiser."

"Nope." The trees on either side marked a straight path before him. "Almost all the great modern-day officers served on destroyers. 'Tin cans' are special, small, close-knit. With only two hundred men, you have to work together. The commanders train you in all departments, from gunnery to engineering to communication, so any man can step in where needed."

"That makes sense."

"And destroyers are scrappy little ships."

"I see. And that makes a strapping good officer."

"I hope so." The Navy had plotted an excellent course for him, and he couldn't wait to see which career they'd point him to.

"Well, the Boston Navy Yard is known for its destroyers. You'll love the *Atwood*."

Jim smiled down at the familiar, unfamiliar face. "You know, this might be the longest conversation you and I have ever had."

"I'm sure of it." Mary's eyes sparkled. "With Quintessa around, how could we have gotten a word in edgewise?"

His chest contracted. He hadn't spoken or heard that name in years, yet it never left his thoughts. He forced a light smile. "True."

"I never minded. I could enjoy fun evenings out without being responsible for conversation. And Hugh and Quintessa were so entertaining."

The sound of his former best friend's name hurt even more, but it was his turn to respond. "Are you—still in contact?" The question scraped on his throat.

"Oh yes. She's my dearest friend in the world, and we write every week. She's in Chicago now. It was best for her to leave town after . . ." Her voice petered out.

After Hugh cheated on Quintessa while she was away at college, got the other girl pregnant, and married her. "Still can't believe he did such a thing."

"Of course not. You're an honorable man. All those years you pined over Quintessa, but you never—"

"What?" He stopped beside a basswood tree, the fountain behind him tinkling like Quintessa's laughter. "She was Hugh's girl. I'd never—"

"I know." Mary gave him a compassionate look that saw right through him. "We knew you'd never interfere. You're not that kind of man. But we also knew you were crazy about her."

Jim's mouth tightened, and he marched toward the brick church building. "I was a fool."

"Nonsense. We were all dazzled by her."

He still was. "Main reason I haven't gone home much since I graduated. It wasn't right, being crazy over another man's girl. I needed to break free."

"Me too, in a way."

"How's that?" He faced her.

Mary reached up to a low-hanging branch still waiting for its leaves. "I was content living in her shadow. No one paid attention to me, and I liked that. But my parents said I needed to step out and find out who I was and what I could do, and my grandfather found me this job with his old friend."

"Did it work?"

"I think so. I love my job. I'm using my talents for a good

purpose." She smiled and fluttered the bare branch in front of her face like a fan. "And I can still hide in obscurity."

Jim laughed. After his time in the Academy, with everyone angling to get noticed, to be liked, to get ahead, Mary's attitude was refreshingly foreign.

3

Friday, March 28, 1941

Mary curled up in her armchair in the bay window of her apartment, sipped her morning cup of unpatriotic tea, and tucked her bathrobe around her slippered feet. If she nudged aside the lace curtains and tilted her head, she could gaze up Charlestown's Monument Avenue to the Bunker Hill Monument.

What more could she say in her letter to Quintessa? The poor dear was lonely in Chicago and still reeling from heartbreak. Almost two years had passed since Hugh's betrayal, but they had dated close to five years, waiting for Quintessa to graduate from college.

Except Hugh couldn't wait.

After all Quintessa had done for her, all the years of deep friendship, Mary longed to do something to ease her pain.

All she could offer was a cheerful letter. She traced her handwriting on the stationery. Her news about seeing Jim Avery would pique Quintessa's interest, as would the mystery at the shipyard. How many hours had the girls spent huddled over Nancy Drew books in junior high, sharing good-natured arguments about who would make the better detective—Quintessa with her confidence and ability to talk to anyone, or Mary with her analytical ways and ability to listen? In reality, they worked best as a team.

Mary tapped her pen on her stationery. One more paragraph.

She glanced up to the sailboat painting over the radiator for inspiration. She'd bought it to honor her New England home, for the peaceful blues and the zip of red on the lighthouse in the background. The boat leaned into the waves, its sails plumped with wind, and spray leaped behind it. Although she liked her life quiet and orderly, the sense of exhilaration and boldness spoke to her.

"Why is that, little boat?" she said.

"You must not talk to yourself." Yvette Lafontaine stumbled in from her bedroom, her brown hair tousled and bathrobe askew. Mornings were the only time she didn't look glamorous.

"You talk plenty to yourself when you're fully awake, *ma petite amie*," Mary cooed to her in her best French accent.

Yvette fumbled with the coffee percolator. "Your French is horrible, but that is fine. You have other charms."

Ah yes, her charms. Mary arched one eyebrow. People complimented her clever mind, her kindness, and her quiet ways. If only men found such things enchanting.

★ ★ ★

Mary shifted her notebook and clipboard, straightened the jacket of her dove gray suit, and turned into the drafting room. She loved this part of her job, visiting the various departments and collecting reports for Mr. Pennington.

Rows of drafting tables filled the room, with draftsmen hard at work crafting plans into blueprints. Mary poked her head into the naval architect's office. "Mr. Winslow?"

He coughed, pressed something between his lips, and drank some coffee. "Miss Stirling. You're early."

"Sorry to startle you." Never before had she seen the man flustered.

Mr. Winslow stood to greet her, his slight build wrapped in an expensive suit, his brown hair sleekly styled, his every move full of the patrician elegance expected of the heir to the Winslow Shipbuilding Company fortune. Even though he'd forsaken it to work at the Boston Navy Yard. "Good morning, Miss Stirling. How are you today?"

"Fine, thank you." She shook his manicured hand, feeling large and clumsy.

"I have your weekly reports." He swept them from his desk and handed them to her. "By the way, have you seen Mr. O'Donnell? I have a project for him. If the man spent as much time on his work as he did on his confounded politics . . ."

"If I see him, I'll tell him you're looking for him." She made a note in her notebook.

"Thank you." Mr. Winslow returned to his desk.

Not the best time to ask her usual questions about his wife and little boys. Perhaps the architect was flustered because of all the bad news from London, his wife's childhood home.

Mary headed outside under the graying sky and shivered. She should have brought her coat. Spring hadn't quite arrived. Oh well. Her rounds wouldn't take more than an hour.

She quickened her pace toward the docks, past all the men hard at work. When she'd started working at the Boston Navy Yard in 1937 at the height of the Depression, men lined up outside the gate looking for sparse work. Now with the Navy building destroyers to replace those they'd traded to Britain, the shipyard bustled with activity.

At Dry Dock Two, she crossed the gangplank to a destroyer under construction. While the Navy Yard built some ships on traditional shipways and launched them down the ways into the harbor, they built some ships deep in the dry dock, then flooded the dry dock to float the ships for launching.

This destroyer's keel had been laid, then the bulkheads set in place, dividing the ship into compartments. Then equipment was lowered into position and decks placed on top like lids. This destroyer had its first layer of decking.

Mary worked her way down the ladder.

"Let me help you, Miss Stirling." A work-roughened hand reached up to her.

"Thank you." She took Ira Kaplan's hand, hopped to the steel deck, and smiled at the scaler. "Have you seen Mr. Fiske?"

The young man took off his cap, ran his hand through black curls, and jutted his angular chin toward the stern of the ship. "I saw him over there a few minutes ago, talking to Bauer. Glad of it. Need to keep an eye on that Kraut. Everyone knows he's trouble."

Sharp opinions ruled at the shipyard, but Mary stayed above the fray. "Thank you for your help." She picked her way over cables, lines, and tools.

Since Heinrich Bauer had emigrated from Germany only four years earlier, he prompted many rumors. Mary angled herself into the welder's line of sight. "Excuse me, Mr. Bauer?"

He raised the leather welding mask that protected his face from sparks. "Yes?"

"I'm looking for Mr. Fiske. Have you seen him?"

"Over there," he said in a heavy German accent and pointed to starboard.

Although she'd worked with him for almost four years, she knew nothing about him. "How are you doing?"

He lifted suspicious blue eyes to her. "Fine."

She smiled and fingered the edge of her clipboard. "How's your family? Do you have a wife? Children?"

Those eyes hardened to blue marbles. "Why do you ask?"

Mary gestured around the shipyard. "I like to know the people I work with."

"Good for you." Mr. Bauer snapped down his welding mask. "Please stand back. You don't want to get hurt."

Mary blinked and backed up. Oh my, he was prickly. But then if everyone distrusted her because of her accent, she might be prickly too.

Over to starboard, Frank Fiske wrote on a clipboard. Stocky and middle-aged, with graying blond hair, the leadingman ran this crew well.

"Good morning, Mr. Fiske."

"Right on schedule." Fiske scribbled his signature and handed her the form.

Mary tucked it away. "How's your son? Any new letters?"

The leadingman's broad brow wrinkled. "Hates Army life. He'll be out in November unless Roosevelt has his way and gets us into a shooting war by then."

Mary murmured her sympathy. It wasn't her job to argue one side or the other.

He crossed his beefy arms and cracked a grin. "You had a chat with the police, I heard."

She laughed and flapped her hand. "It was nothing. The bottle had been unattended for some time. Anyone could have tampered with it. Since I noticed something was wrong and alerted Mr. Pennington, they didn't suspect me."

"Who's the suspect? Do you know?"

"Only what I read in the papers."

"They're idiots. A jealous lover?"

Mary scanned the ship—dozens of workmen, stuttering rivet guns, and whining machinery. If anyone was dangerous, Frank Fiske would know. "Do you think it was someone here?"

He ran his finger across his upper lip. "All I know is this

28

war's behind it. The men say there's a saboteur. Talk about seeing people where they don't belong, tools out of place. Something's going on."

Goose bumps rose under the sleeves of Mary's suit jacket. Out in the harbor, the *Atwood* floated under the gray clouds, awaiting her commission. Jim would be aboard with his congenial smile and easy laugh. People had a right to protest but not to harm good men.

"Keep your eyes open, Miss Stirling," Mr. Fiske said, his voice somber.

"I will."

"Hey, Fiske." George O'Donnell lumbered over, a few years older than Fiske and many pounds heavier. "Here's the blueprint."

"Thanks." Fiske took the rolled-up document.

"Oh, Mr. O'Donnell," Mary said. "Mr. Winslow's looking for you."

He pulled a tin of chewing tobacco from his pocket and stuck a wad in his mouth. "I'm sure he is."

Fiske unrolled the blueprint on a crate. "Don't envy you working with that fop."

"He loves England so much, why doesn't he go fight for them, leave us alone?"

"I doubt he could lift a gun, much less fire it." Fiske looked at Mary over his shoulder. "Sorry 'bout that. Forgot there's a woman present."

"That's all right." It happened to her a lot, but she didn't mind. People said things around her they might ordinarily hold back. Mr. Pennington called her his little spy.

Ira Kaplan strolled over and set down a coiled hose. "Say, Mr. Fiske, glad to see you're keeping an eye on Bauer. The man's shifty, up to no good."

O'Donnell chuckled. "You'd like that, wouldn't you?"

"Like what?" Kaplan straightened to his full, lanky height.

"Like us to have some German saboteur here, just like in those warmongering Hollywood movies you Jews keep churning out. Then everyone would catch your war fever."

Mary eased back, heart pounding.

"Yeah?" Kaplan jabbed his finger at O'Donnell. "Maybe they should. If Hitler knocks out Britain, where do you think he'll come next?"

O'Donnell scrunched up his thick face. "Over here? Over thousands of miles of ocean? You're crazy."

"Hitler's got friends in South America. Don't you know anything? You're crazy if—"

Mary sent Frank Fiske a pleading glance, but he was already stepping forward, setting one big hand on each man's shoulder.

O'Donnell shook his finger in Kaplan's face. "Shame on you. I'm old enough to be your father."

"Then you're old enough to know better."

"Stop it, men," Fiske said.

"You're right, I'm old enough." O'Donnell glared from under iron-gray brows. "Old enough to remember how the Brits bamboozled us into the last war."

"That's enough, George." Fiske tightened his grip on the draftsman's shoulder.

"All right, Frank. All right." O'Donnell held up both hands and stepped back.

"Back to work, Kaplan." Fiske's voice rang with authority.

"Yes, sir." The young man walked away, flexing his hands open and shut.

Mary's heart rate settled down, and she continued on her way, climbed the ladder, and strolled down to the next dock.

Her brand-new notebook beckoned her, and she opened its crisp pages. On the top of one page, she wrote "Heinrich Bauer" in shorthand, then divided the page into two columns. On the left, she wrote all he'd said, which wasn't much. On the right, she recorded what others had said about him.

Then she flipped the page and repeated the process for Ira Kaplan and George O'Donnell.

Maybe she *had* read too much Nancy Drew. She couldn't do anything with this information. Everything she'd recorded could be discounted as rumor and gossip.

Besides, showing it to someone and seeking praise would be prideful. Her favorite verse, Philippians 2:3, said, "Let nothing be done through strife or vainglory; but in lowliness of mind let each esteem other better than themselves."

She'd learned the importance of humility the hard way.

Yet something deep in her belly solidified. A record needed to be kept, and who better to take notes than an invisible secretary?

4

On the fantail of the *Atwood*, lined up with his eight fellow officers for the commissioning ceremony, Jim had never felt taller. Although 199 men in dress blues crowded the deck, the only sounds were the pennants flapping in the breeze and the voice of Rear Adm. William Tarrant, commandant of the Boston Navy Yard, as he read a speech.

This was why Jim had joined the Navy—the tradition, the camaraderie, the sea. He'd enjoyed his service on the battleship USS *Texas*, but being a "plank owner," one of the crew at a ship's commissioning, was a great privilege.

So was serving with Lt. Cdr. Calvin Durant, the *Atwood*'s commanding officer. Jim's older brothers had both sailed with the captain and spoke highly of him. An admiral-maker, Dan called him. Jim didn't share Dan's and Rob's lofty ambition, but he certainly didn't mind floating behind them.

Admiral Tarrant said, "In accordance with this authority, I hereby place the United States ship *Atwood* in commission. Hoist colors."

The band on the pier played the national anthem.

Behind Jim at the stern, a sailor would be raising the

American flag, while at the bow another sailor would be raising the union jack with its white stars on a dark blue background. In his line of sight, a sailor ran the *Atwood*'s commissioning pennant up her mast. Now she was an official ship in the United States Navy, ready to protect American shores.

Jim glanced at the empty platforms for the 5-inch gun mounts. Well, she'd be ready once they finished fitting her out.

After the ceremony, Jim headed down to the wardroom for dinner with the other officers. Since Durant had just arrived in Boston the day before, this would be the first official gathering.

Jim took his seat toward the foot of the table with Arch and the other junior officers, while Durant sat at the head.

Tall and trim, with receding sandy hair fading to gray over the temples, the commanding officer leaned back in his chair and scanned the men at the table. "Tell me about yourselves."

Jim chuckled at the confused looks on the other officers' faces. He'd been warned about Durant's abrupt questions and commands.

Durant leaned his forearms on the table. "Yes, tell me about yourselves. Who you are and where you're from and why you're in the Navy. I expect you to do the same with those under your command. Respect them as men, and they'll respect you as an officer."

Only the formality of the wardroom restrained Jim's grin. As Dan and Rob said—a commander who ran a tight ship but didn't lord it over his subordinates.

As the introductions circled the table, Jim assessed the officers and their personalities. A fine group of men. He'd like working with them.

"And our ensigns." Durant gestured toward the foot of the table, at the man across from Jim.

"Mitch Hadley, sir." The ensign directed his dark-eyed gaze around the group. "Grew up in St. Louis. Big family. Hard life."

Jim smiled at Hadley, whom he recognized from the Academy class before his.

Hadley didn't smile back but jutted out a heavy jaw. "Unlike some people, I didn't grow up with privileges, had to work hard for everything."

Jim and Arch exchanged a glance. That comment was obviously meant for them.

"Always glad to have a hardworking young man on board," Durant said. "What are your goals?"

"Command, sir. I'm here to learn everything I can about the ship and about leading men. And there's no one I'd rather learn from."

Durant looked down at his place setting, one side of his mouth twisted to the side.

Jim made a mental note. Flattery didn't impress the captain, not that Jim ever resorted to flattery.

"And you?" Durant addressed Arch.

"Arch Vandenberg, sir. I'm from Connecticut, an only child, and I've always loved the sea." The sparkle in his sea-blue eyes confirmed his words.

Jim bit back a smile at what Arch didn't mention—the family estate, the trust fund, the yacht.

"As for my goals . . ." Arch sent half a grin to Hadley. "I've always dreamed of command too. You have competition."

"Friendly competition only, boys." A growl rumbled in Durant's throat, but then he turned a warm gaze to Jim. "And Mr. Avery. I barely need an introduction. I know your brothers well."

Hadley let out a quiet snort.

Jim ignored it and rested his clasped hands on the table. "Thank you, sir. I'm proud to be their brother." Arch's privilege came from wealth, but Jim's came from connection—his maternal grandfather who had served in the House of Representatives and two older brothers who had elevated the Avery name in the Navy.

Lt. Vince Banning, the executive officer, crossed his arms. "The captain might not need an introduction, but the rest of us do."

"Of course, sir. I'm Jim Avery, from the small town of Vermilion, Ohio, on Lake Erie. My dad builds fishing boats and yachts, so I grew up on the water. And I'm the third of seven children." Maybe the reference to his big family would soften up Hadley.

Durant's lean face creased in a grin. "And your goals?"

"Wherever the Navy wants to use me."

The creases flattened. "Explain."

Jim shrugged. "I float. As long as I can work with people, I'm happy."

"You . . . you float?" Now the creases migrated to the captain's forehead.

"I'm easygoing. I go wherever the wind takes me." So far he'd managed to float to the top of his high school class, into the Naval Academy, and right onto this destroyer. And for Jim, floating was a far safer policy than pushing into the wind. That's how people got hurt.

Durant leaned back in his chair and folded his hands over his stomach. "Every sailor knows if you let the wind direct you, at some point you end up on the rocks."

Instead of showing his commander he'd be easy to work with, Jim had made himself sound lazy. "Don't worry, sir. I'm a hard worker."

"He sure is," Arch said. "Near the top of his class at the Academy."

"Right behind Arch." Jim flicked his friend a grateful look.

35

"Only because you tutored me in calculus."

"If I'd known . . ." Jim shook his head in mock self-reproach.

Durant didn't reply but motioned in the stewards with the meal.

Air ballooned in Jim's cheeks. That hadn't gone well, but it wouldn't take long to win over the captain.

After dinner, Jim headed up to the deck with Arch. To starboard, the setting sun silhouetted Boston's skyline, with the Custom House standing tall above all else. To port, the lights were flickering out at the Navy Yard.

At the bow of the *Atwood*, Jim gazed down the narrow length of his ship. Couldn't wait to set out and see what she could do.

"I suppose she's done working for the day," Arch said.

"Who?" Jim followed his friend's gaze to the Navy Yard. "Mary?"

"Yeah. Nice girl. Pretty too."

A sour taste filled Jim's mouth. "Don't let Gloria hear you talk that way."

Arch whapped him in the arm. "You numbskull. I'm talking about you. She'd be good for you."

"Mary?" Jim strolled down the starboard side of the destroyer, away from the Navy Yard. "Sure, she's pretty, but you know I prefer bubbly blondes. Always have."

"Because of . . . what's her name?" Arch snapped his fingers. "The girl back home with the strange name."

Jim's shoulders went taut. It wasn't a strange name at all. The most beautiful name he'd ever heard. "Yes, her."

"You always date the same type of girl, but no relationship you've had lasts more than a month or two."

Jim skirted the platform for the number two 5-inch gun. "So?"

"So maybe there's a reason."

The reason was clear—no one held a candle to Quintessa Beaumont.

Arch stepped over a coiled line. "Maybe you should pursue a quiet brunette instead."

High above, the superstructure for the bridge climbed into the darkening sky—the pilothouse, the signal deck, and the gun director, all stacked in order. As assistant gunnery officer, Jim would spend most of his time caged in the gun director. "I'm not going to pursue anyone right now, not when we're shipping out soon."

"Well then, spare me any more double dates. All those bubbles make me dizzy."

On the far side of the superstructure, Charlestown came into view again. "Mary seems to like our evenings on the town. As long as the poor thing can put up with you and me, you'll get a reprieve."

Arch's breath huffed out into the cool evening air. "Poor thing indeed."

5

Saturday, April 19, 1941

Mary stepped out of the movie theater into the teeming Saturday night crowd on Washington Street. Neon lights flashed on marquees offering films that intrigued her—*The Lady Eve . . . Western Union . . . Road to Zanzibar . . . That Night in Rio*. Anything had to be better than *Flying Wild*.

Gloria adjusted her gloves. "That was a waste of a dime."

"Four dimes, you mean. Thanks, Jim." Arch punched his friend in the shoulder.

Jim bumped into Mary. "Hey, I did it for Mary. I thought she'd like the sabotage theme."

She laughed. "Oh, don't blame me. I didn't have a vote."

A rainbow of neon lights reflected in Jim's eyes. "Come on. I know it made you think."

"Definitely." She followed Arch and Gloria down Washington Street. "It made me think I would have preferred that." She pointed to a poster for *The Monster and the Girl*, showing a gorilla-like creature carrying an unconscious damsel in his arms.

"Next week then."

"Maybe I'll stay home." She tried for a mysterious smile.

"Ah, you wouldn't leave me alone with the lovebirds, would you?"

"I suppose not." How could she? For the past several weeks, every Saturday evening Jim loped up the steps of her building and asked her out to nightclubs and movies and restaurant dinners. Not only did she get to go out on the town, but she enjoyed such pleasant company. Even if it was only pleasant and never romantic.

What did she expect? A man who'd doted on vivacious Quintessa would never fall for her.

That pleasant young man hailed a cab. "Come on. Admit it."

Mary's cheeks tingled. He couldn't have known what she was thinking. "Admit what?"

"The sabotage plot. It made you think." He held open the door of the taxi.

A relieved laugh spilled out. "All right, it did." She climbed into the backseat, squished in the middle with Gloria, between the two officers.

Jim draped his arm across the seat back behind her—not touching her—just to make room. "Are they still talking sabotage at the Yard?"

"Constantly." She swung her mind from Jim's warm strength pressed up to her side and onto the situation at work. "The champagne incident shook everyone up. They see sabotage everywhere. They see people and tools where they don't belong. Everyone's suspicious."

"Sounds like mass hysteria." Gloria raised one brow.

"That's what my boss thinks."

"What do you think?" Arch said.

With all three sets of eyes trained on her, Mary forced herself to breathe evenly. But she wasn't talking about herself, only about the situation. "I'm trying to sort it out. What if something is truly going on?"

Gloria flapped her gloved hand. "I hope you haven't been listening to that interventionist propaganda."

Arch barked out a laugh. "Since when have you become an isolationist? Have you been listening to Charles Lindbergh and Father Coughlin behind my back?"

"Nonsense. That's propaganda too. All I know is I don't want us to go to war. I don't want you to leave me."

Arch murmured in his girlfriend's ear.

"This is why I need you around, Mary," Jim said.

"I'm glad I can help." Her breath hitched. With his arm curved behind her and his face so close in the darkened car, how could she think straight?

"So, you say you're sorting it out. What have you been up to? Taking the suspects downtown and grilling them under a solitary lightbulb?"

She smiled. "They cower under my interrogation."

"Who wouldn't?"

Behind Jim, lights and buildings flashed past. "I'm a secretary. I take notes."

"Notes?"

She hadn't told anyone about her rapidly filling notebook, but discussing it with friends would be all right as long as she didn't seek praise. "I record what people say. Separate pages for each person, noting what they say and what was said about them. The workers are used to me taking notes anyway. I'm sure it sounds silly."

"No, it sounds useful." Jim shifted in his seat. "What if something happens at the Navy Yard? Then you have all that information."

An image flew through her mind—an FBI agent flipping through her notebook, stabbing his finger at the page—"That's him! Why didn't I think of it?" Then they'd arrest the guilty party and hold a press conference and drag Mary to the podium . . .

She shuddered and shut off the movie in her mind. "I hope it never comes to that."

"I hope so too. But I'm sure they're doing their own investigation."

"They are, but the men don't talk to the agents like they talk to me."

"What do you mean?"

Mary fiddled with the supple leather of her cream-colored handbag. "I'm quiet, so people open up to me and know I won't blab. And—well, I tend to fade into the background and people forget I'm there, so they speak in an unguarded way."

Jim fell silent. Perhaps he'd forgotten her presence too.

Out of the corner of her eye, she glanced over. He looked straight at her with a rather unnerving gaze.

"Here we are." Arch leaned forward and tapped the driver on the shoulder.

The taxi pulled to the curb in front of the Hotel Statler.

Up in the Terrace Room, the maître d'hôtel led them to a table inside the ballroom, where Howard Jones and his orchestra played "Stompin' at the Savoy" and couples danced.

Mary smoothed the skirt of her periwinkle spring dress. With short sleeves, a scoop neckline, and a flared knee-length skirt, it was simple enough for the movies but elegant enough for dancing.

They settled around the table, ordered beverages, and then Jim turned question-filled eyes to Mary.

No more talk about her. "How's life at sea?"

"At sea?" Jim crossed his ankle over his knee. "I wish. Nothing but inventories and training and stocking supplies and installing equipment."

"Since Roosevelt promised American escort to British convoys, I'm sure they're trying to get you ready as soon as possible."

Jim ducked his chin and sent Arch a sidelong glance. "Well . . ."

Mary's chest tightened. "I'm sorry. I know you can't say anything."

Arch draped his arm around Gloria's shoulder. "We just have to be careful to only discuss public information and keep classified information secret."

"Roosevelt's promise to send you boys to protect British ships was in the papers." Gloria shuddered. "I still can't believe it."

"Remember, those British ships carry American supplies," Arch said.

Gloria sniffed. "Let them use their own escorts."

Jim and Arch laughed together. "They don't have many left," Jim said. "And the British have to cover the Mediterranean too. Hitler just took Yugoslavia, Greece won't last long, and he's driving across Libya toward Egypt. If the Germans take the Suez Canal, Britain won't stand a chance."

Mary tensed at the chilliness in Gloria's eyes, a look she'd seen from the diehard isolationists at work, those who said, "Fine. Let Britain fall. Just leave us out of it."

The chill transformed to worry. "Do you think the war in the Mediterranean will distract Hitler from what we're doing? Not only are we sending supplies to his enemy, but we just set up bases in Greenland. Won't he see that as aggressive?"

"That's the idea." Arch squeezed Gloria's shoulder.

Jim leaned his elbows on the table. "Not aggressive, necessarily, but strong. And smart."

Mary traced the lines of her artfully folded napkin. "It's only a matter of time, isn't it? If we come between U-boats and their prey, eventually something will happen. If it's big enough . . ."

The silence and solemnity around the table answered her question.

"All this heavy talk depresses me." Gloria sprang to her feet. "Please, Arch."

"Shall we dance?" He stood and led her to the dance floor.

"Shall we join them?" Jim offered his elbow. "Although I doubt this song will lift anyone's mood."

Mary took Jim's arm and tuned her ears to the band, which played "I'll Never Smile Again." She laughed. "I don't suppose that song's good for morale."

"No, but it's good for dancing." He pulled her into his arms at a friendly distance, appropriate for conversation.

Mary followed his lead in a foxtrot. "Back to my original question—how's life on board ship?"

"Cramped, stuffy, and smelly."

"Is the food all right?"

"Excellent. The Navy's famous for feeding sailors well."

"And you and Arch share a cabin. That's wonderful. Is it better than on the battleship?"

Jim tilted his head and peered at her with one eye, like a comical detective. "I see what you're doing, Miss Stirling."

"You do? What am I doing?"

"This is how you do your spy work. You ask lots of questions and listen with that intent little look on your face as if every word were fascinating, and your victim keeps talking and talking."

"You make me sound sinister." The thought tugged up the corners of her lips.

He rocked her into a turn. "Not sinister, just modest. I've noticed you don't talk about yourself if you can help it. Why is that?"

Mary glanced away, at the swirling mass of dancers, the men in tailored suits, the women in colorful spring dresses thanks to the unseasonably warm weather.

"Come on." He squeezed her hand. "'Fess up."

The warmth of the room pressed on her. "I don't like attention."

"And why is *that*?"

The teasing look in his hazel eyes coaxed up a teasing smile in response. "Gloria didn't come for heavy conversation, and I didn't come for psychoanalysis."

A shift in the musical tempo, and the band transitioned into "You Turned the Tables on Me."

"The song inspired me." Jim swung her around. "I'm turning the tables and interrogating you."

"Must you?"

"I must. Favorite color?"

"Blue."

"I can tell." He glanced at her dress. "You wear it a lot."

"You're very observant for a man. And what's your favorite color?"

"I'm a Navy man. Of course it's blue, but you're being naughty and trying to flip things around again and I won't have it. Why'd you choose secretarial school?"

Giggles fluttered in her throat. She'd never been called naughty before. "I'm too squeamish to be a nurse and not authoritative enough to be a teacher, but I can type like lightning and I was second in my class in shorthand."

"Second? Why not first?"

Why had she bragged? Mary's step faltered. At graduation, the top student was presented a plaque up on stage. "I . . . I let her win. She wanted it more than I did."

"You failed deliberately?"

She stared at the knot of his black tie, stark against his white shirt. "Yes."

"Out of kindness, or modesty, or . . ."

Fear. "Yes. All of those, all mixed up."

"Hmm."

Mary couldn't bear to see his expression. Would it be pity? Or disgust? Or confusion?

"There's definitely a saboteur at the Boston Navy Yard."

"What?" Her gaze jerked up to him, to warm eyes and an understanding smile.

"You. Sounds like you sabotage your own success to avoid attention. Am I right?"

A sour gelatinous mass formed in her throat, but she swallowed it and nodded. "I suppose."

"There. You survived my psychoanalysis. Now for my spiritual advice—don't hide your candle under a bushel."

She smiled her thanks, even though that advice ran counter to the spiritual theme of her life, avoiding the evils of putting herself above others.

"Now for the fun part of the evening." He grinned at her and whipped her around in a wild circle.

She laughed and held on to his broad shoulder. She'd have to be very careful not to fall for this man.

6

"It's been a while since I've had a blonde on my arm." Jim scratched at his upper lip as they stepped out of the orange El train at the Park Street station.

"Don't scratch. You'll undo my artwork." Mary swatted his hand. "I worked hard to make it halfway realistic. Besides, if I can resist scratching under this wig, you can control yourself too."

Jim rubbed at the dark eyebrow pencil marks staining the tips of his fingers. "Still have my mustache?"

"For now. But if you keep it up, you'll blow our cover." Her accent sounded for all the world like some gun moll in a gangster movie.

"Unlikely." Not only was Jim new to town, but the contrast of his gray civilian suit, fedora, and fake mustache to his usual dress blues would throw off anyone but his shipmates.

And Mary? He couldn't help but laugh again. She wore the curly blonde wig Arch had bought for a roast at the Academy, a red suit borrowed from her roommate Yvette, and a giant red disc of a hat perched on the side of her head. Only her

46

soft eyes and the notebook in her hand would identify her as Mary Stirling.

That notebook was why they wore disguises. While everyone expected Mary to take notes at the Navy Yard, why would she do so on a Saturday stroll downtown? She didn't want to draw attention to her detective work. Better to play the role of lady reporter.

"This is so much fun." Her step bounced as they headed down the platform. "I can't believe we're doing this."

"More fun than visiting the Bunker Hill Monument." Arch had taken Gloria to Connecticut to visit his family for the weekend, and Jim had hoped to coax Mary on a historical excursion this morning. But when he arrived at her apartment, he found her working on her saboteur notebooks. The more they talked about the escalating situation at the Navy Yard, the more Mary wanted to investigate. Then Jim remembered the America First rally at Boston Common this afternoon, and their plan flew together.

"Oh!" Mary's gloved hand pulled on Jim's arm. "I was so busy showing you my notebooks I forgot to tell you about the incident this week."

"Incident?" He gave her his best attempt at a detective scowl.

But she laughed at him. "You have a hard enough time looking serious, much less dangerous."

The curse of having a boyish face. "Just tell me about the incident."

She scanned the station as if her suspects might be listening. "They installed some decking on one of the destroyers. It passed inspection before installation, but then it failed."

"So the inspector . . ."

Mary smiled and adjusted her hat. "Frank Fiske. He's been at the Yard over twenty years. He catches a lot of mistakes. In fact, he told me Heinrich Bauer has made some errors lately."

"The German, right? Did he do it?"

"Ira Kaplan worked on that section. Bauer's most vocal opponent. Fiske says Kaplan must have gone back and altered his work after the inspection, and Kaplan says Bauer did it to frame him. He got everyone stirred up, and Fiske had to break up a fight. It's a mess."

Jim climbed the stairs. "Do you think it's Bauer? Or Kaplan?"

She waved her notebook. "Those are just two of the men. Over ten thousand people work at the Yard."

"But they targeted your bottle of champagne. It must be someone who knows your work habits and routines."

"I agree. And this incident, if it's really sabotage, narrows it down to one crew."

"So let's look at motive. Bauer's would be obvious. A Nazi—"

"If he is one."

Jim nodded. "A Nazi would want to keep our ships off the seas so the U-boats can hunt unmolested. But what about Kaplan? He's an interventionist, right?"

"Right. Here's where it gets tricky. Kaplan wants us to fight, wants us to enter the war. What would be a better motive for America to join the battle than if the enemy attacked us on our own shores?"

Jim paused outside the exit, right on Boston Common, and he blinked in the sunshine. "So if they could make it look like Nazis were sabotaging our ships in our own harbors, the American people would get riled up."

"That's the theory." Mary pointed to Park Street Church rising in red brick stateliness in front of them, with its tall white steeple pointing to heaven. "Say, do you think I should dress like this for church tomorrow?" She sent Jim an exaggerated wink. Completely out of character.

Yet it wasn't. For a quiet girl, she had a nice adventurous streak. "I dare you."

"I don't think so. Now, where's the rally?"

"The paper said it was at the Parkman Bandstand."

"I know where that is." Mary led him around the station entrance and away from the church.

On the green in Boston Common, people headed toward the bandstand. Some would go because they agreed with the America First organization, which wanted to keep the United States out of the war. Some would go out of curiosity. And some would go to heckle.

Jim's civilian suit felt like a coat of protective armor. Boston, like New York, tended to strong isolationism. Many of the immigrants, especially the Irish, Italians, and Germans, had no interest in supporting Britain or in fighting their own cousins overseas.

"Let's stick to the fringes of the crowd," Jim said.

"Yes." Mary's gaze darted around the mass of people, several hundred perhaps.

"We won't let that happen!" a man cried from the bandstand, a round platform with a domed roof suspended on white pillars.

"Who is that?" Mary said. "I don't recognize him."

"Me neither."

The speaker stabbed the air with his finger. "They fooled us during the First World War. Remember all the propaganda the British fed us? The Germans were committing grave atrocities, butchering Belgian babies, and ravishing Frenchwomen. We believed it. We fell for it. Then we got over there and what did we find? Did we find those atrocities?"

"No!" the crowd roared.

"No, we didn't. All lies. All so we'd go and fight Britain's battle for them. All so Britain could maintain their mighty empire—with American blood. Will we let that happen again?"

"No!"

Next to Jim, Mary scribbled in her notebook, filling the page with loops and lines.

Jim looked over her shoulder. "If I didn't know you were using shorthand, I'd say you had the worst handwriting in the world."

"It's my secret spy skill." Mischief sparked in her eyes. "Except every secretary in America can read it."

"What are you writing?"

She gestured to the crowd. "Harvey Mills, George O'Donnell, Curly Mulligan, Ralph Tucker. Let's go that way."

He followed her around the edge of the crowd, gripping her elbow but glancing over his shoulder at the speaker.

The speaker tugged on the hem of his suit jacket. "And now what are the British telling us? Oh, those Germans. They're committing atrocities, butchering Jewish babies, ravishing Frenchwomen. Do they think we're stupid?"

"You're stupid if you *don't* believe it!" someone shouted from the far side of the crowd.

Mary peered over. "We need to go over there."

Jim let her lead but kept her to the fringe. If things turned violent, he'd want to get her away in a hurry.

The speaker rocked back and forth on his heels and gestured to his hecklers. "And now a word from London, eh, folks?"

Laughter romped through the crowd.

"No! A word from the real world. You're a Fifth Columnist, that's what you are, convincing people to weaken our defenses so when the Germans—"

The crowd booed so loudly Jim couldn't hear, but Mary plunged onward. Perhaps now was not a good time to float with the current.

"Weaken our defenses?" the speaker said. "Who's weakening our defenses? Our president, that's who. Sending our new ships and planes to England. If anyone attacked us, where would we be? Undefended, that's what. No arms to Britain. Arm America first!"

The crowd cheered and punched the air with their fists.

Mary stopped and wrote hard and fast.

Jim nudged her to the side a bit. "See someone?"

"Yes. The hecklers. Morton Anders, Ira Kaplan. My goodness."

"You want to defend America?" one of the hecklers called. "Then defend freedom. Defend the democracies. Defend Britain. We're stronger together. Down with the dictators!"

Several members of the crowd surged forward, shouting insults. The hecklers shouted back, brandished fists.

"Okay, that's enough." Jim steered Mary away across Boston Common toward the Public Garden.

Mary resisted and glanced back, like Lot's wife. "Oh! Al Klingman, Weldon Winslow—and he brought his wife? But she's English."

"That's enough for today, Agatha Christie."

She kept writing as they walked. "Oh my. Oh my. It sure got heated, didn't it?"

"That's why we're going to the lagoon, where sweet little families sail on Swan Boats and feed the ducks and eat wholesome picnics."

Mary closed her notebook and stashed her pen in her purse. "I'll fill in details tonight. Goodness. One page per person is no longer enough."

"Are you going to show someone? The FBI?"

"Heavens, no."

"Maybe it's time. Something's going on. You should speak up."

Mary's forehead creased, and she shook her head.

"Wow. You really don't like attention, do you?"

She glanced around at the budding trees. "It's wrong to call attention to yourself. Pride comes before a fall."

"Sure, but there's nothing wrong with taking a little pride in a job well done or in accepting a little attention for it."

Her mouth scrunched up. "Such a fine line between gracious acceptance and reveling in the limelight. Best to avoid attention altogether. Far less dangerous."

"Dangerous?" This was the same woman he had to drag from a potential riot.

"I know. I know from experience." Her voice quavered, and she pressed her hand over her mouth.

What could have made her so afraid? "Why? What happened?"

Mary raised startled blue eyes, a strange contrast with the fearless red suit and hat.

If she didn't want to talk about it, he wouldn't force her. That wasn't his way. He never pushed, never made waves.

Jim tilted his head across the street to the Public Garden. "Come on. Let's enjoy the park. Then we'll get some ice cream, catch the El back to Charlestown. You can get out of that fool wig and we can see Bunker Hill. What do you say to that?"

"All right." Head lowered, she proceeded.

Jim crossed the street and ambled along the flower-lined pathway, but his stomach clenched. He could usually perk people up and encourage them, but he'd deflated Mary's spirits.

She made a good friend, a good companion, but he still couldn't figure her out. One moment timid, the next bold and determined. Quiet and modest, but she loved to explore and try new things. And he wanted to figure her out, find out what made her tick.

He puffed out a breath and glanced her way. He wasn't

falling for her, was he? Getting confused by the blonde wig? Nah. She was a nice girl, a pretty girl, but not for him. He liked women who overflowed with energy and joy and confidence.

At least she didn't seem to be falling for him. None of that simpering and hair-twirling and fussing over him. Of course not. She knew better. She remembered him as a fool, drooling over the unattainable Quintessa Beaumont.

Just as well. Wouldn't be long until they shipped out, and who knew what port they'd call home?

A miniature suspension bridge stretched across the lagoon, and Jim and Mary strolled onto it. On the silvery green waters, ducks floated, bobbing under to feed. Mary stopped and gripped the railing, and Jim leaned against a stone pillar.

On the near bank, a trio of children played with toy sailboats. One of the boats twisted into the wind and toppled over.

"That's me," Mary said.

"Hmm?"

She pointed, forehead puckered. "It hoisted its sail into the wind so proudly. 'Look at me! I'm wonderful!' And it capsized."

Jim frowned at the boat, at the child wading into the lagoon to right it. "I don't under—"

"In sixth grade. The Christmas pageant at school." Mary traced one finger along the railing. "I was chosen to play Mary. Not only did I have the right name, but I had a lovely voice, Mrs. Cassidy said, the best in class. It was the most important role, and I was proud, so proud. My mother warned me and told me not to put myself above others, but I ignored her. I'd been chosen because I was wonderful. I reveled in the attention."

"Oh." Jim sank his hands into his trouser pockets, warmed inside that she trusted him with her story.

"You already know what happened." She turned a guarded gaze to him.

"I do?" He searched his memory. So long ago. But he did remember one year, going to see his little sisters Lillian and Lucy as angels, and . . . "There was an accident, wasn't there?"

She tucked in her chin. "You could say that. More like I *had* an accident."

"Oh." He cringed for her sake.

"I was so excited, so proud, that I forgot to use the restroom beforehand. There I was in my blue gown, holding baby Jesus—the most beautiful porcelain doll I'd ever seen. I was kneeling beside the manger, and I stood up with baby Jesus to sing 'Silent Night' and—" She shuddered.

Now he remembered. He remembered the laughter spreading through the auditorium and his mother's iron grip on his knee to prevent him from joining in.

Mary covered her face with her hand. "I had to walk to the front of the stage for my solo. Everyone behind me could see. I can still hear the laughter. Mrs. Cassidy realized what had happened, and she screeched and ran to me on stage and lifted up the gown, insisting she had to get me out of my wet things. I couldn't stop her because I was trying not to drop the doll, and I . . . well, she didn't know I was only wearing my little slip underneath. I was mortified."

He made a face. "And you ran and fell—"

"And the doll shattered. One of the boys cried out, 'She broke Jesus!' That's all I could hear. All I could think about. I did it. In my pride, I broke Jesus." A breeze blew fake blonde curls across her cheek, and she didn't brush them away.

Jim let out a low whistle. "I can see why you don't like the stage."

"Do you blame me?" Her voice came out small and strained.

"Not at all." He rubbed the scars on his palms. "Some moments sear themselves in your memory."

She nodded, her face still covered.

Now for some encouragement. "But look at you now. Miss Independent Career Girl, living in the big city and standing up to saboteurs."

Mary peeked at him and raised a tiny smile. "Am I?"

"Absolutely." He gave her his best serious look.

The smile grew. "Your mom helped."

"My mom?"

"She was my Sunday school teacher. She heard the snickers in class, saw me becoming more and more withdrawn. So one day she kept me after class and coaxed it out of me, my guilt for breaking Jesus. Your mom sat there watching me, and then she said, 'I broke Jesus too.'"

A smile twitched on Jim's lips. "Good old Mom."

"I didn't understand. So she told me when we sin, we break Jesus's heart. And then he went to the cross, willingly breaking himself so we could be made whole. I'd heard the story all my life, but that was the first time it made sense, the first time I felt the weight of my sin and the need to be saved."

Jim sighed and nodded. He'd felt that weight himself, that burden.

"Your mother was wonderful. She explained breaking the doll wasn't a sin, just an accident, but I'd done other things to break Jesus. I knew I had—my awful pride—and I prayed and asked for forgiveness and received it."

"Mom always cuts through the nonsense and leads you back to truth."

"Quintessa helped too."

Jim's heart jolted at the name, but he kept the same expression. "I'm sure she did."

"She moved to town that summer and took me under her wing. When school started, everyone wanted to be friends with her, but she told them, 'Anyone who wants to be my friend has to be nice to Mary.' Believe me, that put an end to the teasing."

"It would." He stared at the dancing blonde curls. That was what was missing in the women he dated. They matched Quintessa for vivaciousness, but none had her compassion, her willingness to stand up for the underdog. "She's unforgettable."

Mary brushed aside the fake blonde and gave him a soft smile. "You still love her, don't you?"

His face scrunched up, and he glanced away to a Swan Boat being pedaled across the lagoon with half a dozen families and couples on board. "Don't know if I'd call it love. Just a foolish, one-sided crush."

"Unrequited love is still love."

"And foolishness is still foolishness." Something restless squirmed inside him, and he pushed away from the stone pillar. "Now, come on. I promised you ice cream."

Mary swiped aside the curls. "Then I'll let you help me burn this wig."

He headed across the bridge. "Arch will be heartbroken. It's his favorite."

She rewarded him with an amused sidelong glance. Good. He'd actually cheered her up. Even if it meant he had to admit something he preferred to keep hidden. But so had she.

Now her fear made sense. It did. An embarrassing moment like that couldn't be forgotten.

No wonder she hated attention. No wonder she didn't want to draw attention to herself, even for something as noble as catching a saboteur.

Jim stopped in his tracks, and Mary gave him a quizzical look.

Before him rose a statue of George Washington. He circled to the front. The great general rode on horseback, sword drawn and ready to attack, to defend. "Our founding fathers were willing to fight for what was right, to risk their lives for the sake of freedom."

"True." She inclined her head.

"You don't want to report your findings for fear of drawing attention to yourself. But what if something happens? Someone gets hurt?"

Her eyes went from blue peace to silver shock.

Above them, George Washington stared down the future, ready to take on any enemy for the sake of liberty.

"So . . ." Mary cleared her throat. "So I should be willing to stand up and speak out."

He tweaked her pancake of a hat. "And maybe wear a little red."

Her expression solidified, and something new lit in her eyes. "Maybe I will."

7

Tuesday, April 29, 1941

Mary climbed Monument Avenue on her way to work, note-books in her arms, her camel-colored spring coat swinging unbuttoned around her knees.

"You shouldn't do it." Yvette's heels clipped on the side-walk beside her.

Basswood trees waved their new spring leaves above Mary's head. After all the hard work of talking herself into this, she didn't need any discouragement. This was the right thing to do, and as long as she didn't yield to the temptation of taking pride in her actions, she'd be fine. "I need to let Mr. Pennington know my suspicions and ask his advice."

"Americans are so naïve. You do not see the danger."

"But I do see the danger. That's why I need to act."

"You do not understand." Yvette waved her red-tipped fingers in front of her face. "The war will come here. The Nazis will not stop. They are ruthless and powerful."

"If that's true, I need to help."

Yvette's brown eyes riveted her. "Do you not see? If the Nazis are here, sabotaging our ships, do you not think they will hurt those who stand in their way? They are brutes. Man, woman, child—it matters not. They can hurt you and no one will ever know."

Mary let out a sigh. Strange that the thought of public acclaim frightened her more than physical danger. "Don't you always say the biggest mistakes the French made last year were trusting in false security and ignoring the warning signs?"

"Yes, but—"

"I won't make the same mistake." The Bunker Hill Monument rose high before her on a green hill, the granite obelisk puncturing the blue sky. Almost two hundred years earlier, colonists had hunkered behind wooden ramparts, outnumbered, fighting against impossible odds.

Surely one secretary could dare to share her notes.

At the northeast corner of Monument Square, they turned right, down the hill toward the Navy Yard, past Charlestown's neat brick homes.

Mary filled her lungs with warm spring air. Jim would be proud of her, and her heart leaped. How ridiculous to let herself develop a crush on him. He liked gold, not silver, and he still loved Quintessa, for heaven's sake.

Mary crossed Chelsea Street and frowned. Was she being shallow? She hadn't been interested in him in high school, so why now? The only thing that had changed was the breadth of his shoulders.

That wasn't completely true. In high school, they rarely spoke. Hugh and Quintessa did all the talking, and Jim and Mary listened, enraptured. This was the first time they had truly conversed.

The lovesick boy had become a bright and funny man, kind and insightful, adventurous and thoughtful. And not one bit lovesick.

The whole thing was quite hopeless.

Mary straightened her shoulders. Regardless, she'd enjoy his friendship and encouragement until he shipped out.

She and Yvette showed their photographic identification passes and entered the gate to the Boston Navy Yard. They passed the octagonal Muster House, such a darling Victorian building for a military base. To her left, the long narrow building of the ropewalk stretched for a quarter mile, where men spun hemp fibers into rope for the entire US Navy. They turned left and entered Building 39, a solid structure of brick trimmed with granite blocks.

Yvette headed for Accounting, while Mary headed for Mr. Pennington's office in Personnel.

After she hung up her coat, she set up her desk for the day, her notebooks beside her. Today would be perfect to talk to her boss, in the lull between the busyness of Mondays and Fridays, and before the end of the month with its rash of reports.

Mr. Pennington swept into the office, tossed his hat onto the rack, and hung up his suit jacket. "Good morning, Miss Stirling. Don't you look lovely today?"

"You say that every morning."

"Because it's true, my dear. You have your grandmother's eyes and her sweet spirit." He tapped his temple. "You know I had my eye on her until your grandfather stole her from right under my nose."

"I'm glad he did."

Mr. Pennington laughed and smoothed his semicircle of white hair. "So am I. Gave me my most efficient secretary ever."

Mary grabbed her notebooks and followed him into his office, where he plunked into his chair and tugged his vest down over his belly. Now was the time. She inhaled a deep breath and exhaled a quick prayer. "Mr. Pennington, I'd like to discuss something with you."

"Oh?"

Her ankles wobbled. "You know there's been a lot of unrest among the men lately, a lot of accusations."

"Ah yes, the saboteur," he said in a conspiratorial whisper. "I wouldn't worry about it. The entire nation is on edge. First the US declares the Western Hemisphere off-limits to Axis ships, but the British are quite welcome. We've chosen our side, and some people don't like it."

"Yes, sir."

He spread out his hands. "And here in America our great hero, Charles Lindbergh himself, appears at an America First rally at Madison Square Garden and tells us the only way to save our country is not to fight. And then our great president calls our great hero a defeatist. And then our great hero resigns from the Army Air Corps."

Mary smiled. "It's been a busy week."

"That it has. So I expect some grumbling from our boys on the docks."

"I've been keeping track."

Silver eyebrows rose. "Hmm?"

She shifted her weight from one shaky ankle to the other. "You always call me your little spy, so that's what I've been doing. I record everything the men say about the sabotage." She set the first notebook before him.

"It's in shorthand."

"Yes. I can take down over two hundred words a minute, so I can write faster than they speak. Since they're used to seeing me take notes, no one thinks anything of it."

He leafed through. "Very smart, young lady."

The compliment swelled inside her and threatened to turn to pride. "I'm just doing my duty. Then in the evening, I transcribe my notes into other notebooks. I started with a page per person, but it wasn't enough." She opened the second notebook.

"It's still in shorthand."

"In case anyone happens upon it. The left column is what the person said. The right is what others said about him."

"Very organized."

"Do you think I should show it to the FBI?"

His head jerked up. "The FBI?"

"They're still investigating, aren't they? Perhaps they'd find this useful. People say things in front of me they'd never say to an FBI agent."

Mr. Pennington rubbed his heavy jowls. "This is very clever and foresighted of you, but it's nothing but gossip. Smith says this about Jones. Jones thinks Smith is a fink. Am I right?"

"Yes, sir."

He settled back in his chair. "The FBI wants cold hard facts, not rumors. I'm afraid if you showed this to them, they'd think it was rather silly."

Mary gathered her notebooks, her chest tight. Innuendos and grudges and name-calling might seem like gossip, but they might point the way to those cold hard facts.

She headed to her desk.

"But Miss Stirling . . ."

"Yes?" She turned in the doorway.

Twin furrows divided his forehead. "It never hurts to keep a record. Keep it up."

Mary hugged her notebooks. "I plan to."

8

Friday, May 9, 1941

The giant crane grumbled as it lowered the number two gun mount to the deck in front of the bridge. Workmen shouted over the noise, pointed, and yanked lines to direct the gun into position.

Jim stood by the bow, out of the way but close enough to watch the installation. The *Atwood* would have four of these multipurpose 5-inch guns, two fore of the bridge and two aft, useful against ships, surfaced submarines, and aircraft.

He looked up to the new Mark 37 fire director, the tank-like steel compartment on top of the bridge superstructure, where the gunnery officer and his crew would direct gunfire during battle. Looked like the head of Frankenstein's monster, with three portholes for eyes and the optical rangefinders sticking out on each side like the bolts.

That would be his responsibility. Well, the responsibility of Lt. Dick Reinhardt, the gunnery officer. Jim served only as his assistant, thank goodness. Better that way.

"Getting arthritis, old man?" Arch nudged him.

Jim was rubbing his hands again. He chuckled to cover a grimace. "Old scars. They get tight sometimes."

"How'd it happen? Haven't heard this story before."

Jim could still hear Lillian's screams, see the torn flesh of her leg, smell the blood, feel the bite into his hands. All because he'd tried to make waves for once. And his little sister paid a lifelong price. "Ah, you know. Kids messing around." He pointed at the workers. "There it goes."

The crane settled the gun compartment onto the platform that elevated number two above the level of number one. The weight tipped the destroyer slightly down at the bow.

"Excuse me, Arch. I should see if Reinhardt needs me." He passed the men at work and climbed up to the wing of the bridge. Lieutenant Reinhardt leaned against the rail, chatting with Mitch Hadley.

"Hi, Floats," Hadley said with a flat smile.

Stupid nickname, but it hadn't stuck. Only Hadley used it. "Mr. Reinhardt, Mr. Hadley. Some sight, eh?" He nodded to the crane.

"Second gun we've had installed." Reinhardt narrowed his grayish eyes at Jim.

So the man didn't care for enthusiasm. He'd have to find another way to win him over. "Here's hoping we never fire them."

"That'd make for a dull job." Reinhardt adjusted his khaki cover over his red hair and gazed across Boston Harbor toward the open Atlantic.

Hadley snickered. "If you like to float, dull is best."

Jim dug his fisting hands into the pockets of his khaki trousers. "Actually, I prefer a little excitement in life, but either way I'll do my job and do it well."

Reinhardt nodded once, his gaze unmoving.

A sigh filled Jim's cheeks, but he swallowed it. Once they set sail, Reinhardt would see Jim as an asset. He'd already befriended most of the enlisted gun crews, black men and white. He'd figured out most of the men's strengths and weaknesses. He'd be able to motivate and encourage them better than cool-as-an-icicle Reinhardt.

Nothing wrong with floating anyway. Not everyone wanted to be an admiral. Jim just wanted to do good work with good people. And he didn't want to hurt anyone along the way.

Down by the number two mount, the workmen swarmed around, welding and tightening bolts.

"Kaplan! Kaplan!" One of the workers beckoned another. "I need that wrench and now."

"Coming, Mr. Fiske." A lean, dark-haired man strode over.

Jim squinted at the men. Kaplan? Fiske? Weren't those two of the men Mary had mentioned? "Say, Mr. Reinhardt. Anything you need from me?"

A slight shake of the head. No one would accuse the man of wasting words.

"See you later." Jim worked his way down to the gun platform and over to the laborers.

The older man who seemed to be in charge—that was Fiske. He took the wrench from Kaplan. "How's it coming?"

"It'd be coming along a lot faster if Bauer weren't on the job." He gestured with his thumb toward a man squatting nearby with a welding torch.

Bauer? Another suspect. Jim restrained a smile and stepped closer. Maybe he could play detective and pick up some tidbits for Mary.

The welder got to his feet, took off his mask, and ran his hand through blond hair.

"Thanks for the job you're doing." Jim stuck out his hand. "Ensign Jim Avery, assistant gunnery officer. Those are my guns you're working on."

"Heinrich Bauer." He shook Jim's hand and glanced away.

"How long have you been a welder here?"

"Four years. Why do you ask?"

"Just being friendly."

"You need not watch me. I am not a Nazi." His tone cut like a razor, and his blue eyes blazed. But something around the edges of his eyes—a flutter—spoke of fear. A purplish bruise covered his cheekbone.

"Say, what happened?"

Bauer's mouth tightened. "May I work, sir?"

"I'll tell you what happened." The dark-haired fellow, Kaplan, came over. "He got too close to his buddy's 'Sieg Heil!'" He thrust up one hand in a Nazi salute, then mimed grabbing his own cheek in pain.

Jim stepped between them. "I'd suggest you both get back to work."

Bauer marched away. "How can I work with this—this nonsense?"

"Yeah, that's right. Slink back to Herr Hitler, report your spying, your sabotage." Kaplan leaned forward.

Jim planted a hand on his chest. "I wouldn't do—"

"Kaplan!" Mr. Fiske grabbed the younger man's shoulder. "Get back to work."

He backed off, but sparks arced through his dark eyes. "Yes, sir."

Emotions certainly ran high on that crew. Jim had findings for his detective friend. Too bad he didn't know shorthand.

"Hey, Avery!" Mitch Hadley called down from the bridge. "You floated into a mess there. You've got to be careful where you let the wind blow you."

Jim fixed a hard stare on his fellow ensign but bit his tongue and headed to his cabin to change out of his casual khaki uniform into dress blues for dinner. Hadley's words held the sting of truth.

He climbed down a ladder below deck and crossed through the empty wardroom to officers' quarters.

In the cabin he shared with Arch, his friend buttoned up his white shirt. "Time to get ready."

"Need to take some notes for Mary first." He opened a desk drawer, pulled out a notepad, and wrote down what he'd heard.

"For Mary, eh?"

"Yeah. Some of her saboteur suspects got into an altercation up there."

Arch glanced up. The ammunition handling room for the number two mount lay directly overhead. "Should we worry?"

"With all those people watching? Nah." He finished his notes. "Mary will love this."

"Is that so?" Arch bent over to knot his tie in the mirror on their locker. "Gloria thinks you should ask her out."

Jim winced, tossed his cover onto his bunk, and ripped off his khaki tie. "We go out almost every weekend."

"As friends."

"Yes, as friends." He unbuttoned his shirt. "That's what we are."

"I think you're crazy."

"And I think you're a nag." Jim flashed a grin and shrugged off his shirt. "She's like another kid sister to me. There's nothing romantic between us."

Nothing at all. Sure, she was pretty. Sure, she intrigued him. But she wasn't anything like Quintessa.

Besides, Mary acted like a kid sister around him, no flirting or self-consciousness—just normal. That was best. Things might get awkward if she developed a crush on him.

Jim made a funny face in the mirror over Arch's shoulder. "She'd have to be stupid to fall for a fool like me."

"Thank goodness the woman's smart."

He punched his friend lightly in the shoulder. "Thank goodness for that."

9

Saturday, May 24, 1941

Mary eased her way down the ladder to the USS *Constitution*'s gun deck, inhaling the scent of ancient oak, brine, and history. "Old Ironsides," the US Navy's legendary oldest ship, had asserted America's budding strength in the War of 1812. Now she rested in well-earned retirement at the Boston Navy Yard, restored in the 1920s in a campaign partly funded by schoolchildren. Mary had contributed her own pennies for the project.

"Look at all these guns." Jim bounded ahead with Arch behind him. "Can you imagine reloading shot after every firing? Now our 5-inchers can pump out fifteen rounds a minute, and with a range up to ten miles."

"Someone's been studying his *Naval Ordnance and Gunnery Manual*." Arch ran his hand along a gun's iron barrel.

"I'd better." Jim knelt to study the contraption the gun rested on.

"They're like two little boys," Mary said to Gloria. "They're having more fun than if we'd taken them to Revere Beach."

Gloria wore a slim leaf-green dress, and she set one gloved

hand on the peplum on her hip. "I hope it warms up before Arch ships out. I have a simply darling new two-piece swimsuit, and I want to show it off at the beach."

Mary forced a smile. Gloria was one of the golden ones who could show off and not be punished. It didn't seem fair.

Gloria eyed Mary head to toe. "You have a cute figure. Maybe if we get the boys to the beach, Jim will finally notice you."

Thank goodness Jim was too far away to hear and too immersed in discussing the gun's mechanics. "I'm not trying to be noticed. We're just friends."

"But I so enjoy watching people fall in love."

"Then watch yourself with Arch."

She patted her upswept hair under a matching green hat. "We're a boring old couple now. He'd better ask me to marry him soon. All these tests are so tiring."

"Tests?"

Gloria leaned closer, bringing a whiff of perfume with her. "He's so skittish, thinks girls only love him for his money. He wants a girl to be unimpressed by his wealth, even to disdain it."

Mary studied the handsome blond officer, who peered down the barrel of a gun. "That makes sense. I'm sure he wants someone to love him for who he is."

"Except wealth is part of who he is, part of what makes him attractive. And it's so hard to pretend."

"Pretend?" The word tasted like dust.

"Just between us girls, okay?" Gloria winked. "The Vandenberg estate is spectacular. Who wouldn't want that? And the money? Heavens, you could buy anything you wanted, never have to count pennies. I'd be a fool not to want that. But with Arch, I have to wrinkle my nose and pretend the whole thing is quite distasteful. The sooner we get married, the better."

Mary swallowed the dusty mouthful. Gloria might not be a gold digger, but she was standing in the stream with a pan, ready to sift out a nugget.

"Come on, ladies. Come see." Jim beckoned them over.

For the next ten minutes, the men showed them how the gun worked, how the sailors hauled it back and forth on its wheels, loaded the shot, rammed it in place, lit it, and protected their hearing with the tips of their neckerchiefs jammed inside their ears.

Gloria made appreciative noises—another act? How could she pretend to like and dislike in opposition to her own tastes, in order to trick Arch into marriage?

"Look at that, Mary. Twenty-four-pound shot." Jim patted a cannonball.

"That's incredible." She didn't have to pretend, nor would she ever do such a thing.

Mary could watch him all day, the way his smile tilted slightly higher on the right, the boyish glint in his hazel eyes, the smooth cut of his hair, the perfect fit of his double-breasted jacket, his long fingers and the way he moved them.

She ripped her gaze away. Who was she kidding? She was as guilty of pretending as Gloria. Every day she pretended not to be attracted to Jim, pretended the sound of his voice didn't scramble up her insides, pretended the thought of him shipping out and not returning to Boston didn't leave her aching.

The men led the ladies down another hatch to the berth deck, filled with dozens of hammocks.

Arch fingered the canvas. "Our enlisted men should be required to come aboard the *Constitution*, see how sailors lived in the nineteenth century. They'd be more appreciative."

"That works for us too." Jim leaned through a door. "Officers' quarters. They have hammocks too. Although I sure wouldn't mind that desk."

Mary poked her head inside. A gorgeous oak desk topped with green felt, adorned with antique telescopes and sextants and things. "I assume your accommodations are less colorful."

"Plain old steel." His grin flashed, far too close to her face, then he strode away, back to the hatch.

Mary followed the group up the ladders, not easy in a skirt and heels. Perhaps it would be best if the *Atwood* didn't return to Boston. Sure, she'd miss Jim and his friendship, but then she could recover from her crush.

On the main deck, Mary drew in a breath of cool air. A mild overcast hinted at coming rain. Wind played with the skirt of her dress, and she anchored the blue fabric sprigged with sweet little white and yellow flowers.

Arch and Gloria headed for the bow, but Jim circled the main mast, face tipped up and glowing. "Two hundred twenty feet tall. Can you imagine her with sails unfurled, flying with the wind?"

"She'd be marvelous." Mary imagined yards of snowy canvas snapping above her, sailors climbing the rigging and calling to each other. "It's sad to see her sails trussed up to her masts, isn't it? She can't fly."

"All she can do is float with the current." Jim's eyebrows bunched together. "She can't let the wind move her. She can't set her own course."

Mary laid her hand on the polished oak railing surrounding the mast. What a contrast to the painting in her apartment. In her painting, the tiny sailboat charged ahead, sails full, charting new territory. Yet here this grand old ship sat stagnant.

She let a sigh join the sea breeze. Her sails were bound up tight. She might not capsize, but she didn't go anywhere either.

Jim frowned up at the swooping lines. "My sails are trussed too."

"You?"

His gaze turned to her, a bit bleary and unfocused, and he made a wavy motion with one hand. "I float wherever the current takes me. I don't make waves, don't push, and no one gets hurt. So far the current's taken me exactly where I wanted to go."

That did fit his easygoing personality.

He jutted his hand out. "But I don't control the direction. The current chooses. Not me. Not the Lord."

She studied his intent face. "Your sails are trussed for a different reason than mine."

He grasped one of the lines hanging limp alongside the mast. "We have to hoist our sails. We have to let the Lord fill them. Then we have to resist the current if necessary to stay the course."

A sense of peace, of rightness, of exhilaration filled her lungs. "Then we can fly with the wind."

Jim looked deep into her eyes, his own awash with emotion.

Mary caught her breath, capturing the peace and rightness and exhilaration and sealing it with the joy of shared experience. She'd never felt such an intense connection with another human being.

In the cloud-filtered sunshine, his eyes gleamed green as spring, full of hope and promise. "Hoist your sails high, young lady. Let's see how fast you can go."

Affection for him swelled inside, burst her restraints, and flowed into her smile. "And let's see where your course lies."

10

Sunday, June 1, 1941

Jim stepped out the door from the bridge superstructure to the main deck, and a cool mist tickled his face. Boy, did it feel good to get out to sea.

Well, out to harbor at least. Under an overcast sky, the *Atwood* chugged past the islands in Boston Harbor, with the neat white tower of the Long Island Head lighthouse rising to starboard.

Finally the *Atwood* was out for her shakedown cruise, to see what she and her crew could do. For a month, the men would perform drills and drills and more drills, until they functioned as one. He couldn't wait.

And yet . . .

Jim gazed past the destroyer's two funnels, where he could barely make out the piers of the Boston Navy Yard. Right after the *Atwood* had shoved off, Mary had come, waving a handkerchief, looking small and pretty in her light brown coat.

Made him feel good to know she'd be there when he returned.

Jim stepped down through a hatch, his hands guiding his descent down the ladder as his feet glanced over the steps. Like an old sea salt.

He ducked his head at the bottom, but not in time. The top of the doorway scraped his scalp. After a quick glance to make sure no one had seen, he snatched up his cover and shoved it back on his head. Old sea salt indeed.

More like a giant puppy, bounding around with his tongue hanging out. No wonder Mary wasn't interested in him. A quiet soul like her would prefer a man of suave sophistication.

Did he want her to be interested in him anyway? Sometimes when she smiled up at him, he wanted to draw her close. Her gentle ways soothed him, intrigued him, balanced him.

He'd never imagined himself with anyone but a perky blonde, but now he longed for Mary's company. Strange. He'd have to wait and see what happened.

Jim entered the forward boiler room and shed his navy blue jacket. Heat pressed in, and the roar of the machinery assaulted his ears. At some point he'd have to do his turn down here with the "black gang" in the engine and boiler rooms, but he wouldn't volunteer.

Working his way through the maze of pipes and cables, he kept a respectful distance from the hot steam pipes.

Up ahead, Arch studied a gauge and made a note on a clipboard. His blond hair curled around his forehead.

"Hey, Curly!" Jim called.

Arch shot him a withering glare and jammed his cover over the disobedient locks. "What's the matter? Assistant gunnery officer has nothing to do in peacetime?"

"Nothing to shoot but the breeze." Jim gave him a jaunty smile and a sheet of paper. "But I do have an important memo from Durant. Jim Avery, assistant messenger boy, second class."

Arch smiled, skimmed the message, and slipped it onto his clipboard. "Ah, soon they'll give us both plenty to do."

"I know. Got a practice loading drill at 1500 hours."

"It'll be a busy month. Glad we're coming back to Boston, though. Good home port."

"Does Gloria like it here?" A drop of sweat broke free from Jim's hatband.

"Sure. She likes her job well enough." He marched down to the next gauge. "But she'd follow me anywhere. I'm quite a catch, you know."

Jim winced at the cynicism in Arch's voice. How many times had they been through this? "You don't think she loves you only for your money, do you?"

"I don't know." Arch peered at the gauge and adjusted a valve. "Thought she was different, but all she talks about lately is money, shopping, how wonderful it is to buy nice things."

"Because of her job or because of you?"

He shrugged. "Does it matter?"

"Look, we're coming out of the Depression. Most of us had to scrounge and save and do without. She sounds like every other American girl with a good paycheck right now."

"I'm sure that's all it is." His tone contradicted his words. "Say, you don't think we'll see any action this month, do you?"

Jim laughed. "Along the New England coast?"

"We'll be in this war before the end of our cruise, mark my words. You heard the news—Germany says escorting convoys is an act of war. And here we are committed to escorting convoys in the near future."

"Yeah. The Battle of the Atlantic's really heating up." Steam hissed overhead. Jim shuddered at the thought of the thousands of men who had perished the past week in the sinkings of the British battlecruiser HMS *Hood* and the

German battleship *Bismarck*. The war at sea had claimed many ships, many lives, and now the US Navy was skipping right into the middle of it.

Arch dashed to the source of the hissing steam and tightened a valve. "Gloria might need to find another checkbook to raid, because we'll be at sea longer than a month."

Even if Congress declared war that day, they'd have to return to port in a month to restock. But correcting Arch when he was in a mood like this would only waste words. "See you later, buddy. Off to pretend to fire my guns."

Back up topside, Jim took a bracing breath of cool air. The deck rolled gently beneath his feet. Far to starboard, the old brick Graves Light signaled the outer reach of Boston Harbor. Jim wouldn't set his feet on land again for a month.

He sighed. He'd also miss his little sister's college graduation. His older brothers, Dan and Rob, would too. At least his parents, Lillian's twin, Lucy, and the two youngest boys would attend.

In Lillian's last letter, she sounded downcast. Most of her pharmacy school classmates had jobs lined up, but not Lillian, despite her excellent grades. No one wanted to hire a woman, especially one who was missing her left leg below the knee.

Jim coiled his hands into fists, the scars on his hands tightening. Anyone who couldn't look past her prosthesis and see a bright capable young lady—well, they ought to be keelhauled.

Men were already assembling by the practice loading machine between the aft superstructure and the searchlight platform. Reinhardt wanted each of the four gun crews to practice on the loader for half an hour each day. Not a popular decision with some of the seamen, but Jim would do his best to make the gunnery officer's orders understandable and palatable.

Lieutenant Reinhardt hailed Jim and handed him a stopwatch. "Time them."

"Aye aye, sir." Jim smiled and bit back the "And good afternoon to you too" on the tip of his tongue.

The crew for the number two 5-inch gun rolled up the sleeves of their chambray shirts. All the men were black except the gun captain. While the segregated Navy only allowed Negroes to serve as stewards, cooks, and mess attendants, when general quarters sounded, everyone had a battle station.

Jim found the gun captain, Gunner's Mate First Class Homer Udell. "Good afternoon, Udell. You fellows ready?"

The petty officer nodded. "Aye aye, sir. Good crew here. Number one crew is whining about the number of drills, but my boys know the more they practice, the better they'll get."

"Maybe we should get some friendly competition going."

"Yeah?" Udell's sun-wizened face cracked in a grin. "We'll show 'em number *two* gun is number one."

Jim laughed, clapped the man on the back, and climbed the ladder onto the aft superstructure, about eight feet above the main deck. Standing on the platform for the machine guns, he'd have a good view but wouldn't be in the way.

"Mr. Reinhardt! I'm ready." Jim leaned his elbows on the rail and held his thumb over the stopwatch.

Below him, the crew took their positions around the practice loading machine. Lieutenant Reinhardt raised his hand high. "Ready, set, go!"

The men sprang into action. After the spade man opened the loading tray, the powder man placed a dummy powder case in the tray, and the projectile man hefted up a fifty-pound target practice shell filled with sand and laid it forward of the powder. Then the projectile man rammed them home. The case and shell dropped into a collecting tray, and the hot case man returned them to be used again.

Over and over they repeated the process, grunting with

exertion. Jim cheered them on. He'd seen similar drills on the battleship, but this crew was slower. They kept getting in each other's way. They fumbled a pass, and a projectile clanged to the deck. They placed the powder case backward and had to flip it.

Udell directed them with practical advice, but Reinhardt regarded them with granite silence.

Jim winced. This was the first time the crew had performed the drill. Slowness was to be expected. Over time they'd improve, but only with guidance and encouragement.

"Come on, men! You can do it," he called.

"One hundred," the projectile man shouted.

Jim clicked the stopwatch off.

The crew stepped back, leaned over, hands on knees, the backs of their shirts dark blue with sweat.

Lieutenant Reinhardt looked up at Jim. "Time?"

"Eighteen minutes, forty-two seconds."

The gunnery officer's mouth screwed up. "Eighteen . . . ?"

Udell stepped forward. "Remember, sir. This is our first practice together."

Icicles were warmer than Reinhardt's glare. "That was the most pathetic drill I've ever had the indignity to witness. Mr. Avery, please tell me how many seconds they took to load each shell."

He'd already done the math in his head, but he didn't like the number. "Eleven seconds—eleven point two—"

"Eleven seconds? Eleven!" The gunnery officer paced in front of the offending crew. "That's fewer than six shells a minute. Six. We need to fire at least fifteen. Four seconds per shell, you hear me? Four seconds. Do you realize the Nazi U-boats have been at war almost two years? In the time it takes you loafers to load one shell, they'll sink us."

"Aye aye, sir." Udell stood tall, his hands behind his back. From above, Jim could see the petty officer's hands ball up.

"And don't think your lazy performance gets you fewer drills." Reinhardt didn't raise his voice, but he didn't have to. "A good crew can do five drills in half an hour. So you'll do five drills too—ten if you don't speed it up."

A single groan rose from below, quickly quenched.

If only Jim could help. At their current rate, the seamen had ninety minutes of hard physical labor before them. And to run through all four crews . . . well, they'd be at work long past dark. "Udell," he called down. "You're an old hand at this. What did you see? How can we improve?"

Udell glanced up at him with a mixture of surprise and gratitude, then he turned to Reinhardt. "Permission to speak freely to my men, sir?"

"Granted."

The gunner's mate's shoulders relaxed, and he gathered his crew around him, using lots of hand signals, his voice too low for Jim to hear.

"Mr. Avery!" Lt. Cdr. Calvin Durant stood off to the side, beckoning Jim to come down. When had he arrived on the scene?

Jim climbed down to the deck and found the commanding officer. "Yes, sir?"

Durant pointed his chin toward the gun crew. "I like what you did."

"What I did, sir?"

"The petty officers are the best asset on any ship, far better than any of us with an Academy ring." The CO flashed his own gold ring. "Udell knows guns and he knows his men. If we get out of his way, he'll do his job."

"Yes, sir." Warmth rose in his chest. He'd done something right.

Durant glanced over his shoulder. "You're a good match for Reinhardt. Between the two of you I might have myself a good officer."

Jim's left eye twitched. That was only half a compliment then. One more reason to hoist his sails and stop floating.

"Are you a Bible-reading man like your brothers?" Durant's blue eyes homed in on him.

"Yes, sir."

"Read Nehemiah."

"All right." But he frowned in confusion. Why would his CO want him to read about the rebuilding of Jerusalem's walls?

"Something you said to Udell reminded me of Nehemiah. See if you can find it. Come to think of it . . . Mr. Reinhardt!" He waved over the gunnery officer.

"Yes, sir?" Reinhardt stepped over with a lot less steel in his gaze.

"Read Nehemiah. In the Bible." Durant pointed his finger, swept it from bow to stern. "All of you—all my officers are going to read it. No one could lead like Nehemiah. Tomorrow night we'll discuss it over dinner. Pass the word, both of you."

"But . . ." Reinhardt gazed toward the bridge. "But what about Shapiro? He's Jewish."

"All the better." Durant slapped Reinhardt on the back and strode away. "Last I checked, Nehemiah was Jewish too."

How many times had Dan and Rob warned Jim about Durant's strange sudden assignments? Jim laughed.

Reinhardt sent him a baffled look, the first truly human look Jim had seen from the man. "Nehemiah?"

Jim grinned at him. "Guess we have some walls to build."

11

Boston Navy Yard
Tuesday, June 3, 1941

The air in the drafting room stood still, and Mary halted inside the doorway. All the draftsmen sat at their angled desks, pens silent, ears cocked toward Mr. Winslow's office, toward the sound of raised voices.

Mary crossed the room as if nothing were wrong and opened her notebook to a fresh page. Since she was there on official business, no one would think anything unusual about her presence.

She paused outside the office and peered around the burly shoulders of George O'Donnell to catch Mr. Winslow's eye. At the naval architect's nod, she stepped just outside the doorway and leaned against the wall to wait.

And to take notes.

"Mr. O'Donnell," Mr. Winslow said in his cultured tones. "It's hardly uncommon for a supervisor to check the work of his subordinates. In fact, it's expected."

"You don't trust me? I've been a draftsman since before you were born. Subordinate, my foot."

"I appreciate your experience, but—"

"But you think your fancy college degree makes you qualified to judge my work."

"It isn't a matter of judging—"

O'Donnell cursed. "You and your hoity-toity ways. Questioning my work and rushing me."

"I hardly think asking you to be at your desk during working hours is rushing you." Winslow's voice quavered.

Mary's pen flew over the paper, but she kept a nonchalant look on her face as if she were doodling to pass the time.

"You can't fool us." O'Donnell's voice lowered to a growl. "We all know why you're rushing us—to get more of *our* ships into British hands."

"As you know, these ships are being commissioned into the United States Navy."

"Yeah. To do England's dirty work for her, escorting ships carrying American goods across the Atlantic to feed them—and for free. Lend-Lease? It's outright theft. Why should we help them when they've never done anything to help us?"

"We help them . . ." Winslow's voice rose and shook. "We help them so more innocent people don't die. I'll have you know my wife's nephew died in London a few weeks ago—ten years old—killed in a German air raid. If we don't help them, who will?"

Mary drew in her breath. Ten years old. What horrors the British faced.

Mr. O'Donnell snorted. "And I'll have you know my cousin was killed in the Irish War of Independence back in 1920. By the British. America didn't send help to Ireland. Why should we help the Brits now?"

"I'm not asking you to help Britain. I'm asking you to do your job."

"My job? My job is to build ships for America. For America.

Lindbergh's right, I tell you. We need new leadership in the United States."

Mary scribbled hard and fast. A few days earlier, Charles Lindbergh's speech at an America First rally in Philadelphia raised an uproar. What did the aviator mean by "new leadership"? Some said he was calling for an immediate overthrow of Roosevelt's presidency. Some said he was referring to the lawful election process.

O'Donnell stormed out of the office, chomping on his tobacco, rolled blueprints in hand. Every eye in the drafting room watched him leave.

Mary waited a few seconds to finish her notes and to give Mr. Winslow time to gather himself. Then she pulled out the report from Mr. Pennington and entered the office. "Good morning, Mr. Winslow."

He set down a glass of water and swallowed hard. "A bit late for that, I'm afraid."

"From Mr. Pennington." She offered him the report and a soft smile.

"Thank you." He took the papers with a shaking hand and turned his chair away from her.

She had no intention of further assaulting his dignity by asking questions about the incident, so she made her exit.

And she made up her mind. Mr. Winslow allowed Mr. O'Donnell to intimidate him, but Mary refused to let her fears intimidate her any longer.

It was time for her lunch break and time to visit the FBI agent.

Mary returned to Mr. Pennington's office in Building 39 and grabbed her new loose-leaf notebook filled with her typed-up notes. The carbon copies resided in a similar notebook in her apartment. This past weekend while she typed, Yvette kept peeking over her shoulder and warning her, but Mary wouldn't be swayed.

She poked her head into her boss's office. "I'm going on my lunch break."

"Yes. Yes. You're welcome." His snowy head was bent over the papers on his desk.

Mary smiled. He never made sense when he was immersed in his work. "I'll see you in half an hour." She hadn't asked his permission, but she didn't need it. As a private citizen, she had a right and a duty to share her suspicions.

Down on the first floor, Mary entered the cramped temporary office set up by the FBI.

Agent Paul Sheffield stood at his desk, his back to Mary, loading papers into a cardboard box. With his slight build and thin sandy hair, he looked nothing like the dark and dashing G-men in the movies.

"Excuse me?" Mary rapped on the back of the door with her knuckles. "Agent Sheffield?"

"Yes?" He shoved his glasses up his nose and squinted at Mary. "We've met, haven't we?"

Memorable as always. "Yes, sir. I'm Mary Stirling, Barton Pennington's secretary. I set up the champagne."

"Ah yes." He grinned and motioned for her to take a seat. "Have you come to confess?"

She laughed and sat down. "I'm afraid not."

"What can I do for you?" He settled into his chair behind the desk.

Mary ran her thumbs along the notebook. "As Mr. Pennington's secretary, I collect and deliver reports to various departments. I hear a lot."

Thin sandy eyebrows drew together. "What have you heard?"

"I—I hear lots of things. Nothing threatening, but I—well, I take notes on what people say, and I've typed them up. Would you be interested in seeing?"

He let out a long sigh and held out one hand, his fingers opening and shutting.

Mary laid the notebook in front of him, pleased with how neat and organized it looked. "Each page—or pages—is for a separate person. On top is the person's name and position, plus his possible motive, means, and opportunity to commit sabotage. In the T-shaped chart below—on the left is what he said and on the right is what others said about him."

Agent Sheffield flipped through the notebook, and Mary returned to her seat, watching his face for any glimmer of interest, but he remained impassive.

At last, he pushed the notebook away and leaned back in his chair. "What you have here is a long—and exceptionally organized—account of all the shipyard gossip."

Mary's gut twisted. "I suppose so, but it does show each man's frame of mind, his personality, his motives, and how he's perceived. I think it would be useful in your investigation."

"The investigation is over." He gestured to the box on his desk. "After this afternoon's commissioning ceremony, I'm closing up shop."

"But the champagne—"

"A single incident. The local police are in charge. As for this perceived sabotage . . ." He shrugged. "Tensions are high throughout the nation, and they're concentrated here because of the work you're doing. The problems people have seen are the normal mistakes you'd see at any shipyard. But since everyone's convinced there's a saboteur in your midst, they interpret every error as sabotage most foul. Mass hysteria."

Mary pulled her lips between her teeth. His statement did hold truth.

The agent stood and placed more papers in the box. "In fact, the Bureau is convinced our presence here is only inflaming the situation. If we leave, show them we think nothing's wrong, everything will settle down to normal. Besides, we have more pressing matters, real spies to hunt down."

"But what if something is actually happening here?"

He put his hands on his hips and tilted his head. "Let me guess—the Case of the Shipyard Saboteur."

Mary's breath caught. That's what she'd taken to calling it. She'd almost written it in her notebook.

The agent shook his head. "How many Nancy Drew books did you read?"

Book covers flashed through her mind—*The Secret of the Old Clock, The Mystery at Lilac Inn, The Sign of the Twisted Candles*. At least a dozen books—all the mysteries that had been published before she graduated from high school and set aside her girlhood heroine along with her schoolbooks.

Mary smoothed the skirt of her blue dress—the color Nancy Drew favored in her wardrobe as well. "A few."

Agent Sheffield chuckled and pulled file folders from a desk drawer. "We see this all the time at the Bureau—eager young ladies who fancy themselves amateur sleuths able to catch clues we bumbling blind professionals miss."

Mary gasped. "I assure you, sir, that wasn't my intention. Not at all. I just thought I could aid the inves—"

"And I assure *you*, miss. There's nothing in your pretty little notebook we don't already know."

Her throat burning, she picked up her notebook, said good-bye, and retreated. She'd hoisted her sails and had capsized. She hadn't hoisted them in pride, but he thought her prideful, thought her pushy and condescending.

Mary strode down the hallway, her vision blurring. Had she been prideful after all? She examined her words and actions, and she rejected the notion. No, she only wanted to help. The last thing she wanted was attention or recognition.

Back on the second floor, she leaned against the wall outside Mr. Pennington's office and opened her notebook, her eyes still damp. The first page was for Morton Anders, a riveter on Frank Fiske's crew and an outspoken interventionist.

Mary screened her notes—she'd seen Morton Anders at the isolationist rally on Boston Common. She'd worn that itchy blonde wig and that bold red dress. And she'd been with Jim.

Her lips warped, and tears filled her eyes. Jim didn't scoff at her. Jim didn't think her investigation was silly or prideful. In fact, he believed in her.

Mary bowed her head and clutched her notebook. If only she could talk to him right now.

She could almost hear his deep voice encouraging her. She could almost feel his strong hand patting her shoulder. She could almost see his hazel eyes sparkling to cheer her up.

He'd only been gone two days. How could she miss him so much?

12

Off the Coast of Maine
Wednesday, June 11, 1941

"Good night, men." Jim raised one hand in farewell to his fellow officers and left the wardroom.

"Going for your evening constitutional?" Arch asked.

"Yeah." Although Jim had never favored solitary strolls, the smooth seas, clear skies, and pleasant temperatures on this cruise called to him.

He left the stale smell of tobacco smoke in the wardroom and made his way to the main deck and the fresh smells of ocean air. Here he could chew over the evening's conversation. Most nights this week, between discussions of shipboard happenings, baseball scores, and news events, the captain had brought up another aspect of Nehemiah's leadership for discussion.

Jim hadn't been able to figure out what in the Bible passages referred to him until Durant pointed it out tonight. During the practice loading drill, Jim had asked Gunner's Mate Udell, "How can we improve?" The word *we* was what Durant had liked.

When Nehemiah arrived in Jerusalem and wanted to enlist the help of the Jewish leaders, he told them, "Ye see the distress that we are in, how Jerusalem lieth waste, and the gates thereof are burned with fire: come, and let us build up the wall of Jerusalem."

"We. Us. Collaboration," Durant had said. When a leader inserted himself into the problem and the solution, he didn't blame his subordinates or look down on them. Then the subordinates rallied behind the leader. That's what he said Jim had done.

The memory of those words and a lungful of cool night air puffed out Jim's chest, but he had a long way to go. Durant hinted at it. Jim's natural style was to gather people together. That came easily to him. But what about when an unpopular or dangerous decision needed to be made?

Jim's chest deflated. "That's where I need to improve."

At the stern of the destroyer, Jim leaned against the empty depth charge racks, which stood ready to roll ash cans of explosives down to submarines if they ever went to battle.

The ship's wake fanned out astern, and the song "Moonglow" played in Jim's mind, slow and romantic. Before him, the full moon cast silvery light on the blue waters.

Why was he drawn here every night?

A peaceful view, entrancing, and somehow familiar. Not from earlier trips to sea. It was more like a connection, a reminder. Something about the sight made him feel relaxed and strong and confident. Like . . . like . . .

Like when he was with Mary. *Those eyes.*

That was it. Mary's sparkling, peaceful, entrancing eyes. Boy, did he miss her. Much more than he thought he would.

Mary had a glow rather than a flash about her. With her, he felt like he could become a better man and help her become a better woman. A friendship and yet more.

What now? Jim pushed away from the depth charge rack

and strode toward the bow, past the number four gun mount, the number three. Something about his relationship with Mary felt right, but she'd never shown any signs of being attracted to him, and their friendship was comfortable. Best to wait and see if anything happened.

Jim passed the machine gun platform, the practice loading machine, the searchlight platform. Wait and see? That sounded like floating. Could he float into love? Wouldn't a real man charge ahead and pursue the lady?

He winced and passed the aft funnel, the torpedo tubes, the forward funnel. Whenever he pursued a woman, he came across like a drooling fool, acting as he had with Quintessa. That was surely how Mary remembered him.

Behavior like that wouldn't impress a sensible woman like Mary. No, he'd have to be subtle and suave.

"Jim Avery suave?" He laughed and made his way down the narrow passageway around the bridge superstructure. He wore a suave uniform and had manners any mom would be proud of, but he still acted like a frisky colt most of the time.

"Mr. Avery? Is that you, sir?" A rough voice came from ahead.

"Yes." Jim squinted in the faint light from the foremast, range, and side lights overhead. A man in a petty officer's uniform headed toward him. "Udell?"

"Yes, sir. I was looking for you."

"For me?" Jim met up with the gunner's mate.

"Yes, sir." Udell rubbed the back of his neck. "Something isn't right in my mount, down in the handling room. I talked to Mr. Reinhardt yesterday, and he said it was nothing, but . . ."

Jim frowned and crossed his arms. "What is it?"

"Water."

He swallowed a comment about being at sea. "Water?"

"My men noticed some drops on the deck the other day.

We wiped them up. More the next day in the same place. Nowhere near the doors. Sir, you know we keep things dry down there 'cause of the powder."

It didn't seem like a problem—except Udell thought it was. "Mr. Reinhardt said it was nothing?"

Udell let out a growl. "He says we're on the ocean. He says be more careful. Sir, I joined this Navy twenty years ago, when you and he was still in knee pants. I know when things ain't right."

Jim clapped him on the shoulder. "Show me."

Udell led him to the ammunition handling room directly underneath the number two gun. Racks of 5-inch projectiles and brass powder cases lined the walls. In the center of the small room, the projectile hoist and powder scuttle extended to the gun compartment above. Udell and his crew kept this room spic and span.

"Here, sir." Udell pointed to the panel boxes by the central column. Three droplets of water spotted the deck, and the petty officer wiped them up with a rag. "Just since I left to find you."

Jim squatted. The droplets lay beneath the panel boxes. "What's in the boxes?"

"Controls for the projectile hoist." Udell unlatched a panel box.

Jim looked inside. The usual switches and dials seen on any control panel. However, the left-hand third of the box was walled off with a tiny padlock securing the door. "What's back there?"

"Don't know, sir. And I don't have a key. That's not right. I'm the gun captain."

"And Mr. Reinhardt—"

"Wouldn't come look."

Jim jiggled the padlock. "Are the other turrets like this?"

"Don't know."

"Let's find out." Jim scrambled outside, down a hatch, and into the number one handling room. He greeted a crewman and opened the panel box. Smaller than the panel box in the number two mount. No walled-off area. No padlock.

An uneasy feeling writhed in Jim's belly. What about all that talk of sabotage at the Navy Yard? Weren't the men who installed that mount the same men on Mary's suspect list?

But water? In a locked box? Nothing about it made sense.

"What do you think, sir?" In Udell's weathered mask of a face, concern flitted in his brown eyes.

Jim scratched at the stubble on his chin. "I don't know. But I agree with you—something isn't right."

"You gonna tell the captain?"

Go straight to Durant over Reinhardt's head? That didn't seem wise, and it certainly wouldn't make Reinhardt warm up to him. But the gunnery officer had already dismissed Udell's observations. Wouldn't he dismiss Jim's too?

But reporting to Durant would create a monstrous wave.

The image of those three drops on the deck filled his mind. He'd talk to Durant in private. If nothing came of it, he'd ask the captain not to say anything to Reinhardt.

He had to do this. He had to make a little splash. Besides, no one would get hurt.

"Come on, Udell. Let's go find the captain."

"Thank you, sir."

Durant would be up on the bridge. He said he always had to say good night to his ship, and he believed in long good nights. Jim had served as junior officer of the watch a few times late during first watch and mid-watch, and there was Durant, still saying good night.

Jim led Udell up to the bridge, high above the deck.

Sure enough, Durant stood behind the helmsman in the pilothouse. He glanced at Jim. "Mr. Avery."

"Captain, may we have a word with you in private, please?" He motioned to the petty officer behind him.

"Very well." The corners of Durant's thin mouth turned down, and he showed them into his tiny cabin just aft of the pilothouse and shut the door. "What's up?"

"Sir, it's probably nothing, but . . ." Jim relayed the situation as concisely as possible without mentioning Reinhardt's name.

"A padlock?" Durant perched on the edge of his desk. "Why would we keep anything locked up in a handling room? Udell, have you ever seen anything like this?"

"No, sir."

"Odd." The captain leaned out the door. "Mr. Banning, go with Mr. Avery. He'll brief you on the way. I'll take the conn."

"Aye aye, sir." The executive officer led them back down to the main deck.

As they walked to the gun mount, Jim repeated the story.

Lt. Vince Banning shifted his square jaw to the side and raised one eyebrow. "Water?"

"I know. But why is there water in the panel box? Why a padlock? The other turrets don't have a lock. Something doesn't seem right." No need to mention the sabotage rumors.

Banning glanced behind him. "Well, I trust Udell. If he says something's wrong, something's wrong."

"That's what I thought." Jim threw a smile behind him to the petty officer, glad Reinhardt seemed alone in his disrespect. "Say, Udell. We might need a hacksaw for that lock."

"I'll get it, sir."

In the handling room, Jim showed Banning the setup. As he did, a lone drop fell from the seam of the panel box and splashed on the deck.

"I've got a hacksaw." Udell clambered through the door.

Jim stepped aside to let the man work.

After a few minutes of sawing, Udell pried off the lock and opened the door. "Holy mackerel!"

Jim peered over his shoulder. A tin can sat inside on a film of water. Wires protruded from the side and poked into a block of—

Holy mackerel indeed! "Is that TNT?"

"Don't touch a thing." Banning cussed, lunged for the telephone, and explained the situation to the bridge.

Jim sat on his heels, his heart pounding. The rumors were right. There was a saboteur.

Within seconds, the siren clanged overhead and the loud-speaker announced general quarters.

Jim's blood went cold. They'd run the collision drill every day at sea, preparing for any type of hull breach, from collision, stranding, a torpedo hit—or an explosion. He never dreamed they'd put it into practice so soon.

All around the ship, men would be running to their stations, closing watertight doors and hatches, preparing the damage control and medical teams, and readying the whale boats and life rafts.

Banning motioned with his thumb to the door. "Go on, Avery. Get out of here. You too, Udell."

"No, sir," the men said in unison.

"Fools." Banning stared at the bomb and rubbed his hand over his mouth. "Let's see what we have here."

"Why the water?" Jim ran his finger through the puddle in the bottom of the panel box. "It's leaking from the can."

"All right." Banning wiped his upper lip, then gingerly slid the contraption out of the box.

Udell got down low and peered up at the device. "There's a tiny hole in the bottom."

Jim tossed aside his cover and ran his hand through his hair. "It's designed to leak. Very slowly."

"So the water level inside falls," Banning said.

"Maybe something's floating inside," Jim said. "Like a cork."

"Yeah." Udell clapped his hands. "When the water runs out, two wires meet, and boom!"

"Boom." Jim's breath ran out.

"Throw it overboard," Udell said.

"Then we'd lose the evidence. They wouldn't be able to track down the saboteur." And Mary would never forgive him. "Let's cut the wires, take off the TNT."

Banning frowned at the bomb for a long moment. "Go ahead."

While Banning held the can and Jim held his breath, Udell pulled his clasp knife off his belt and sliced through the wires. No boom.

All three men released deep sighs.

"Okay. Let's tell the bridge. Then we'll show the captain." Banning pried off the TNT. "They'll want all of this for the investigation—the can, the padlock, the explosive. Mr. Avery, call up to the bridge."

Jim got on the telephone. Soon the siren sounded three times overhead, and a voice on the loudspeaker called, "Secure."

But were they secure? If the saboteur left one bomb, might he have left another? Jim had to tell Durant about the rumors at the shipyard and Mary's concerns.

Right there in the handling room, surrounded by powder cases and explosive shells. If the bomb had detonated, it could have blown off the bow of the ship and taken many—if not all—of the crewmen to the bottom of the sea.

Thank God, they'd caught it in time. Yes. Thank God.

Jim closed his eyes and did just that.

When he opened his eyes, he looked inside the panel box again. What kind of man would do such a thing? What kind of man had so little regard for human life?

95

What was that? Dark marks on the wall of the panel box, hidden in the shadows.

Jim pulled his flashlight from his trouser pocket and shone it inside. A bright red swastika marred the steel.

And the words "Sieg Heil!"

13

Boston
Thursday, June 12, 1941

Over Boston Common, the setting sun spilled golden light on the grassy slope. Only six weeks earlier, she and Jim had played detective at the rally.

Now he was in danger.

Mary shuddered as she stood on the corner outside Park Street Church. This morning, Mr. Pennington had told her the USS *Atwood* was coming back to Boston prematurely.

They'd found a bomb on board.

No one had been hurt, thank goodness, but they all could have been blown to pieces.

All day, Mary had been shaken. All day, she'd prayed for safety for the crew and justice for the saboteur.

Word hadn't leaked out into the Navy Yard, but it would, and chaos would ensue.

Due to the news, Mary had almost broken the resolution she'd made on Sunday. But she refused to be swayed. It was time.

Mary climbed the steps, opened the church door, and made her way toward the choir room.

While she didn't want Jim back in town for such a horrid reason, she still longed for his return. The fanciful part of her thrilled at the memory of his voice and the dream of romance, but the reasonable part of her listened to the truth in Quintessa's last letter.

A month before, her best friend had asked if anything romantic was stirring between Jim and Mary. Mary kept her feelings private and merely said Jim never acted gaga around her. In this week's letter, Quintessa confirmed that Jim couldn't have a crush on Mary. The poor man wore his heart on his sleeve. If he were interested, everyone in Boston would know.

Mary drew a deep breath. Quintessa was right, and Mary would be fine. It was only a mild crush, after all, and she truly enjoyed their friendship.

She paused outside the open door to the choir room. Sounds of conversation, laughter, and a tinkling piano drifted into the hallway.

Time to hoist her sails. Mary strode into the choir room. About forty people milled around inside. At the piano sat a middle-aged lady, her graying blonde hair rolled into a low chignon—Hilda Gunderson, the choir director.

Mary lifted her chin and approached the piano.

Mrs. Gunderson gave her an expectant smile. "Well, hello. Who might you be?"

"Mary Stirling. I came to inquire about joining the choir."

"Do you like to sing?"

"Very much."

"Can you read music?"

"Yes." Thanks to Mother's insistence that a lady should know how to play the piano, even if she played poorly.

"And can you hold a tune?"

"Yes, ma'am."

Mrs. Gunderson squinted at Mary through her glasses. "Soprano?"

"Yes, ma'am."

"Splendid." Her fingers fluttered over the keys, sending up a bounty of notes. "We're always short on sopranos. Very high turnover."

"Did I hear we have a new soprano?" A young lady gave Mary a dimpled smile.

"Yes." Mary's heart jumped as if she'd met a celebrity. Claudia Richards, a red-haired beauty, frequently sang solos on Sunday mornings.

Claudia clasped her slender hands in front of her chest. "Ooh, you can sit with me. Please do."

"I'd love to." She'd only been there five minutes, and she'd already made a friend.

Mrs. Gunderson gestured to a bookshelf. "Claudia, please show Mary where to find her music. After practice we'll find a robe that fits."

"Oh." Mary's face tingled. She should have told the choir director earlier. "I—I won't be able to sing on Sundays."

"Do you have to work?"

"No. I . . . I . . ." She twisted her hands together.

Mrs. Gunderson looked up at her with kindly green eyes. "Stage fright, dear?"

Mary's breath rushed out. "A severe case."

"You realize the choir sings up in the gallery behind the congregation."

"Yes, ma'am." That fact gave her hope.

For a long moment, the choir director studied her. "So why are you here?"

Only the truth would do. "Because I love to sing, and the only way to conquer a fear is to face it, right? And Jesus tells us we shouldn't hide a candle under a bushel. Someday I hope to sing on Sundays."

"Good." Mrs. Gunderson played a scale. "Put your candle on a candlestick so it can give light to all. 'Let your light so shine before men, that they may see your good works, and glorify your Father which is in heaven.'"

Inside Mary, that truth wrestled with other biblical principles of humility and not putting oneself above others. There had to be a balance, but she hadn't found it.

Mrs. Gunderson plunked out a chord and raised a sudden bright smile. "Welcome, Mary. Come and shine with us."

"Yes, do come." Claudia motioned her to the bookshelf. "Sit with me, and I'll tell you what's what."

Mary followed her. "Thank you."

Claudia pulled a leather-bound folder from the shelf. "Are you new to Park Street?"

"I've been coming here for four years."

"Four years?" She gave her a blank look. "I've never noticed you."

"I like to be invisible."

One red eyebrow twitched. "You really don't like to sing for an audience? Why ever not?"

Only Jim had heard the story, and she certainly didn't want to tell it to a new acquaintance. "Why do you *like* to sing for an audience?"

"Oh, I love it." She batted her big blue eyes. "It's the most exciting thing in the world. As I'm sure you know, I'm the main soloist."

"Yes. You have a beautiful voice."

Claudia headed for the front row in the soprano section and patted the seat next to her, a glint in her eye. "I suppose I don't have to worry about competition from you."

"Definitely not." Mary sat. If only the ladies in the back row had invited her to join them instead.

"Good." Another dimpled smile from Claudia. "I'm glad we can be friends."

Mary smiled back, but cautiously. Friends? Only as long as she didn't threaten Claudia's position. Even though Mary had no intention of doing so, that was not a good foundation for a friendship.

"Everyone, please find your places." Mrs. Gunderson tapped on a music stand with a baton, while an elderly gentleman sat at the piano. "First, we'll sing 'Joyful, Joyful, We Adore Thee,' which will be the opening hymn on Sunday. Please stand."

One of Mary's favorites. With Claudia's help, she found the music in the folder.

The piano played the opening chords, Mrs. Gunderson waved her baton, and everyone sang. Mary joined in, her voice soft so as not to stand out.

After the first verse, the choir director motioned for them to halt. "The beauty of a choir is all the voices rising together, mingling as one, in perfect harmony. But that beauty can only be realized when each of us sings fully. So sing out, all of you, in joy to our Lord."

Mrs. Gunderson gave Mary a quick pointed look, then waved her baton. That speech was meant for Mary alone, but the director had been kind enough not to single her out.

They began again with the first verse, and Mary let her voice build in volume. Why not? Her voice was only one of many. She wasn't putting herself on display or parading like a peacock.

Mrs. Gunderson gave her an approving look and made a fluttering, boosting motion in front of her chest.

Since Mary knew the hymn, she closed her eyes and let Beethoven's music and the message flood through her. Her voice melded with the others, singing for God's glory, not personal acclaim.

Her eyes sprang open. That was the point, wasn't it? The purpose behind your actions. Shining your candle to call attention to yourself was prideful, but when your purpose was to call attention to the Lord, then it was right and good.

With abandon, she let her voice rise, her eyes drifting shut from the sheer joy of it.

> Mortals, join the mighty chorus
> Which the morning stars began;
> Father-love is reigning o'er us,
> Brother-love binds man to man.
> Ever singing, march we onward,
> Victors in the midst of strife;
> Joyful music leads us sunward
> In the triumph song of life.

The hymn ended with a swell of music. Why had Mary let her fears trap her for so long? Why had she kept herself away from such delight?

"Excellent. Excellent." Mrs. Gunderson went back to the piano. "Mr. Fanarolli, please come work with me on your solo. The rest of you, please study the anthem."

Claudia leaned over and flipped through pages in Mary's folder. "Well, you're certainly making yourself at home."

"I am. It's exhilarating, isn't it?"

"Yes. Well." Claudia sneaked a glance to the piano, then gave Mary a sympathetic look. "Do remember, despite what Mrs. Gunderson says, we all know only a few voices in this choir are presentable. The rest of you . . ." She shrugged. "Keep it down to a soft background."

Was this why the soprano section was so weak? Why turnover was so high? "Thank you for the advice." Mary infused her voice with polite distance. "But I'll take direction from Mrs. Gunderson. I'm sure you won't mind."

Claudia's blue eyes snapped. "Of course not."

For the rest of the practice time, Claudia spoke not one

word to Mary, and afterward she flounced out without saying good-bye.

A wry smile tilted up Mary's lips. So much for the new friendship.

Mrs. Gunderson beckoned Mary to the music stand. "Thank you for joining us this evening. You have a lovely voice, and you sang with courage."

Mary laughed. "I don't know about courage. But I sang with joy."

"The same thing. 'The joy of the Lord is your strength.'"

Perhaps it was—or should be.

Mrs. Gunderson patted Mary's arm. "Please join us again next Thursday."

"I will." How sweet that she didn't pressure Mary to come on Sunday.

In the hallway, two elderly ladies waited for Mary. "We didn't meet, dear." The tinier of the ladies—and they were both tiny—held out her crepe-paper hand. "I'm Bertha Wilkins, and this is my sister, Edith."

"Hello." Mary shook both their hands. "I'm Mary Stirling. I'm pleased to meet you."

"Not as pleased as we are to meet you." Edith peered up with cloudy gray eyes. "Not often someone stands up to Claudia. Thinks she's the queen bee, that one. Drives off all the sopranos, she does."

"Never you mind her." Bertha gave a sharp nod. "Come sit with us next week, if you'd like."

Warmth rose in Mary's chest, as energizing as the singing. "I'd like that very much."

14

Jim bounded up the stairs to Mary's apartment and rang the doorbell.

Within seconds, the door swung open. "Oh, Jim! I'm so glad you're safe."

He just stared. Mary wore a dress of silver-blue, just like her eyes. Starry clips held up her night-dark hair. She was stunning. He cleared his throat. "You got my message."

"Yes, Yvette told me." She headed across the room. "Dining at the Normandie and dancing at the Totem Pole Ballroom. I'm so excited. I've always wanted to go there."

"Mm-hmm." He followed her inside. So much for being suave. Why didn't he tell her she was stunning instead of staring at her like a fool?

"Pardon me. I need to switch purses. Are Arch and Gloria waiting in the cab?"

"Yes."

"I'll only be a moment." She leaned over a little cabinet and rummaged inside.

Why hadn't he noticed her figure before? Really noticed it? The curves of her legs, her hips, her waist, her—well, everything was just right.

"We'll have lots to talk about tonight, won't we?" Mary pulled items from one purse and stuffed them into another, her skirt swinging around her knees. "Goodness, when I heard they'd found a bomb on your ship, my heart stopped. I'm thankful no one was hurt."

"Mm-hmm."

She glanced at him. "Are you all right?"

"All right?"

"You're quiet."

Because she'd addled his thinking. He wrangled up a smile. "The shakedown cruise was a lot more eventful than expected."

"You poor thing." She glided over to him, her brow furrowed, her red lips pinched into a bow. "Are you sure you want to go out tonight?"

Not at that moment. At that moment, he wanted to close the distance between them and greet her properly. But assaulting her with a kiss wouldn't be suave. Instead, he offered his elbow. "Nothing I'd like better than an evening on the town with a beautiful lady."

"Thank you. Let me get my wrap." She swished past him to the coatrack as if he hadn't complimented her at all.

Jim followed and helped her with a little cape thing. Either Mary didn't realize how much he'd meant that compliment— or she did realize and chose to ignore it.

On the cab ride and over dinner at the Normandie, Gloria prattled about the big bands and the new movies and even the latest on the Boston Red Sox—how Ted Williams was batting over .400 and how Lefty Groves was heading for his three-hundredth win. Impressive for a woman, but not what Jim wanted to discuss. Mary kept looking at him with

Through Waters Deep

concern in those starry eyes and questions perched almost visibly on those pretty lips.

After dinner, they walked next door to the Totem Pole Ballroom. A huge dance floor faced the stage, which was flanked by two colorful totem poles. Surrounding the dance floor were the ballroom's famous couches, with velvet upholstery and high backs and sides. Emory Daugherty and his Tom-Tom Boys played a lively rendition of "Cherokee," and Arch and Jim led the ladies to one of the couches.

Jim sat and crossed his ankle over his knee. If only the couch had a low back, he could drape his arm behind Mary's shoulders. That would be subtle.

Arch leaned over and grinned at Mary. "Our amateur sleuth can't wait to give us yet another interrogation."

"It's true." Mary smoothed her silvery skirt. "Wait— *another* interrogation?"

Jim clasped his hands over his knee. What else could he do with them? "We came in late last night. We spent all day talking to the FBI, the Navy brass, and folks from the Navy Yard. I must have shown them where I found the bomb a dozen times."

Mary gasped. "You found it?"

Gloria leapt to her feet. "Oh, Arch. I can't stand to talk about this. Please, let's dance. The thought of you being hurt . . ."

Arch led her to the dance floor but flashed Jim a "what else can I do?" look over his shoulder.

"Did you?" Mary scooted a few inches farther from Jim but swiveled to face him. "Did you find it? How?"

"One of my petty officers. The gun captain. He noticed drops of water below a panel box—there was no source of water inside. I investigated and told the captain. That's when we found it."

She covered her mouth, her eyes enormous. "Oh my. I'm glad you investigated."

He smiled and nudged her with his elbow. "Thanks to you."

"Me?" Her slender hand lowered from her mouth.

"If you hadn't talked about your suspicions, all those rumors, I wouldn't have thought anything of it."

She raised a playful smile, and a defiant glint flashed in her eyes. "So my Nancy Drew ramblings aren't so silly after all."

"Of course not. Never were."

"Thank you. It means so much that you believe in me." Her expression softened, and she laid her hand on Jim's arm. "Have they said anything about the suspects?"

Suspects? The only thing in his consciousness was her hand on his wool-encased arm. What would be most gentlemanly? To cover her hand with his own? To squeeze her hand? To raise it to his lips with a debonair smirk?

"Well?" she asked. "Have they?"

Jim blinked. "No. But they think it's a Nazi because of the swastika."

"The swas—" She clapped both hands over her mouth. "Swastika?"

Jim had lost his hand-holding or hand-smooching opportunity, but he leaned closer and lowered his voice to a whisper. "The saboteur painted a red swastika in the panel box behind the bomb. And the words 'Sieg Heil.'"

Mary leaned back in the divan and gazed out over the swaying couples toward the stage, where the band played "Moon Love."

He knew that analytical look. "What are you thinking?"

She crossed her arms. "I don't know. It's too obvious, don't you think?"

"That thought occurred to me. It's like a scene out of a low-budget spy movie, with a dastardly Nazi villain twisting his tiny Hitler mustache."

"Yes." She snapped her gaze back to him. "If I wanted to

sink a ship, I'd use a bomb, but why the swastika, the note? If the bomb exploded, the note would be obliterated. Why bother?"

"It's as if he wanted the bomb to be found."

"As if he wanted it to look like a Nazi planted it."

"As if he wanted to frame the Germans."

"Yes." Mary's eyes darted, sparking with ideas.

Jim drew nearer. The thrill of thinking together, of completing each other's thoughts—that made his heart float higher than thousands of bubbles would have.

"So many suspects." She tapped her fingers on her crossed arms. "Ira Kaplan—he can't stand Heinrich Bauer and lets everyone know. He certainly has the technical expertise and the access to the ship. And he's brilliant. He studied for two years at MIT, then dropped out to work at the Navy Yard, his bit to support the Allied war effort."

"He's that hothead I saw on board the *Atwood*, right? He even said, 'Sieg Heil' when he mocked the German man."

One corner of Mary's mouth puckered. "Yes, he's hot-headed, but I don't think he's dangerous. Then there's Mr. Winslow. He has even more of a desire to see us in the war than Mr. Kaplan does. He's smart enough, and he knows naval architecture, but I've never seen him on board ship. And he doesn't seem strong enough. Oh, and there are so many more."

Jim loved watching her face as she thought things through, the flashes of insight in her eyes, the doubt twisting her lips, the glow of delight in the puzzling-out process.

Mary said something about notes and the FBI and vindication.

"Mm." He tried to concentrate on her words but failed.

"Are you sure you're all right?" Once again, she laid her hand on his arm.

Another chance, but he froze. "All right?"

"You look dazed. You're not your usual sunny self."

He shrugged. "Tired, I guess."

"You poor thing. And we dragged you out. Let's call a cab and get you back to quarters."

"No!"

Mary pulled back her hand, her eyes round.

"I mean . . ." Jim scratched together what little dignity he'd retained. He stood and offered a smile and his arm. "Just need a chance to wake up. How about a dance?"

"Sure." She gave him a quizzical look, but she rose.

Jim led her down the steps, over carpet emblazoned with piano keyboards and musical notes and the words "Totem Pole." Suave had eluded him, but he could at least grasp for an impression of sanity.

Out on the polished dance floor, he swung Mary into his arms. The band played "Two Sleepy People," a bit too appropriate, but slow enough to require a foxtrot rather than a full jitterbug. He savored the firm, warm curve of Mary's waist.

"Have they found any more bombs?" she asked. "I assume they've looked."

"We tore the ship apart—as much as we could at sea— and didn't find anything. They'll tear her apart even more at the Yard."

"You're not staying on board, are you?"

"No, they put us up in the officers' quarters on shore." Jim gave her a mischievous grin, determined to be the sunny man Mary seemed to miss. "Once again, Miss Stirling is asking all the questions and not talking about herself."

"I told you I went to the FBI. Although you listened about as well as Agent Sheffield."

He laughed. "I'll pay better attention now, I promise. What else have you been up to the last two weeks? Did you follow the ways of Nancy Drew and get locked up in any towers or cellars or freezers?"

"No." A smile twitched. "But I joined the choir at Park Street."

"You did?" He twirled her in a big circle and made her laugh. "Good job. I knew you could do it."

"Well, I'm only partway there. I'm singing at practices but not on Sundays yet. Someday I will. I'm determined to overcome my fear."

"Nehemiah was afraid too."

"Nehemiah?"

Not the typical dance-floor or wardroom conversation topic. "When the king asked him why he was sad, he was afraid. He wasn't allowed to be sad in the king's presence. In fact, he was 'very sore afraid.'"

Mary's lips bent into an appealing little smile. "Not just sore afraid, but very sore afraid? I know how he feels."

"But what did he do? He prayed, and then he spoke boldly."

"So I should pray . . . and sing boldly."

"Watch out, world." Jim thrust Mary's hand high out to the side, and he charged her down the dance floor as if doing the tango. "Mary Stirling is coming your way."

Her bell-like laugh rang out, and at the front of the stage, Jim twirled her under his arm and back into his embrace. "I'm proud of you," he said.

Mary lowered her chin and cast her gaze to the side.

He'd embarrassed her. One glance around the room proved it. A lot of people watched them and smiled at them. "Sorry. Didn't mean to call attention to you."

"It's all right." She looked up at him, her eyes warm. "That was fun."

"I'll restrain my exuberance from now on."

"Please don't. I—your exuberance is part of who you are."

Exuberant like a giant puppy. Ladies cooed over puppies and patted them on the head, but Jim didn't want a pat on the head. Not this time, not from Mary.

As he glided her around the dance floor, other men gave her appreciative looks. Mary was a gem. Why had he taken so long to notice? She didn't dazzle like Quintessa, but she had a soft glow from within. Now that she'd caught his eye, she'd caught it indeed.

If only he could catch her eye and then capture her heart.

He gazed down at her hair rolled back from her forehead, pulled up on the sides in sparkly clips, and falling in dark waves to her shoulders. Begging to be touched.

All those years, she'd been right under his nose and he hadn't bothered to notice. Now she was in his arms, and he didn't want to let go.

15

Monday, June 16, 1941

Mary turned the corner and paused in the hallway, her breath bundled up inside her. Outside Agent Sheffield's office, Jim leaned against the wall, gazing the other way toward the main entrance. He wore his dress blues, his hands in his trouser pockets, his long legs crossed at the ankle, his raincoat tucked under one arm.

He cut such a dashing figure—dashing her hopes that her crush would die a quick death. At the Totem Pole Ballroom he'd acted oddly enough to fan her dream that he might return her affections, but on Sunday morning at church, he'd been perfectly normal.

Raindrops beat on the window of the main door. This weather wouldn't help the workers get the *Atwood* repaired so the ship could spirit her assistant gunnery officer back to sea where he belonged.

In the meantime, she had a job to do and a façade to maintain. She stood tall and headed down the hallway.

Jim turned to her, grinned, and pushed off from the wall. "Good morning."

"Good morning. You know, you don't have to do this."

"I want to. I'll let you do the talking, I promise. But he knows me from my lengthy interrogation. He likes me, and I think he'll accept your ideas better if I show respect for you."

"You mean he'll be less likely to call this my pretty little Nancy Drew notebook?" She patted the notebook in her arms.

Jim grimaced. "He said that?"

Mary pressed a finger to her lips. "Shh. He's partly right."

"We men can be dolts." He held open the door for her.

Why did she long to pat his cheek and tell him what a darling dolt he was? Mary entered the office and hung her raincoat and umbrella on the coatrack.

Agent Sheffield stood beside his desk, pulling papers out of a cardboard box. At another desk against the wall, a large dark-haired man in a charcoal gray suit did likewise. Sheffield gave Mary a wry look. "I thought you might be back."

Time to be brave. "I thought you might summon me."

"Ensign Avery." The FBI agent stepped forward and shook Jim's hand. "Are you acquainted with this young lady?"

"Yes, sir. We went to high school together."

"Please have a seat." Agent Sheffield motioned to one chair and pulled a second from the corner. "May I introduce my partner, Agent Walter Hayes?"

The younger man shook hands, quiet and dark and brooding, looking far more the part of an FBI agent than his slight, rumpled, light-haired partner.

"We're all glad you found that bomb in time. No fingerprints, of course, but plenty of useful evidence. I'd hate to see it destroyed." Agent Sheffield settled into his chair, rummaged in his breast pocket, and pulled out a cigarette case.

Jim shot Mary a comical look, and she had to look away so she wouldn't laugh. All business, this agent—more concerned with the evidence in the bomb than a whole shipload of men.

Mary smoothed the skirt of her pale gray summer suit. "Agent—"

"I'm impressed with your keen observations, Ensign." He lit his cigarette.

"Only because of Miss Stirling." Jim gestured her way. "If she hadn't raised my suspicions, I wouldn't have investigated."

Agent Sheffield turned to her as if seeing her for the first time. "Tell me again what you have."

"Yes, sir." Mary laid the notebook on the desk and repeated everything she'd told him two weeks earlier. "As you see, I've recorded each person's possible motive, means, and opportunity, plus my notes."

"The gossip."

Her mouth tightened. "I transcribe conversations."

"Entire conversations." Jim leaned his elbows on his knees. "She can take shorthand over two hundred words per minute."

Agent Sheffield leaned back in his chair and blew out a column of smoke. "All right. Tell me your theories, Miss Marple. Although you're too young to play *that* amateur sleuth."

She'd pretend she hadn't recognized his patronizing tone. "The obvious suspects are any Nazi sympathizers, perhaps members of the German-American Bund."

"I agree. Any names come to mind?"

"No, sir. A lot of people suspect Heinrich Bauer, but he's never said or done anything wrong that I know of. He just happens to be German."

"A suspiciously silent German. Does he talk to you?"

"No, sir. But it all seems rather obvious, don't you think? The swastika and the 'Sieg Heil'? If he wanted to be subtle, he failed."

Agent Sheffield tipped his head in an indulgent manner. "One thing I've learned in this business is criminals have immense egos. They want to draw attention to their cause or to their own brilliance. And the folks in the German-American Bund are thugs. They don't know anything about subtlety."

Mary sat forward. "But do they want to be seen as saboteurs? They want to rally Americans to their cause, not drive them away. It seems more likely that the saboteur is an interventionist who wants to make it look as if the Nazis are wreaking havoc. That would fan a public uproar, wouldn't—"

"The other thing I've learned in this position." Agent Sheffield rocked forward, and the front legs of his chair thumped on the floor. "The obvious scenario is usually true. The obvious suspects are usually guilty. Framing is very rare outside of Hollywood."

Mary tucked away her theory that an isolationist could be framing an interventionist, making it look as if *he* were framing a German. Agent Sheffield would burst into laughter at her convoluted logic.

Jim turned his cap in his hands. "Mary's idea makes sense to me. I think the saboteur wanted the bomb to be found. Why would he hide it in a busy place like a handling room?"

"If it weren't such a crudely designed bomb, you wouldn't have discovered it."

Jim gave Mary an apologetic look.

"Listen." Agent Sheffield thumbed through Mary's notebook. "I can't tell a bright young girl not to think, but you'd be better off not trying to figure this out. Let us do our work. Now that we have facts and evidence, the investigation will go into full swing. And your notes might prove useful. I appreciate the work you've done."

"Thank you, sir." Somehow his condescension allowed Mary to accept his praise. "And I'll continue—"

"No!" He fixed a strong gaze on her. "Leave the investigation to the professionals."

"I can still take notes. They might—"

"No. Absolutely not. It's only a matter of time until people figure out you're spying on them. This saboteur is dangerous. He was willing to kill two hundred men for his cause. He won't hesitate to hurt you. Leave it to us."

Mary rose from her chair, her legs wobbly. "Thank you for your concern, sir."

"And thanks for listening." Jim stood and shook the man's hand.

"Yes. Well, keep an eye on this young lady. Make sure she keeps her dainty little hands out of this. Of course, you know how women are."

"Don't worry, sir. Miss Stirling is smart. She'll do the right thing." Jim held the door open for her.

Mary gathered her belongings and scrutinized Jim as she left the room.

He gave her a wink, shut the door, and headed down the hallway. "Have time for lunch?"

She glanced at her watch. "Barely. What did you mean by that?"

Jim laughed and slipped on his raincoat. "I meant you're too smart *not* to keep investigating. That you'll keep doing the right thing."

What a good friend she had in him. She pulled on her coat too. The rain hadn't relented all morning.

Jim reached for her umbrella. "May I? I doubt your dainty little hands could hold it."

Mary laughed and handed it to him. "The man's impossible."

"And I'm selfish." He nudged the door open and raised the umbrella. "The only time an officer is allowed to use an umbrella is when he's shielding a lady."

"Taking advantage of my friendship so you can stay dry?"

"Guilty as charged." He offered his arm.

116

Mary clutched it, taking advantage of the umbrella to stay near to him. Guilty, although she hadn't been charged.

Jim strode forward through the rain toward the yard restaurant. "Agent Sheffield might not want to hear your theories, but I do. What are you thinking? One of the interventionists?"

"Yes. Someone who wants us to fight."

"Like Kaplan—that's his name, right?"

"Right. He's making a lot of noise, asking why Bauer hasn't been fired, much less arrested."

"Who else? Winston somebody?"

Mary hopped over a puddle. "Weldon Winslow, naval architect."

"Now that's a highbrow name. Sounds like he'd associate with Archer Vandenberg and his friends."

"Perhaps. He's heir to the Winslow Shipbuilding fortune."

Jim stopped and faced her. "Why does he work here?"

A raindrop scuttled down Mary's collar. She guided Jim back along the way. "His family rejected him when he married a working-class British girl. He renounced his inheritance."

Jim's lower jaw crept forward, and his eyes narrowed. "I don't understand."

"People are saying he lied about the feud, that he wants to undermine work at the Boston Navy Yard so his family's company will receive more Navy contracts. Plus, he loves England and desperately wants to help the British people."

"Because of his wife. Makes sense."

"But Mr. Winslow says he thinks his family sent the saboteur."

"Ah, to discredit the wayward son."

"Yes."

"Complicated." His eyes sparkled.

"Not as complicated as my other theory."

"What's that?"

Mary held his arm tight and frowned. "What if an isolationist is framing an interventionist?"

"An isolationist . . . ?"

"Think about it. What's one of the strongest isolationist arguments? That the British used false propaganda to trick us into fighting the First World War. Now, what would happen if an interventionist made it look as if the Nazis were trying to sink our ships and kill our men? How would the public react?"

Jim nodded. "They'd be furious. It might tip the scales and make people want to enter the war."

"Exactly. But what if that interventionist were proven to be framing the Germans? What if he were caught in the act of tricking the public?"

"I see. Then the public would be even more furious that they'd been fooled. They'd be even more opposed to entering the war or helping the Allies. Say, that's clever, Mary."

She stopped at the entrance to Building 28. "I don't know about clever. Remember what our dear FBI agent said about the obvious scenario usually being right. He's far more experienced than I am. Reading mysteries isn't the same as solving them."

Jim opened the door for Mary and shook out the umbrella. "Well, keep up your work. I promised him I'd keep an eye on you, after all."

"Now who's being clever?" Mary stepped inside and unbuttoned her raincoat.

"One thing's for certain—the saboteur succeeded in his primary purpose. My ship is not at sea, and everyone here is busy putting her back together instead of building new ships."

Mary sighed and hung her coat on a row of hooks. "And with all the tensions whipped into a frenzy, productivity has slowed to a crawl."

Jim shrugged off his coat. "All the more reason for Mary Stirling to continue her amateur sleuthing."

"I will."

In the restaurant, the tables were crowded with workers. Mary smiled at some of them and greeted others. After four years, they felt almost like uncles and cousins. Some were rough around the edges, but they were the salt of the earth, hardworking and trustworthy.

How could any one of these men commit sabotage? Would any of them really try to hurt her?

"Mary?" Jim's voice sounded husky.

She faced him. "Yes?"

He gripped her arm, right above the elbow, with an intensity in his gaze she hadn't seen before. "Be careful."

In that crowded room, surrounded by boisterous conversation, all she could see was the concern in his eyes. "I will."

16

Lieutenant Reinhardt signed the form with a flourish and passed it to Jim without a glance. "Take that up to the captain."

"Aye aye, sir." Jim exchanged a look with Gunner's Mate Homer Udell. Ever since they'd discovered the bomb, Reinhardt had rarely looked them in the eye. Could be he was angry at Jim and Udell for going over his head. Or it could be he was embarrassed that they'd been forced to do so, that he hadn't acted himself.

Either way, Jim handled the gunnery officer as he would a caged bear. Feed him regularly with work well done. Don't provoke him. Don't get caught alone in a room with him.

Jim stepped out the door of the handling room onto the main deck. He fanned his khaki shirt against his sweaty chest. In the high eighties today with plenty of humidity and a chance of thunderstorms.

For the past two weeks since they'd returned to Boston, everyone had worked hard tearing the ship apart and putting her back together again—under the supervision of armed Marine guards. Would they get liberty before they shipped

120

out for their second attempt at a shakedown cruise? Jim hadn't seen Mary since their meeting with Agent Sheffield.

The granite and brick buildings of the Navy Yard taunted him with their nearness. How could he pursue Mary if he never saw her?

Jim huffed out a breath and climbed up to the bridge. Friday was the Fourth of July. Surely Durant would give the men a break for the holiday.

Durant's voice floated down from the bridge—and another, more familiar voice. Jim doubled his speed up the stairs. Could it be?

Sure enough, out in the sunshine on the wing of the bridge, Durant stood chatting with Jim's oldest brother, Lt. Daniel Avery, wearing dress whites in contrast to the khakis worn by the crew of the *Atwood*.

"Dan!" Jim sprang forward to shake his brother's hand. "I mean, Mr. Avery. Good to see you, Mr. Avery."

"Good to see you too, Mr. Avery." Dan's hazel eyes sparkled beneath strong dark brows, and he gave Jim a hearty handshake.

"What are you doing here?"

"The *Vincennes* put in to Hampton Roads. I have a week's leave. Thought I'd see how my little brother is getting along."

Although Jim stood two inches taller than Dan, he still felt like a gangly, goofy kid next to him. Dan had a way about him, had it all his life—commanding, confident, no-nonsense.

"Your little brother is doing well for himself." Durant nudged Dan in the arm. "Earned a medal. He's the one who found the bomb."

"And Gunner's Mate Udell, sir. He alerted me to the situation. And don't forget Mr. Banning gave the orders."

Durant and Dan gave him matching appreciative looks—both men valued competence and disdained boasting.

Why did Jim feel like a puppy receiving a pat on the head? Ridiculous. He was a grown man. He pulled himself tall, glad of his height, and gave the report to the captain. "Sir, from Mr. Reinhardt. All four 5-inch guns are back in working order."

"Good. Good." Durant perused the form. "Sooner we can get this ship in shape the better."

"We need destroyers out there," Dan said.

"I know." Durant nodded to Jim. "Your brother's ship has been out on Neutrality Patrol."

Now Jim felt like the boy being asked to sit at the grown-up table for Thanksgiving dinner. Best to keep his opinions to himself in case he sounded foolish. "What's it like out there, Da—Mr. Avery?"

A flicker of a smile from Dan. He'd never been much of one for laughter. "Tense. As you know, we aren't escorting convoys yet. But we patrol the Security Zone and report any German ships."

Roosevelt had extended the Security Zone past Greenland, almost reaching Iceland, making a giant portion of the Atlantic off-limits to Axis ships.

"Anything to report?" Durant asked in a confidential tone.

Dan edged closer. "Our sonar operator made a sound contact, but it disappeared in minutes. Could have been a whale."

Despite the heat, a chill raced up Jim's arms. "Or it could have been a U-boat."

Dan adjusted his white cover. "I like to think the *Vincennes* scared it away."

"The Nazis can't afford another mistake after they sank the *Robin Moor*," Durant said.

The Avery brothers murmured their agreement in unison. In late May, a U-boat had sunk the freighter in the South Atlantic, although she flew under the neutral American flag and was unarmed, as were all American merchant ships. The crew had survived, but only after spending two weeks in lifeboats.

A light breeze cooled Jim's face. "The Nazis won't provoke us—not when they're fighting on two fronts now."

"True," Dan said. Germany had shocked the world the previous week by invading the Soviet Union, turning on their former ally. "Hitler may have spread himself too thin."

"Not at sea." Durant crossed his arms, the report from Reinhardt fluttering in his hand. "The war with Russia is a land battle. The U-boats are free to roam. England might not have to worry about invasion for a while, but she can still be starved of food and supplies. The sea's her lifeline. Her strength—and her great weakness."

Dan wrapped his hand around the railing. "It's hard for Brittania to rule the waves when U-boats lurk underneath."

"Say . . ." Durant glanced at his watch and then at the halyard lines stretching to the yardarm at the top of the mast. "I thought Mr. Shapiro was going to drill his flag crew at 1100 hours. Mr. Avery, please remind him."

"Aye aye, sir." Back to messenger boy.

"I'll go with you." Dan clapped the captain on the back. "Don't forget about our dinner plans, Cal. I'm looking forward to it."

"Me too. See you at 1800."

Jim led the way up to the signal deck, on the roof of the pilothouse and at the base of the gun director. He gave Dan a teasing look over his shoulder. "Calling the captain by his first name, eh?"

"We go a long way back."

"You're only four years older than I am."

"That's a long way back." Dan's eyes glowed with the pride of accomplishment. He'd already made a name for himself with the brass.

Up on the signal deck, Lt. Maurice Shapiro chatted with two sailors. "Hey, Mr. Avery!"

"Hi, Mr. Shapiro." Normally they called each other Mo and Jim, but not with Dan right behind him. Jim introduced his brother to the communications officer.

"I assume the captain sent you. We're ten minutes late with our drill." Mo's green eyes twinkled, a startling contrast with his olive skin and black hair. "Go ahead and keelhaul me."

Jim frowned at the water some forty feet below. "Hard to do at port."

Shapiro clicked his heels and saluted. "I shall commence posthaste."

"Good. Good," Jim said in his best Durant imitation. "Posthaste."

One of the sailors slouched against the flag bag. "Ah, posthaste means fast, don't it? All we do is drill, drill, drill. When're we gonna get liberty? We're tired."

"I know what you mean." Jim sent him a smile of commiseration. "We could all use some liberty. Best way to get it is by doing these drills crisp and fast."

Dan cleared his throat and tilted his head toward the far side of the little deck.

Jim followed and turned to see the drill. He loved watching the sailors string up the colorful signal flags.

"Jim," Dan said in a low voice. "Don't let the boys talk like that."

"Like what?" But a sinking feeling told him the truth. He'd breached etiquette.

"The grumbling. And definitely don't join in. It's bad form. Believe me, when you're out at sea with the gales blowing and the sea heaving, those boys will wish they were back at port running drills—especially when this turns into a shooting war."

"Only a matter of time, eh?"

Dan's eyes darkened. "Very soon."

"All the more reason to give the men some time off. I know I could use some." The Bunker Hill Monument rose to starboard, with Mary's cozy apartment at its base. "I'd love a night out dancing."

"Do you have a girl?" Dan's voice curled in disapproval.

Jim hadn't even told Arch about his intentions, in case an innocent slip or a not-so-innocent jest undid his efforts at subtlety. "Four of us. Arch and his girlfriend, Gloria, and my friend Mary Stirling from back home. She works here at the Navy Yard."

"Stirling?" Dan's dark eyebrows drew together. "Any relation to Harriet Stirling? She was in my class. Popular girl."

"Probably. Mary has two older sisters, but she's quite a bit younger. They aren't close."

"This isn't that silly blonde girl your friend Hugh was dating."

Jim swallowed hard. "No. In fact, Quintessa is Mary's best friend."

"Quintessa." Dan shook his head. "How could I forget a name like that?"

For Jim, forgetting her came easier every day.

Dan squinted at the signal flags racing up the halyards. "Well, see you don't get involved."

Jim read his brother's message as easily as he read the flags. "Ah, yes. The philosophy of the eminent Aloysius Howard." Dan had studied under the admiral at the Academy and then had served under his command at sea—and he wanted to follow in every one of his hero's distinguished footsteps.

"He's right." Dan straightened his white tunic. "A woman slows down the serious naval officer. She cries when you go into danger, so you hold back. Or she has her own ambitions for your career and pushes you in the wrong direction."

Jim smiled at the bright red and yellow and blue and white

flags flapping above him. Mary was brave enough to send him to sea and gentle enough not to manipulate him.

"More importantly . . ." Dan tapped Jim's arm with the back of his hand. "What if you face a situation at sea? What if your destroyer is escorting a convoy, and a U-boat approaches? The proper thing is to make an aggressive attack and protect the convoy. But what if you have a pretty wife at home, maybe a couple of children? You might be tempted to save your own neck for their sakes. That would be wrong."

How could he resist a tease? "What about Durant? He's married, has four of the cutest girls you've ever seen."

Dan glanced behind, below. "Why do you think he's only commanding a destroyer? At his age, he should be a lot further along. He's a good man, probably the best I've served with, but his family slows him down."

Never mind that the Navy strongly encouraged officers to marry. Never mind the long line of new ensigns waiting to wed at the Academy Chapel on graduation day and parading their brides through Annapolis in horse-drawn carriages. When Dan Avery fixed on an idea, he couldn't be budged.

Jim shrugged. "The captain seems happy."

"And he deserves that." Something in Dan's tone said he thought Durant deserved more.

Another line of signal flags shimmied up to the yardarm. Jim wouldn't float his way into a career or a relationship. He needed a plan for both. He needed God's guidance for both. "You have to decide what matters most to you."

"I want to make admiral."

"And you will." Jim's goals seemed flimsy in comparison. What exactly did he want? To serve in the Navy. To work with people. On shore or at sea, it didn't matter. And he wanted a family, a pretty wife at home waiting for him, and the picture in his dream had changed to a blue-eyed brunette.

"What do you want, Jim?" Dan's gaze prodded him—not to tear him down but to build him up. "You have it in you too. You could make admiral."

The corners of Jim's mouth eased up. "I'll have to see which way my path lies."

17

Thursday, July 3, 1941

The El train shivered its way out of the City Square Station in Charlestown. The Boston Navy Yard passed by on Mary's left. What fun to have an afternoon off to shop with Yvette.

The southbound Winter Line train clattered across the Charlestown Bridge, and steel girders flashed by Mary's eyes.

"Now do you believe me?" Yvette whapped a headline in the *Boston Globe*. "The Nazis are here, and they are dangerous."

"I know." All week Mary had been reading every news article she could. In New York City, the FBI had arrested thirty-three members of the Duquesne Spy Ring, most of whom had been born in Germany and had become American citizens.

"Do you see?" Yvette bowed her head over the paper, and the feathers on the front of her hat bowed with her. "They worked at defense factories, on passenger ships—and on the docks."

"I know." The train pulled into North Station. Dozens of people disembarked, and dozens more boarded.

"Why not Boston?" Yvette's golden-brown eyes beseeched her. "The FBI found thirty-three, but—"

"How many more? And are there any at the Navy Yard?"

"They put a bomb on your friend's ship."

Mary crossed her legs and rearranged the skirt of her blue-and-yellow floral shirtwaist dress. "We know someone put a bomb on the ship, but we don't know who."

"Pssh." Yvette folded the newspaper. "We don't know the names, but they are the *Boche*."

"The Germans? Possibly." A good detective, even of the amateur variety, needed to keep her mind and her eyes open.

"Possibly? Pssh. If it is not the *Boche*, I will . . . I will . . ."

"Eat American cheese?"

Yvette's thin brown eyebrows sprang high. "Never again. Not even if the Nazis conquer America and we have no other food. I will starve."

Mary laughed and patted her friend's hand.

The train went down an incline and entered the subway system. Lights flashed by in the dark tunnel.

"See? You must stop." Yvette rapped Mary's hand. "No more notes."

"I have to." Mary raised her voice to be heard over the magnified train sounds. "We have to catch the saboteur before anyone gets hurt. If I can help in any small way, I must."

"The FBI told you to stop. You must obey."

"I'm not breaking the law. They're afraid I'll do something stupid and interfere with their investigation, but I won't."

"They want you to be safe, and so do I."

Mary raised a satisfied smile. "Then I must help. No one is safe until the saboteur is caught."

Yvette mumbled a long string of French words, none of which Mary understood.

They each had their code language. Yvette had French, and Mary had shorthand. She kept her notes about Yvette in shorthand and didn't type them up. Rumors circulated around Yvette because she was a foreigner, and some of the things she said might sound incriminating to someone who didn't know her. A solid record could protect her friend in case of accusations.

Mary gazed out the window to the platforms of the Haymarket Station. Unlike Yvette, Jim encouraged her investigation, and that meant so much to her. Whenever she prayed, she felt a sense of stirring rightness. Unless that changed, she'd continue.

In her letters home, she hadn't mentioned a word to her parents or sisters—they'd think her sleuthing was silly. But Quintessa was delighted and full of questions and ideas. If only her dear friend were here to puzzle over the mystery.

Mary sucked in a breath. But then Jim would forget Mary existed. In Quintessa's brilliant presence, Mary faded away. In the past, Mary preferred it that way, but now she didn't want to fade away in Jim's sight.

All her life, she'd avoided attention, but now she wanted attention—from Jim.

At the Devonshire Station, more people exchanged places, and Mary sorted out her views. Seeking attention usually stemmed from pride and selfishness, but not in this case. She cared for Jim and hoped he'd return her affections. Love wasn't a selfish goal when both people benefitted.

The whole thing was more complex and nuanced than she'd led herself to believe.

If only she could see him. Jim hadn't had liberty since his first weekend back in Boston, and neither had Arch. Gloria called Mary every day, sounding more frantic with each call, and Mary soothed her each time. No, Arch hadn't forgotten her. The men were hard at work.

"Here we are." Yvette stood and made her way down the aisle.

Mary followed and stepped off the train onto the underground platform, keeping her purse clutched to her stomach as they pushed forward.

Up the stairs and through the tunnel they went, then down some steps straight into Filene's Basement. Yvette charged into the crowd, but Mary hung back to get her bearings.

Upstairs, Filene's carried eight stories' worth of gorgeous goods, but down in Filene's Basement bargains reigned.

For Bostonians, it was a game and a gamble. Products came downstairs with low prices, then were marked down 25 percent after twelve days, 50 percent for six more days, 75 percent for six days, and then donated to charity. The longer you waited, the greater the bargain—and the greater the chance someone else would snatch it up.

Mary searched until she found a bin of summer dresses in her size. Half a dozen women pressed around, grabbing dresses, examining them, thrusting them back. One woman stripped off her dress, down to her slip, and tried on a green-and-white striped dress.

If only the bargains came with dressing rooms.

Mary's eyes were drawn to a short-sleeved sailor dress, and she held it up. How sweet—white with blue trim around the collar and sleeves, and with a darling princess-seamed cut and a flared skirt.

Wouldn't she look smart walking next to Jim in his naval uniform? Or would she look like she was angling to be a sailor's girlfriend?

She grumbled, reached to put it back, then stopped. Someone else might grab it. She should at least try it on.

A flash of red blurred by her face as a woman tossed a dress back into the bin.

A bold red dress, yet in a silky fabric and softened with passementerie trim on the bodice. A year ago, she would have adored a similar dress in blue, but never in red.

Now she grabbed it, her heart quickening. How silly. She wasn't doing anything heroic, just trying on a red dress.

At a nearby table, Yvette riffled through a pile of blouses.

Mary worked her way over. "I'm going to find someplace less exposed and try these on."

"You are too modest." Yvette gestured at the women in their slips all around her. "Not all Americans are."

Mary gave her a wink. "I'm from Ohio."

Yvette gasped and touched the red dress. "*C'est bon!*"

"The dean of my secretarial school told us never to wear red because it excites the men."

"Isn't that what you want?"

Perhaps she did. Just a little. "I'll try it on. I might not like it."

"*Oui, oui.*" Yvette waved her to the corner.

Mary found a spot behind a rack, where she could be as prudish as she wanted. She unbuttoned her shirtwaist dress and quickly slipped the sailor dress overhead and pulled up the side zipper.

It fit perfectly. She gathered her things and found a mirror, waiting her turn to catch a view of herself. Oh yes, she loved it. So summery.

Someone jostled her out of the way, and Mary returned to her secluded spot. Off with the sailor dress and on with the red.

No one stood by the mirror now, and Mary studied her unfamiliar reflection. The fit flattered her figure, and the red—why, it brought out pink in her cheeks and a glow in her hair.

She only needed one new dress. Both appealed to her for different reasons. Both suited her. Both were marked down 25 percent. Which should she buy?

For heaven's sake, she was choosing a summer dress, not a husband. Mary darted back to her spot and changed back into the safe floral dress her mother would approve.

Yesterday, a letter had arrived from home. Mother was concerned about Mary's decision to join the choir. Wouldn't that lead her down the same road of temptation? A good Christian girl should be humble and not flaunt herself. She should put others above herself. She should avoid praise at all cost, because praise led to conceit and all sorts of vain foolishness.

Mary did up the buttons. Her mother was only partly right. Humility was a great virtue, but did humility require hiding in the corner? Nonsense. The Lord had given her gifts, and he wanted her to use them for his purposes. Not for herself, but for him. As long as she kept her priorities straight, she would be fine.

Mary held up the two dresses and studied them until a decision made her smile. She'd buy both.

★ ★ ★

Off the Coast of Maine
Tuesday, July 15, 1941

"Target sighted. Action starboard. Target is barge, bearing three-zero. Start tracking." Up in the gun director on top of the bridge, Jim looked through the telescope of the slewing sight through a porthole. Above the tops of the waves, the outline of an old barge rhythmically flashed into and out of view. The Navy had anchored the barge a hundred miles off the Maine coast for target practice.

Beside Jim, the director trainer cranked his hand wheels, rotating the whole gun director on its giant ball-bearing ring, changing the flow of the breeze. "On target."

Meanwhile the pointer adjusted his equipment for elevation. "On target."

Behind Jim, the range-finder operator peered into a thick horizontal tube that connected the two optical range-finders and computed the distance to the target. "Range five-one-double-oh." Fifty-one hundred yards.

Electrical signals from the trainer, pointer, and range-finder were transmitted to the mechanical computer in the plotting room, which would calculate a solution and automatically elevate and rotate all four 5-inch guns to bear on the target.

"Mr. Reinhardt, target angle three-zero. Target horizontal speed double-oh." Jim spoke on the intercom to the Interior Communications and Plotting Room, several decks below. Sweat trickled down his breastbone.

Reinhardt repeated the message, to verify with Jim and to relay the input values to the computer operators. A short pause. "Solution computed and transmitted to guns."

"Thanks. Captain, do we have permission to fire?" The intercom connected Jim to the bridge directly below.

"Yes, Mr. Avery. Commence firing."

Jim hauled in a breath. This was the first time he'd been in command of the director for a gunnery drill, and he needed to make it count. "Aye aye. Fire salvo."

Down on the main deck, two guns on the bow and two on the stern craned their barrels skyward. Rings of orange fire, belches of gray smoke, a thunderous noise, and the deck beneath Jim's feet heaved. Better than the Fourth of July.

Except now he didn't have Mary Stirling next to him in a red dress, her eyes lit up by the fireworks over the Charles River, her narrow waist begging for his arm to circle it. He'd come close. His heart keeping tempo with Arthur Fiedler and the Boston Pops, Jim had placed his hand on the small of Mary's back to guide her through the crowd at the Hatch Shell. But then he'd let go, unsure whether embracing her would be suave or foolish or welcome.

He shook his head and counted the eight seconds it should take the target projectile to reach the barge. Maybe Dan was right about women distracting an officer from his work.

Through the slewing sight, he followed four orange tracers streaming behind the projectiles and converging on the barge. Spouts of water rose, about one hundred yards short.

"Up one-double-oh, bearing true." Jim wiped sweat from his upper lip. Firing a naval gun required skill. Both the destroyer and its target could change location, speed, and direction—and the motion of the sea constantly altered the angle of the guns. The Mark 37 gun director had a mechanical computer and a stable element to compensate for all the variables, but gunnery remained as much an art as a science.

"Mr. Avery, we have a new solution," Reinhardt said on the intercom.

"Thank you." Jim eyed that old barge, determined to land a sand-filled projectile right on top. "Commence firing."

The guns fired their shots.

Jim planted his hand on the steel wall of the enclosure so he wouldn't lose his balance, and then he trained his sight on the target and counted off the seconds. Plumes of water, just aft of the barge, about five degrees.

He made a face. "Right zero-five." In today's drill, the *Atwood* maintained the same speed and bearing, the target was stationary, and the weather was sunny and mild. They wouldn't have conditions like that in battle.

And battle loomed nearer each day. Only a week earlier, US Marines had occupied Iceland, relieving the British troops guarding the strategically vital island from German invasion, and the US Navy had taken joint responsibility with the Royal Canadian Navy in escorting convoys from Canada to Iceland.

The veil of neutrality was fraying.

Jim wiped sweat from under his eyes. The three portholes and three overhead hatches didn't admit much of a breeze, and the sun beat on the metal enclosure.

Through his headphones, he could hear Reinhardt barking

at the computer operators in the plotting room. Poor fellows. Just doing their jobs as best they could.

Jim spread an encouraging smile around the cramped space. "Come on, men. Let's sink that old barge. I know we can do it."

The crew nodded, engrossed in their jobs. These men had trained hard in this technical work and didn't need pats on the back. They also didn't need Reinhardt's verbal haranguing. Hadn't Reinhardt learned anything from Nehemiah? The importance of everyone working together, side by side, the leaders acknowledging everyone who helped, from the greatest to the least?

"Do we have a new solution?" Jim said.

"Yes, Mr. Avery."

Jim braced himself. "Commence firing."

Another set of booms and rumbles and shakes. Eight seconds ticked by. No plume of water, but the barge rocked. "I think we hit it."

"Yes, sir. We did." The range-finder operator lifted his head and grinned. A red rim circled his eyes from the rubber gasket of the eyepiece.

Jim put on his best Western accent. "Good shootin', cowboy."

One hit out of three. Reinhardt had done worse. He'd done better too, but he'd done worse.

"Okay, men. Let's clean up shop and get some fresh air."

The second shakedown cruise seemed to be going well. The constant drills annoyed some of the men, but most saw the worth. They were faster, smoother, and better coordinated. A few more weeks of this, and they should be ready for any crisis.

Then back to Boston. Jim stuck his face in the square porthole and inhaled fresh cool air. Arch had invited Gloria, Jim, and Mary for a sailing weekend at his parents' seaside

Connecticut estate. Partly for fun, and partly to test Gloria again. How she reacted to the mansion, the yacht, and the lush grounds on her return visit would determine the fate of their relationship.

Poor girl didn't stand a chance. Jim saw the way she ogled the wares in the windows of Boston's finest shops.

Not Mary. She'd exclaimed over how little she spent on her new dress. She'd be satisfied with a modest income. Good. Unlike Arch, Jim wouldn't inherit wealth.

Jim pulled off his headphones and followed the crew out the narrow doorway and down the ladder to the bridge.

"Not bad for your first time, Mr. Avery." Durant clasped his hands behind his back.

"Thank you, sir." Jim squared his cover back on his head. "That was fun."

"Glad to see you can take Reinhardt's place if he's officer of the deck."

Or if Reinhardt became a battle casualty. Every man needed to know more than one job in case of emergency. "Will I get another chance to practice, sir?"

"We'll see. We don't have a lot of target projectiles, but we plan to use them all before we return to Boston."

"Good." They'd have to make more room for live ammunition anyway. Next time they put out to sea, they'd escort a convoy across the North Atlantic, protecting merchant ships and scouting for U-boats.

Jim headed down to the wardroom to complete his paperwork. *Lord, make me ready.*

18

Boston
Friday, August 8, 1941

If only she could catch a breeze. Mary tipped up her face into the muggy air but found no relief. After she fanned herself with her notebook, she crossed a catwalk and stepped down to the main deck of a destroyer under construction.

A giant crane lowered a section of the superstructure into position as men guided it with ropes.

Mary kept her distance and made her way toward the stern of the ship, where she thought she'd spied Frank Fiske.

"Joe DiMaggio, he's my man," said a worker—Al Klingman—coiling a cable around his bent arm. "Fifty-six-game hitting streak. Beat that."

Ira Kaplan socked Klingman on the shoulder. "Ah, go back to Brooklyn where you belong, old man. You're in Boston now, and Lefty Grove got his three-hundredth win."

Morton Anders swept up a pile of metal shavings. "And Ted Williams is batting over .400. I'd put my money on him over DiMaggio any day."

Mary shaded her eyes from the sunshine and gazed around the deck.

"Hiya, Miss Stirling," Kaplan said. "Looking for Fiske?"

"I am. Have you—" Mary gasped. A green-and-yellow bruise surrounded Ira Kaplan's eye, and a bandage covered his chin. "My goodness. What happened?"

The friendly smile fled, and his gaze dropped to the side. "Got jumped last weekend by some thugs in brown shirts."

Anders cussed, then sent Mary an apologetic look and ran his hand into blond curls at the nape of his neck. "Bunch of good-for-nothing German-American Bund boys."

Mary's stomach twisted. "Oh dear. I'm so sorry."

"They beat up this young man. Today's his first day back, been out all week." Klingman set a protective hand on Kaplan's shoulder. "Want to know what else they did?"

Kaplan shrugged off the older man's grip. "Come on. That's enough."

"No. People need to know." Under wiry dark brows, Klingman's brown eyes pierced more than any tool on the deck.

"What happened?" Mary asked.

Anders's round face turned stormy. "I'll tell you. Those swine left him for dead and threw pamphlets on top of him. Pamphlets about how America should support Germany. How the Jews are ripping apart our country, driving us to war. How Christians should unite—"

"Enough." Kaplan stuck out one hand and walked away.

Anders called after him. "I go to mass every Sunday, and I think those pamphlets are a bunch of stinking lies."

Mary pressed her free hand to her roiling stomach. How could some Christians forget their own Savior was Jewish? "I'm so sorry."

"Yeah?" Kaplan wheeled around. "I am too. Sorry the FBI isn't doing its job. Why haven't they arrested number thirty-four?"

"Thirty-four?" Mary asked.

"Heinrich Bauer." He gestured with his thumb toward the stern, where the welder worked. "The FBI arrested thirty-three Nazi spies in the Duquesne Ring. They missed one."

Mary stared into Kaplan's eyes, one wide, one swollen half shut. "You—you have proof?"

"Proof? That's what the FBI wants." He pointed to his bandaged chin. "How much more proof do you need?"

Breath raced into Mary's lungs, pungent with the smell of hot metal. "He was one of the thugs?"

"No, but he was behind it. I'm sure of it."

Al Klingman crossed arms thickened by decades of manual labor. "Looks like those spies, don't he? Did you see that two-page spread in *Life* magazine with those pictures? All just run-of-the-mill types, nothing special. Not like those spies you see in the movies."

"I suppose it's best for a spy to blend in and not be noticed." That was what Mary depended on.

Anders tapped his temple. "Yeah, well, we notice Bauer. Keep our eyes on him. Even if Fiske did divide us into the sheep and the goats."

Mary allowed a small smile. Last week, the leadingman had divided his crew into isolationists and interventionists, assigning them to separate areas to increase productivity. "Speaking of Mr. Fiske . . ."

"Oh yeah." Kaplan's wide grin reappeared. "Here we are distracting you from your work. He's over there." He pointed to the stern.

There he was, not far from where Mr. Bauer talked to another workman.

"Thank you, Mr. Kaplan. I'm glad you're feeling better." Mary headed aft, smiling to herself that she was thinking in nautical terms.

Mr. Bauer took an envelope from the workman, and the

other man departed. Bauer opened the envelope, read the contents, glared in the workman's direction, crumpled up the paper, flung it overboard, and strode away.

The wind tossed the paper back onto the deck behind him, and Mary rushed to pick it up. She smoothed it open.

Bauer how is yore friend Adolph? Be careful Natsi or something will happen to you. Think about Magda she sure is prety and yore babys to.

Oh no. Mary dashed to the welder and tapped him on the shoulder. "Mr. Bauer!"

"*Ja?* Yes?" He faced her, looked down to the note in her hand, and his long face went slack.

"How many of these have you received? Have you shown the FBI?"

His jaw shifted from side to side, and he stared at the note, his blue eyes awash with indecipherable emotions. "The FBI is police, *ja*? I do not trust them."

"But they want to help. They want the truth."

"They want—" His features turned to ice. He snatched the note from Mary's hand and crammed it into his pants pocket. "I want to work. I want to feed my family. Let me be."

Her heart kept pace with the riveting gun to her right, and she scribbled down the contents of the threatening note in her book. Regardless of what Bauer said, the FBI needed to know. Why wouldn't Bauer tell anyone? Did his reticence mean noble restraint—or concealment of guilt? If he was innocent, silence only put him in more danger. Didn't he realize that?

Mary looked up. Where had Mr. Fiske gone to now?

There he was, striding along the port side of the ship.

Mary passed three men installing a watertight door on the aft superstructure, all isolationists.

George O'Donnell talked to them as they worked, but why was he down on the docks? Didn't the draftsman belong in the drafting room . . . drafting? Mary slowed her pace and angled her path to skirt past the group, her notebook and pen poised.

"Roosevelt lied to our boys." O'Donnell stuffed idle hands in his trouser pockets. "He promised if they were drafted, they'd only serve one year."

Ralph Tucker paused in his work and glanced up at O'Donnell. "You heard the Senate passed the law extending the draft. The House had better shoot it down."

"It'll be close, I heard." Curly Mulligan adjusted his cap over his namesake hair. "Let's hope common sense wins out."

"Common sense?" O'Donnell jabbed one finger in the sky. "How can we have common sense in America? Our president's the playground bully, picking fights with the Germans, and now the Japanese. Freezing their assets? Cutting off their supply of oil? He's asking for it, but we're the ones who have to pay."

Mary took notes as she passed, but their comments on the news were predictable and didn't shed any light on the sabotage.

Now where had Mr. Fiske gone? She scanned the busy deck and stepped over an electrical cable. The leadingman stood by one of the ship's funnels, writing on a clipboard.

Mary made her way over, ignoring further conversations. Mr. Pennington said she could only sleuth if it didn't interfere with her work responsibilities, and reports did need to be delivered and collected.

Frank Fiske spotted Mary, smiled, and waved her over. "Good morning."

"Yes, if a bit warm." She fanned herself, a futile gesture in such heat and humidity, even in her light blue, short-sleeved linen suit. If only ladies didn't need to wear slips and girdles and stockings that made them sweat in a most unladylike fashion.

She exchanged paperwork with Mr. Fiske. "How's the separation of the sheep and the goats working?"

He laughed. "I heard that's what they're calling it. They disagree on who's who."

Mary smiled. They disagreed on almost everything. "Is it helping?"

"Fewer fights, that's for sure, but now they spend too much time gabbing, getting each other riled up."

Speaking of getting the men riled up . . . "Do you know why Mr. O'Donnell's here?"

Fiske squeezed his eyes shut and groaned. "He's still here? I'll have to talk to him. One of my oldest friends, but he's distracting my men and spreading rumors. What's he up to?"

Revealing how closely she listened didn't seem wise. "I think they were talking about the bill to extend the draft."

Eyebrows bunched together over his deep-set eyes. "I don't blame them. It's a betrayal."

Mary gave him a compassionate look. "Your son would be affected?"

"He's the only family I have." His mouth squirmed. "My parents gone. My wife gone. He's all I have."

"I'm sorry."

"He's supposed to be out in November. That was the deal. But now . . ."

"I know." If the country went to war while his son was still enlisted, he'd be committed for the duration of the conflict.

Fiske's expression shifted, and he glanced aft toward O'Donnell and his pals. "I have bigger problems around here than O'Donnell."

"Mr. Bauer?"

He barked out a short laugh. "You sound like the FBI.

They won't leave the man alone, especially since a section he worked on failed earlier this week, looked suspicious."

"Oh dear."

Fiske flapped his broad hand. "It's not that simple. I inspected his work the day before. It passed. Then the next day it failed when we fitted it to the next section."

Mary's mind swam. "Do you think he—someone—altered it after the inspection?"

"I know someone did. And I know who. Found a pair of gloves right there, labeled with a name."

"Gloves?" A clue Nancy Drew would love. "Whose?"

"A man who keeps misplacing his gloves. A man whose mother sewed his name inside." Fiske leaned closer. "Ira Kaplan."

"Oh dear." Mary glanced over to the tall young man, hard at work with his friends. "Did you tell Agent Sheffield?"

"He wasn't impressed. Kaplan did work in that area."

Mary's heart sank. "I hope you're wrong."

"Me too. He's a good kid, a hard worker. I like the boy, I do, but he and his buddies want us in that war. They don't care who gets hurt."

"Does Mr. Pennington know?"

"All the details are in the report I gave you."

"Thanks." She headed for the catwalk.

Heinrich Bauer walked in the same direction, about ten feet in front of her.

"Hey! Hey, Kraut!"

Bauer stiffened and stopped, then plowed forward.

"I'm talking to you." Ira Kaplan marched over, arms swinging high. "Nazi."

Mary hung back, pulled out her notebook, and watched wide-eyed.

"I am not," Bauer said.

"Sure you are. You're a stinking Nazi."

"You know nothing." His voice was hard and stiff.

"I know one thing. You stole my gloves." Kaplan shoved him.

Mary sucked in a breath. A crowd formed, sheep on one side, goats on the other. Wouldn't anyone break this up? Where was Mr. Fiske?

Bauer stumbled, then straightened. "I am not a thief."

"You're a thief and a saboteur, and now you're trying to frame me." Panic chased around the edges of Kaplan's voice. "The FBI's questioning me, but I know what you did. You stole my gloves, altered your work after Fiske's inspection, then—"

"I did not. You know nothing." Bauer stared him down, then turned for the catwalk.

"Thief, saboteur, coward!" Kaplan rushed at him, and the men erupted in shouts, urging them on.

Why wouldn't anyone help? Mary searched the crowd, pushed her way toward where she'd last seen the leading-man. "Mr. Fiske!"

He was already on his way, elbowing workmen aside. "Break it up!" He shoved Bauer and Kaplan apart like Moses parting the Red Sea. "What on earth do you think you're doing?"

Some of the older men grabbed Kaplan by the elbows.

He strained against them. "Let me go. Let me at him. He's the saboteur."

Fiske stepped right in front of Kaplan. "Back off and let the FBI do their work. They'll catch the saboteur."

"Yeah? Then why is Bauer running free?"

"They can't arrest a man without solid proof." Fiske patted Kaplan on the shoulder, a gesture both fatherly and menacing. "You should be very glad of that."

"What?" Kaplan's dark eyebrows twisted. "What do you mean by that?"

Mary knew perfectly well what he meant, and she scribbled as fast as she could in her notebook.

"All right, boys, back to work. All of you." Fiske's voice didn't allow argument. "Kaplan, you're taking the rest of the day off. Without pay. I'll deal with the union."

"What about—"

"Bauer didn't start it. Get out of here. Come back tomorrow when you've cooled down."

Grumbling, Kaplan crossed the catwalk, and the men returned to work.

Mary backed up and took down every detail in her notebook, her pulse thrumming in her veins. Both Bauer and Kaplan thought they were being framed. How curious.

George O'Donnell ambled over to Fiske, about ten feet from Mary. "I tell you, Frank, those warmongers are bound and deter—"

"George, why are you here?"

O'Donnell stepped back, dark eyes narrow. "Chatting with the boys."

"About the war, the draft, all that."

"Of course."

"You're slowing down work."

O'Donnell stood still, his gaze fixed on his old friend. "I guess I am."

With a brisk nod, Fiske walked away.

Mary frowned. Was that a reprimand of O'Donnell's actions—or approval? How very odd. She recorded every word in her book.

By the time she'd finished, her heart rate had almost returned to normal, but energy coursed through her. Agent Sheffield hadn't seen that fight or heard those words. In fact, if he'd been around, none of it would have happened.

A smile tugged the corners of her lips as she crossed the catwalk to the dock. Who said amateur detectives were useless? Who said pride played a role? She wasn't undermining the FBI but aiding it.

She strode across the wharf toward Building 39. This investigation made her feel as if she were doing some good. This weekend she'd type up her most recent notes, and she'd turn them in to Agent Sheffield on Monday. He wouldn't be pleased that Mary was still involved, but he'd be pleased with the information she presented.

She hummed "Joyful, Joyful, We Adore Thee" as she strolled along. As of September, she'd sing in the choir on Sunday mornings, even if Bertha and Edith Wilkins had to prop her up between them. They treated her more like a third Wilkins sister than a girl young enough to be their great-granddaughter. At choir practice, they giggled like schoolgirls. On several occasions, poor Mrs. Gunderson had needed to hush them.

Three naval officers in summer whites passed Mary, smiled, and tipped their caps.

She smiled back. Oh, how she missed Jim. The shakedown cruise was supposed to last about a month—any day now. Arch had mentioned a possible sailing weekend at his parents' seaside Connecticut home. That would be wonderful.

The air felt lighter, cooler, and her step more buoyant. A whole weekend together. Maybe things would change. Even if they didn't, even if her romantic dreams fizzled and died, a whole weekend enjoying Jim's company and friendship would be delightful.

Her music, her friendships, the thrill of confronting her lifelong fear—how it all filled her sails.

19

Stonington, Connecticut
Saturday, August 30, 1941

"Little more to port." Jim grasped the helm above Mary's hand, guiding her, his bare arm brushing hers. Heat rushed through him.

Thank goodness he'd decided not to stand directly behind her and help her steer with both hands. If he had, he'd throw common sense into the balmy breeze, wrap his arms around her, and nuzzle in her sun-warmed neck. Scare the poor girl half to death.

Instead he stood behind her right shoulder, far enough away to look suave, but near enough to help and too close to ogle her figure. He was still aware of every curve in that dark blue swimsuit covered with little white spots, as orderly and feminine as Mary herself.

Up by the mast of the Vandenberg yacht, wearing swim trunks and deck shoes, Arch adjusted lines. He called forward to Gloria, who lay in the sun in a skimpy swimsuit, a giant hat clamped over her face.

"How's this, Jim?" Mary glanced over her bare shoulder, her dark hair sweeping back in the wind.

Jim schooled his face not to erupt in a goofy grin. "Good. Almost time to change tack."

"Still seems odd that you have to zigzag to move in a straight line."

"The wind doesn't always blow in the direction you want to go."

"So true."

Her thoughtful tone massaged his brain. All his life, he'd had favorable winds. His family loved and supported him. He had the personal traits needed to excel and the opportunities to do so. It might not always be that way. It wasn't for most people.

Arch's parents wanted their only son to take over their business, but he'd bucked their desires and joined the Navy, straining against the current.

Running with the wind wasn't the only—or even the best—way to sail.

"Ready about," Jim called to Arch.

"Aye aye." The yachtsman gathered up the sheet lines, ready to spring to action. "Hard-a-lee."

"All right, Mary. Turn her hard into the wind."

She did so. The sails loosened, and Arch ran out lines to compensate.

The bow pointed straight into the wind, and the boat paused, holding its breath.

"Oh!" Mary paused too.

"No. Don't stop now." Jim gripped the wheel and kept it moving. "We'll be in irons."

"In irons?" The sails luffed, jangled on their rings, and snapped in the wind.

"Stalled. Stuck."

Arch ran out more lines, the mainsail puffed up on the other side, and the boat sailed smoothly.

"Hold her steady." Jim wrapped his hand around Mary's slender wrist. "Very good."

"That's exciting, isn't it? A lot of noise and motion."

He released her wrist for his own sake. "As you saw, when the sails start luffing, you can't let the noise and motion distract you. You have to keep moving."

"Hmm. I understand."

"Good. This weekend we'll make a sailor out of you."

Mary smiled, snatched the white cover from Jim's head, and snugged it over her wind-whipped hair. Much cuter on her. Very cute.

The goofy grin—he could feel it undoing months of hard work trying to look sophisticated. He plopped onto the seat in the stern. "You have the helm, Captain. Since I've been demoted to landlubber."

Her laugh sparkled. "So what shall we talk about, since Arch has forbidden all talk of war and sabotage?"

Arch wanted to placate Gloria by avoiding her least favorite subjects. If Gloria failed this weekend's test, it wouldn't be due to lack of effort on Arch's part to satisfy the girl's demands.

Too bad, because the events in the news would give them plenty to discuss. President Roosevelt had signed the bill to extend the draft, increasing the length of service from twelve to thirty months. US Navy planes now flew from Iceland, covering Allied convoys. And still the carnage continued in the North Atlantic, with multiple freighters and tankers falling prey to Nazi U-boats almost every day.

"Well?" Mary looked like a pinup girl in Jim's cover, her nautical bathing suit, her playful smile, and too many curves for Jim's well-being.

He leaned back, draped one hairy leg along the brass railing, and laced his hands behind his head. "Anything you want."

"Anything?"

"Anything." But the way she squinted and pursed her lips made him regret it.

"I've been wondering . . . about your hands."

"My hands?" The scars constricted, curling his fingers into his briny hair.

Mary tilted her head, gazing ahead. "Sometimes you rub your palms, but you stop when anyone notices. And when we dance . . . just now when you touched me . . ." She set one hand on the wrist he'd held only moments earlier.

Jim swallowed. Above his head, the edge of the sail ruffled. He sprang to Mary's side. "The wind shifted. Head a bit to starboard."

Mary complied, and the ruffling ceased. "If you don't want to talk about it, that's all right. I understand."

A sophisticated man didn't have scars, but Jim uncoiled his hands before her. Shiny scars ran along the fleshy ridges of his palms.

"Oh," Mary sighed. "How did that happen?"

He returned to his seat, elbows on his knees, the evidence on his palms facing the clear blue sky. "The first time I tried to take charge, to make waves."

"What happened?" She had such a soft way of asking, without accusation.

"The day Lillian lost her leg."

"Oh dear. I knew she had an accident, but no one talks of the details."

"She was five, so I was seven, Rob nine, Dan eleven. Lillian and Lucy might be identical twins on the outside, but they couldn't be more different on the inside."

Mary tipped up a smile. "True."

"Lucy liked to stay home and play dolls, but Lillian was a tomboy, always wanted to tag along with us boys. I liked to play with her, but Dan and Rob didn't, so they always prevailed."

"I understand. My older sisters didn't let me tag along either."

The boat rose and fell with the waves, the constant reassuring hiss of water on wood, the wake spreading white behind them, spray cooling Jim's skin. "One day we boys were heading into the woods, and Lillian wanted to come. She begged me. She never used tears to manipulate me, but this time she cried. So I told her to follow us at a distance. Then when we arrived at the fort we were building, she'd show up. Dan and Rob would be annoyed, but they wouldn't send her home, and they'd see how much fun she was."

"You're a sweet brother."

Jim glanced away, toward the homes along the shore, the lighthouse on the point. "She followed my instructions too well. She kept off the path so she wouldn't be seen, but she strayed too far. Halfway to the fort I heard a scream."

"Oh no."

The memory of that sound ripped through him, fresh and raw and primeval. "I raced back. Dan told me to stop, because a wounded animal was dangerous, but I knew it was Lillian. Knew it."

"It was a trap, wasn't it? I remember."

Never once had Jim been seasick, but now nausea cramped his belly. "You can imagine—strong enough to hold a wild animal—and her little leg." The mangled, crooked, bloody mess.

Jim's fingers bent down, working their way into the imaginary trap. "I tried—I tried to open it, but I wasn't strong enough. I wasn't thinking, didn't care about my hands, just wanted to save her."

"Of course you did."

"Then Dan and Rob arrived. Dan flipped the release lever, calm as can be, and he carried her home."

"Poor Lillian."

"They couldn't save her leg, amputated the same day."

"And your hands . . ."

He curled up his fingers, the tips resting on the hard smooth scar tissue. "For a while, I wished the doctor would amputate my hands too."

"Oh, Jim . . ." Mary's voice wavered.

"Hey, Avery!" Arch shouted.

He jerked up his head. The boat, the sails, the course. He hadn't been paying attention. "Yeah?"

"Ready about?"

"Yeah. Yeah." He stood, his legs wobbly. "Ready, Mary?"

At Arch's command, she swung the helm and switched tack, smooth as maple syrup.

"Well done," Jim said, glad to change the topic.

Mary looked up at him with a liquid gaze. "Do you blame yourself?"

Every single day. "If I hadn't intervened, she wouldn't have been hurt."

"Does she blame you?"

He smashed his lips together. Three months out of pharmacy school, with excellent grades, in a booming economy, and she still didn't have a job. Only one reason stood out—no one wanted to hire a woman they'd label a cripple. "If she does, she's forgiven me, or at least acts like she has."

"You were both so young. It was an accident."

Jim had heard that countless times, but hearing it on Mary's pretty lips—somehow he believed it for the first time.

20

Mary stretched flat on her stomach, the sun dissolving her bones, the waves rocking her. Only Jim's voice kept her awake, his deep cheerful voice, laughing and talking to Arch as they tied the yacht to the pier.

His behavior was more mysterious than that of the sabotage suspects. One minute open and friendly as usual, then the next he'd replace his smile with blank apathy. Yet he'd stayed at her side most of the afternoon, and he'd touched her far more than necessary to teach her to sail, touches that sent warmth vibrating through her.

If she couldn't figure out Jim Avery, what made her think she could solve a complicated mystery? If only she could discuss the latest developments with Jim, but the silly moratorium on talking about war and sabotage stifled her. She blew out a breath, cooling her forehead.

Beside her on the deck, Gloria Washburn heaved a sigh and sat up, leaning over her bent legs and stroking them. "I can't believe the government seized the entire supply of silk. Whatever shall we wear for stockings?" Her voice drifted well past Mary.

Yet Arch laughed at something else and tossed a line down to Jim on the pier.

To relieve Gloria's embarrassment at being ignored, Mary pretended Gloria had intended to converse with her instead. "We'll have to make do. I have a pair of those new nylon stockings, and I like them. The government needs silk for parachutes for all the planes we're building, and Jim says silk is used in powder bags for the large guns on battleships and—"

"Oh, the war. I'm so tired of it, and we haven't fired a shot." Gloria leaned back and rested on her palms. She frowned in her boyfriend's direction. "He hasn't paid me any attention all day."

Mary laid her cheek on her crossed forearms and gave Gloria a sympathetic smile. Gloria certainly flaunted herself, with her tiny light green two-piece swimsuit and many provocative looks and poses. In comparison, Mary felt dowdy in her modest one-piece.

Gloria glanced over to the pier. "Well, Jim's paying attention to you. What'd I tell you? All you had to do was show off your figure."

Mary winced. She flipped to see the pier, see if Jim had heard, but he was chatting with Arch and tying a line to a cleat. Relief poured out in a sigh. She faced Gloria again. "I'm not trying to show off."

"Maybe not, but he's noticing."

"Do you think so?" Mary kept her voice low. Maybe that would encourage Gloria to do likewise.

She laughed. "Oh, honey, I know so. He likes you."

Hope fluttered in her chest, and she ventured another glance at him. He looked so good in his swim trunks as he climbed back onto the boat with long muscular legs. More than hope fluttered inside her, but her common sense squelched it.

She raised herself on her elbows. "I don't think so. Not like that. In high school, he was madly in love with my best friend. He couldn't take his eyes off her, practically drooled over her. He doesn't act that way with me. Not at all."

Gloria tapped Mary's elbow with her toes. "He isn't a schoolboy anymore. He's a grown man."

Grown nicely too. As he lashed down a sail, the muscles of his chest and arms worked. Once when she'd stood at the helm, he'd squeezed behind her, his chest hair brushing the back of her arm. Her cheeks heated at the remembered intimacy.

"See how he watches you?" Gloria said. "He's been doing it all day."

Sure enough, Jim's gaze flitted to her. She smiled, he smiled back, and he returned to his work.

"Is she watching me?" Gloria said in a fake masculine voice. "Did she see me flex my muscles? Better do it again, make sure she sees."

Jim did seem to flex his muscles a lot more than required for his work.

Hope and amusement bubbled into a giggle. "Stop it, Gloria."

Jim rested one hand on the mast and looked Mary's way, a long look, as if studying her, querying her, and it pressed her heart hard against the polished wooden deck.

In high school Jim had loved vivacious golden girl Quintessa, but maybe he could grow to like Mary's subdued silver ways. Perhaps he already had.

How could she encourage him? What did she know about flirting or romance? She'd had so few boyfriends and hadn't dated for almost two years. Yet something natural flowed through her, took over, and raised a soft smile.

He flipped up a grin, spun around, and grabbed a line, back to work.

Gloria groaned and flopped onto her back. "Arch used to look at me like that. More so. He was enthralled."

Mary didn't want to offer false encouragement. Who wouldn't notice the tension between them this weekend? "I'm sure Arch just has a lot on his mind."

"What good is a great figure and a killer-diller swimsuit if I can't snag a rich husband?"

Although she cringed, Mary kept her voice gentle. "Maybe he doesn't want to be snagged. Maybe he wants to be loved for who he is."

Gloria sat up and leaned close, her golden hair falling over one golden-tan cheek. "I do love him for who he is. Can I help it if 'who he is' owns this spectacular estate and this yacht and an enormous thriving business?"

Mary's stomach soured. "He gave up the business to join the Navy."

Gloria shoved back her hair. "That won't last. He says he'll stay in the Navy forever, but he won't. He'll miss all this. Who wouldn't? His Navy salary won't satisfy him. How could it when he's used to having everything he desires?"

Mary studied the perfect symmetry of Gloria's face. "What if he doesn't miss it? What if he's satisfied with a simpler life?"

A startled look raced through Gloria's eyes.

Just as Mary thought—Gloria planned to make Archer Vandenberg quite dissatisfied with Navy life.

"All right, ladies." Arch stepped closer, pulling on a khaki shirt. "Time to head ashore and dress for dinner."

Mary rummaged in her bag, pulled out her one-piece play-suit, stepped in, and buttoned it up, still tickled to have found a playsuit in navy-and-white polka dots to match her swimsuit.

Gloria sauntered down the length of the boat, hips sway-ing, swinging her bag, and she sang the new hit song "You Made Me Love You."

Arch hopped to the pier, reached out a hand to his girlfriend, then retracted it. "Do you have something to put on over that? Shorts and a blouse like Mary has?"

Gloria put one hand on her hip. "Are you ashamed of me?"

His shoulders sagged. "Come on. I told you my parents are old-fashioned. Please put some clothes on and don't make a scene."

Without a word, Gloria threw her bag to the deck and opened it.

"Mary?" Jim stood on the pier, his hand outstretched, and he tilted his head as if to say, "Let's get out of here."

Mary took his hand, hesitated as she studied the watery gap between boat and pier, then jumped across.

He leaned down, his face only inches from her ear. "Let's give them some space."

How could she breathe with him so close and his hand still wrapped around hers? She wouldn't let go. He might, but she wouldn't. "All right." Her voice came out too breathy.

"Here. Let me take your bag."

She'd rather he hold her hand than her bag, but he took it from her and strode up the wharf to the shore, his unbuttoned khaki shirt flapping behind him.

Mary followed him up the stairs to a winding, climbing path across the manicured estate grounds.

She and Jim strolled side by side. Stone benches beckoned from under shady trees, and colorful flower gardens rested in the bends of the path. At the top of the slope, the Vandenberg home sat long and stately and white, trimmed with gray stone. In the center of the home, the wall bowed outward, graced with huge windows in the ballroom upstairs and the enormous sitting room downstairs. Off to one side lay the tennis courts and horse stables.

Mary could admire such opulence without coveting it, but unlike Gloria, she'd never seen it as an option. In a way, she felt sorry for the girl.

Faint snapping voices rose from down by the water.

"Oh dear," Mary said. "I do hate when couples argue."

Jim slung both his bag and Mary's over his shoulder. "They won't be a couple for long."

"I was afraid of that."

"It was inevitable." He waved one arm over the grounds. "Arch says he wants a woman with middle-class sensibilities, then expects her to share his upper-class indifference to luxury. It's happened before, and unless he wises up, it'll happen again."

"And he's such a nice man."

"He is. He's a good man, a good officer."

"It's too bad that wasn't enough for Gloria."

"Yeah." A wry smile crinkled one corner of his mouth. "I have a hunch it never was."

"And the more she feels him slipping away, the harder she tries."

"And the harder she falls. The Vandenbergs don't like show-offs, and they despise scenes."

The path curved around a maple tree, and Mary ran her hand under the green leaves, soon to be a brilliant orange-red. "If the Vandenbergs don't like show-offs, I'm surprised they allow maple trees on their property."

Jim laughed, stopped, and faced Mary. "They're show-offs in autumn, but they pay penance in winter. Maybe that's why they haven't been chopped down."

Mary joined his laughter. Jim's shirt hung open over the long lean expanse of his chest, and a sudden playful impulse leaped inside her. She grasped his open shirt and did up a middle button. "Why, you're a show-off too. You heard Arch. Put some clothes on and don't make a scene."

He stood stock-still. Silent.

What was she doing? Her fingers froze and fumbled with the button, and her breath grew ragged. He must think she was either forward or ridiculous. Somehow she had to save face, so she straightened his collar points. "There. You're a big boy. You can do the rest yourself."

She mustered up a smile and looked him in the eye.

His expression turned her knees to mush—the question in his eyes, the parting of his lips, the softness, as if he wanted—as if he wanted to—

Footsteps stomped behind them. "I can't believe you said that, Archer Vandenberg. Just who do you think I am?"

"Come on, Gloria. Come back here. Let's talk in private. Don't make a scene."

Jim's expression warped. He stepped back and did up his buttons with his free hand, giving Mary a tight-lipped smile. "So much for the relaxing weekend, eh?"

With effort, she nodded, but the world felt topsy-turvy beneath her feet.

Gloria stormed past them on the path, properly clad but cursing Arch in improper language.

Jim glanced behind them. "Arch will stay on the pier for a while. I know him."

"Oh. All right." Mary's voice squeaked and embarrassed her.

"Come on. Let's get dressed for dinner."

"All right." No squeak this time, thank goodness, but she couldn't help but sigh. Had she imagined that moment? That look in his eyes? As if he wanted to kiss her?

Her lungs filled with perfumed ocean air. She'd dreamed of a whole romantic weekend, but she'd had one romantic moment. For now, that would have to do.

21

Boston
Sunday, September 7, 1941

After the last rousing chord of "God of Our Fathers," Jim
sat down next to Arch in the pew at Park Street Church.

Time for the choral anthem. Behind him, up in the gallery,
he could barely see Mary in her black choir robe. The choir director waved her baton, and the musical introduction started.

Jim's grip tightened on the stiff brim of his cover in his
lap. *Lord, hold Mary up.*

She met Jim's eye. He gave her a huge smile and mimed
hauling on a rope to hoist a sail, despite the odd look Arch
gave him. Mary rewarded him with a brief smile. Right now
it was more important for Jim to be a good friend than a
debonair suitor.

Some debonair suitor he was. The previous weekend in
Connecticut he'd had several opportunities to push their
friendship over the threshold into romance. And he'd wasted
every one. He could still see her buttoning up his shirt, her
dark head bent close to his, her silvery eyes glancing up to
him full of affection and self-consciousness.

He'd wanted to stroke her cheek, to embrace her, to tell

her he needed help with the rest of his buttons, to burrow in her hair, to kiss her forehead, kiss her lips. Torn between so many good options, he'd frozen. Then when Gloria stormed by, all the options evaporated.

All week he'd told himself the timing had been wrong. Starting a romance the same day Arch and Gloria broke up would have been insensitive.

Jim's leg jiggled. Yet how much time did he have before they shipped out again? Not much.

The voices of the choir rose in a triumphant anthem. Was it his imagination, or did the soprano section sound stronger? Perhaps Mary's courage had bolstered the rest of the ladies. Courage did that.

Arch shifted in the seat beside him. Thank goodness Durant had given them liberty today. Not only did Jim want to cheer for Mary the first time she sang with the choir, but Arch needed a distraction.

Since the breakup, Arch had alternated between stony and melancholy. He was furious with Gloria for being more enamored with his inheritance than his heart, and he was furious with himself for being snared by another gold digger.

In a few weeks, Jim could talk to Arch about his unrealistic expectations, but not now. Now Arch needed his fury.

The song ended, and Dr. Harold Ockenga approached the pulpit, prayed, and started his sermon.

Jim had enjoyed every one of the pastor's sermons he'd heard, but today he couldn't concentrate. He wanted to see Mary and find out how she was doing.

No one else in the building knew the fullness of what today meant for her, how she'd faced her worst memory and deepest fear. His satisfaction that she'd confided in him and his admiration for her strength filled his chest.

What a wonderful woman she was, and how blessed he was to call her a friend. And perhaps soon, something more.

Finally the organ played the recessional. Jim strode down the aisle and out to the second-floor lobby. Mary came down a spiral staircase on his left, her choir robe swinging around her shapely calves.

He dashed to her. "Good job. I'm proud of you."

"Thank you." She gave him a twitchy smile and clutched her choir book to her chest. Her hands shook.

If only he could take her hands and smooth away the tremors, but a church service was no place for a romantic overture.

Mary stepped aside to let other choir members pass. "I need to put away my robe and book."

"Oh, sure. Sure. I'll meet you outside." Would he ever attain suave? He joined Arch and went down one of the twin spiral staircases to the ground floor, then down to the sidewalk.

Arch was quiet, gazing up at the red brick façade and the white spire, but Jim paced until Mary glided down the steps in a flowery dress.

"Wasn't the sermon wonderful?" She even smelled like flowers. "Isn't it remarkable that he spoke on Isaiah 43? Exactly what I needed, and perfect for you, Jim."

"Yes, perfect." He sent up a quick prayer that she wouldn't probe further, but guilt jabbed him. Should he really pray for God to conceal his lack of focus during a sermon? He took a step of courage, into honesty. "Actually, I was distracted."

Her gaze swung to Arch, and she gave Jim a sympathetic smile. "It's been quite a week, especially with the *Greer* incident."

Jim had failed again. Couldn't she see he'd been distracted by her, not by his best friend's heartbreak or even an international naval incident?

Arch was already talking about the injustice of it, funneling his personal anger into the story—how a German U-boat had fired upon the destroyer USS *Greer* in the North Atlantic, and how the *Greer* had fired back with depth charges.

Jim's own anger hardened into a lump. He knew a fellow on the *Greer*, and someone had tried to kill him. Why Congress hadn't immediately declared war, Jim didn't know, but they hadn't. No ships had been sunk. No sailors harmed.

Mary clutched her purse to her stomach. "I'm surprised we aren't at war."

Jim sighed. "That's all anyone's talked about on the *Atwood*—how many men have to die to tip the balance?"

She gazed up at them as if relaying a confidence. "I've heard men at the Navy Yard say we fired deliberately, either to enrage Germany into declaring war on us, or to enrage the American public into calling for war ourselves."

Some of the sailors did talk about provoking an incident, but talk didn't mean action, especially when their own lives would be at stake. "I don't believe that for a second."

"Me neither." Mary adjusted her hat, a little straw thing with flowers on it. "Will you be in town long? I know you can't give me specifics . . ."

Jim put on his cover. "A bit longer. The Navy's adding new equipment and loading us up with supplies. New crew members too."

He and Arch exchanged a glance. They couldn't say they'd taken on a full load of live ammunition. They couldn't say they'd soon escort a convoy from Newfoundland to Iceland, with British ships relieving them at the Mid-Ocean Meeting Point. They couldn't say they might end up in an international naval incident themselves.

A pretty young redhead came down the steps and approached Mary, turning her shoulder to exclude Jim and Arch. "I was so surprised to see you in choir this morning. I was afraid you'd faint."

Jim's hands coiled around the hem of his white tunic. She had to be Claudia, the soprano diva Mary avoided.

Mary gave Claudia a stiff smile. "Edith and Bertha prayed with me beforehand."

"If I didn't know better, I'd think you were angling for a starring role in the Christmas pageant."

"Oh, never," Mary said with force.

"Good." Claudia patted Mary's arm. "As I'm sure you know, the role of Mary has always been played by a soprano, and you and I are the only ones young enough."

"Don't worry. Your role is safe."

Jim smiled at the sarcasm in Mary's voice.

"I know, but I'd hate to see you disappointed." She fluttered a wave at Mary and departed.

Arch tapped Mary on the shoulder. "Why didn't you introduce us? I'm single now, and she's my kind of woman. Such kindness. Such sincerity."

Jim joined Mary's laughter. Good. Arch was already switching back from melancholy to charm.

Two tiny elderly ladies came out and headed straight for Mary. "There's our girl," one of them said, clasping Mary's hand. "We're so proud of you, dear."

Now Mary's smile was relaxed and true. "I couldn't have done it without you. Oh, you must meet my friends, Jim Avery and Arch Vandenberg. Jim and Arch, please meet Bertha Wilkins and Edith Wilkins."

Bertha shook Jim's hand. "Well, Mary, aren't you blessed to have two handsome young men fighting over you?"

Mary's laughter rivaled the pealing church bell. "Not like that, Bertha. They're my friends."

Jim winced. Maybe he was the only one who wanted that to change.

Edith peered up at Arch. "Are both you boys single?"

"Yes, ma'am." Arch's eyes sparkled.

Edith clapped her hands. "What a coincidence. So are Bertha and I."

Laughter eased the hurt somewhat. Was he making a fool of himself again? Reading too much into the act of slipping a button through a buttonhole?

Arch lowered into a bow. "Would you three ladies do us the honor of joining us for lunch?"

Mary turned to Jim and raised an eyebrow and a smile. Yes, Arch was turning on the charm full force. The sermon must have raised his spirits.

"We'd love that. Wouldn't we, Bertha?"

"On one condition." Arch bent closer, his face drawn in mock seriousness. "I must know. Are you only after my money?"

"Oh no, sweetie." Edith pinched his cheek. "I'm after your handsome face."

Arch grinned at Jim. "If I'd known all the lovely ladies were in choir, I would have joined ages ago."

"I think he's feeling better now," Mary murmured to Jim.

He looked into her twinkling eyes. "Arch has never had trouble finding a date. Only in finding the right woman."

"How about you, dearie?" Bertha asked from his other side. "Which gives you troubles?"

The women's gazes skewered him from opposite ends, making him feel like corn on the cob, sweating over the grill. "Huh?"

"You're still single, young man," Bertha said. "Which gives you troubles? Finding a date or finding the right woman?"

Jim tried to swallow, couldn't. The right woman stood beside him, but he couldn't say so—not here, not now, not like this.

Mary leaned in front of Jim and cupped her hand over her mouth. "As you can see, Jim has trouble finding the right words."

He smiled and nodded. For once, playing the fool suited him fine.

22

Agent Sheffield snuffed out his cigarette in an overflowing ashtray and flipped a page in Mary's notebook. "Doesn't look good for Ira Kaplan and his pals."

"No, sir. It doesn't." The leaden feeling in Mary's chest wouldn't go away. Mr. Kaplan had always been kind to her.

"He has experience with wiring, you know. Studied engineering at MIT for two years, then dropped out to work here two years ago. He's smart enough, all right."

"Mm-hmm." At his desk facing the wall, Agent Hayes nodded and made notes.

Mary sighed. "I still can't imagine him—"

Sheffield slapped the notebook shut. "That's why you leave the investigation to us. In this work, there's no room for feminine sensibilities or women's intuition. Cold hard facts and the insight into the criminal mind that comes from training and experience."

Mary leaned forward and eyed her notebook. "Anything useful in there?"

"I have to admit, yes. And I appreciate how you transcribe the conversations without any editorial input."

"Yes, sir. Only cold hard facts."

Sheffield rewarded her with half a smile. "I should give you my weekly lecture about keeping your little nose out of this, but you won't listen, will you?"

Mary's mouth twisted in what she hoped was a mysterious way. "Oh, I'll listen."

He groaned and rolled his eyes. "Women."

The office door burst open. Ira Kaplan barged in and slammed a small metal item onto Sheffield's desk. "There. You wanted proof. Here's your proof."

Agent Sheffield rolled his desk chair back and narrowed his eyes. "Mr. Kaplan, I'm in the middle of a meeting."

"Oh." Mr. Kaplan spun to Mary and gave her an apologetic look that turned to curiosity.

Mary lowered her eyes to the empty notebook in her lap. To maintain her cover, she tried not to be seen in the FBI agents' office. But any harm was already done, and now her own curiosity took over. "Go ahead, Mr. Kaplan. Don't mind me."

Agent Sheffield poked the metal disc with his pen. "A German-American Bund pin."

Kaplan held his chin high. "It belongs to Heinrich Bauer. I saw him drop it."

"Did anyone else see him drop it?" Sheffield gazed at the young man over the top of his reading glasses.

"No, but—"

"Bauer says you're framing him, then you show up with a Bund pin with no proof it's his."

"No proof?" Kaplan thrust a shaking finger toward the door. "The rat dropped it."

"I'll hang on to this and make a note of it, but without any witnesses . . ." The agent shrugged his slim shoulders.

Out of habit, Mary's fingers itched to take shorthand notes, but Sheffield was hearing the conversation anyway. Still, she wanted it recorded word for word.

Kaplan's gaze bounced between Sheffield and Hayes, who hadn't even faced the young man. He breathed hard, his fingers working at his sides. "Search his locker."

Sheffield shook a cigarette from a pack. "His locker?"

"Bauer's. He's hiding something in there, we all know it. A bomb or something. He keeps it locked—no one else does—and he's sneaky, shields it from view when he opens it, won't let anyone look inside."

In silence, Sheffield pulled out his lighter, lit his cigarette, and puffed it.

Mary held her breath. A man acting sneaky wasn't hard proof, especially when everyone suspected him of a crime, and yet . . . what *was* Mr. Bauer hiding?

Agent Sheffield shoved back his chair and stood. "Agent Hayes, fetch Mr. Bauer and meet me at the locker room. And Miss Stirling . . ." He paused in front of her and bowed his head. "Would you like to come along as my personal stenographer and record these proceedings?"

She sprang to her feet. "Yes, sir."

He raised one eyebrow at her. "I figured you'd follow me anyway."

"Perhaps." She clutched her empty notebook.

The agents put on their hats and departed. Mr. Kaplan led the way, his long legs setting a brisk pace. Mary had to put an extra skip in her step to keep up, almost like walking with Jim.

Except Jim would laugh and chat as they walked, with an easy swing in his step.

Mary followed a set of railroad tracks and gazed out to where the *Atwood* was moored. Perhaps Jim would have liberty tomorrow night and come to church on Sunday. Seeing his encouraging face in the congregation bolstered her. If only he could be with her right now. No matter what happened today, she'd certainly have plenty to discuss with him this weekend.

Mr. Kaplan led Agent Sheffield and Mary into Building 42.

Agent Sheffield paused outside the door to the locker room. "Wait here. I'll make sure no men are inside."

While Kaplan paced by the door, Mary opened to a clean page in her notebook. Her stomach squirmed. Although she was excited to be part of an official investigation, her role today might make the men wonder about her note-taking on the docks. Without her invisibility, how could she sleuth?

Agent Sheffield opened the door and beckoned them inside. "All clear."

Kaplan marched in, past several rows of steel lockers with benches in the aisles. He jangled a small padlock. "Here it is. See—the only one with a lock."

Mary glanced around. Not quite, but very few did have locks.

"Go ahead. Open it." Kaplan rattled the locker door.

Sheffield sighed, leaned back against the bank of lockers, and puffed on his cigarette. "We won't have to wait long."

Sure enough, loud voices rose in the hallway and the door banged open. Agent Hayes led Heinrich Bauer by the elbow, and a dozen men followed, jeering, shouting, arguing with each other.

Frank Fiske strode behind the mob. "Back off, boys. Leave him alone. Let the FBI do their work."

Mary eased away from the crowd and set her pen in motion. In secretarial school she never imagined using her skills like this.

Bauer's blue eyes stretched wide, his forehead creased. "What is wrong? I have done nothing."

Fiske stepped right in front of Agent Sheffield. "What's going on here? You drag my man away from his job and start a disruption. How can I get any work done? We have a timetable to meet."

The agent leaned around Fiske and addressed Mr. Bauer. "May I look inside your locker?"

"My . . ." He looked at his locker, at Kaplan, at Sheffield, his face pale. "I have a coat, a lunch. That is all."

"Good." Sheffield gestured at the locker.

Bauer moistened his lips. "This is America. I thought it was different here. Do you not need a—what is it named?"

"A search warrant. If you don't agree to the search, I'll get a warrant. But if you have nothing to hide, why not open it now and shut these fellows up for good?"

"Yeah, Bauer." Al Klingman pointed at the locker. "What are you hiding?"

More shouting, more accusations.

Mary shifted to the side to get a better view through the pulsating crowd.

Agent Sheffield shrugged. "With or without your cooperation, I'm getting inside your locker."

When Bauer nodded, Agent Hayes dropped the man's elbow. Bauer wiped his upper lip, slid a key from his pocket, and opened the lock. For a second he stood still, his head bowed, then he slipped off the lock and opened the door.

Dozens of pamphlets fluttered to the ground, stark red and black and white.

Bauer gasped and stepped back. *"Was ist—"*

"See! Proof!" Kaplan snatched up a pamphlet and waved it before the men. "Nazi propaganda, courtesy of the German-American Bund. I knew it. I knew he was a Nazi."

"I am not a Nazi." Bauer's voice came out high-pitched. "These are not mine."

Mary could scarcely take her eyes off the drama long

enough to take notes. But she had an official job, and she'd do it.

Kaplan flicked a pamphlet in Bauer's face. "The evidence says otherwise."

"Yeah." Morton Anders raised a fist toward the German. "Lying Nazi saboteur."

Bauer backed against the lockers, his eyes wild. "I am not. I—"

"Remember?" Kaplan faced the men and held the pamphlets high. "Remember when those Bund thugs beat me up a few weeks ago? They threw trash like this on top of me."

Bauer lunged at Kaplan and grabbed his collar. "You! You did this to me!"

Heart racing, Mary gasped and stepped back.

"Get off me!" Kaplan shoved him away.

As shouts rose, Bauer socked Kaplan in the gut. Pamphlets and fists flew through the air.

Rough hands grabbed Mary's arms from behind.

She cried out and glanced over her shoulder to see Mr. Fiske. She sighed in relief.

"Get out of here, Miss Stirling." He guided her back, away. "You'll get hurt."

Something fierce and determined stirred within her, and she wriggled out of his grasp. "No! I'm taking notes for Agent Sheffield. He asked me to. I need to stay."

His deep-set eyes narrowed. He glanced at her notebook, the open page covered with shorthand scrawls, and he frowned.

"Excuse me." She turned back to the melee and tried to make sense of it.

Bauer pinned Kaplan to the ground. "You did this. Why did you do this to me?"

"'Cause you're a stinking Nazi." He spat in Bauer's face.

Men pulled Bauer back. Kaplan stumbled to his feet, darted forward, but other men grabbed him from behind.

Bauer strained against his captors, his eyes flaming, blood dripping from the corner of his mouth. "I am not a Nazi. I left Deutschland to escape the Nazis."

"Baloney!" Kaplan rammed an elbow into the chest of the man to his right, but he failed to get free.

Mary scrawled down the words she couldn't believe—Mr. Bauer had left to escape the Nazis? How could that be? What would such an Aryan-looking man have to fear?

Bauer's shoulders rounded, like a bull ready to charge. "I am not a Nazi," he growled.

"Sure you are, German pig!" Kaplan struggled, arms flailing. "You hate the Jews, think you're better than us."

"My *wife* is Jewish!" Bauer startled, cried out, then ducked his head, curling his hands before him as if to protect himself.

The room hushed.

Mary's lips tingled while her fingers took down the words. His wife was Jewish. His wife—no wonder he'd fled.

Bauer shook his head behind his raised fists. *"Meine Magda. Meine liebe Magda."* His voice cracked. *"Es tut mir leid."*

Mary didn't speak German, but shorthand was phonetic, so she did her best, though her heart broke for the man.

"Your wife . . . ?" Kaplan's voice quavered through the silence. "Your wife is Jewish?"

"Ja." Bauer looked up, his face stricken. "That is why we escaped. She was not safe."

Kaplan sagged back, his arms hanging loose. "You—you never said anything."

"She is not safe here either. You should know. Folk hate the Jews. It is wrong."

Kaplan's eyes widened, and his hand rose and covered his mouth and nose like a cage. "You—you aren't the saboteur."

No, he wasn't, and Mary almost smiled. No wonder Bauer was so secretive—he feared for the safety of his family. Thank goodness he wasn't guilty.

"No, he isn't." George O'Donnell stepped forward and jabbed Kaplan in the chest. "But now we know who the real saboteur is. You."

"What?" Kaplan's face scrunched up. "That doesn't even make sense. Why would I—"

"Why would you frame Bauer?" Curly Mulligan joined O'Donnell. "Hmm. I don't know. Maybe to make it look like a German was blowing up our ships. That'd get us in the war right quick, wouldn't it?"

In tandem, realization and horror dawned on Kaplan's face. "You think I—I didn't—I couldn't."

Mary's mouth drooped open. Nothing insincere in his reaction at all. "He didn't do it either," she whispered.

Agent Sheffield picked up a handful of pamphlets and displayed them in front of Kaplan. "Be truthful, son. These are the same pamphlets the Bund members threw down on you, aren't they?"

Kaplan blinked over and over, his chest heaving.

"Wrinkled, soiled." Sheffield lifted one of the pamphlets. "And look. This one has a blood smear. What do you want to bet it's your blood type? Easy enough to find out."

"I—I—" Kaplan's breath huffed out. "I thought Bauer—I thought he was guilty. I thought he was dangerous, and you said you needed proof, more proof, and—" He cussed and grabbed his head, his knuckles white.

"And what, Mr. Kaplan?" Agent Sheffield said in a calm voice.

He gestured to the locker. "Look, all I did was put the propaganda in his locker, slipped it through the cracks, but I didn't plant a bomb. You've got to believe me. I couldn't—"

Shouts rang out from the isolationists, while Kaplan's interventionist friends backed up, disgust carved into their expressions.

Mary shook her head and forced herself to take notes. He admitted to framing Mr. Bauer? But not to the sabotage? If he were guilty of both, wouldn't he either deny both or confess both?

"Yes, he could." Mr. Fiske's voice rang over the shouts and silenced them. He turned to the FBI agent. "He could've planted that bomb."

The agent dipped his head. "Continue."

Fiske faced Kaplan. "I'm sorry, Ira, but I won't cover for you. The day we installed that gun mount, I sent you to the handling room when we were done, to clean up."

"Yes, but—"

"You were there a long time."

"Five minutes." Kaplan spread his hands wide, disbelief warping his features. "Five minutes."

Fiske turned back to Sheffield, his face solemn. "A lot longer than that. Plenty of time to install that lockbox. And he helped me with the final inspection before the *Atwood* shipped out. I left before he did. That must be when he planted the bomb."

"What?" Kaplan cried. "This is ridiculous."

The FBI agent cocked his head toward his partner, who stood in the corner.

Agent Hayes slipped handcuffs out of his pocket. "Ira Kaplan, you're under arrest."

"I can't—I can't believe this is happening." He held out his arms and didn't resist the handcuffs. "I can't believe it. I can't believe it."

Mary couldn't either, because the devastation on the man's face proved his innocence.

The FBI agents led Mr. Kaplan out, and the noise in the locker room built again.

"All right, men. Enough." Mr. Fiske made a patting motion with both hands above the men's heads. "Simmer down.

It's over. The saboteur's finally been caught. Now get back to work, all of you."

After the men filed out, Mary sank to a bench, light-headed. Yes, Kaplan was guilty of framing Bauer, but he wasn't the saboteur.

The guilty party was still at large.

23

With creaking of wood and a giant splash, the new Gleaves-class destroyer *Knight* slid down the ways into Boston Harbor and joined her sister ship, the *Cowie*, launched earlier that day.

Jim and Arch joined the applause, the band played "Anchors Aweigh," and pennants flapped in the sunshine. All around the nation, Liberty Fleet Day was being celebrated. Shipyards were launching the first fourteen Liberty Ships, mass-produced cargo ships designed to be sturdy, reliable, and quickly constructed. At the Boston Navy Yard, two new destroyers had been launched and two others laid down.

Up ahead, Mary weaved through the crowd in her red dress.

Something constricted in Jim's chest. Everything about today—except the weather—reminded him of the day he and Mary had become reacquainted. Had it really been six months? Back in March, he'd barely noticed her, and now he couldn't take his eyes off her. Back in March, he'd thought starting a romance before shipping out would be stupid, and

177

now his greatest regret was not starting the romance before he shipped out this evening.

More than anything, he wanted to kiss her good-bye at the docks. But not their first kiss. Not in front of everyone. Because he'd tried to be suave instead of bold, he'd have to wait until after they returned. He'd still acted the fool, only a different kind of fool.

"There's Mary," Arch said.

"Mm-hmm." Jim hadn't told Arch about his changing feelings for Mary. Why should his best friend know before the lady?

Mary caught his eye over the crowd and waved. How good to see her smile again. The previous Sunday, she'd been dismayed by the arrest at the shipyard.

If only he could have comforted her alone. If only he'd had *any* time alone with her this month, but Arch had accompanied them to church and on Sunday afternoon excursions.

"You're here." Mary's face lit up. "I thought I'd lost the two of you to Bertha and Edith."

"Never." Jim tried to make his voice sound deep and meaningful, but it didn't sound the way he intended. He could never be an actor.

"Done with your responsibilities for the day?" Arch asked her.

"I am." Mary clasped her hands under her chin. "Oh! Have you seen the Fletchers we laid down this morning?"

"Not yet," Jim said. "Waiting for you."

"Listen." Arch set his hand on Jim's shoulder. "I've had enough festivities for one day. You two go have fun. I'll make sure everything's squared away on board."

"All right." Jim put on a stiff smile. Finally he had time alone with Mary, but in a crowd. Fat lot of good that did.

"Good-bye, Mary." Arch shook her hand, then tapped

his wristwatch. "Get him back by seventeen hundred or he turns into a pumpkin."

"Seventeen hundred?"

Jim leaned down to speak into her ear. "We're shipping out."

"Oh."

Her clean scent scrambled his brain, but he straightened up to see her reaction.

Sadness turned down the corners of her eyes, but she smiled. "They need you out there. So many ships being sunk. It's tragic."

She cared, but she'd never hold him back.

Jim could have kissed her right there, crowd or no crowd. But a public kiss? For a woman who hated attention more than anything else in the world? Might as well slap her.

He swallowed the impulse. "They do need us."

"You'll do great, I know it." She tilted her head. "But may you and your guns be completely bored."

Time for a joke. "Our guns are always bored."

"Oh, brother." Arch bowed to Mary. "I apologize for my friend's bad pun. The bore of a gun . . ."

"I understand." Mary's twinkling eyes said she didn't mind puns. "So, Mr. Avery. You have four more hours on land. How would you like to spend them?"

With her. Every minute. "I want a hot dog, I want to see those Fletchers, and I'd like you to see me off."

"I'd be honored."

"Au revoir." Arch lifted one hand in farewell. "Seventeen hundred."

Jim offered Mary his arm and threaded his way through the crowd. Sailors and shipyard workers mingled on the wharves for the festivities.

Jim followed his nose to a food stand and bought two hot dogs and two Cokes. He took a big bite and savored the perfect blend of sausage and mustard. The Navy fed them well, but nothing beat a hot dog eaten outdoors.

Mary led him toward the dry dock where the keels for two new Fletcher-class destroyers had been laid down. As much as he wanted to talk about ships, he wanted to hear about Mary more.

Jim swallowed the last of his hot dog and wiped mustard from his lips. "How have things been around here since the arrest?"

"Much quieter. More peaceful." But she frowned.

"A big uproar in the papers."

"For a day or two, but now they're more interested in the World Series coming up. Some people aren't happy about that. They expected national outrage, and there isn't any."

Jim shrugged. "No national outrage when the *Robin Moor* was sunk, or the *Steel Seafarer*, or when a U-boat fired on the *Greer*. I don't know what it takes."

Mary sipped her Coke. "The uproar over Mr. Kaplan was muted to begin with. The FBI is being circumspect. I hope it's because they doubt his guilt. I pray so, because he isn't the saboteur, and I feel awful that my notes helped put him behind bars."

He stopped so she'd have to face him. "Why do you say that?"

"The things he said, that I recorded, they sound so incriminating."

"But you don't think he did it."

"I know he didn't. Oh, Jim, you should have seen his face. Yes, he tried to frame Mr. Bauer, which was horribly wrong. But he was motivated by a vigilante sense of justice. He was convinced Bauer was the saboteur and needed to be arrested. Once he realized Bauer was innocent, he instantly regretted his actions. You could see it."

Jim squinted at her. "Which means Kaplan isn't guilty, and our saboteur is still out there."

"Yes." Mary's shoulders slumped. "But not one clue since Kaplan was arrested."

"Looks like you have some detective work to do while I'm gone, eh?" He offered her a smile and his elbow. "Now, show me those Fletchers."

At Dry Dock 2, they gazed down at the two bare hulls side by side on their wooden scaffolds.

"The *Guest* and the *Hutchins*," Mary said. "I can see why you sailor boys are so eager to sail in them."

He laughed at her sarcastic tone. "Just you wait. Our Gleaves-class destroyer is only 1630 tons, but the Fletchers will be 2100 tons and 28 feet longer. They can carry more guns and torpedo tubes, and are more rugged. Sleek design too."

"Interesting."

Was it? Was it interesting to a young woman? "I'm boring you, right?"

"Never." A lock of hair covered her mouth, but not the amusement in her eyes. "Remember, this is my business too."

A surge of emotion rose inside, and he lifted his hand to brush away her hair, to linger.

But she beat him to it and shook her hair off her face.

He used his raised hand to scratch the back of his neck. Either a drooling fool or a frozen one. He'd chosen his path—why couldn't he follow it?

★ ★ ★

Mary stayed close to Jim's side. Two hundred men and officers of the USS *Atwood* crowded the wharf, all in gleaming white uniforms, along with wives and sweethearts and children. What an honor to be invited to see Jim ship out.

All around, women cried into shoulders or put on brave stoic faces. She understood their fears. The sea itself was dangerous, especially the frigid storm-tossed waters of the North Atlantic where everyone knew—but no one could say—the *Atwood* would be sailing.

In those same seas, U-boats sank dozens of ships each month. Only a matter of time until an American warship was sunk, until they went to war.

But the Bible said, "There is no fear in love; but perfect love casteth out fear," and Mary would rest in that. If she loved Jim—and she was pretty sure she did—then fear had no place. Her fear would only burden him and paralyze her. The Lord loved Jim and would keep him safe, even if safety lay in heaven rather than on earth.

Jim faced her, breathtakingly close in the press of the crowd. "I'll miss you."

She wanted to drink in the warm expression on his face, to etch it into her memory. "I'll miss you too."

"It's good to know you'll be here when I get back."

"*When* is a nice word." Her voice came out too whispery, whittled away by the intensity of his gaze. Perhaps when he came back, things really would change. If only she could communicate her wish to him without sounding forward or desperate.

Someone jostled Jim and clapped him on the back. Jim smiled at the man. "Hi, Mo."

"Hiya, Jim." The officer led a petite dark-haired woman by the hand toward the gangplank.

Jim gestured with his thumb. "Maurice Shapiro, communications officer. That man over there with the four little girls—that's the captain."

"Lieutenant Commander Durant," she said.

The man embraced a lady who held a little girl on her hip and a cheerful smile on her face. They kissed, and the captain patted the other girls on their heads and climbed the gangplank.

His wife held up the pudgy hand of the tiniest daughter. "Say good-bye to Daddy, girls. He's off on a grand adventure."

What a tender scene, and what a brave wife and mother.

"Well, I'll be." Jim nudged Mary and nodded toward a red-haired officer, who was engaged in a passionate kiss with a pretty blonde. "I'd heard rumors Reinhardt was married, but somehow I never believed them. Glad I was wrong."

Lieutenant Reinhardt boarded the destroyer, and other officers after him, each kissing someone good-bye. Only Arch and Jim didn't have sweethearts to kiss good-bye. This had to be painful for Arch.

Arch strode to the foot of the gangplank, faced the crowd, and pressed his hand over his heart. "Alas, I have no one to kiss good-bye. Any patriotic volunteers?"

From the edge of the crowd, a feminine shriek rang out, and a young lady pushed her way forward, one of the other secretaries at the Navy Yard. "Me! Me! I'll volunteer!"

"Oh my goodness," Mary said.

Jim gave her a stunned smile. "Guess he's over Gloria. Or pretending he is."

The brunette dashed to Arch. He pulled her into an embrace, dipped her low, and planted a quick kiss on her lips.

The crowd erupted in laughter and applause, and Mary and Jim joined in. The patriotic volunteer sashayed away, fanning herself, while Arch swept a bow and climbed the gangplank.

Near the top, Arch wheeled around and leaned forward, bracing himself on the guide ropes. "Your turn, Mr. Avery! Kiss her!"

Mary gasped and shrank back. Oh goodness, no. Already dozens of heads turned to her.

Jim stood stock-still, his hands fisted, gaze cemented on his best friend.

"Yeah, Mr. Avery, kiss her!" another officer shouted from up on the deck.

"Kiss her! Kiss her!"

Mary sucked in a breath, willing away the nausea.

Everyone stared at her, smiling, laughing, chanting, "Kiss her!"

Jim spun to her, eyes wide. "Mary, I—I'm sorry. I'm sorry."

Her stomach squirmed, not only from the attention, but because Jim didn't even want to kiss her. "It—it's all right."

Jim swatted at the chanting men on the ship. "Knock it off, fellows. Leave her alone."

"What's the matter, Mr. Avery? Chicken?"

"Yeah, if you don't want to kiss her, I will."

Mary's face tingled. They'd keep chanting until he kissed her or left her. In an instant, her concern flipped from herself to him. If he didn't kiss her, the crew would tease him the entire cruise. How could she allow that to happen to him?

Mary tugged his sleeve. "Would it be so bad?"

"Huh?" Jim turned to her again, his face red.

"Would it be so bad? One kiss? Just a friendly kiss." How could she say such a thing? But how else could she end the attention? How else could she protect Jim from teasing?

Jim stared down at her, his eyebrows twisted. "A . . . friendly kiss?"

Oh, for heaven's sake, the man would never act. Only she could end the shouting, the laughter, the tension.

"Kiss her! Kiss her!"

Mary threw her arms around his neck, drew his head down, and kissed him full on the lips.

He stiffened, but then his arms circled her waist and gathered her close.

Was he? Yes, he was kissing her back.

Around her, the chants melted away and disappeared in a blue haze. All she sensed, all she cared about, was the gentleness, the firmness of his kiss, his embrace, the way every bone in her body turned to jelly and only the strength of his arms held her up.

But how long had they been kissing in that glorious blue haze? A split second . . . or a week?

Mary eased back.

Slowly, Jim opened his eyes. Never had she seen them so close—the brown mixed with green, the tiny golden rays, the intelligence and humor and thoughtfulness she adored.

Oh dear. What would he say? Her breath caught and her lips wouldn't move, swollen by the kiss. Should she apologize? Should she blurt out her love for him? What?

One corner of his mouth bent up. "Just a friendly kiss, eh?"

So that's how they'd handle it. "What kind of friend would I be if I let those men tease you?"

Then he gave her the grin she loved, but fuller than ever, and he tipped his cap to her. "Till I return." Up the gangplank he went, his stride long. At the top, he turned and waved at her.

She waved back, her own grin bursting forth. Oh goodness, it wasn't her imagination, not at all. Something was happening—something *had* happened.

Only then did she realize no one was chanting or laughing or staring at her anymore. How strange that she'd dissipated the attention by accepting it and stepping into the limelight for one blissful moment.

Mary hugged herself and bounced on her toes. Oh, what one kiss could do.

24

Like a pretty red beacon on the wharf, Mary grinned and waved.

With great effort, Jim resisted the urge to race back to her. It had really happened. She *had* kissed him. She had *kissed* him. If that was how she said good-bye, he couldn't wait to say hello.

Only one problem. *She* had kissed *him*. Why hadn't he initiated that kiss? After all, she invited him, gave him permission, but he'd just stared at her like an imbecile until she'd been forced to act.

At least he'd had the presence of mind to kiss her back. He'd have to make up for it when he returned. His smile returned, he gave her one last wave, and he stepped onto the deck of the *Atwood*.

Arch leaned against the bridge superstructure. "Well, well, well. Jim Avery has suddenly acquired a taste for quiet brunettes."

Jim tried to look noncommittal. "Just a friendly kiss, she said."

"Friendly? She didn't kiss me like that."

"Guess you're not her friend."

Arch laughed and clapped him on the shoulder. "It's about time, old man."

Yeah, it was. Joy erased his noncommittal façade. "I'd better get to my station."

"Me too. The engines won't run themselves."

Jim headed forward, where he'd help the executive officer, Vince Banning, with the deck gang as they hauled up lines for shoving off.

In the narrow space alongside the superstructure, Jim squeezed past Mitch Hadley heading the opposite direction.

"What do you know?" Hadley said. "Jim Avery even floats with the dames."

The muscles in Jim's neck went taut. "You don't know anything about the situation."

"I know the poor girl had to kiss you, because you don't have the guts." He stuck out that thick jaw of his. "You have no initiative at all."

"Excuse me. I have a job to do." Jim continued on his way before he took the initiative to sock the jerk in the chin.

His arms swung hard by his side. No initiative? No initiative?

Jim's lips set in a solid line. That was going to change.

★ ★ ★

Twirling on the sidewalk in front of the Bunker Hill Monument wouldn't be mature. Not at all, so Mary indulged in a touristy gaze upward at the white granite obelisk, circling to view the charming neighborhood. There. She'd twirled without twirling.

Why shouldn't she twirl? Jim had kissed her.

Well, she had kissed him, but he didn't seem to mind. Her chest expanded, and her eyes drifted shut. Oh, the look of wonder on his face afterward.

Even if he wasn't falling in love with her, at least he was attracted. Maybe the kiss had awakened something. Maybe that was the first time he'd seen her as a woman, not just as a friend. Either way, it was bliss.

Mary strolled down Monument Avenue toward her apartment. "Bring him home soon, Lord," she whispered, but guilt pricked her conscience.

Jim had important work to do. If the *Atwood* could scare off the U-boats, the lives of countless merchant marines could be saved, and thousands of tons of valuable supplies could be delivered to Britain.

Her prayer needed editing. *Lord, help him do his job well and bring him home safely—in your time.*

The tune of the new song "Yours" flowed up inside her and out of her mouth. For once, she didn't care who heard her singing. An older woman passed by and gave her an appreciative smile. Mary closed her eyes. She refused to let praise do its harm, but she also refused to let fear silence her song.

She climbed the stairs to her apartment and swung open the door.

"Mary! There you are!" A beloved voice, a beloved face, a beloved pair of arms enfolding her in a hug.

"Quintessa?" Mary hugged her back. Relief surged through her that Jim wasn't there, but how could she be so selfish? Thinking only of herself?

Mary pushed back and held her best friend by the shoulders. "My goodness! What are you doing here? I wasn't expecting you."

Quintessa's golden-green eyes sparkled. "I wanted to surprise you, sweetie."

"You did. Oh, it's so good to see you."

"Don't you look swell?" Quintessa stroked the sleeve of Mary's dress. "I've never seen you wear red, and it's marvelous on you. And I love your hair like that. A little longer, isn't it? So is mine. We have to stay with the times, don't we?"

"We do." Mary fingered her friend's shoulder-length blonde curls. "Oh, it's good to see you. But what brings you here? How long—listen to me. I haven't even invited you in yet."

"I'm already in." Quintessa raised that infectious smile of hers.

Mary laughed and motioned her to the couch. "When did you arrive?"

"Right before noon." Quintessa sat and smoothed the skirt of her yellow dress, patterned with swirls of pale green leaves. "Your friend Yvette recognized my name, said you talked about me all the time—you sweetheart—so she let me in. When she said you'd be gone all day, I took the El downtown, looked around, and . . . met my new boss."

Mary blinked. "Your new . . ."

"Yes." Quintessa's shoulders lifted. "Oh, I was miserable in Chicago. Yes, I needed to get away from Vermilion—I can't stand seeing *him* with *her*—but I was so lonely in Chicago. I liked my job at Marshall Fields, but I got to thinking. I can do this job in any city in America. Why not with my very best friend in the world? So I applied to Filene's, and they were impressed with my business degree, and they hired me. I'll have to work the floor in sales for a year, but then they promised to move me into the business offices."

Mary gripped her friend's hand. "You're staying in Boston?"

"I'm so excited. I haven't been this happy in over two years."

"Wonderful. Wonderful." It took every grain of effort to keep selfish disappointment from marring her face. Quintessa would still be here when Jim returned.

"Do you suppose . . . I hate to spring this on you, but Mr. Garrett at Filene's said finding an apartment in Boston is near impossible with the shipyards booming. Do you suppose . . . ?"

"You could live here?" It was difficult to swallow and smile at the same time. "My room is plenty big. We could fit another bed, another dresser, but of course I'd have to ask Yvette."

"She loves the idea. In fact, she's the one who suggested it. Cut the rent, you know?" She winked, cute as ever.

"This is wonderful." Mary built it up in her mind. She'd finally have a dear friend in town to do things with, to—"Oh! Now I can show you my notebooks for the Case of the Shipyard Saboteur."

"I can't wait." Quintessa clasped her hands together. "I couldn't stand how you were having this delightful mystery adventure without me. You've been having all the fun this year. And with Jim Avery in town too."

Jim Avery, who had a lifelong infatuation with Quintessa Beaumont.

Mary's heart deflated. "He shipped out an hour ago."

Quintessa pressed her hand over her mouth. "He did? When will he be back?"

How could she face Quintessa and talk about Jim? She went to the kitchen, since she had to make dinner anyway. She grabbed her favorite apron from the hook by the kitchen door and tied it around her waist. "I don't know how long he'll be gone. A month or so, I imagine."

"Oh, bother." Quintessa followed Mary and untied the apron from behind. "Don't you dare make dinner. I'm taking you out. I was hoping Jim would be here too, but oh well."

Mary studied her golden friend in her golden dress. "He'll be happy to see you."

"Do you think so?" Quintessa patted her throat. "Pardon me, but may I have something to drink? I'm so thirsty."

"Would you like some iced tea?" Mary opened the refrigerator and pulled out the pitcher she'd made this morning, before Liberty Fleet Day. Before the kiss.

Pain squeezed her heart, and her hand squeezed the pitcher handle.

"Did you forget something?" Quintessa asked.

Yes, she'd forgotten how gold outshone silver. She lifted a smile. "The glasses are in the cupboard behind you."

Quintessa spun around and pulled out two glasses, always thinking of others, and she set them on the table.

With a deep breath to steady her hand, Mary poured the iced tea. "Sugar?"

"No, thank you."

"Come, let me show you something." Mary led her friend back to the living room. "Sit in that chair, lean toward the bay window, and look up the street."

Quintessa did so, brushing aside the lace curtains. "Oh, look! You can see the Bunker Hill Monument. How thrilling."

Only minutes earlier, Mary had wanted to twirl in its shadow. Now she stood behind her best friend to conceal her face. "It's my favorite spot."

"To tell you the truth, Jim is one of the reasons I came to Boston."

"Oh?"

Quintessa swirled the tea in her glass. "You said the two of you are only friends—you know I'd never interfere in a budding romance—but your letters got me to thinking. He was madly in love with me in high school, but of course I overlooked him because I had a boyfriend. But now . . . if he's turned out as well as you say he has, he sounds like a real catch. If he adored me then, he might adore me again. I thought to myself, why not?"

"Yes," Mary choked out. "Why not?"

Quintessa turned and took her hand. "Do sit down, sweetie. I want to see your lovely face."

Just when Mary didn't want her face observed, but she obeyed and sat on the couch.

"He's a good man, isn't he? He always was, but I was young and stupid and only wanted a handsome, charming football player, so I never looked twice at poor Jim. But now I know the worth of a good man."

All Mary had to do was nod, but her swollen throat made the act torture.

Quintessa leaned back in the chair, looked out the window, and fiddled with the lace curtain. "When I think of how Jim used to look at me with complete and utter adoration—oh my. Feelings like that, feelings so deep, don't truly disappear."

No, they didn't. Mary's vision blurred. She'd seen his face when Quintessa's name was mentioned. His feelings for her hadn't changed. They never would.

"Mary?" Vulnerability softened Quintessa's voice. "Do you think he could care for me again?"

Something green and cruel and selfish inside wanted to say no, but she couldn't lie, couldn't be cruel to the one person who had offered her friendship when she was an outcast, couldn't envy the one person who had always encouraged her, a person who had been miserable for two years and deserved happiness again.

Yet her voice didn't work. She traced the rim of the glass, cold to her fingertip, and she forced herself to nod.

Quintessa's face lit up. "Do you really think so? That would be marvelous. I knew I should take a chance and come to Boston, take a chance on Jim. Maybe he'll take a chance on me."

And Mary's chances dribbled away.

25

Off the Coast of Newfoundland
Tuesday, September 30, 1941

Thank goodness Jim never got seasick.

Since the gun director sat high on top of the bridge superstructure, the motion there was the greatest. Swaying a good twenty degrees from side to side, Jim scanned out the porthole with his slewing sight for ships on the horizon.

The *Atwood* stood on Condition Three, with only one gun and the director manned, and with assistant gunnery officers trusted to control the weaponry. This close to Newfoundland, the Royal Canadian Navy and US Navy aircraft helped deter U-boats.

Jim glanced to both sides at Task Unit 4.1.5—four other American destroyers, the *Babbitt*, *Broome*, *Leary*, and *Schenck*. All but the *Atwood* were "four-stackers" built during the last war. Along with four funnels, the older destroyers had lower fuel capacity, which might cause problems if they faced storms. Or battle.

"There! Straight ahead." Juan Dominguez, the director

pointer, looked through his prismatic telescope, his white "Dixie cup" cover perched on the back of his head.

Jim trained his telescopic sight on the horizon, where a line of dark shapes emerged. "I see them. Our first convoy."

Convoy HX-152, fifty-five cargo ships steaming from Halifax, Nova Scotia, escorted by the HMCS *Annapolis*, one of the old US destroyers transferred to Canada a year earlier under the destroyers-for-bases deal with Britain.

Dominguez adjusted a dial on his telescope. "They'll be ours for over a week, huh, sir?"

"We're supposed to reach the MOMP on October 9." At the Mid-Ocean Meeting Point south of Iceland, British warships would relieve the Americans and escort the ships the rest of the way to Liverpool.

"Then we get to see sunny Reykjavik." Dominguez tipped up his brown face. "Work on my suntan."

Jim laughed. "I doubt we'll get off the ship much. Word is the citizens of Iceland aren't so keen on the American invasion."

"They invited us, didn't they?"

"Only under British pressure." He gave Dominguez a mock scowl. "Let's not make them long for Nazi occupation."

"Not me, sir." The pointer raised one hand as if taking an oath. "Nothing stronger than milk for me, and I'm true to my girl. Mama would know if I strayed. She'd know, and she'd swim all the way from Los Angeles to whip me."

"She would too." Bert Campbell, the director trainer, looked up from his telescope next to Dominguez's. "Once, back when we were with the Pacific Fleet, Juan and I had liberty in LA. Saw that woman light into him for cussing. Ain't never heard him cuss since."

Dominguez nudged his buddy. "Watch your grammar too. She'll get you."

Nothing like the camaraderie of men who served together.

Jim smiled and studied the cargo ships ahead, their shapes becoming more distinct each minute. "Let's see if I remember. Mostly British ships, some Dutch, Norwegian, Swedish, Greek, and one American ship heading to Iceland."

"That's a lot of cargo," Campbell said.

"Tons and tons." Oil, grain, sugar, peanuts, scrap metal, tobacco, and mail. "Britain needs that cargo, and we need to keep it safe, plus the merchant marines and a couple hundred passengers. This isn't a drill."

"No, sir," Dominguez said, "and I'm glad, 'cause I'm sick of drills."

Jim remembered his brother Dan's warning that someday these men might long for drills. *Lord, keep the U-boats away, but if they must come, let us do our jobs well.*

Only two weeks earlier, President Roosevelt had commanded US ships to shoot on sight any German or Italian vessels in US waters or any vessels attacking ships under American protection.

"Neutrality?" he muttered. Only on paper—and in the eyes of the folks back home. Even if the civilians didn't know it, the United States was already at war.

HX-152 was the third Halifax-to-Liverpool convoy escorted by American warships. So far, no cargo ships had been lost under their care—but no attacks had occurred either. How long could that last?

Jim's fingers stiffened on the dials of his sight as he studied the steel ships coming his way in a square grid of ten columns, each ship in an assigned, numbered position. How many of them would be sunk on the way to Iceland? To Liverpool?

The *Atwood* veered to starboard.

"Looks like we're taking station." The destroyers would keep station on the perimeter of the convoy, with one at each corner of the square and one sweeping in front of the convoy. Since the destroyers steamed faster than the cargo ships, they could patrol back and forth if U-boats were suspected in the area, and they could dart out toward sound contacts. To attack.

The *Atwood* plowed through the waves, driving toward her destination, heedless of the wind or current. Reminded him of that passage in Isaiah 43 Mary recommended. "Thus saith the Lord, which maketh a way in the sea, and a path in the mighty waters. . . . Remember ye not the former things, neither consider the things of old. Behold, I will do a new thing; now it shall spring forth; shall ye not know it?"

A sense of determination poured into Jim. God had made a way. God was doing a new thing. Jim would choose his path and charge forward, here at sea and—if he returned safely—in Boston with Mary Stirling.

Mary with the silvery eyes and the soft lips.

Was he falling in love? He didn't feel at all like he did in high school with Quintessa. But that was a one-sided crush. What he had with Mary felt real, steady, deep—and quite mutual.

He could still feel her weight sagging into him, still see her eyes, bleary from the kiss, her lashes low. Why on earth hadn't he marched right back down that gangplank, kissed her again, declared his feelings, and sealed her for himself?

Jim shook his head hard. Why on earth wasn't he paying attention to his job?

One corner of his mouth edged up. Wasn't distraction a symptom of falling in love?

★ ★ ★

South of Greenland
Sunday, October 5, 1941

For the first time in his life, Jim had been seasick.

On the darkened deck just before midnight, Jim clutched

the lifeline with both hands as he made his way to the bridge for his turn as junior officer of the watch. Everyone had gotten sick tonight, even the hardiest sea salt among them.

Waves towered above the *Atwood* in the darkness, and rain stung Jim's cheeks and froze. The bow punctured a wave, and seawater gushed over the forward section of the deck. Jim braced his feet, turned his back, and gasped as icy water sloshed over his feet. He'd never seen so much "green water," waves breaking across the deck, as he had the last few days.

Two giant steps and he reached the door to the superstructure. In he went and up the ladder, timing his steps to the motion of the waves, keeping a firm grip on the handrails. At the top, he burst into the pilothouse and slammed the door behind him.

"Look what the sea washed in," Captain Durant said. "Another drowned rat."

"Yes, sir. Junior rat of the watch reporting for duty." Jim shed some of his outerwear, took the towel offered by one of the seamen, and wiped himself down.

In the red light required to preserve night vision, the bridge equipment glowed—the helm, engine telegraph, gyrocompass, and communication equipment. For the past half hour, Jim had rested in a darkened room to develop his night vision. If only he could have slept, but the seas interfered as badly with sleep as they did with digestion.

"I'm afraid you'll have a tough night." Durant nodded to Jim and to Lt. Vince Banning, who was scheduled to serve as officer of the deck. "Keep in close contact with your lookouts. In seas like this, we haven't been able to relieve them every two hours as we should. Make sure they're awake and alert and reporting."

"Aye aye, sir." Jim didn't envy those men out in the wet

and dark and cold, expected to keep constant vigilance to prevent collision and to watch for U-boats.

"We've been on the TBS all evening." Durant gestured to the telephone-like Talk Between Ships radio system. "You'd think after two years at war, these merchantmen would value a tight convoy. But they keep trying to spread out, and they keep putting up their lights. Unacceptable. We need to avoid collisions, but we mustn't attract U-boats."

Jim planted his feet wide to allow for the thirty-degree tilt of the ship in each direction. The seasoned merchantmen didn't think too highly of their green American escorts, just as their civilian crews didn't think too highly of military discipline and order.

Jim peered through the portholes into the darkness. Night was the most dangerous time. The submarines could attack on the surface unseen and undetectable by sonar. How would the storm change things? The heaving seas would make an attack more difficult, but would also make it harder for the convoy to spot the U-boats. And the Germans were aggressive, attacking in coordinated groups nicknamed "wolf-packs."

Vince Banning leaned over the plotting table. "Where are we at, Captain?"

Durant tapped the navigational chart several hundred miles south of Greenland and briefed them on their current location and bearing and speed and weather, the planned zigzag course for the night, and how the Navy's "Fox" long-range radio broadcast predicted no U-boats on their course based on direction-finding radio transmissions.

Jim paid careful attention. His duties included making routine entries in the log book, taking stadimeter and range-finder readings, and inspecting above and below decks if weather permitted.

"Any word on the *Svend Foyn*?" Banning asked.

Jim murmured his concern. The Norwegian ship had straggled behind the convoy four nights earlier in heavy weather. Not only did she carry a crucial load of twenty thousand tons of fuel oil, ten bombers, and two tanks—but she carried 220 passengers. Stragglers were easy pickings for U-boats.

"No word. But also no word of a sinking, so keep those souls in your prayers." Durant relayed the last bits of information they'd need for their watch, then retired to his cabin behind the pilothouse, within shouting distance if needed.

Banning took his position behind the helmsman, and Jim at the log table. He made the change of watch notations in the log, keeping his handwriting as neat as he could with the ship rolling side to side and pitching bow to stern. Destroyers were lively ships, quick and easy to maneuver, but prone to violent motion in rough seas. Serving on a battleship had been less dramatic, but also less fun.

"Sir?" The talker turned from the telephone to Banning, eyebrows bunched together. "We had a sound contact."

Jim's stomach lurched, and not from nausea this time. In the sound room, deep in the lowest section of the bow, the sonar operators listened to the constant ping-ping-ping of the sonar emanating from a dome under the hull. Now something had pinged back.

Vince Banning's expression remained impassive. "*Had* a contact?"

"Yes, sir. Norris says he heard what sounded like propeller noises for about thirty seconds, but they disappeared."

Jim checked the time on his watch and made the proper notation in the log. Why was the executive officer so quiet? What decision would he make?

Banning gazed out the porthole, his arms crossed over his mackinaw. His fingers dug into the thick fabric, and he cussed. "I have no choice. We have to follow Cinclant procedure and stay within two thousand yards of the convoy."

The Commander-in-Chief of the Atlantic Fleet had issued convoy escort protocols that cautioned against jumping on minor sound contacts and against leaving the convoy for more than an hour to chase U-boats.

"This is insane." Banning strode to one end of the bridge, wheeled around, and strode back the other way. "What are we supposed to do? Wait for them to attack? We need to hunt them down and kill them before they kill us."

Jim chuckled to lighten the mood. "That would violate the Neutrality Laws just a smidgen, don't you think?"

Banning leveled a glare at him in the strange red light. "Our job is to protect this convoy."

Jim had misjudged the situation. With no food in his stomach and a possible U-boat in the vicinity, Vince Banning didn't want jokes. Jim gave the XO a solemn nod. "And we can't protect if we can't fight. Cinclant makes us fight with our hands tied behind our back."

With one eyebrow lifted, Banning signaled the resumption of his respect for Jim. "As an officer, I must obey the commander of this task unit and of the Atlantic Fleet, but as a man, I tell you, this procedure stinks."

"Let's hope this procedure doesn't sink." Jim held his breath. So much for not making jokes.

However, Banning chuckled. "Yes. Let's hope." He turned to the talker. "Anything else?"

"No, sir. No further sound contacts."

Jim registered the information in the log book. Most likely, they'd heard a whale—a whale that should be thankful he hadn't lost a fin to the *Atwood*'s depth charges. Or it could have been a U-boat, zipping in on reconnaissance, then zipping out to call in his buddies for the slaughter.

Without a doubt, someday soon Jim would be tested in

battle. He tugged off his gloves and blew on his hands. His fingers tingled with renewed warmth, and his mind tingled with the determination to be bold, strong, and decisive.

If only that sound contact had come nearer. Jim was ready to prove himself.

26

Boston
Thursday, October 9, 1941

Quintessa set a New England pot roast on the kitchen table between Mary and Yvette. "I feel so Bostonian. It smells heavenly, if I do say so myself."

"It does." Mary inhaled the savory scent. "When did you become such a good cook?"

Quintessa took her seat. "I was a single gal alone in Chicago. Cook or starve."

"Well, thank you for sharing your skills. I'm glad you moved in with us."

"You're just saying that because now you only have to cook twice a week." Quintessa winked.

Mary laughed and winked back. "Now, if we could just find three more roommates . . ."

"Oh!" Yvette pressed one hand to her chest. "Only if they aren't detectives."

With bright eyes, Quintessa turned to Mary. "Speaking of detectives, what's new in the case?"

"Must we?" Yvette shuddered. "This talk of sabotage ruins the appetite."

"Ten minutes." Quintessa darted out of her chair, grabbed the egg timer, and set it on the table. "No more than ten. Girl Scout promise."

Mary waited for a nod from Yvette, then proceeded. "Everything's been quiet since Mr. Kaplan was arrested, although Mr. Fiske still complains about shoddy work."

Yvette sliced her pot roast and took a bite, her fork remaining in her left hand in the European style. "I saw the FBI agents today."

Mary concealed her smile. For someone who claimed sabotage talk destroyed her appetite, she always participated in the conversation and showed a great deal of interest in Mary's typed-up notes. "They still have an office in my building."

Quintessa's eyes danced. "That means they must have other suspects."

"All Agent Sheffield will tell me is they're building their case." Mary divided a perfectly boiled potato. "But when I asked if he meant his case against Kaplan, he just smiled."

"Ooh! He does have another suspect. Who do you think it is?"

Mary measured her words. "Everyone thinks it's an interventionist, Mr. Kaplan or one of his buddies, who made it look as if Mr. Bauer planted the bomb."

"Or . . ." Quintessa gazed at the ceiling and tapped her fork on her sliced pot roast. "Or it could be an isolationist who framed Mr. Kaplan to make it look like he was framing Mr. Bauer."

Yvette drew back her chin. "That is crazy, as you Americans say."

But Mary laughed. "As different as you and I are, Quintessa, we do think alike."

"You are both crazy."

Mary leaned forward. "No, think about it. Everything about the bomb was so overt, as if to say, 'Look! An evil Nazi was here.'"

Yvette leveled her brown-eyed gaze at Mary. "An evil Nazi *was* here."

"Perhaps." Mary shrugged and took a bite of tender beef.

"If not a Nazi, who? George O'Donnell?"

Mary stared at the Frenchwoman, who was concentrating on her plate. What a strange leap to make. "Why him?"

"I have been in the drafting room. My friend Henri shows me his work. It is fascinating. But Mr. O'Donnell is angry. I ask about his drawings, but he . . ." She snapped her fingers.

"Snaps at you?" Mary said.

"Yes. Snaps at me."

Quintessa rested her chin in her hand. "If only we had another clue."

"We don't." Which wasn't good for Mr. Kaplan.

"They're trying to lull us into complacency." Quintessa lifted her chin high. "But no, not us. We will not be lulled. We will be vigilant."

"You're wasting your talents at Filene's." Mary took another bite.

"Not at all. I love my job. For a whole year, I get to explore every department as a salesgirl so I understand how a store is run. After that, I can put my business degree to work in management. I do hope they like me."

Mary gave her a fond smile. "How could they not?" Not only was Quintessa smart and charming, but she had a way of making everyone feel special. "Everyone likes you."

"I hope Jim does." Quintessa's smile turned dreamy. "Every time I look at his service portrait or reread one of your letters about him, I fall a little more in love."

The bit of beef turned to stone in Mary's throat, and her

eyes watered. If only she could enjoy Quintessa's company without hearing Jim's name.

Quintessa frowned at Mary. "The other day, I had a horrible thought. You and Jim have been such good buddies recently. I hope you don't think I'm stealing your friend."

Mary sipped her coffee to clear her throat. "No. No, of course not."

"Because I won't. We can double-date. You said his best friend is single, right? And you know I'm not one of those jealous sorts who won't let her boyfriend talk to another girl."

"I know." Mary grabbed her plate and headed for the sink. Not only did she need to hide her face, but she couldn't eat another bite.

"You talk as if it is fait accompli," Yvette said.

Quintessa's laugh bubbled up. "I do, don't I? I don't mean to sound arrogant. I don't, but Jim simply adored me in high school, and now I'm wise enough to appreciate him."

Mary scraped her plate over the trash can, her vision blurry. In six months of friendship, Jim had never fawned over Mary as he had over Quintessa. He'd never shown any true interest in her. The moments she'd interpreted as romantic could easily be interpreted as friendly or chivalrous. She'd deluded herself.

And the kiss? The more she thought about it, the less romantic it seemed. If he'd wanted a kiss, he would have kissed her himself. Sure, he responded to her kiss, but he was a man. Any red-blooded male would respond to a kiss. For heaven's sake, Arch had kissed a complete stranger.

The egg timer dinged.

"Oh, Mary!" Quintessa called. "Look at the time. You need to leave for choir."

She blinked away the haze in her eyes and glanced at her watch. "Oh dear, I do. I hate to leave a mess."

"But it's Thursday," Quintessa said. "My day to cook and

clean. Don't you worry about a thing. Go use your lovely voice and have fun."

Mary worked up a smile, blew her friend a kiss, grabbed her coat, and left.

As she rode the El downtown, her thoughts descended underground with her. Mary drew her coat tight. Part of her wanted to tell Quintessa how she felt about Jim, to fight for the man she loved. Quintessa would back down, mortified that she'd interfered in Mary's romance, and she'd wish Jim and Mary every happiness.

But a scene played like a movie in Mary's mind. Jim returning from sea, mounting the stairs to her apartment with that grin, Mary throwing herself into his arms. Then, over Mary's shoulder, Jim would see Quintessa, the woman he'd always loved. Something would pass between Jim and Quintessa, the spark of mutual attraction. But Jim would feel compelled to date Mary and would pass up his chance with Quintessa, his dream.

Mary turned to the window and rubbed away more tears. Confessing her love to Quintessa might be honest, but in a selfish, mean-spirited way. What could be crueler than coming between two people who longed for each other?

Quintessa was already falling for Jim, and she hadn't even seen him yet—the brilliance of his smile and his mind, the depth of his voice and his heart. Once she did, she'd be lost in love.

Mary pressed her fist to her mouth. She owed her best friend so much. Quintessa could have chosen any girl in Vermilion to befriend, but she'd chosen Mary, the school outcast. Mary could still see her in the schoolyard in her pink drop-waist dress, her bobbed blonde curls shimmering in the sun, her fists planted on her hips, chastising the other girls for picking on her friend.

Quintessa saved Mary from a youth full of misery and isolation. If Mary loved her best friend, she'd want her to be happy. Only a little while ago, Mary had wished she could do something, anything to make Quintessa happy again, and now she had her opportunity.

And Jim? A sob gurgled in her throat, but she shoved it down. If she truly loved Jim, she'd want him to be happy. She'd want to help him fulfill his dream. She'd make any sacrifice for his sake.

How could she do otherwise?

★ ★ ★

Sandwiched between Bertha and Edith, Mary let the music comfort her. When Jim returned, the Lord would see her through. She was doing the right thing, she knew it, and the Lord would reward her with peace.

The final song finished, and Mary took her seat.

Mrs. Gunderson tapped the music stand with her baton. "As you know, the Christmas pageant is only two months from now, and it's time to announce parts."

In the row in front of Mary, Claudia Richards scooted forward in her chair and smoothed her red hair.

Bertha nudged Mary and smiled at her. The two sisters had dared Mary to try out with them for the parts of the three angels, and she'd accepted. What fun it would be to sing with these two sweet friends. And the angels sang from up in the gallery. Behind the congregation.

Mrs. Gunderson lifted a sheet of paper and adjusted her glasses. "The part of Joseph will be played by Ed Fanarolli, Mary by our very own Mary—Mary Stirling—Gabriel by—"

After Claudia gasped, Mary's ears shut out everything else. Quintessa's pot roast turned green in Mary's belly and threatened to reappear. No, no, no. She couldn't be cast as Mary. She couldn't. She hadn't even tried out for it. She didn't want it. She wouldn't take it. She refused.

General motion and conversation let her know Mrs. Gunderson had finished the cast list and choir was dismissed. Bertha and Edith were congratulating her, but the words jumbled together.

Claudia dashed to the choir director. "There must be a mistake. I tried out for the role of Mary, not for an angel, and I sang quite well that evening."

"Yes." Mrs. Gunderson raised a stiff smile. "You sang angelically."

"But—but I've played Mary five years in a row."

"And it's time someone else had a turn."

Now was the moment. Mary scrambled over, almost knocking over two wooden chairs. "Please, let Claudia have the role. I don't want it."

Claudia jutted out her chin. "See?"

"This is how it will be this year." The choir director gathered her papers and tapped them into a neat stack on the music stand. "Mary, you've done so well on Sundays. You're ready for something more."

"Yes." She wrapped her arms around her stomach. "Like an angel."

Mrs. Gunderson peered at Mary and Claudia in turn over her glasses. "My decision is final."

Claudia's face turned cherry red, and she stormed out of the choir room.

"Come with me." Mrs. Gunderson took Mary's arm and led her to the corner of the room. "I thought you'd recovered from your stage fright."

Her eyes burned. "I—I have. But a starring role? As Mary? I can't. Please let Claudia—"

"No. I prayed about this all week. For several reasons, I feel this is what the Lord wants." Mrs. Gunderson's eyes were so soft and encouraging. "First, you have a lovely voice, and a little push would be good for you."

This wasn't a push but a shove. She hugged herself harder, willing the nausea away.

"Second, you're right for the role. Mary needs to be a young soprano, and I only have two. For the past five years, I haven't had a choice, but this year I do. The mother of our Lord was the essence of humility and gentleness, just like you."

Mary shook her head, blinking hard. If only the choir director knew how she struggled with pride and selfishness.

"Third, and this is just between you and me." Mrs. Gunderson glanced over Mary's shoulder and lowered her voice. "Claudia is a gifted singer, but she's proud and divisive. She doesn't represent our church well, and she definitely doesn't represent our Lord. You may notice she hasn't had a solo for some time. I've been featuring the men and the altos."

Mary nodded. She'd heard Claudia complain about that several times.

Mrs. Gunderson stashed her music in the cabinet. "I've decided to remove Claudia from the limelight for her own sake and for the sake of the church. Pride is a nasty, destructive sin."

How well Mary knew. She could still feel the swell of pride in her chest, the weight of the blue robe on her shoulders, the pressure in her bladder, the warmth gushing down, the clammy cloth stuck to her legs, the sharp cold of nakedness and humiliation, the darts of laughter. She could still hear the crash, see baby Jesus shattered before her, one glass eye staring at her accusingly.

"I can't," she said. "I can't do it. You don't know what you're asking of me."

Mrs. Gunderson squeezed Mary's arm. "When the mother of our Lord heard the angel Gabriel's announcement, I imagine she felt the same way. How could a simple peasant girl—and not yet married—raise the Christ as her own child?"

Mary swiped at the tears tickling her cheek. "I can imagine."

"What did Mary say? 'Behold the handmaid of the Lord; be it unto me according to thy word.'"

According to his word? This was God's will? Yes, it was. It was punishment. Somehow, without even knowing it, she'd let pride worm its way back into her life—in choir, in her investigation, with Jim—and this was her punishment.

She had to relive the most humiliating moment of her life.

27

South of Iceland
Monday, October 20, 1941

An eerie stillness hung in the frozen air, and Jim gripped the lifeline. Oil slicks stained the water black, and wreckage littered the waves. Something macabre inside him scrutinized each lump in the water to see if it was a body. He'd already seen two.

Convoy SC-48 had passed through these seas on her way to England. From October 15 to October 19, U-boats had sunk nine freighters and tankers, a British destroyer, and a British frigate. Three American destroyers had been diverted from escorting Convoy ON-24 to help. On October 17, a U-boat torpedoed the USS *Kearny*. Although she remained afloat, eleven American sailors had perished, the first to die in this war.

Jim gave his head a sharp shake and moved on. He was scheduled to relieve the torpedo officer, Ens. Reggie Parkinson, for the afternoon watch at 1200. While waiting at the Mid-Ocean Meeting Point for Convoy ON-26 to arrive from Liverpool, the *Atwood* had been sent to search for survivors from the slaughter of SC-48. They hadn't found a soul, and the crew tensed, scouting for U-boats.

Jim headed amidships, where the quintuple torpedo tube mount sat between the two funnels like five fingers, ready to point to starboard or port to fire at enemy vessels.

Reggie waved Jim over with his customary grin on his long face, and he briefed Jim on his station's condition and readiness. Since U-boats often remained in the area after a battle to prey on rescue ships, the *Atwood* stood at Condition Two, prepared for attack. Like Nehemiah's men, they had one hand at work and one ready to fight.

Reggie motioned toward the stern. "I was about to check on the fellows down at the depth charge racks and the Y-gun."

"I'll take care of that. Go get some rest." Jim clapped him on the back and sent him on his way. With calm seas for now, the men were stocking up on food and sleep.

"Ahoy!" Up on the wing of the bridge, a lookout yelled and pointed.

Jim's heart jolted, and he followed the lookout's line of sight to port. Without binoculars, all he could see was a gray shape in the water. Wreck or U-boat?

On the bridge, Durant joined the lookout, peered through his binoculars, then returned to the pilothouse.

The general quarters gong sounded, and Jim froze along with everyone else on board, waiting for the signal to specify the drill.

The bugle sounded "Assembly," and the boatswain's mate's pipe sounded "Away fire and rescue party." A rescue operation.

The *Atwood* made a sharp turn to port, heading for the hulk. The harder Jim squinted, the more he could make out what looked to be the upside-down stern of a ship. The rescue party gathered by the whaleboat, and the deck gang prepared to lower the boat by its davits to the water.

Jim made his way to the stern. He didn't have specified duties during a rescue drill, but he needed to make sure the depth charges were ready in case of attack.

He passed the Y-gun, already loaded with two 300-pound depth charges, which could be propelled starboard and port. The gun crew was alert and ready.

Down at the stern, 600-pound depth charges lay in two angled racks. Hydraulic controls allowed a man on the bridge to flip the release lever and drop one "ash can" at a time.

The talker was speaking into his microphone, so Jim joined him. He saluted Jim. "Good day, sir. The captain wants us to prepare to drop a pattern at 100 feet, 150, 200, and 250, at five-second intervals."

Jim returned the salute. "Very well. Tell him the Y-gun is loaded and ready."

"Aye aye, sir." He waved over the petty officer, Marvin Hill, and relayed the pattern.

Hill passed on the order. Two seamen got to work with special wrenches to turn dials on the ends of the ash cans to set the depth at which they'd explode.

"Hey, everyone!" one of the Y-gun crewmen shouted. "Survivors."

Jim jogged over to the rail. Sure enough, half a dozen men sat on what remained of the stern of their ship, waving frantically. "Thank God." Jim smiled at the glimmer of hope in the middle of the destruction.

The *Atwood* slowed to a stop, and the whaleboat swung out on its davits, loaded with the rescue party, blankets, and rum. Durant's voice came over the loudspeaker. "This is the USS *Atwood*. Stay where you are until the rescue boat comes to you."

But one of the men stood and jumped into the water.

"No!" Jim cried, echoed by the men around him. The man would die in under twenty minutes in the frigid water, and several minutes would pass before the whaleboat could row to him.

"No!" Durant barked into the loudspeaker. "Do not come to us. We will come to you."

Jim's breath froze. "What if they don't speak English?"

Two more men jumped in and swam toward the *Atwood*. Vince Banning marched down the deck. "Drop the cargo net. Now!"

The deck gang sprang to work and heaved the net over the side. If only the men in the water could make it to the ship in time. If only the whaleboat could be lowered more quickly.

"Hurry, hurry," Jim muttered.

The alarm clanged, and Jim whipped around to face the bridge. What now?

"General quarters" blasted on the bugle. "Man your battle stations."

They must have made a sound contact.

"Oh Lord, not now!" Jim stared at the three men in the water, swimming, each stroke slower than the last in the icy water. The whaleboat hovered just off the gunwale, nowhere near the surface.

"Haul in that boat," Banning shouted. "Now!"

Everything in Jim wanted to scream his protest. A few more minutes and they might save those men.

But in a few minutes, they could be pierced by a German torpedo. Those three men—and all two hundred men aboard the *Atwood*—could die.

"Throw them a life raft," Banning called, but defeat hollowed his voice.

The American naval life rafts were large rings with netting in the center. They kept men afloat but didn't get them out of the water. They wouldn't drown, but they'd die of hypothermia.

The destroyer's engines rumbled, propelling the ship away,

smothering the cries of the dying men. Jim squeezed his eyes shut, but the image of three outstretched hands, three panicked faces burned into the backside of his eyelids. *Lord, be with them.*

Durant had to make a speedy decision. He had to be bold. And he'd made the right choice for the greater good. Nehemiah had done hard things too, rebuking those who did wrong and tossing out those who violated God's law. Neither man was afraid to be unpopular.

Jim ran down to the stern for the depth charge attack. Could he be like Durant? Like Nehemiah?

"Range five-double-oh," the talker called out. "Ready charges."

Five hundred yards. Jim's breath curled in the air. The destroyer drove forward at about twenty knots. At that speed they'd reach the sub in about two minutes. "Everyone ready?"

"Clear the racks," Hill called. "Charges ready to roll from the forward to the after detent."

"Just a second." A sailor leaned into the narrow space between the smoke generator canisters and the starboard depth charge rack, his arm down through the triangle formed between two depth charges and the lower rack rail. "Dropped my wrench."

"Get out of there, Ozzie! Now!" Hill grabbed the hem of the man's mackinaw and yanked.

A click, and the depth charges rolled to the end of the rack.

Ozzie's scream punctured the air.

Jim leaped forward. "What happened?"

"His hand." Hill cussed. "It's caught."

Ozzie screamed, swore, writhed.

Jim dashed to the other side to get a better look. One of the 600-pound steel drums had smashed two of Ozzie's fingers against the vertical bar supporting the rails. Blood dripped from tears in his gloves.

Still cussing, Marvin Hill flipped the release lever to manual control, overriding control from the bridge. "Everyone! Roll back the charges. Step to it!"

"Range three-double-oh," the talker called.

Jim's lungs filled with lead. Only a minute left to roll back all five depth charges on the rack and free Ozzie's hand—what remained of it.

Two of the men wrestled with the top depth charge, barely budging it. Ten men would be required to roll back all the charges, if they could even squeeze into the cramped space. How long would that take? More than a minute. Much longer. Then the destroyer could only drop half the depth charges, completing only half the pattern. The chance of the U-boat surviving to torpedo them would be doubled.

But what about Ozzie? The young man's face wrenched in agony, sweat beaded on his forehead, and his arm twisted at an awkward angle to relieve pressure on his smashed fingers.

Jim's breath came hard. He gripped the upper rails of the rack as if they were the jaws of an animal trap, as if he could pry them apart and save Ozzie's hand, Lillian's leg.

But he couldn't. Lillian lost her leg. Ozzie would lose those two fingers.

"Range two-double-oh. Sound contact lost," the talker said. "Mr. Avery, sir, should I tell the captain we're down to one rack?"

Jim stared at the man in his headphones. They were close enough to lose sound contact. They had to release the depth charges in thirty seconds. If they did, Ozzie would lose the other two fingers on that hand. What if the contact was a whale? A pocket of cold water? What if Jim sacrificed Ozzie's hand for nothing?

But what if it was a U-boat? What if they only dropped half the charges, and the U-boat survived to sink the *Atwood* with Ozzie and two hundred other men on board?

Jim had to decide, and he had to decide now.

Time to be an officer. Time to be bold. He straightened up. "Hill, switch back to bridge control."

"What? He'll lose his hand."

"That's an order. Do it now."

Hill's square face agitated, but he leaned over and flipped the lever.

"Please don't," Ozzie cried. "Please, sir. Please don't."

"Call for a medical team," Jim told the talker, then he circled the rack and set his hand on Ozzie's shoulder. "Get as much of your arm out of the way as you can. I'm sorry, but we need to sink that sub before it sinks us."

The man scrunched his eyes shut, tears streaming down his cheeks, and Jim clenched his shoulder.

Behind Jim, the port rack clicked, and a depth charge splashed into the water, set to explode at one hundred feet.

Five seconds. Ozzie's muscles tensed beneath Jim's hand.

Five, four, three, two, one.

The lever clicked. The charges rolled forward. Ozzie screeched.

As soon as the charge rolled by, Jim grabbed his shoulders and pulled him free. "Come on, men. Get him out of here."

Sailors dragged the screaming man away from the racks, to the open space behind the number four gun mount.

A loud hollow explosion sounded behind the ship. The stern heaved out of the water, and Jim fought to keep his balance. The water turned white in a rapidly spreading circle, then a giant plume erupted in the center. The first depth charge.

Two more depth charges rolled off the stern. Three more explosions fired, churning up the sea.

Jim leaned back against the smoke generator, his breath galloping. A group huddled around Ozzie. Some of the men held him down while a pharmacist's mate wrapped gauze around four bloody stumps.

The *Atwood* shifted to a circling pattern, and the Y-gun fired both 300-pound depth charges.

No further sound contacts. No torpedo wakes in their direction. But no oil or debris rose to the surface.

Jim stood there, gloved hand splayed on the cold steel of the smoke generator, while blood froze on the depth charge rack and the medical team helped young Ozzie Douglas down to sick bay to start a new life without the fingers on his right hand.

A vile taste filled Jim's mouth. For the second time in his life, he'd acted boldly. And for the second time in his life, someone had been maimed.

28

Boston
Friday, October 24, 1941

Mary leaned in to Mr. Pennington's office. "I'm off to see Agent Sheffield. I'll be right back."

Her boss shook his white head. "I do wish you'd stop. Your grandfather will have me tarred and feathered if anything happens to you."

"Thank you for your concern, but nothing will happen. I only take notes." She waved and departed. No need to tell Mr. Pennington how daring she'd been lately, even sitting behind suspects in the cafeteria to record conversations. Inadmissible evidence, Agent Sheffield told her, but still valuable information.

Mary's heels clicked down the hallway. The FBI agent's sudden appreciation for her skills should have served as vindication but instead only reminded her of the role she'd played in Ira Kaplan's arrest. That guilt motivated her to find the real saboteur.

She descended the stairs. Things were heating up. At first

the errors in the shipyard looked like sloppy work, but now it looked like a deliberate attempt to slow production.

Rumors of sabotage abounded in Massachusetts lately. Down in Fall River two weeks before, a fire had broken out at the Firestone plant, destroying thirty thousand tons of crude rubber, 12 percent of the American stockpile. No one knew how it started, but everyone had a theory.

Mary paused at the base of the stairs and gripped the banister. If only she could discuss things with Jim. Never again. She had to release him, and how it hurt.

Why had she kissed him? That complicated matters. Now he knew she cared. Now he'd feel sorry for her when he chose Quintessa. How cruel it would be to force him to choose. No, she couldn't have that. She had to assure him that she wanted him and Quintessa together.

She hauled a breath into her burning lungs. If she loved Jim, if she loved Quintessa, she could do this.

Mary straightened her shoulders and entered the FBI agents' office. Frank Fiske leaned over Agent Sheffield's desk, examining a blueprint.

The agent smiled at Mary. "Ah, Miss Stirling. This week's report?"

Mary's smile stiffened. She didn't care to have anyone other than the FBI agents and Mr. Pennington know about her notes, and now Mr. Fiske gave her a curious look.

"Perfect timing." Agent Sheffield took her report, skimmed it, and set it down. "I have another job for you. I already have permission from Mr. Pennington."

"Oh?" The excitement of being included in the investigation mixed with her frustration at being singled out. She respected Mr. Fiske but kept him on her suspect list. After all, he had motive, means, and opportunity, and she wouldn't be impartial if she excluded him.

"A job?" the leadingman asked.

Agent Sheffield rolled up the blueprint on his desk. "You want me to talk to Weldon Winslow. Miss Stirling took thorough and accurate notes when Mr. Kaplan was arrested, and I'd like to employ her stenography skills again. I'll see you later, Mr. Fiske."

Agent Hayes unfolded his long form from his desk chair, gave Mary a silent nod, and held open the office door for her.

After the leadingman headed back to the docks, Mary followed the two agents next door to Building 38. "May I ask what this is about?"

Once inside, Agent Sheffield climbed the stairs. "I don't want to confuse you with technical details, but Fiske's crew has had problems."

"I heard. The holes were drilled too large for the bolts, so several entire sections had to be scrapped. Then they assembled another section using too-small bolts, which weakened the structure."

The agent stood on the landing and raised an eyebrow at her. "Yes."

Mary raised her sweetest smile. "A girl picks up some technical know-how in four years at a shipyard."

He continued on his way. "Mr. Fiske checked again. Everything had been constructed according to the blueprints."

In the hallway, Mary fell in beside the gentlemen. "So the blueprints are the origin of the errors?" The blueprints came from Mr. Winslow's office.

Thoughts careened in her mind. Mr. Winslow, with his desire to aid Britain, had motive, but he hardly seemed the radical bomb-building type. Did he have the mechanical expertise to build and install a bomb? She'd never once seen him on the docks.

The agents marched down the aisle in the drafting room, and all the draftsmen stopped and stared. The scrutiny made

Mary's skin crawl. She wasn't trying to display herself, yet everyone was looking at her.

Agent Sheffield knocked on Mr. Winslow's door and entered the office.

Mr. Winslow's eyes widened, then he stood and offered his hand. "Agent Sheffield, Agent Hayes. To what do I owe the pleasure? And Miss Stirling. Always a pleasure."

Mary shook his slight, soft hand, noting his clean, manicured nails. Did the man even know how to use a hammer or a wrench? How could they think him guilty of sabotage?

Agent Sheffield pulled up a chair for Mary, then sat across from Mr. Winslow's desk, thumping his shoes onto the desktop. "Do you know why I'm here?"

Mr. Winslow stared at the agent's shoes, his lips thinned. "I can't imagine."

"Why don't you tell me how your plans make it into blueprints and end up on the docks?"

Mary opened her notebook and started a new page of notes.

Mr. Winslow straightened the blotter on his desk. "It's rather straightforward. I draw up preliminary plans with all the specifications. I pass them on to the draftsman assigned to that project. He draws up the final diagram, has the blueprint developed, and delivers it to the leadingman."

Agent Sheffield lit a cigarette without offering one to Mr. Winslow. "Have you heard about the bolts on the Fiske crew?"

"Yes, I have. I can't imagine what happened. It's all rather strange."

"Here's the situation." The agent angled cigarette smoke over the desk. "We had an independent inspector come in. He verified the construction was performed exactly to the specifications on the blueprints."

"Exactly? That can't be. Do you—do you think I made a mistake? Even if I did, it hardly seems like the FBI's jurisdic—

wait. You don't think I did it on purpose?" The edge of the blotter rolled in Winslow's grasp.

Agent Sheffield shrugged and tipped his wooden chair back. "Tell me—what should I think?"

Mary took notes rapidly, her gaze darting back and forth between her notebook and the men. She didn't want to miss even one nuanced gesture.

Mr. Winslow's fingers skittered around as if he were typing on a miniature typewriter. "Why would I do anything to jeopardize our ships or our men? I want to help Britain, and the best way I can help is by getting these destroyers out to sea. Why would I slow production? You ought to look at the men who want to keep us off the seas and out of the war."

Mary anchored her tongue between her teeth so she wouldn't mention the theory that Winslow could be framing someone to stir up public sentiment in favor of the war.

Mr. Winslow thumped his fists on the desk. "O'Donnell!"

"O'Donnell?" Agent Sheffield sounded as if he'd never heard the name before, although it appeared in each of Mary's reports.

"George O'Donnell." Mr. Winslow ran his hand over his pomaded brown hair. "Of course. He's the loudest isolationist I know. He's the draftsman assigned to Fiske's crew. He draws up the blueprints from my plans. He could alter them. He's the one. It's him, I tell—"

"You'd like that, wouldn't you?" A gruff voice rose from the office entrance.

Mary whipped around.

George O'Donnell filled the doorway. "You'd love to make me look bad. You're the one who altered the plans, you and Kaplan in cahoots, I bet you. Then you pin it on me. Pin it on the isolationist. That'd get the papers in a fit, drive us right into the war."

Mr. Winslow rose from his chair, his fingers still working

on the desktop. "I could say the same about you. You altered the plans to make me look guilty, make it look as if I were trying to get us into the war."

O'Donnell entered the office, fists clenched by his side. "You and Kaplan. Yeah, you'd need help, someone willing to get dirt under his nails. I wouldn't be surprised if that French girl were in on this too, always sticking her nose into things around here."

"French girl?" Mary said, pen still. "Yvette?"

O'Donnell looked down at her, his heavy salt-and-pepper brows drawn together. "Yeah. Young. Brunette. Long foreign name."

Mary doodled on the corner of her page to look indifferent. Yvette had mentioned her fascination with drafting, the time she spent in the drafting room.

Agent Hayes stood and grasped the doorknob. "Excuse us, Mr. O'Donnell. This is a private meeting. We'll speak with you later."

A twitch in Agent Sheffield's upper lip told Mary he was perfectly happy listening to the men incriminate each other.

Agent Hayes shut the door behind Mr. O'Donnell and took his seat.

A long stream of cigarette smoke rose from Sheffield's mouth. "Then there's the matter of Winslow Shipbuilding Company. Your family."

"They're not my family." Mr. Winslow's voice went taut, and he fiddled with his fingers. "They may have raised me, but they aren't my family. My wife and children are. I made my own way in this world, no thanks to them, and I have no share in their lives or in their company."

Agent Sheffield rested his forearms on the desk and cocked his head. "You're shaking pretty hard, Mr. Winslow. Perhaps you should see a doctor about that."

The men stared each other down, and Mary held her

breath. What sort of message had passed between them? What was that about?

Mr. Winslow's hands dropped to the handle of his desk drawer. "I'm fine. Why wouldn't I be shaking? I'm not accustomed to such accusations."

"Of course not. A gentleman like you." Agent Sheffield planted his hands on his knees, grunted, and stood. He reached across the desk to shake Winslow's hand, blowing cigarette smoke in his face. "As you said, always a pleasure."

Mr. Winslow drew away and choked back a cough. "Yes. A pleasure."

Mary capped her pen. She'd never seen such bad manners from the FBI agent, as if he were deliberately trying to annoy the patrician naval architect. He'd succeeded.

"Come along." Sheffield motioned for Agent Hayes and Mary to follow him.

Mary turned back to give Mr. Winslow a polite farewell. "Good-bye."

"Yes. Good-bye." His smile stretched over his teeth. In his open desk drawer, his hand clenched a small object.

For a man who insisted he wasn't guilty, he sure acted guilty. And yet the idea of Weldon Winslow rigging and installing a bomb seemed ludicrous. Unless he had help.

Mary followed the agents into the hallway.

"What do you think?" Agent Hayes asked.

"I think . . ." Sheffield glanced at Mary, then leaned closer to Hayes, his voice low. "I think a spring wound this tight is bound to pop."

Whatever did he mean by that? Mary resisted the urge to write it down, but she memorized it.

Both Winslow and O'Donnell did act tightly wound, but when—and how—would they pop?

29

"Ever since we said good-bye, I couldn't wait to say hello."
Jim rehearsed his line as he strolled past the Bunker Hill Monument toward Mary's apartment, his head ducked against the rain.

In the gleam of the street lamps, raindrops shimmered in the puddles. Surely Mary was at home on a rainy Saturday evening. Perhaps he should have called first, but he wanted to surprise her. Since she wouldn't have gone to work today, she wouldn't know the *Atwood* had come into port this afternoon.

After the ordeal of their first convoy escort, Durant had given all the men liberty tonight except a skeleton crew. Jim couldn't shake the images of Ozzie Douglas's mangled hand and of those three bodies in the water when they'd returned to the sunken freighter. At least they'd been able to save the other three sailors—Norwegians who didn't speak a lick of English.

Tonight he could talk with Mary. The other officers praised Jim's actions that day and said he'd done the right thing.

Even Mitch Hadley and Dick Reinhardt were impressed. But the accolades sat wrong, like an ill-fitting uniform. Mary would listen. She'd understand.

He headed down Monument Avenue. If it weren't for the rain, he wouldn't even need his overcoat. After the North Atlantic, forty-five degrees felt balmy. Besides, he felt warm inside. In just a minute, he'd hold Mary in his arms and give her the hello he'd imagined all month.

He broke into a jog. At her building, he glanced up to the window. A dark figure, silhouetted by golden light, parted the curtains. Jim waved and grinned. She waved, and the curtains dropped.

Jim took the stairs two at a time and raised his hand to knock. Excited feminine chatter on the other side of the door made him pause. Didn't sound like Mary or Yvette, but it did sound like his return was welcome.

"Ever since we said good-bye," he murmured, "I couldn't wait to say—"

The door flung open. "Hello, Jim."

A beautiful blonde stood in his path, everything about her as dazzling as in his memories. "Quintessa?"

"Look at you, poor thing. Out in the rain without an umbrella." She sprang forward, pulled him into the entryway, and took off his cover. "But don't you look wonderful?"

Jim smoothed his hair as if the gesture would smooth his thoughts. "When—when did you get into town?"

"Over a month ago. The day you left, would you believe it?" Her eyes danced, all green and gold. "But I've had a swell time. I'm working at Filene's, and it's the best job I've ever had. I haven't been this happy in ages."

"Filene's? You have a job? Here?" He couldn't breathe, couldn't think. This was the longest Quintessa had ever aimed conversation his direction. She'd never been rude, just focused appropriately on Hugh.

"I moved to Boston. Isn't it exciting? I'll tell you all about it over dinner. When I heard how much fun you and Mary were having, I just had to come."

Mary—the reason he was here. He tore his gaze from Quintessa.

There was Mary, standing by the telephone in a brown suit, the receiver cradled to her cheek. "Yes, that's right. Two for seven. Thank you. Good-bye."

"Mary." Her name flowed out, full of hope and longing.

"It's good to see you. I'm glad you came home safely." She hung up the telephone. "Now, if you'll excuse me, I need to serve Yvette her soup. She's been sick in bed, poor dear. You two go have fun. Everything's set."

You two? "What?"

"You have so much catching up to do." Mary headed for the kitchen door. "Besides, Quintessa came all the way to Boston just to see you."

"Oh, Mary." Quintessa clucked her tongue. "I came to see you too."

"Of course you did." Mary raised a teasing smile and went into the kitchen.

Quintessa sighed and laid her hand on Jim's arm. "I admit, it's partly true."

"What?" Jim blinked hard and faced Quintessa, everything heaving him around like the seas off Greenland.

Quintessa gazed up at him through long lashes. "I have to admit, I was a bit jealous of Mary having so much fun with our handsome naval officer, and I had to come."

He couldn't swallow, couldn't see straight. He'd always adored Quintessa, and now she looked at him . . . adoringly. But Mary—he loved Mary. And what was she doing?

"Bye. Have fun." Mary leaned out the kitchen door and gave them a smile and a wave as if sending her little brother out on a date.

What on earth? Didn't she remember their kiss? He swallowed the thick lump in his throat. "You're coming with us, aren't you?"

"Me?" She turned away and tied an apron around her waist. "Don't be silly. I wouldn't dream of interrupting your special date."

Jim's hands balled up. Interrupt? Interrupt? Mary was supposed to be his special date.

"Poor confused Jim." Quintessa giggled. "That's why I have our evening all planned out. I have for over a week, in case you came home. As soon as Mary spotted you coming down the hill, she called the Normandie for me. We have reservations at seven, so we'd better hurry. Let me freshen up. Won't take but a moment."

Jim nodded absently, but as soon as Quintessa left, he hung up his damp overcoat and marched into the kitchen. "Mary?"

"Hmm?" She stood at the stove, her back to him, ladling soup into two bowls.

He stopped and stared at her, the blue apron tied around her tiny waist, her dark hair curling on her shoulders, begging for his fingers. *Ever since we said good-bye . . .* this wasn't how he'd imagined hello.

"Yes?" Mary glanced over her shoulder at him.

Jim cleared his throat. "What's going on?"

"Isn't it wonderful?" She leaned back against the stove and wiped her hands on her apron. "All your dreams come true. Sometimes a broken heart allows a woman to see the good in a man she'd overlooked."

He shook his head, comprehending but not comprehending. "I don't under—" He waved his hand south, in the general direction of the docks. Didn't she remember? Didn't she still feel that kiss as he did? "When I left—when we said good-bye—"

"Oh, that." She tilted her head, one corner of her mouth dimpled. "You don't have to worry about me."

"Worry . . . ?"

"The kiss," she whispered, and she peeked past him through the doorway. "I know it didn't mean anything. I know it was just for show. You don't have to worry about me building a silly fantasy."

His jaw hardened. It didn't mean anything to her? She thought he'd kissed her back just for show? Well, she might not have built a silly fantasy, but he had.

"Just a friendly kiss," he said through gritted teeth.

"Yes." She turned to the stove. "Quintessa doesn't know, and you don't have to worry about me pining away for you. I know you've loved Quintessa forever. I'm so happy for both of you."

"I'm ready, Jim," Quintessa called.

The smell of chicken soup filled his nose, paralyzing him like a drug. The kiss meant nothing to Mary. He meant nothing to her. Nothing at all.

"Go on." Mary gave him an eager smile. "The girl of your dreams is waiting for you."

He spun away, his chest hot.

Quintessa stood in the entryway, twirling in a dark green dress. "How do I look?"

"Beautiful," he said over his clenched jaw.

She strolled over to him, blonde curls bouncing. "And look at you. So handsome in your Navy uniform. Even more handsome than Mary said. Of course, she was just looking at you with the eyes of a friend."

His ribs felt like a vise on his heart and lungs. Mary had her back to him again, ladled soup again, oblivious to his presence again. The eyes of a friend indeed.

Jim wheeled to Quintessa, flashed a grin, and offered his elbow. "What are we waiting for? Our evening of dining and dancing awaits. Just the two of us." Did he sound testy? So what? Mary didn't want him.

But Quintessa did—brilliant, sparkling, vibrant Quintessa with the golden-green eyes—eyes that saw him as a man, not just a friend.

As she chattered and laughed, he helped her on with her coat, slipped on his coat and cover, took Quintessa's umbrella, and led her out into the rain to hail a cab.

If his dream had just come true, why did he want to wake up and end it?

30

Mary bent her head over the music for the closing hymn, "O, That I Had a Thousand Voices." Her choir robe burned, taunting her to rip it off and flee the church. How could she sing about hope and joy when her heart felt wrung out, when her mouth ached from smiling late into the night as Quintessa related every delightful detail about her delightful date with delightful Jim?

His manners—impeccable. His dancing—lively. His company—attentive to her every word. He was quieter than Quintessa remembered, but then she did prattle on, didn't she? Thank goodness he wasn't as gangly and goofy as she remembered. She'd never cared for that about him, but he'd outgrown it. Wasn't she the happiest girl in the world?

Mary's voice cracked.

Claudia Richards glanced back at her and smirked.

Mary focused hard on the words. A thousand voices? If only she had one voice that behaved.

Down below her in the sanctuary, Jim sat in the pew in

his dress blues, with Arch on one side and Quintessa close, close, close on the other.

This morning's headline deepened her longing for their friendship. The destroyer USS *Reuben James* had been sunk by a U-boat in the North Atlantic on Friday, taking 115 men down with her, including all her officers. Did Jim know any of the men? What did he think would happen next? Surely America wouldn't sit idly by after Germany sank one of her warships?

For one heart-piercing moment, Jim looked up over his shoulder and met her eye. Her brain felt fuzzy, woozy. If she wasn't careful, he'd see her heartbreak. No, she'd chosen the role of a supportive friend, and she'd play it well, for his sake and for Quintessa's sake.

Bertha nudged her and tapped the sheet music. "We skipped verse two," she whispered.

Heavens, that was right. Mary furiously scanned to find her place, the words and notes tumbling before her eyes. She waited until they started the fourth verse and joined in, her voice alone among the sopranos. Oh, heavens above. The altos were leading this verse, weren't they?

Claudia's shoulders shook in suppressed laughter, and Mrs. Gunderson shot her a concerned look.

Mary's eyes stung with hot tears. What had she done wrong? What had she done to deserve this pain and humiliation?

Her sails luffed, jangling on their rings, announcing her failure for all to see. Mousy Mary Stirling honestly thought she had a chance with handsome Jim Avery, thought so much of herself that she grabbed him and kissed him as if he'd enjoy it. And she'd joined the choir, parading herself on stage. And the investigation? Putting herself where she didn't belong, getting an innocent man arrested, and impeding the FBI.

The choir robe—so hot. She wiped sweat off her upper lip and yanked the collar away from her neck.

Why hadn't she stayed in hiding, in obscurity where she was safe? Oh, that's right. Pride. Pride lured her out. Mary Stirling could catch a saboteur. Mary Stirling could catch a man. Mary Stirling could publicly display herself in a bright red dress and a choir robe.

She stumbled through the final verse, her voice faint and quavering.

At last, they were dismissed. Mary dashed down to the choir room, the two flights of spiral stairs making her dizzy.

Claudia hung back at the door and snickered as Mary passed her. "Someone isn't ready for a solo."

No, someone wasn't. Someone never wanted it in the first place. Mary ripped off her choir robe and almost lost her balance.

"Steady there." Edith braced her. "Mary, dear. Are you all right?"

Overcome by the compassion in the ancient gray eyes, Mary shook her head, her mouth screwed shut.

"You don't look well. Your cheeks are too red, your eyes bleary." Bertha pressed her hand to Mary's forehead. "Land sakes, you're burning up."

"I am?" Mary felt her own forehead. It was indeed warm. "My roommate's had the flu."

"Go straight home, young lady, and put yourself to bed."

As much as Mary would like that, she couldn't. "I have to wait for Quintessa. She'd wonder where I went."

"I see your young Navy friends are back. Such a shame you're sick."

"Yes. Such." But a smile edged up. Now she had a legitimate excuse to skip lunch and the afternoon excursion she'd dreaded all night.

Mary headed out to the sidewalk. A friendly greeting, a

quick explanation, and a polite good-bye. That was all. She could do it.

Quintessa waited, one hand wrapped around Jim's elbow, the other stretched to Mary. "There you are."

Mary held up one hand. "I caught Yvette's flu, I'm afraid."

Quintessa stopped short. "Oh, you poor dear."

"Sorry you're not feeling well." The coolness of Jim's voice should have felt like a balm to her fever, but it pricked her soul.

Mary worked up a cheery smile and turned to Arch. "I'm afraid that means I'll have to abandon you to third-wheel status. I should go home."

"I'll go with you." Quintessa dropped Jim's arm and stepped closer. "You've been fussing over Yvette all week, and now it's your turn to be fussed over."

"Nonsense." Mary eased back. "You told me Jim won't be in town long, so you should enjoy every minute together. You certainly don't want to get sick."

"No, I don't." Quintessa embraced Jim's arm and gazed up at him.

Now Mary really did feel sick. She turned for the Park Street subway station. "I'll see you later, Quintessa. Have fun, everyone."

"Hope you feel better," Arch called after her.

Highly unlikely. Even chicken soup and hot tea couldn't cure her.

★ ★ ★

In the length of the train ride home, Mary's symptoms deepened and clarified. Every muscle ached, her face flamed, and her head felt stuffed full of wool. She longed to shed her heavy new coat—a dark, showy red. With a matching hat. She should shove them both in the nearest Salvation Army bin and retreat to safe, modest brown.

She huddled by the window, her cheek pressed to the cool glass. Should she even continue with the investigation? She was bound to stir up more trouble. Bound to.

But the work satisfied her and would distract her from Jim. This flu would keep her home from work all week. If she didn't have anything to do, she'd go crazy. She could type up her remaining notes and organize her notebooks filled with all the carbon copies she'd kept.

Perhaps new patterns would emerge, new clues, new directions. Or perhaps she'd see the folly of her ways and give it up for good. Either way, she had a purpose.

Mary got off the El at the City Square Station. Breed's Hill rose high and formidable before her, although she climbed it every day. She trudged up Main Street, light-headed. Before she tucked herself into bed, she needed aspirin and Yvette needed more cough syrup. They were out of both.

Maybe Quintessa would get sick too. Wouldn't that be nice?

Mary clutched her hot, cruel head. What was wrong with her? How could she wish illness on her dearest friend out of jealousy for a man who didn't even love her? A man who'd never been interested in her in the first place? A man who preferred gold to silver, and why shouldn't he?

Mary caught her breath and found her bearings on Main. The lights were on in Dixon's Drugs, open every Sunday at eleven.

Mary headed inside, past the soda fountain and the cosmetics and the household goods, back to where the proprietary medications were stored close to the prescription counter.

The pharmacist, a heavyset man in his sixties with thick gray hair and thicker glasses, talked to a patient wearing an overcoat and a fedora. On the counter, a hand-lettered sign read "Pharmacist wanted. Inquire with Mr. Dixon."

Mary blinked her heavy eyes. If only she could apply, be hired, get away.

What on earth was she thinking? She wasn't even a pharmacist. Oh, she needed aspirin badly.

But getting away . . .

Why not? She was a secretary, qualified and experienced. She could work anywhere in the country. Shipyards were bustling from Bath, Maine, to Charleston, South Carolina, from Seattle, Washington, to San Diego, California. Even on the Great Lakes.

Why did she need to be in Boston? She didn't. What was keeping her here? Nothing.

The pharmacist slipped an amber glass vial into a paper bag. "Your consumption of codeine has increased greatly the past few months."

Mary backed away, not wanting to intrude on a private conversation.

"I'm aware of that," the patient said in a familiar, cultured voice. "My nerves have been acting up lately, the pains in my arms and legs."

Mary recognized that voice, the slight frame in the well-cut coat and expensive hat.

The pharmacist shook his head, his jowls shifting. "See that you cut back. You don't want to become an addict."

"We wouldn't want that, would we?" With a wry chuckle, Mr. Weldon Winslow, naval architect, slapped down some cash and grabbed the paper bag.

Mary's mouth went dry. He was addicted to codeine?

She spun away and slipped down an aisle, her head lowered. The jittering, the shaking. What had Agent Sheffield said? "Maybe you should see a doctor about that." He knew—he knew what the shaking meant.

How many times had Mary seen Mr. Winslow swallow something furtively or hide small objects?

Palpitations shivered in Mary's chest. What did this mean to the investigation? Was Mr. Winslow's addiction causing him to make errors others interpreted as sabotage? Or was it driving him to abandon common sense and commit sabotage? Addicts often turned to crime to support their habits, didn't they?

Mr. Winslow's steps approached, and Mary angled her back away from him, pretending to examine a bottle in her hand. Milk of magnesia? She didn't need milk of magnesia.

This was a new clue, an important clue. But should she report it? Agent Sheffield already suspected something. Let him discover it on his own. Mary couldn't afford to get another innocent man locked up. For goodness' sake, Mr. Winslow had a wife and children who depended on him. How could she ruin four lives with her meddling?

It was high time she retreated. She needed to keep her suspicions and gossip and nonsensical theories to herself.

Tears scalded her eyes. Why hadn't she left well enough alone?

31

Lately the sea felt more stable to Jim than land. Here on the *Atwood*, things ran as they should, but once he stepped off the gangplank, he felt ill.

In the captain's office, Jim stared down into his cup. The gentle motion of the ship at pier rippled his coffee, the same deep brown as Mary's hair. He wanted to go back to sea.

Two weeks for resupply and repairs, they said. The storms had ripped off life rafts and ladders and lockers on the deck. The Navy Yard was also replacing the old Y-gun with six new K-guns to fire depth charges. Since the Navy needed every possible destroyer on escort duty, work proceeded quickly.

Lieutenant Commander Durant flipped a page in Jim's report. "Everything looks fine, Mr. Avery."

"Thank you, sir."

Durant set down the papers and folded his hands over his flat belly. "Have you given any further thought to your career direction? Now that you've had some time at sea, some experience?"

"Yes, sir. I think I might be good in training, perhaps in personnel."

"Why do you say that?"

Jim swirled his coffee, competing with the ship's motion. "I work well with people, motivate them."

"Those traits are needed in a line officer too."

"Yes, but . . ." He sipped his coffee. How could he put the truth into words?

Durant sat in silence, but his silence never meant he'd forgotten the question.

Jim's sigh ruffled the surface of the coffee. "I don't trust my ability to be bold in a crisis. I told you when I first came on board I've always floated through life. I'm easygoing. That's a great trait until Mr. Easygoing has to make a hard decision. Both times in my life I've tried to be bold and decisive, someone's gotten hurt."

"Ozzie Douglas."

"Yes, sir."

Durant's blue eyes held a strange concoction of compassion and scrutiny. "Could that have been avoided?"

"He would have lost two fingers. That couldn't be helped. But he didn't have to lose all four."

"What if that sound contact had been an actual U-boat? What if they'd attacked?"

Jim's grip on the cup handle tightened. "I know. I know."

"You made the right decision." The pigeonhole cubbies on the captain's steel desk held envelopes and supplies in perfect order, the sign of an organized mind, a man who knew the right thing to do.

Jim took a sip of lukewarm, bitter coffee. "I know I made the right decision, but I don't like how I made that decision."

"Explain."

He shoved the cup away, disgusted by the contents. "I started that cruise with one intention—to be a bold, competent officer.

240

That's what drove that decision. I wanted to be seen as bold."
But he hadn't prayed. That's what hurt most. Nehemiah always
stopped and prayed. Always. That's what made him such a
powerful leader.

Durant scratched his chin. "Did you weigh the conse-
quences of both decisions?"

"Yes, but—"

"Did you consider the needs of Ozzie Douglas? The needs
of all the men on the *Atwood*? The role of the *Atwood* in
the convoy as a whole?"

Jim closed his eyes and tried to remember. "Yes, but—"

"If you weighed your options, considered the good of all—
not just one man, not just your own reputation, but the ship
as a whole and our role in the war effort—then you made the
right decision and you made it well. You only had one minute
to make that choice. Don't expect too much from yourself."

Jim scrunched up his nose. One minute was plenty of
time to pray.

"Enough of that." The CO raised a smile, but one without
humor. "Remember, that same day I made a decision that
doomed three men to death. Do I wish I could have saved them?
Absolutely. But I'd make the same decision again, and I won't
beat myself up about it. An officer can't afford to do that."

Jim nodded. Not one man on the *Atwood* doubted the
captain's decision to abandon those men in the water. And
come to think of it, after Marvin Hill's initial resistance, not
one man had criticized Jim's decision to drop those depth
charges.

"Your hands are weakened."

"What?" Jim spread out his fingers. Looked fine to him.

"Remember our friend Nehemiah? When his enemies
spread lies and rumors, Nehemiah said they were trying to
weaken his hands so the work wouldn't be done."

The scars on Jim's palms broadcast his ancient fear that if

he made waves, people would be hurt. And that fear weakened him and held him back.

"What did Nehemiah say?" Durant's voice held both power and kindness.

Jim's fingers coiled, the muscles working, covering the scars, warming him inside. "'O God, strengthen my hands.'"

"Yes." Durant slapped his knees and stood. "Now, I intend to enjoy my Saturday night out. I expect you to do likewise."

On the outside Jim smiled, but the warm feeling oozed away. If only he could enjoy his evening.

Arch wanted to see the new detective film *The Maltese Falcon*. He insisted they take Mary and Quintessa. The ladies would expect them. They knew the *Atwood* was in port. They knew the men would probably get liberty.

Staying on board would be cowardly. But so tempting.

Jim made his way down the passageway to the cabin he shared with Arch, dreading the upcoming land-sickness.

Last week Mary acted as if she were bequeathing Quintessa to him, and Quintessa acted as if she'd granted him a huge favor by bestowing her affections on him. Well, where was his say in the matter?

Jim banged the door open.

Sitting on his bunk, Arch jumped and stared at him.

"Sorry." He offered a limp smile.

Arch stood and grabbed his cover and overcoat. "Are you ready?"

"Suppose so."

"You sound like a man heading to the gallows rather than a man about to spend a night on the town with his dream girl."

Jim shrugged and punched his arms into his overcoat.

Arch straightened his collar in the mirror. "Dream girl isn't so appealing after you've spent the majority of 1941 falling in love with her best friend."

Jim's jaw clenched to see his heart splayed out in front

of him. Playing the fool, once again. "She doesn't see me as anything but a friend. She made that very clear to me. She's thrilled that Quintessa is interested in me. Thrilled. Does that sound like she's interested in me herself?"

"All right. Let's leave Mary out of the equation." Arch led the way down the passageway. "What about Quintessa? Is she everything you remember?"

"More so." Every bit as sparkling but less silly, tempered by time and heartbreak.

But she wasn't Mary.

Jim huffed out his breath and climbed the ladder to the main deck, where crisp autumn air tickled his nose. Yes, he had to leave Mary out of the equation, because Mary didn't want to be in the equation. That left Quintessa.

The lovely Quintessa Beaumont, who came all the way to Boston to see Jim. "I'll see what happens with Quintessa. It's only fair."

Arch trotted down the gangplank. "You're floating again."

Only a month earlier, he'd stood in this same spot, waving to Mary, his lips warm from her kiss. He snapped. "What do you expect? Mary doesn't want me, but Quintessa does. So leave me alone."

Two blond eyebrows rose. In over five years of friendship, Jim had only snapped at Arch a handful of times, and usually during final examinations.

An apology was expected and deserved, but Jim dug his hands into his overcoat pockets and marched down the pier. Later. He'd apologize later.

He'd been testy with Mary too. She didn't deserve it either. She was only being honest with him. How could she know she'd hurt him? She didn't know he loved her. He'd never told her, and now it was too late. If he told her now, he'd make a fool of himself, embarrass Mary, and hurt Quintessa. He might even damage the ladies' friendship.

A fine mess he'd floated into.

Now he'd snapped at Arch for telling the truth. Jim's sigh turned white in the cool air. "Sorry, buddy."

On Chelsea Street, Arch raised an arm to hail a cab. "Perhaps each of us should refrain from commenting on the other's love life."

Jim chuckled. "Perhaps."

They climbed into a cab and directed the driver to the ladies' apartment. Arch insisted on waiting in the taxi, and Jim drew a deep breath of fortitude and climbed the steps.

"Jim, darling!" Quintessa pulled him inside and kissed him on the cheek. "I'm so glad you're here. Please tell me you're here to take me out. It's been a dreadful week at work."

"Arch thought you ladies might like to see *The Maltese Falcon*."

"I'd love to. Humphrey Bogart is the tops. Let me change into something pretty. Won't take but a moment."

Quintessa dashed to the bedroom, and Jim turned to find Mary curled up in a wing chair by the bay window with a book in her lap.

He refused to be testy with her again. Besides, he missed her. "Hi, Mary."

"Hi, Jim." Her voice sounded deep and husky.

Everything inside him wanted to buck the current. He motioned over his shoulder with his thumb. "What are you waiting for? Go get ready. Arch can entertain Quintessa, and you and I can catch up."

Her light eyes widened, then she smiled back. "How kind of you to include me, but I'm still not well. I've been home from work all week, and I should rest."

Compassion drew him closer, and he sat on the couch across from her. She looked pale and tired, her hair tugged back in one of those net-like things. What were they called? "How are you feeling?"

"Much better, thank you. I should be able to return to work on Monday."

"Good." He took off his cover to give his hands something to do. "Anything new in the investigation?"

"I haven't been to work all week. How's your family?"

Back to her old trick, eh? Turning questions back on others so she wouldn't have to talk about herself. He hadn't heard anything about the sabotage case in over a month. Surely something had happened. But he'd play along. "My family? They're doing well. Rob's still in San Diego, and Dan's out at sea." Rumor was the USS *Vincennes* had been assigned to escort a convoy of Canadian troops to South Africa in the first leg of their journey to India.

Mary covered her mouth and coughed. "San Diego must be nice. And the others?"

"Ed and Charlie are busy with school, and Lucy with her home. But Lillian . . ."

"What's wrong with Lillian? I thought she just graduated from college." Her pink lips pulled together, no less tempting without lipstick.

Jim flipped his cover in his hands. "Yes, in June, but she still can't find a job. She's getting discouraged."

"Oh." She closed her book, her eyes darting about, more like the Mary he knew—and loved. "She's a pharmacist, isn't she? Do you think she'd be willing to move to Boston?"

"If it meant a job, sure."

Mary unfolded her legs, set her sock-clad feet on the floor, and leaned over her knees, her eyes bright. "Dixon's Drugs on Main Street is looking for a pharmacist. Down by City Square. You should inquire."

"Great idea. Thanks for the lead."

"Oh! If she'd like, she could live here. We'd love a fourth roommate to help with the rent, and there's so little housing in town."

"I'm sure she'd like that." He grinned, hoping she'd reciprocate and reestablish their connection.

But she glanced over his shoulder. "Oh, Quintessa, don't you look lovely? I knew that dress would be even prettier on you than on the hanger."

Jim stood because it was expected.

Quintessa twirled in a wine-colored dress, asking for attention, for a compliment. Mary never asked. Not once had she asked, and now he'd give anything to shower her with attention and compliments.

"I knew it," Mary said. "I told you Jim would be speechless."

Quintessa struck a pose, one hand on her hip. "I'm sure you can come up with something, Jim. An intelligent man like you."

An intelligent man sticking his oars into the current, fighting the flow. Why were these women making assumptions, putting words in his mouth, assigning thoughts to his silence?

The earth rocked beneath him. He'd prefer a good storm at sea.

If he didn't compliment Quintessa, she'd feel insulted. "You look nice. Are you ready?"

"Oh, I am. What a treat. A night out with not one, but two handsome officers." She sighed and gave Mary a sympathetic look. "Next time, when you're feeling better, you can join us and keep Arch company."

Mary curled up with her book again, covered her mouth with her fist, and coughed. "We'll see."

Where was the Mary he knew? The Mary who couldn't wait to discuss the sabotage case with him? The Mary who wanted to know all about his life at sea while respecting the limits of censorship? The Mary who loved a night on the town and an afternoon exploring the city?

A cavity formed in his chest, aching. Why hadn't he said anything when he had the chance?

"Are you coming?" Quintessa stood by the door, pulling on her gloves, a quizzical look on her face.

With a nod, he joined her. Because he'd failed to walk the path he'd chosen, that path had closed and another had been marked out for him.

He had only himself to blame.

32

A month from today, two destroyers were scheduled to be launched and two more laid down, so Mary had four ceremonies to coordinate.

At her office desk, she broke into a coughing fit, then waited for the light-headedness to pass. Perhaps she wasn't well enough to return to work, but a week away had put her behind schedule. Besides, work would take her mind off Jim. How she missed him as her companion and sounding board.

If only she could follow Jim and Quintessa's wishes and double-date with them. At least she'd enjoy Jim's company. But she wasn't mature enough or strong enough. In time, she'd accidentally reveal her feelings, and the pity, awkwardness, and attention would be unbearable. No, she'd keep her distance.

Mary reviewed her checklist. The sponsors had already been arranged. Today Mary would order the flowers for the sponsors and write the first drafts for the ceremony programs. By the end of the week, she needed to deliver the final programs to the printer.

She opened her planning notebook to find the florist's telephone number and blinked her eyes from the heaviness.

Thank goodness her fever had dissipated along with her feverish delusions. A whole week with nothing to do but read and pray helped her sort out her thoughts and intentions.

Had she been prideful in joining the choir? Not at all. She was using her gifts to glorify God, and somehow he'd even see her through the Christmas pageant.

What about with the investigation? No, she was doing good work for a good purpose and trying to stay invisible for her own safety.

With Jim?

Mary sighed and rested her eyes. What was wrong with hoping the man you loved could come to love you? Misguided, perhaps, but not prideful.

All she'd done this year was change direction, tack into the wind. She could still smell the salt air from that day sailing. She could still feel the resistance at the helm as she changed tack and the sails luffed and jangled. She could still hear Jim's deep voice in her ear: "When the sails start luffing, you can't let the noise and motion distract you. You have to keep moving."

That's what was happening in her life. She'd changed directions, tried new things. Some luffing was to be expected. She couldn't get distracted. She had to keep moving.

And her next move would be away from Boston. While home last week, she'd called a long list of shipyards on the Great Lakes, far from destroyer bases. Several asked for her resume and a letter of recommendation. This morning she'd worked up the nerve to ask Mr. Pennington. He'd objected but promised to write a letter today. Tomorrow she'd send everything out in the mail.

The phone rang, and she picked it up. "Mr. Pennington's office, Miss Stirling speaking."

"Ah, Miss Stirling. Agent Sheffield here. I'm glad you're back at work. May I speak to Mr. Pennington, please?"

"Yes, sir." Mary transferred the call to her boss's line. Since her call to the florist would have to wait until they got off the phone, she rolled a sheet of paper into her typewriter and organized her notes for the launching ceremony programs.

"Miss Stirling?" Mr. Pennington stood in his office doorway with concern on his face. "Agent Sheffield has requested your shorthand skills again. This is the third time, and I don't like how he puts you in the middle of danger."

"Oh." Mary chewed on her lips. Would her boss's worries keep her from an exciting new assignment? "What did you tell him?"

He waved one hand to the door. "How can I say no to the FBI?"

"Why does he need me? What's happening?" She sat up straighter, her toes tapping.

"You won't believe this. I certainly didn't. The FBI received an anonymous tip last night. They searched Mr. Winslow's home and found a bomb."

Mary gasped and covered her mouth. "A bomb?"

"I find it hard to believe. A civilized young man like that."

"Oh dear." Apparently he had the expertise after all. She'd underestimated him.

"They arrested him last night, and they brought him to his office this morning for some reason. They want you to take notes." He tugged down his suit vest. "Do me a favor, young lady, and tell this FBI agent to hire his own secretary."

How sweet he was. If he weren't her boss, she'd kiss him on the cheek. After she thanked him, she grabbed her pen and notebook and hurried to the drafting room.

Just inside the doorway, George O'Donnell and Frank Fiske stood talking together.

Mr. Fiske greeted Mary. "Did you hear the news? Mr. Winslow got himself arrested."

"I heard. I can't believe it."

"I can." O'Donnell crossed his big arms over his chest. "Always knew that pansy was up to no good."

Fiske shook his head. "Never thought he'd be building bombs in his basement. They found a whole crate of equipment down there. Didn't know he had it in him."

"Excuse me. Agent Sheffield is expecting me." A polite smile, and Mary headed into Mr. Winslow's office.

Agents Sheffield and Hayes stood in front of the desk, and Mr. Winslow sat in his chair, his head in his hands, his suit rumpled.

When she entered, the agents looked her way. "Thank you for coming, Miss Stirling. Shut the door and have a seat."

"Thank you." Mary did as asked and readied her pen and notebook.

"I swear it isn't mine." Mr. Winslow dug his fingers into his unkempt hair. "It's my friend's."

"Is it common for your friends to bring bombs to Sunday night supper?"

Winslow groaned and shook his head in his hands. "It was a meeting, nothing more. English expatriates and Anglophiles like me. We discuss ways to aid Britain, ways to show America the dangers of trusting Nazi Germany. Peaceful ways."

Sheffield released a hard chuckle. "Nothing more peaceful than a good bombing."

Winslow raised his head, revealing dark shadows under his eyes. "It's my friend's. I—"

"Your friend Cyril—"

"Cecil. Cecil Dalton. Yes, he wanted to set it off at an America First rally, but I talked him out of it, talked him into giving me the bomb. I planned to dismantle it and dispose of it today. Then you showed up."

"So we did."

Mary frowned as she transcribed their words. Mr. Winslow was lying. His story didn't explain the crate of bomb-making equipment in his basement. He was either building the bombs or providing a location for Cecil Dalton to do so.

Mr. Winslow opened his drawer and rummaged inside, shoving aside items.

"Looking for this?" Agent Sheffield pulled an amber prescription bottle from his suit pocket.

Winslow's face stretched long, and he reached for it. "Please. I need it. I have pains in my arms and legs from an old childhood illness. It's a legal prescription, I assure you."

Mary ducked her chin. Her conscience had led her to call Agent Sheffield last week to report what she'd seen and heard at Dixon's Drugs.

The agent turned the bottle in the light from the window, inspecting it. "Codeine sulfate, one-half grain. Your physician verifies this is a legal prescription, but said you use more and more every year. In fact, this past month, you've doubled your dose."

Winslow let out a series of rough breaths, and his fingers tangled with each other. "My nerves have been acting up with the upheaval here at the shipyard. I need it to do my job."

"Addicts . . ." Agent Sheffield narrowed his eyes. "Addicts behave erratically."

Tremors ran through Mr. Winslow's arms. "I do my job, sir. I do it well."

"Tell you what." He tossed the prescription bottle to Agent Hayes. "You cooperate, and we'll give you a pill. Sound like a fair trade?"

Winslow's hungry gaze bored into Agent Hayes. "I have

cooperated. I let you into my house last night without a search warrant, didn't I?"

"You did, didn't you?" Sheffield flicked his chin in Hayes's direction. "Give the boy a cookie."

Mary swallowed the nasty taste in her mouth. She might have to transcribe the conversation, but she didn't have to like the interrogation techniques.

Mr. Winslow swallowed the pill like a starving man. Then he smoothed his hair and stood. "You said you'd bring me here to compare my original plans to the blueprints. May we please get started so I can return to the comforts of my prison cell?"

Agent Sheffield unrolled a blueprint on the desk. After Mr. Winslow read something off the blueprint, he went to a filing cabinet. In a minute he pulled out a large drawing covered with numbers and notations.

"You see the coordinating number and date." Mr. Winslow pointed to the bottom corner of each diagram. "Let me examine them. The bolts . . . the bolts . . ."

"The drawings should be exactly alike," Agent Sheffield said.

Mary resisted the urge to lean forward and examine the diagrams herself. She was a secretary right now, not a detective.

"There!" Mr. Winslow jabbed his finger at the blueprint. "Look right there. See, on my original, the numeral one. On the blueprint, the numeral four. And here, the five is an eight. And here. And here." He cussed, then shot Mary an apologetic look.

She chose not to record those words.

The FBI agents inspected the diagrams, and Hayes took notes in a small notepad.

"I told you. It isn't me." Winslow strode to the window and spun to face them. "It's O'Donnell. He's the one. He altered my plans to sabotage our ships and to frame me. That's why he always refused to let me inspect his work. Why'd I let him bully me? Why?"

Agent Sheffield straightened. "O'Donnell has worked on all the affected blueprints?"

"Yes, sir. That's his assignment, the Fiske crew."

"Hayes?" Sheffield cocked his head to the door.

Agent Hayes opened the door and leaned out. "Mr. O'Donnell. Would you please join us?"

Mary tucked her crossed ankles under her chair. Things were about to get explosive.

O'Donnell entered the office, a smug smile on his face, and he opened his mouth.

"Come here." Agent Sheffield motioned him over, apparently not in a mood to listen to O'Donnell taunt his boss. "We've found some discrepancies between Winslow's original plans and the blueprints you drew. See here, and here, and here."

The draftsman bent his iron-gray head over the papers, silent. "Those aren't my marks. Look here—I close up my fours—these are open at the top. And these eights—someone added a line to a five. I always make eights with two circles. That's what I learned in drafting school. See? These are my marks."

"Hmm." Sheffield looked closer, and Hayes made more notes.

So did Mary. Could O'Donnell have deliberately made such marks? Or had someone else done the alterations?

"Look. These marks are thicker than mine too. Someone altered the draft after I finished, but before the blueprints were developed." O'Donnell leveled his gaze at Winslow. "Nice try, boss. You failed."

"You think I'd alter my own plans? That's poppycock." Winslow ran shaking hands over his trousers. "If you didn't do it, one of your friends did. Perhaps your buddy Fiske."

"Frank? You've got to be desperate to accuse him." O'Donnell's thick eyebrows twisted. "I know it was you. I leave the plans on my desk. I never thought I needed an armed guard."

Winslow's mouth and eyes went hard. "If you were at your desk more often . . ."

"It could be anyone here." O'Donnell swept his arm in the direction of the drafting room. "You, any of the draftsmen, that French girl who's always around here. For crying out loud, it could be the janitor. We don't lock this room."

"The French girl," Agent Sheffield said. "Yvette Lafontaine? You mentioned her before."

Mary's breath turned solid in her lungs. Why must he accuse Yvette again? And why did Agent Sheffield remember her name?

"Yeah, some froufrou foreign name like that. She wants us in the war, you know. Wants us to fight her country's battles. Why should we? We need to protect ourselves first."

Mary turned the page in her notebook and coughed.

"What exactly are you doing, Miss Stirling?" O'Donnell asked.

"Me?" Her face tingled as the blood drained out.

"She's an excellent stenographer," Agent Sheffield said. "I asked her to transcribe today's proceedings. You don't mind, do you?"

"Why would I? I have nothing to hide." But his dark eyes scrutinized Mary's notebook.

"We have what we came for." Agent Sheffield stacked the blueprint and the original and rolled them up. "Mr. Winslow, let's go back to your cozy cell."

"Good." O'Donnell jutted out his chin. "He wants you to think someone else altered his drawings, but remember, he's the one who got caught making bombs."

"Possessing a bomb, Mr. O'Donnell. He got caught in

possession of a single bomb. If you're going to spread gossip, get your facts straight." Agent Sheffield opened the office door. "Miss Stirling, I'll expect that transcript tomorrow morning."

"Yes, sir." She attempted a benign smile, but her lips trembled. Her cover had been smashed to pieces. From now on, she'd have to be far more careful.

33

Saturday, November 15, 1941

Jim picked at his patty melt and fries while Quintessa chatted over lunch. She told humorous stories of her stint in Filene's children's department, the improvements she'd made, how she loved working with the children and their mothers, and how the managers were thrilled with her sales numbers.

She was beautiful and animated and engaging. So why wasn't Jim engaged? In high school he could listen to her for hours, enraptured. Why not now? She wasn't selfish either. She asked about his work and family and friends. But he couldn't think of anything to say. He'd had plenty to say to Mary, plenty he longed to say to her right now. Could he talk to Quintessa about his decision with the depth charges? About his doubts and challenges?

Even if he could, he didn't want to.

When he invited Quintessa to lunch today, he had one purpose. The *Atwood* was shipping out this afternoon, and Jim wanted to choose once and for all among the three paths that lay before him.

257

Quintessa laughed about something, and Jim smiled and sipped his Coke, as fizzy as her laugh.

The first path was a broad lazy river. Without any effort, he could float into a relationship with Quintessa Beaumont. She already talked as if she were his girlfriend, although he'd never asked her on a real date or even held her hand. If Quintessa had arrived in March rather than November, he'd have jumped at the opportunity. But she hadn't.

The second path felt like a sneaky, dark alley. He could back out of both ladies' lives. When he returned from this tour, he simply wouldn't visit their apartment. Maybe he could get transferred to another ship. An easy path, but cowardly.

The third path looked steep and rocky with an unknown destination. He could pursue Mary and pray she fell for him. The path of the fool.

Jim took a bite of his patty melt and studied the gorgeous woman across the table from him. Sunlight slanted through the window beside him and lit up her hair. Every word was bright, every gesture sparkled. She was dazzling.

Yes, dazzling. When you fired a gun at night, the flash destroyed your night vision and blinded you. That's what Quintessa did. But Mary had an illuminating glow, like the moon, which allowed him to see more clearly.

Jim's fingers coiled around the crust of his sandwich, and his eyes slipped shut. *Oh Lord, I miss her. I miss Mary. Please show me the right path. Not the path Quintessa chooses for me, not the path Mary chooses for me, not even the path I desire, but the one you want me to travel. Because right now, none of my options appeal to me.*

"Jim?" Quintessa tilted her head. "You're so quiet. Are you all right?"

"Hmm?" He schooled his face into neutrality. He couldn't lie to her, but the truth required more work and thought and prayer. Whichever path he chose affected other people and could alter friendships and bruise hearts.

"Are you feeling all right?" She glanced at his plate and smiled. "You've crushed that sandwich crust to crumbs."

He had. He dropped it, wiped the crumbs off on his napkin, and folded his hands on the table in front of him. "Guess I was full." He tried for a sheepish smile.

She reached across the table toward him, an invitation. "I've been concerned. Mary always talked about how much fun you were, but you've been so quiet and serious since I arrived."

"These are tense times." Not only in the world, but in his own life.

"That's true." Quintessa wiggled her fingers on the table, the invitation even louder.

Jim ignored it, and he leaned closer so as to lower his voice. "We ship out today."

"Today? So soon? We've barely had any time together."

"We're ready. I'm ready."

"Oh." She retracted her hand, and her mouth pinched.

He didn't mean to hurt her feelings. "I can't tell you or anyone else what we're doing out there, but it's necessary. Lives are at stake."

"I understand." She reinforced her words with a smile. "Sorry if I sounded selfish. I know you have important work to do. When do you have to be back?"

Jim checked his watch. "Half an hour."

"Half an hour? Oh my. I thought we'd have the whole day. Well, we'll just have to spend every minute together." She peeked at him through her lashes. "May I see you off?"

His throat glued shut. Images flashed through his mind of the crowd on the wharf, the families embracing, the couples kissing, Mary's soft hands pulling him down, deep into her kiss, his arms around her, his lips on hers—

"I'm sorry." Quintessa glanced away, her forehead puckered. "That was forward of me."

"No, it's fine. Please come. Arch will want to say goodbye too."

"Will he? He's such a good friend for you. We have to find him a new girlfriend. Are you sure he and Mary—"

"No." The word came out too loud and harsh, so he mustered a smile. "Trust me, no. Shall we go?"

Jim slapped down a couple of dollars for the bill and helped Quintessa with her coat.

On the walk to the Navy Yard in the cool clear air, Quintessa walked close to his side, her shoulder brushing his, an invitation for him to offer his hand or at least his elbow. But he didn't want to, didn't want her choosing his path for him, so he jammed his hands into his coat pockets.

At the wharf, a crowd of sailors and family members was forming. On Liberty Fleet Day, the men wore their summer whites, and he had Mary Stirling on his arm in her red dress. Now the men wore navy blue overcoats, and Quintessa Beaumont threaded her arm through his.

Never once had he minded when Mary held his arm. In fact, he offered her his arm all the time, even when he hadn't been interested in her. It was the chivalrous thing for a man to do with a lady. But now Quintessa's touch bothered him, as if her tiny gloved hand staked her claim.

Why did it irritate him? Why this discontent?

His eyes widened, taking in the gray ship and the blue sky and the truth he'd begged God for. This discontent was like sonar alerting him that he was floating toward the rocks.

His path didn't lie with Quintessa, but along that uncertain and unpaved road.

A surge of rightness and determination rushed into his chest. If he showed Mary his interest, told her how he felt, maybe her heart would bend to him. Even if it didn't, even if he made a complete fool of himself and lost his friendship with her, it was the true thing to do. True to his heart, true to where God seemed to be leading him.

If God wanted to lead him into a storm, so be it. He'd promised, "When thou passest through the waters, I will be with thee." The Lord would be with him in the storm, and something good would come out of it, some purpose, even if Jim didn't see it for decades.

All around him, men and officers said their romantic good-byes. Jim needed to get away now, but how could he put this fresh new plan into words, knowing those words would hurt Quintessa?

Nevertheless, it had to be done. He faced her.

"Hey, Mr. Avery! Kiss her!"

Jim cringed. Oh no. Not again. Not with Quintessa. *Please, Lord, make them stop.*

Either the Lord missed his prayer, or the men missed the Lord's promptings, because the clamor built like last time. Only last time he'd longed to kiss Mary—just not in public.

"Kiss her! Kiss her!"

Jim slammed his eyes shut. Everyone was pressuring him, shoving him in the wrong direction. No more. No more.

Two small hands rested on his upper arms. "Jim?"

He opened his eyes.

Quintessa gazed up at him, all dewy-eyed and beautiful. "You have my permission." Her invitation couldn't be any clearer.

Or any less welcome. How many years had he longed for a moment like this, but now he didn't want it. He didn't love Quintessa. He loved Mary, and he'd do everything in his power to win her heart. If she rejected him, at least he'd know he'd chosen the bold but prayerful route.

Voices rose all around him. "Kiss her! Kiss her!"

Quintessa gave him a sly glance. "What are you waiting for?"

Jim settled a firm but kind look on her. "I'm sorry, but I can't."

"You can't?"

"Come on, Mr. Avery! Kiss her like you kissed that brunette last time."

Oh no. Jim groaned.

"Brunette?" Quintessa asked.

His face heated up. He didn't want to involve Mary or cause trouble between the ladies. When he came home again, when he spoke his mind, there would be plenty of trouble, but he'd be there to deal with it. Not now, not when he was about to ship out.

Quintessa's fingers tightened on his coat sleeves. "Who was she?"

"Just a friend." That was true, especially since the kiss meant nothing to her.

"A friend?" Quintessa's eyes widened into green pools. "Not Mary?"

How could he lie? "It didn't mean anything to her. These fellows were acting up like this, and she only did it to shut them up."

Quintessa eased back. "You kissed Mary, but you won't kiss me?"

Countless emotions arced through her eyes—the indignation of a beautiful woman unaccustomed to rejection and the pain of a woman who had been betrayed by a man she'd loved and trusted for years.

Her dismay, the clamor of the sailors, everything acted like a funnel, but he resisted and set his heels.

Jim took both her hands. "Thank you for giving me a chance. I'm honored, and I appreciate it. But it isn't working between us, and it never will."

"Isn't working? What do you mean?"

Jim clamped his lips between his teeth. This would require a long and emotional talk he didn't have time for right now.

Regardless, he couldn't give her false hope. "I have to leave, but we'll talk when I return."

Her mouth thinned into a sharp red line. "Talk?"

"Good-bye, Quintessa." He pressed a quick kiss to her forehead.

Before she could respond, he marched away and up the gangplank.

Good-natured jeers from his shipmates bombarded him, groans of disappointment, offers to take his place. Mitch Hadley made a crack about his eyesight and his manhood.

None of the jabs penetrated.

Nehemiah's enemies tried to distract him and discourage him with taunts and jeers, but he refused to let them disturb his work.

Jim forged ahead. He'd never felt stronger or more assured in his life. With the Lord's guidance, he had set his own course, and he would sail it.

He might sail alone, but he'd sail.

34

Mary did up the side zipper of her dark blue gabardine dress. The sooner she and Yvette left the apartment for their shopping trip, the better. When Jim came to pick up Quintessa for lunch, Mary had managed to be busy cleaning the bathroom, and she wanted to be away whenever they returned.

Jim hadn't even asked about Mary, just spirited Quintessa away.

Her zipper snagged on her slip, and her thoughts snagged on the truth. She worked to free both. Hadn't she done everything possible to discourage conversation with Jim the past two weeks? Why should she be surprised when he no longer sought her out? Wasn't that best in the long run?

Yes, it was. She sighed and closed the zipper.

The front door opened.

Oh bother. Mary had taken too long to get ready.

But only one set of footsteps entered the apartment, feminine heels clicking on the polished wood. The bedroom door opened, and Quintessa came in, her cheeks pink from the cold.

"Back so soon?" Mary asked.

Quintessa crossed to her dresser. "He shipped out."

"Oh." Mary's chest contracted. Into danger again, with things heating up on both coasts. And she never said good-bye. *Lord, keep him safe.*

Quintessa unpinned her hat. "You should have warned me how the men act when they ship out. I had no idea."

Mary opened her jewelry box and pushed around the ear-rings, a silver blur. "Oh?"

"All the men hounding him to kiss me. But I guess you know all about that." She let out a short laugh, tight around the edges.

Every muscle in Mary's body froze. Why had Jim told her? And what could she say that wouldn't make Jim look bad—or hurt Quintessa's feelings? Even the truth sounded suspect, but what else did she have?

She sorted through the earrings, all in silver, for a matching pair. "Just a friendly kiss. I couldn't stand how the men harassed him. I just wanted to end it. It didn't mean anything to him."

Silence from Quintessa.

Time to be brave, so she put on her blandest expression and turned around. "You have nothing to worry about."

Quintessa eyed her up and down, pressed her fingertips to her forehead, and her mouth smiled. Only her mouth. "Strange to think my best friend and I have been kissed by the same man."

That bland expression took more work than any smile. Jim had kissed Quintessa. She hadn't needed to grab him and kiss him. He'd done it himself and eagerly, no doubt, and in only two weeks together. Not six months. Why had Mary deluded herself?

Quintessa's mouth twitched, and she sat on her bed. "I don't have any reason to be jealous, do I?"

The poor thing. Hugh had cheated on her, abandoned her, and broken her heart. Why wouldn't she fear betrayal?

"Oh, honey." Mary dashed over, sat on the bed beside her, and took her hand. "I'd never do anything to hurt you. You're my dearest friend in all the world. I owe you so much. Your friendship is more important to me than any man. Don't you know that?"

Her face buckled, and she covered her eyes with her hand. "I'm sorry. I know that. I know you'd never hurt me. I'm still too sensitive after what *he* did to me."

"I understand. I don't blame you. But no, honey, I'm happy for you and Jim. He's adored you for as long as I can remember, and I'm thrilled you've discovered each other after all these years. You deserve each other." If her mouth said it often enough, someday her heart would agree.

"Thank you," Quintessa said in a cramped voice, and she glanced away.

What her friend needed was a distraction, so Mary squeezed her hand and made her voice cheery. "Yvette and I are going downtown to shop. Would you like to join us? I could use your help picking out a new blouse."

"At Filene's? On my day off? No, thank you. Besides, I have laundry and mending to do. Go have fun."

"All right. But how can I possibly have fun without you?" Mary said in her most dramatic voice.

A flicker of a smile returned to her friend's face. "Somehow you'll manage."

★ ★ ★

Mary turned the display case of gold earrings. She never wore gold jewelry, only silver. Mother said silver complemented her complexion, and Mary preferred its subtlety.

But why shouldn't she wear gold? Wasn't she good enough to wear gold? Maybe she needed flash to attract a man.

Something hardened inside her, and she held a pair of gold

earrings beside her cheek. Why not? She was already wearing a flashy red coat and hat. Why not gold jewelry?

But her image wavered in the little mirror. Would a pair of gold earrings have made Jim fall in love with her? Of course not. He simply preferred the gold inside Quintessa to the silver inside Mary, and what was wrong with that?

She swiped away her tears and studied her reflection. Gold really didn't do anything for her skin. She exchanged the earrings. Yes, silver did look better with her coloring and brought out the light in her eyes.

Silver was best for her.

That hard something melted away. Silver had its own worth, its own beauty, a quieter beauty, a beauty that reflected rather than called attention to itself. There was nothing wrong with that, and nothing wrong with her. Someday, a man would come along who preferred silver.

Perhaps at her new job. A smile rose, wobbly but warming. She'd mailed her resume and letter of recommendation to half a dozen shipyards on the Great Lakes. Surely one would hire her. She'd be closer to home and farther from Jim. Why should she watch Jim and Quintessa fall in love? She'd only get depressed. With a new start in a new city, she could heal and start over. Another change in tack.

Anxious voices rose from the store aisle, all speaking in French. Yvette stood with several of her friends—Henri, Solange, and two others Mary didn't know.

Henri met Mary's eye, frowned, then spoke to Yvette.

Yvette turned and gave Mary a breezy smile, then addressed Henri. *"C'est ne pas un problème. Elle ne parle pas français."*

Mary didn't speak French, but she recognized a few phrases. Yvette was assuring her friends Mary couldn't understand their conversation. Why? What did they need to conceal from her?

She turned to the nearest dress rack and sifted through the selections. Why did Yvette spend so much time in the drafting room, asking questions of Mr. O'Donnell? Was it simply her interest in drawing, or something more sinister?

Why was Yvette always so adamant that Mary stop her investigation and not discuss it—yet she joined in the conversations? Was Yvette involved? Mary couldn't imagine Yvette building or planting a bomb, but what about her friends? Were they working together?

She ventured a glance at the group in their zealous conversation. Their families in France lived in danger under Nazi domination in the north or Vichy French domination in the south. Yvette's friends wanted the United States to enter the war so their homeland could be freed. But were they desperate enough to commit sabotage, maybe even kill?

Mary grabbed a random dress from the rack and fled to the dressing room. Once inside, she collapsed into the chair and rested her head in her hands.

She'd lived with Yvette for a year and a half. She prided herself on her observational skills, but had she overlooked vital clues, blinded by friendship? Why, she barely had any notes for Yvette, and she'd never typed them up or turned them in to the FBI. But didn't Yvette have motive? And her friends might have the means.

What kind of detective was she? An impartial observer would have kept Yvette high on the suspect list.

And her notebooks. How many times had Mary found Yvette flipping through? She had access to the carbon copies typed out in plain English. Wouldn't those be an easy resource to know whom to frame? Had Mary unwittingly aided the sabotage?

She pushed down the nausea, pulled a small notebook from her purse, and started a list. Everything she hadn't recorded— Yvette's comments on the sabotage and the suspects, her access to the notebooks, the conversations she'd overheard when Mary and Quintessa discussed the case, when Mary and Jim discussed the case. Yvette had even loaned Mary that smart red suit and hat for the undercover operation.

Mary yanked a handkerchief from her purse and wiped her face. Tonight, after Yvette went to sleep, Mary would type up her notes on Yvette, as complete as she could make them. Then she'd hide all her notebooks somewhere—her trunk, and she'd keep the key with her at all times. On Monday, she'd give her report to Agent Sheffield.

Her eyes burned at the thought of turning in her friend— but what if her friend had been using her to commit crimes?

"Mary?" Yvette called.

She took a deep breath and prayed her voice would sound normal. She couldn't let Yvette know she suspected her. People who planted bombs on ships wouldn't be concerned about the life of one secretary. "In here."

"Good. I've been looking for you. I wanted you to hold my bags while I tried on this suit. But Mr. Fiske offered to hold my bags. Wasn't that kind?"

"Mr. Fiske?" As Mary's eyes stretched open, they dried.

"*Oui.* From the shipyard."

What was a middle-aged man doing in the women's clothing department? He was widowed, and he had one son. And why did he just happen to run into Yvette?

Mary checked her reflection in the mirror and powdered her face. Thank goodness her eyes weren't too red. She grabbed the hanger from the hook. The dress wasn't very pretty anyway. "I'm done, Yvette. I'll see you outside."

"Don't go far. I want your opinion on this suit."

"All right." Mary stepped out of the room and handed the dress to the attendant. "Thank you, but it isn't for me."

"I'd say not." The attendant arched her brows.

The dress did look about three sizes too big.

Mr. Fiske stood not far from the dressing room area, holding Yvette's bags and purse.

Mary approached him. "What a pleasant surprise. Yvette told me you were holding her bags. How kind of you."

His broad face cracked into a bashful smile. "Well, I remember how my wife liked me to hold her things. Miss Lafontaine looked burdened. I'm glad I could help."

"How kind of you. I can hold them now."

"Thanks." He transferred the bags and Yvette's new black handbag. He wore heavy brown leather work gloves. Black ink stained the right forefinger, and a small tear ran alongside the thumb. Why was he wearing work gloves out on the town? Inside the heated store?

She kept her smile in place but tilted her head at the dress rack beside him. "Shopping?"

"Yeah, well, it's my mother's birthday this week. She'll be seventy."

"How lovely. Is she here in town?"

"Uh, yes." His smile turned to a scowl. "Listen, Miss Stirling, I need to warn you. Watch out for that friend of yours."

"Yvette?" She refused to let her own suspicions color her voice.

He leaned closer, his blue eyes serious. "Watch out for her and her friends. They're dangerous. I bet they're part of Winslow's ring, building bombs in his basement. They found a crate of equipment, you know. Same stuff used to build the bomb found on the *Atwood*. Watch out."

Cold tingles ran through her. "Thank you for the warning."

He ran one gloved finger under his nose and flipped his gaze over Mary's shoulder. "You're much too involved in this investigation. You need to stop. If you think those FBI agents will keep you safe while you poke around, think again. You're a nice girl, and I'd hate to see something bad happen to you."

Mary choked out a thank-you. Was that a fatherly warning—or a veiled threat?

"There you are, Mary." Yvette glided over. "I did not like the fit of that suit. Another day. Oh, you have my bags. Thank you. And thank you, Mr. Fiske. Shall we go, Mary?"

"Yes. Let's." She headed down the aisle. After ten paces, she glanced over her shoulder.

Mr. Fiske walked in the other direction toward the store entrance, without stopping to browse, without any bags.

What about his mother's birthday?

A chill crept into her chest. Didn't Mr. Fiske always say his son was the only family he had in this world? His wife was dead. And his parents?

Dead.

An ashy taste filled Mary's mouth. Mr. Fiske lied to her. He'd followed her and Yvette.

Now Mary had to figure out why.

35

East of Newfoundland
Tuesday, November 18, 1941

Heavy seas tossed the USS *Atwood*, but the interior communications and plotting room enjoyed relative warmth and stability, nestled below the waterline directly under the bridge.

Jim gathered with the four men who ran the Mark 1 computer, a complex piece of machinery, a little bigger than his mom's kitchen stove, filled with gears and levers and cams and electrical circuits. Beside the computer, three men operated the stable element, smaller than the computer but no less complex.

"Director to plot." Mr. Reinhardt's voice came through Jim's headphones from his position in the gun director high over Jim's head. "Captain's ordered us to run a drill using one of the merchant ships as a pretend target. He suggested we aim at the *Manchester Merchant*."

Jim grinned. The convoy commodore's ship. The day before, US Task Unit 4.1.5 had picked up Convoy HX-160 off the coast of Newfoundland. During the night, they'd counted sixteen light violations and had received gruff resistance to their orders to darken ships. One of the captains said he didn't take orders from "gold braids" in tin cans.

Apparently Durant had chosen mock vengeance on the commodore, although the command ship sailed over a mile away from the *Atwood* and the commodore would never know he'd been targeted.

Jim spoke into his microphone. "Ammunition?"

Reinhardt laughed. "Nope. We'll just practice tracking the target, computing the solution, and transmitting to the guns. You're in condition Standby 2, correct?"

"Correct."

"Go to Standby 3."

"Aye aye." Jim looked up. "Standby 3, men."

"Aye aye, sir." The men turned cranks and dials and pushed buttons.

Jim wandered behind the men at the stable element. The gyro inside had already been activated for their current state of readiness. What a great piece of machinery, calculating all the instantaneous compensations needed to overcome the effects of the ship's pitch and roll.

"Target angle three-zero-five," Reinhardt said. "Target speed eight knots."

Jim repeated the initial values aloud, and the computer operators turned little cranks to enter the data manually. Then he called up to the bridge for wind speed and direction, and the operators entered that data too. "At Standby 3," he told Reinhardt.

"Very well. Begin tracking," Reinhardt said.

"Aye aye. Begin tracking."

In front of Jim, the men at the computer operated their dials. The *Atwood*'s speed and course came into the computer automatically, and soon the target's bearing and range would enter the computer by electrical signals from up in the director.

Sure beat the old system of using a plotting board and a ruler and a roll of paper, even if Jim enjoyed learning the method at the Academy.

"Range matched," one of the operators said.

"Bearing synchronized."

"Elevation synchronized."

"Very well." Jim looked over the shoulders of the computer operators, each attentive to his duties. Skilled, technical work—and each man here knew all the other men's jobs as well.

"Solution calculated and transmitted to guns," an operator said.

Jim repeated the information to Reinhardt. In the time it took electricity to travel and motors to turn, the four 5-inch guns would each train and point at the target, with the fuze-setters in the projectile hoists set for the correct range. An engineering marvel.

"Very well," Reinhardt said. "Cease tracking."

Not the most complicated target, moving at a sluggish speed in parallel to the *Atwood*. But the director and computer could make similar calculations even for dive-bombing airplanes.

"Good job, men. Return to Standby 2." Jim appreciated the captain's drills. The monotony, discomfort, and constant vigilance of convoy escort wore on the men's nerves, and having a task to perform helped distract them while honing their skills.

Jim pulled out his clipboard and filled out his report for the drill. The men had been jumpy since they left Boston, and he didn't blame them. After the *Reuben James* was sunk on October 31, the men oscillated between cold terror that the *Atwood* would be next and heated desire to avenge the men of the *Reuben James*.

Neither approach was wise. Jim wanted to help them find a mellow balance, to be prepared and alert, unsullied by fear or fury.

Balance. He tapped his pen on the clipboard. That's what he needed. Just like Nehemiah. Prayerful but bold. A man of analysis and a man of action. A man who gathered and encouraged, yet could also rebuke and stand his ground.

Here at sea, Jim was determined to temper boldness with prayerful caution. And back in Boston?

His breath puffed out his cheeks. He'd made a mess, but he'd sort everything out as best he could. First item on his agenda when he returned—he'd have that long, emotional talk with Quintessa. But why did it have to be emotional anyway? He'd never understand how women thought. Jim had been out with Quintessa only three times, and none of those outings qualified as true dates.

However, he wouldn't return until mid-December at the earliest. Quintessa would have a whole month to think about what he'd said on his departure. She was an intelligent woman. Maybe they wouldn't need an emotional talk after all.

Jim signed the bottom of his report. Yeah, and maybe Hitler would surrender and go back to painting.

Regardless, Jim would be firm and truthful. He didn't love Quintessa. He loved Mary.

And what about Mary? Could he pursue her right away? That depended on how Quintessa reacted. He didn't want to be an insensitive dolt, but how else would it look? Both women saw him as Quintessa's property. Somehow they'd made that decision last time he went to sea.

What would they decide this time?

Jim groaned and rearranged papers on the clipboard for

the rest of his watch. Daytime was quiet on convoy duty. U-boats didn't like to attack during the day, and the merchant ships could keep station more easily. If it weren't for the weather and the difficult nights, it might be relaxing.

He longed to unwind. His short leave in Boston had been almost as nerve-wracking as his time at sea. If only he could have spent his time with sweet, relaxing Mary.

If only he could be there right now. Quintessa had told him enough about the sabotage case to know something was going on, but not enough for him to make sense of it.

And the Christmas pageant was approaching. When Quintessa told him Mary had been cast in a leading role, he was worried. How was she doing? She was strong enough to handle it, but he wouldn't be there to cheer for her, to encourage her.

He should be back for Christmas though.

Christmas. Would Mary go home to Ohio or stay in Boston? If she went home, could he get enough leave to follow her? It might be romantic to declare his love under a Christmas tree. Girls liked stuff like that, didn't they?

And he'd decided on a bold declaration, when it was time. No more trying to be suave. No more foolishness. Just plain brave honesty.

Even though it was too late. He could feel it in his gut, but that wouldn't stop him. Nothing could.

"Back at Standby 2, sir," the computer operator said.

Jim blinked and looked him in the eye. "Very well. Good job, everyone."

The operator gave him a teasing smile. "Daydreaming, Mr. Avery?"

Caught in the act. He chuckled. "Suppose I am."

"The blonde or the brunette?"

The computer crew broke down in laughter. But Jim had two older brothers. He could handle teasing. He laughed right along and clapped the man on the back. "Classified information."

The words gouged him in the chest. Classified information. That's how he'd treated his interest in Mary, and look where that got him.

Jim started a new report sheet, a clean start. Time to declassify.

36

Boston

Wednesday, November 19, 1941

How strange to wear a spring suit the day before Thanksgiving, but when November felt like June, what choice did Mary have?

She headed past the Muster House on her way to work in the unseasonably warm morning sunshine. The newspapers forecasted a record high for today. If only it were still June, with Jim in Boston and Quintessa in Chicago.

Mary scrunched up her nose. What a selfish thought. What kind of person wanted to keep her two favorite people apart? Even if Quintessa hadn't arrived, Jim wouldn't have fallen for Mary. If he hadn't done so in six months, he never would.

She quickened her pace down the elm-lined road between Buildings 33 and 34. At least Quintessa's arrival saved Mary from falling deeper in love with Jim. Thank goodness she'd come when she had.

Several months ago, Jim had told her he rarely went home because seeing Quintessa and Hugh was too painful, because it was wrong to love his best friend's girlfriend. He'd made that decision out of respect for both Hugh and Quintessa, and out of self-respect as well.

It was time for Mary to follow his example and leave Boston, out of respect for both Jim and Quintessa, and out of self-respect. Yesterday after work, she'd received a phone call from the Defoe Shipbuilding Company in Bay City, Michigan, offering her a job.

Today she would give the Navy Yard two weeks' notice. She would fulfill her obligation with the Christmas pageant, spend a few weeks at home for the holidays, then start the new year with a new job and a new start.

If God was smiling on her, she'd be able to leave before Jim returned from his tour. Last time he'd been gone five weeks. If this tour lasted as long, she'd already be home for Christmas.

"There she is." In front of her, in the gap between Buildings 38 and 39, five men approached.

Mary recognized Ralph Tucker and Curly Mulligan, but not the other three. However, she did recognize their demeanor as less than friendly. She gave them a polite greeting and turned toward her building.

The men stepped in front of her, in an arc blocking her path.

She stopped short, hugged her notebooks, and studied five burly, angry faces. "Yes, gentlemen?"

Ralph Tucker crossed his arms over his chambray work shirt. "We understand you've been spying on our friend O'Donnell."

"Spying?" Her voice came out thin.

Curly Mulligan adjusted his cap. "Yeah. Every time we see you, you're writing in one of those notebooks."

"O'Donnell says you're spying for that Frenchie girl," Tucker said. "You're her roommate, aren't you?"

Mary straightened her back and willed away the quiver in her chin. "Taking notes is my job. I'm a secretary. I was taking notes long before this sabotage nonsense began."

"Well, stop." The tallest man poked his finger at her, glaring down a bulbous nose. "We see you taking notes again, we break your pen. Maybe something else."

Her breath ratcheted its way down her throat, and she stepped back. "How dare—"

"Tell you what, Miss Stirling. Why don't you let us look at those notebooks ourselves, see what you're really up to." Ralph Tucker reached for the notebooks in Mary's arms.

She held them closer and took another step back, only to bump into someone large.

"Yeah, lady." The mountain behind her nudged her closer to Tucker. "Show us what you got in there."

She couldn't. All her typed notes about Yvette and Mr. Fiske were in there, for Agent Sheffield's eyes only. "It's none of your business."

"Says who?"

"Says Mr. Barton Pennington." Mary stared down Ralph Tucker. "Do I need to tell him you tried to steal from his secretary? The granddaughter of his oldest friend? That you threatened her?"

Tucker's gaze wavered. Mr. Pennington had plenty of influence over hiring and firing, and the union wouldn't like its name sullied by a workman threatening young ladies.

"Excuse me." Mary shouldered her way past him.

Another group of workmen approached, and Mary sucked in her breath.

"Say, miss." This man looked concerned. "Those hoodlums bothering you?"

The cavalry had arrived, but Mary didn't need them. She turned and gave Tucker and Mulligan an icy glare. "You tell me. Are you bothering me?"

Mulligan dropped his gaze to his shoes. "Wouldn't dream of it."

"Good." She passed the cavalry. "Thank you. I'm glad there are still some gentlemen in this world."

Mary darted into Building 39, but she aimed for Agent Sheffield's office. She'd explain her tardiness to Mr. Pennington later.

The papers rustled in her trembling arms. She flung open the FBI agents' office door, marched forward, and slapped the notebook on Agent Sheffield's desk. "This is my final report."

"Final?" Sheffield arched his sandy eyebrows.

From his corner desk, Agent Hayes gave her his customary silent nod and returned to his work.

"They know what I'm doing." Mary crossed her arms to conceal the shaking. "They know I record their conversations, and they just threatened me. Plus, I have reason to suspect my roommate might have used my notes for improper purposes. I need to stop immediately."

"Have a seat." Agent Sheffield's expression softened, and he motioned to the chair. "Tell me everything."

For the next fifteen minutes, she relayed everything that had happened over the weekend with Yvette and Mr. Fiske, as well as the morning encounter with Tucker and Mulligan.

Agent Sheffield expressed great interest in the meeting at Filene's, perused Mary's notes, added some of his own, and asked several questions. Apparently both Yvette and Mr. Fiske had moved up on the suspect list.

By the time she finished, her shaking had stopped and her determination to quit the investigation had hardened to certainty.

Agent Sheffield closed the notebook and settled back in his chair with an expression Mary had never seen before on his face—respect. "This is very good. Is there anything else?"

"It's all in the notes." How ironic that she'd earned his

respect the moment she quit. "Thank you for listening, for believing in me, but there won't be anything more."

His gaze stayed on her—level, sure, unbending. "As you wish. You're a private citizen. However, I suggest you keep your eyes and ears open, remember what you see and hear, write it down later—not in public—and keep me informed."

"No, thank you." Mary stood to leave.

But one question tickled the back of her brain. While she'd noted the discrepancy in her report, she hadn't called attention to it, since it shifted from fact to supposition.

She paused with her hand around the brass doorknob. "I'm sure you can't tell me, but I'll ask anyway. When you arrested Mr. Winslow, you said you'd found a bomb. You told Mr. O'Donnell that Mr. Winslow wasn't arrested for building a bomb, but for possessing one. Yet twice I've heard Mr. Fiske state that a crate of bomb-making equipment was found in Mr. Winslow's basement. He said it was the same equipment used to build the bomb on the *Atwood*."

Agent Hayes whipped around and stared at her.

One corner of Agent Sheffield's mouth crept up. "You're very perceptive, Miss Stirling."

"Which is it?"

Sheffield tapped a cigarette out of a case. "When we searched his house, Mr. Winslow was agitated when we went through his kitchen cupboards. That's where we found the bomb. But when we went down to the basement, he showed no anxiety at all."

Mary's hand slipped from the doorknob. If he had a crate of equipment in his basement, he would have been nervous. Agent Sheffield, however, hadn't stated what he'd found—only Mr. Winslow's reaction. "What did you find?"

He chuckled. "I can't tell you that, young lady. I can only tell you what was in the public statement, what Mr. Winslow

282

himself was told—that we found a bomb in his kitchen cupboard."

Her mouth drifted open. Agent Sheffield had deliberately told her, in a roundabout manner, that they had indeed found a crate of equipment. No one knew except the FBI.

And Mr. Fiske.

And Mary. "Mr. Winslow didn't know. That means someone else put it there. Someone trying to—"

"I thought you quit, Miss Stirling."

She sighed. She wouldn't be in Boston for long anyway. "No promises, but if I hear anything . . ."

"I knew you wouldn't let me down."

Mary shook her head and departed. This was how Nancy Drew got herself in trouble too, but Nancy always found her way out.

If only real life came with such guarantees.

★ ★ ★

Mary and Quintessa sat on Mary's bed with the door shut, hunched over the section of the notebook dedicated to Frank Fiske.

On a blank sheet of paper, Mary drew a straight line to track the timing. "See?" she said in a hushed voice. "Mr. Fiske's son was drafted last October in the first lottery. Fiske is worried. He had a horrible experience in the First World War."

"Who didn't?" Quintessa whispered.

Although Mr. Fiske was Mary's prime suspect, she still didn't want Yvette to hear their conversation.

"I don't blame him for his concern for his only son." Mary made another mark at September 1940. "Just a month earlier, President Roosevelt agreed to give fifty of our old destroyers to Great Britain. I remember how angry Mr. Fiske was, all the isolationists."

Quintessa tucked a blonde curl behind her ear. "When was the champagne incident?"

"March 18." Mary drew another line and gave Quintessa a pointed look. "Exactly one week after Roosevelt announced Lend-Lease."

"Oh." Green eyes widened. "The isolationists hated that."

"That's about the time I started taking notes." All along, Mr. Fiske had seemed to be the calm voice of reason, yet he was always there, always involved. "All the problems have happened on Fiske's crew."

"That just means the saboteur is probably on his crew."

"That's what I've assumed from the start." Mary tapped the mark at March 18. "The champagne was a call for attention, as if the saboteur wanted the FBI to start looking."

"He succeeded." Quintessa turned a page. "Here's something about decking failure?"

"Yes. It failed after Mr. Fiske inspected it. Mr. Bauer and Mr. Kaplan blamed each other."

Quintessa's lips twisted. "Well, we know it wasn't Mr. Bauer, and Mr. Kaplan's been in jail for a while. And things are still going on."

"Exactly. So it was someone else, someone trying to make Bauer or Kaplan look guilty. Mr. Kaplan wants us in the war. Mr. Fiske doesn't."

"Where does the bomb come in? I still can't believe it. What if something had happened to Jim? To his friends?"

"I know." Mary focused on her notes, trimming out thoughts of the man she loved. "The number two gun mount was installed on May 9. Jim—" She swallowed hard. "Jim was there, and he observed an argument between Bauer and Kaplan that Mr. Fiske broke up."

"Hmm."

"Think about it. Everyone suspects the loudmouths. A smart saboteur would know better. He'd keep a low profile."

Quintessa nodded and ran her finger down the mark on May 9. "Mr. Fiske was there the day the gun was installed."

"Yes, and he sent Mr. Kaplan to the handling room to clean up—that's where the bomb was found. Kaplan said he was only there five minutes." Mary rolled her shoulders. "I think Mr. Fiske sent Kaplan to frame him, so others would remember him going there."

"Wow."

"The *Atwood* shipped out June 1. Fiske and Kaplan returned for a final check the day before. I think that's when he planted the bomb and painted the swastika." Mary darkened the mark. "But it was so flamboyant. Kaplan realized he was being framed, and then he got beaten up by thugs from the German-American Bund. He got desperate. He wanted to create evidence to prove what he believed to be true."

"That a Nazi did it."

"Mm-hmm." Mary gave her friend a small smile. How wonderful to puzzle things out with Quintessa.

"So when did Jim find the bomb?"

Mary turned from the affection and worry in her friend's eyes. "June 11. There was an uproar, but not for long. No one was arrested, and everyone was upset about it."

"Mr. Fiske too?"

"Of course. Then over the next month or so, things started happening again, sections failing after inspection. And here . . ." Mary drew another line. "August 8, right in the middle of the congressional hearings on the bill to extend the draft, which affects Mr. Fiske's son. Mr. Fiske told me Bauer's section had failed after he inspected it—and that he found Mr. Kaplan's gloves at the spot."

"Mr. Fiske just happened to find them, huh?" A skeptical look from Quintessa.

Mary flipped a page. "Look. On August 18, Roosevelt

signed the bill to extend the draft. Mr. Fiske's son is bound to the Army until May of '43. Do you think we'll avoid war that long?"

"I wish." Quintessa let out a long sigh.

"Me too." Mary found her spot in her notes. "Here we are. September 19. That's when Mr. Kaplan was arrested. Mr. Fiske was there, calming the men down. He told the agents he sent Mr. Kaplan to the handling room on the day the gun was installed and later before the *Atwood* shipped out. That bit of evidence tipped the balance."

"Convenient."

"I'll say." Mary glanced up to the ceiling. "Mr. Fiske was happy for a while. There was an uproar again. But it didn't last long, and that made him mad. I remember. He must have realized his plan had failed. He'd successfully framed an interventionist, but public opinion about the war didn't change. He needed more. That's when he shifted to his second plan and found another interventionist to frame—Mr. Winslow."

"Is that when all this stuff with the blueprints started?"

"Yes, in mid-October." Another line. "The bolts didn't fit. Mr. Fiske took the blueprints to Agent Sheffield, showed him how the construction followed the blueprints perfectly but wasn't correct."

"And they started looking at Mr. Winslow." Quintessa had such a gift with names, which certainly helped with sales.

"Yes. Then the FBI received a tip, went to his house, found the bomb—" She clamped her lips shut. They'd also found the crate of equipment, but she didn't feel at liberty to discuss that with anyone else. "And they arrested him."

"Then they discovered O'Donnell's blueprints didn't match Winslow's plans, and they started looking at him—and at Yvette." Quintessa's eyes lit up, as if having a saboteur under their roof would be the grandest adventure ever.

"It isn't her, I'm sure."

"Blueprints can't be altered after they're developed, so they had to be altered in the drafting room."

"Mr. Fiske visits the drafting room, visits with O'Donnell. He knows his friend's schedule, when all the draftsmen take lunch break. And Mr. Fiske is the man who reads the blueprints and puts them into action. He'd know exactly what modifications to make."

"Why would he want to frame his friend? Aren't they both isolationists?"

"Yes." Mary made another mark for the meeting at Filene's. "A hole in his plan. He didn't mean to involve Mr. O'Donnell. He didn't realize the draftsman would look guilty. That's why he's calling attention to Yvette and her friends. But that's a leap of logic, linking Yvette's pro-French crowd with Winslow's pro-British crowd. Mr. Fiske is desperate, and with each twist he gets sloppier and his plans get wilder."

The doorbell rang.

Mary startled. For one second, she thought of Jim, but he was at sea.

"I'll answer the door," Yvette called from the living room.

The front door creaked open, and a male voice sounded. A familiar voice.

"That's Agent Sheffield." Mary closed her notebook and laid it on the bed.

"How exciting. The FBI in our own apartment."

Mary tilted a smile to Quintessa. "That isn't good."

She stood and tugged on Mary's arm. "Let's see what's happening."

Out in the entryway, Yvette stood with Agents Sheffield and Hayes.

"Good evening, gentlemen." Mary's nerves shivered. "Am I under investigation?"

Agent Sheffield chuckled. "Well, we did receive an anonymous tip that you were up to something fishy, but no, we have a search warrant for Yvette Lafontaine."

"Why?" Yvette pressed a hand to her chest. "I have done nothing wrong."

"I need to see your purse, miss."

"All—all right. That is the purse I take to work." Yvette pointed to the coatrack, then she opened a drawer in the mail table. "The other three are in here."

Mary clutched Quintessa's arm. What were they looking for? And what would they find?

Agent Hayes opened the brown shoulder bag on the coatrack, while Agent Sheffield pulled out the purses from the cabinet and dumped the contents from a black handbag.

"I thought so." Using a handkerchief, Agent Sheffield lifted a pen. "I was told I might find this here."

"What is that?" Yvette's voice crimped.

Mary peered closer—a pen, but a strange one, with a wooden handle stained dark brown at the end, two tips, and a screw to adjust the distance. She knew exactly what it was.

"Is that—" Yvette frowned at it, her eyes frantic. "Is that a drafting pen?"

"Yes." Sheffield examined the pen with a smug expression. "I believe we'll find this pen matches the marks on the incorrect blueprints. And I believe this stain is the same color as the chewing tobacco favored by Mr. O'Donnell, and that these tooth marks will match his bite. And I believe we'll find the pen wiped clean of all fingerprints."

Yvette's chest heaved. "You think—I could not. I did not."

However, the agent's tone and words didn't sound accusatory, merely satisfied. He was up to something. Mary rubbed Yvette's shoulder. "I know you didn't."

"That—" Yvette fluttered her hand at the purse. "I do not take that to work. It is too dressy."

"No." A cold rock formed in Mary's throat. "But it is the purse you took when we went shopping at Filene's this weekend. When we ran into Mr. Fiske."

Horror flashed through Yvette's brown eyes. "He held my purse."

"He was wearing gloves." Mary's eyes drifted shut, bringing the memory into focus. "I thought it was strange to wear heavy leather work gloves in a heated department store."

"So he wouldn't get fingerprints on the pen," Quintessa said.

Mary locked her gaze with Agent Sheffield. "There was a black ink stain on the right forefinger. Not a smudgy stain like you'd see with grease, but crisp. His reports are always in blue ink, not black. I know, because it bothers Mr. Pennington."

Agent Sheffield bowed slightly to Yvette. "Miss Lafontaine, I need to take you in for questioning."

She gasped and gripped her hands together. "But I—"

"Didn't do anything. However, this is a game of chess, and he's an excellent player. I'm pretending to fall for his move."

"That makes sense, Yvette." Mary rubbed the tense muscles in her friend's shoulder. "You'll be safer too. If the FBI doesn't take you in, he might get desperate enough to hurt you."

"You'll keep her safe, won't you?" Quintessa asked.

"Of course. Grab your hat and coat, Miss Lafontaine." Agent Sheffield tipped his fedora to Mary and winked. "Fiske doesn't realize it, but I control this game. The next move is mine, and it'll be good. Just watch."

Mary nodded but wrapped her arms around her middle. As long as she didn't have to watch anyone get hurt.

37

South of Iceland
Monday, November 24, 1941

Jim followed Arch through his routine in the engine room, partly to kill time before midnight when he took the mid-watch in the gun director, partly to learn the job, partly to chat with his friend, but mostly to keep warm in the toastiest compartment on the ship.

This convoy escort had been cold and stormy. No ships had been lost, but several sound contacts and depth-charge attacks kept the destroyers hopping and alert. Tomorrow morning TU 4.1.5 would pass Convoy HX-160 to the Royal Navy and escort a handful of ships to Iceland, then later they'd meet up with Convoy ON-41 and return to Halifax.

Jim ducked around the deaerating feed tank, memorizing connections and positions. Durant planned to rotate the junior officers when they returned to Boston so they could learn other duties.

Arch tightened a valve. "This new escort-of-convoy policy works well."

"Makes more sense, that's for sure." The earlier policy required the escorts to stay within two thousand yards of the merchant ships, which allowed the U-boats to sink ships while outside the range of the destroyers' sonar. Now they kept station up to five thousand yards away.

Arch made a notation on his clipboard. "We should be back in Boston before Christmas. If they give us leave, will you go home?"

That depended on Mary and Quintessa's reactions to his declarations, and on their plans. Either he'd be avoiding both ladies or enjoying a romantic week with Mary. "I hope to."

Arch worked his way around a complex of steam and fuel oil pipes. "Any chance I could join you?"

"Sure. Don't you want to go home?"

"When I'm unattached? Not if I can help it. Mother will try to attach me to the daughters of all her acquaintances. Silly snobbish girls who talk of nothing but redecorating the parlor and their troubles with the help."

Jim followed his friend. "Middle-class women can be superficial too. So can men, by the way."

"I know." Arch rubbed the back of his neck. "But I want more."

"I'm sure there are plenty of bright, down-to-earth ladies in your society."

Arch sent him a wry look. "If there are, the ladies hide it well."

"Well, you're more than welcome in the Avery home. Plenty of room."

"Plenty of people too. I don't know how you keep them all straight." A huge smile lit his friend's face. "But thanks. I can't handle my parents right now."

"I under—"

The alarm clanged general quarters.

A sailor stationed at the engine telegraph turned and shouted, "Sound contact. Increase to flank speed."

"See you." Jim clapped Arch on the back and headed out at a brisk pace for the gun director. He followed the mass of men moving in a calm deliberate pattern to their battle stations. All motion went forward and up on the starboard side and aft and down on the port side to prevent sailors from crossing paths and jamming passageways and ladders.

Durant required the men to wear their life vests at all times in a combat area, but Jim checked his anyway and felt for the sheath knife and whistle on the lanyard around his neck and the flashlight in his left trouser pocket. He pulled his gloves from his right trouser pocket and put them on since he'd be out in the elements.

Some of the men were tempted to be lazy and leave their survival gear in quarters, but you never knew when a torpedo could come out of the blue.

The *Atwood* picked up speed, jolting over the waves, but Jim had his North Atlantic sea legs and scampered up the ladder to the deck and forward to the bridge superstructure.

A cold clear night, a half-moon, moderate wind, fair seas—a good night to patrol. And maybe to hunt down a U-boat. No American ship had sunk an enemy sub, and the men longed to avenge the loss of the *Reuben James* and the damage to the *Kearny*.

The destroyer made a sharp turn to port. Jim braced his legs to keep his balance. What was going on? They never deviated from course when chasing a sound contact.

Men shouted and pointed to starboard.

Something pale and phosphorescent streamed toward the *Atwood*.

Torpedo!

Jim grasped the lifeline and watched in horror and fascination, willing the ship to turn faster, harder, to swing the bow out of the way.

But a slimy green feeling filled his stomach. Every calculation of vectors and speed told him they'd fail.

"Hold on!" he shouted. "Brace yourselves!"

The torpedo slammed into the bow below the number one gun mount.

With a sickening shudder, the ship heaved up, settled down. Jim gripped the lifeline, set his feet wide, his heart hammering.

An explosion pummeled his eardrums. A ball of orange fire lit the sky.

"The magazine!" The torpedo must have hit the ammunition stash for the forward guns. "Oh, Lord. The men."

Flames ripped through the bow area. The ship's bell sounded rapidly, and the bugle sounded "fire quarters."

But every man on board already knew they'd been hit.

As the damage control party raced forward, Jim scrambled up to the gun director, his face tingling from cold and fear. How many men had been killed? Wounded? Could the *Atwood* stay afloat? How many more men would perish tonight?

38

Boston
Monday, November 24, 1941

Mary put the finishing touches on her Boston cream pie. Yellow cake, custard filling, chocolate glaze—what could be better? Only two more weeks in this city, and Mary wanted to savor everything.

Magda Bauer said Mary didn't need to bring anything for dinner, but Mary insisted on providing dessert.

What a strange evening it would be. For Agent Sheffield's big chess play, he'd released both Ira Kaplan and Weldon Winslow on Thanksgiving Day, citing insufficient evidence. Today, some at the shipyard claimed he'd released the turkeys.

This morning Mary had made a casual visit to the docks without a notebook. Everyone was in an uproar, arguing whether justice had been done or justice had been violated. Mr. Fiske seemed calm, but Mary didn't trust him one whit.

She untied her apron and hung it by the door. In the afternoon, Ira Kaplan came to Mr. Pennington's office to speak to Mary. Heinrich Bauer had visited him in prison, and the men had come to preliminary amends, with Mr. Bauer refusing to press charges for Kaplan's attempt to frame him. Mrs. Bauer had invited Kaplan to dinner to further make peace. The men decided to invite Mary too because she believed in both of them and had tried to help them. Mary had a hunch her presence was also desired as a neutral buffer.

She set the covered cake plate on the mail table and checked her hair in the mirror. Besides, her other option was to dine alone with a can of Campbell's tomato soup. Yvette had a meeting with one of her French groups, and Quintessa was working late setting up Christmas show windows at Filene's.

The clock read six-thirty. She didn't need to leave for another fifteen minutes. Perhaps she could stop at the store if Mrs. Bauer needed something. With two small children at home, shopping would be difficult.

She pulled her notepad from her purse, found the Bauers' phone number, and rang it. "Hi, Mrs. Bauer. It's Mary Stirling. I'm running early, and I wondered if you needed anything from the store."

"No. Thank you, no." Her voice carried an even heavier German accent than her husband's. "I am glad you called. Mr. Bauer is not here. Maybe another night for dinner?"

"He's still at the Navy Yard?" With the union watching over things, working late was rare.

"He went back fifteen minutes ago. Mr. Winslow called and said Heinrich must come."

"Mr. Winslow?" Mary stared at her own puzzled expression in the mirror. "Why would a naval architect need a welder?"

"I asked Heinrich. He was not happy. Mr. Winslow said he must talk to a welder. A problem in the—how do you call them?—the papers?"

"The blueprints?"

"*Ja*. He wanted to ask a welder in private. It is strange."

Strange? It was downright fishy. Mary rested her hip against the mail table. "Why did he want to talk in private?"

"He said he was at Dry Dock 2 and something was wrong, but he needed to ask a welder about it. Heinrich asked why him? Why not Mr. Fiske? He is leadingman. But Mr. Winslow said he didn't trust Mr. Fiske."

Neither did Mary, but right now she didn't trust Mr. Winslow either.

"He said he'd pay Heinrich fifty dollars to come in." Mrs. Bauer's voice wavered. "Heinrich said he sounded scared."

"Scared?"

"I—I am too, but Heinrich said he must go. He thinks something is happening, and he wants it to end now. He has been beaten and framed and almost arrested. And Mr. Kaplan was arrested when he was innocent. Heinrich says it needs to end."

Yes, it did. But what if Mr. Bauer had walked into a trap? "Thank you, Mrs. Bauer. Please let me know if you hear anything. I'm going to make a phone call."

After she hung up, she flipped through her notepad for the FBI's number. Agent Sheffield had given her a number to call day or night, just in case.

She paused and frowned. Why would Mr. Winslow be at the dry dock? He never went to the work site. Something wormed around inside, niggling her.

Mary grabbed the phone book and scanned the W section until she found the number for Mr. and Mrs. Weldon Winslow. Her hand hovered over the receiver, but then she grabbed it and dialed.

A woman answered. "Hello?"

"Hello. This is Miss Stirling from the Boston Navy Yard. May I speak to Mr. Winslow? I have a question for him."

"He isn't at home," she said in a crisp British accent.

Mary worked her finger through the coil of the phone cord. "Is he working late?"

"No, he had to return for—for an item he left at the office. He should be home any minute."

Any minute? But he'd just called Mr. Bauer. "Perhaps you can help me solve a little mystery. I was just talking to Mrs. Heinrich Bauer. Her husband is a welder at the shipyard. Fifteen minutes ago he received a phone call from your husband summoning him to the docks so he could ask a question."

"That can't be. He went in for only one reason and promised he'd be home immediately. He's a man of his word, Miss—Miss—"

"Miss Stirling. I know he is. That's why it seems odd to me."

"Oh dear. With everything happening at the shipyard, I don't like the idea of him being there alone at night. Someone worked hard to arrange his arrest, and he must not be happy that Weldon's been released."

Mary twisted the cord around her finger. "If you wouldn't mind, would you please tell me why he went in?"

Silence hummed on the wires. Then Mrs. Winslow cleared her throat. "His pills. He has a—a condition, and he needs to take pills regularly."

Mary murmured sympathetically.

"Oh dear. He always keeps one bottle at home and one at the office. This morning I received a call from his office saying his bottle at work was empty, and would I please bring the other bottle to the gatehouse?"

"You said the call came from his office, not that your husband called."

"I didn't think anything of it. I know how busy he is, but Weldon is not happy with me."

The fishy smell grew stronger. "He didn't make the call, did he?"

"No. The man had—well, I thought it was a German

accent, but thinking about it, I realize it sounded like the bad German accents the American actors use in the cinema."

The cord tangled into a knot between Mary's finger and the phone. "Could you tell? Was he young, old, middle-aged?"

"Middle-aged, I think."

Like Mr. Fiske, although half the men at the yard were middle-aged.

"I did as he asked." Anxiety tinged Mrs. Winslow's voice. "I put the bottle in a lunch bag with a sandwich and brought it to the gatehouse. That sounded like something Weldon would ask. He's a private person."

"I understand."

"The guard took the bag and set it on a bench with several other lunch bags."

"And Mr. Winslow never even knew."

"No, he didn't. When he came home this evening and needed to take a pill—well, he was quite cross."

"How long ago did he leave?"

"Oh, it must have been a quarter to six."

Almost an hour ago. "How long should it take him?"

"We don't live but ten minutes away. He—he should be home by now."

Yes, he should. In Mary's mind, the situation changed from fishy to alarming, and she yanked her finger free from the telephone cord. "Excuse me, Mrs. Winslow. I'm going to make another phone call. I'll call you back if I hear anything. And please call me if you hear something." She gave her phone number and hung up.

The FBI. Mary could scarcely rotate the dial, her finger shook so much. Finally the phone exchange answered. "Hello, this is Mary Stirling from the Boston Navy Yard. It's imperative that I speak to Agent Paul Sheffield or Agent Walter Hayes immediately. Something is terribly wrong."

"Mm-hmm." The woman on the other end sounded bored.

"What is your number, please? I'll tell Agent Sheffield you called, and he'll get back to you in the morning when he comes to the office."

Panic pressed on Mary's throat. "That'll be too late. This is an emergency. Please, ma'am. I've worked with them on the sabotage case at the shipyard. Agent Sheffield gave me this number and promised I could reach him night or day."

"Yes, ma'am. But I'm not allowed to bother the agents except in an emergency."

Mary took a long, trembling breath. "That's why I said it was an emergency."

"Ma'am, if I had a dollar for every emergency I hear about, I wouldn't need this job."

"Two lives are at stake." Her voice came out thick. "Does that qualify as an emergency?"

An annoyed sigh. "I'll let Agent Sheffield make that decision—"

"Tonight? You'll call him immediately?"

"I'll call him and tell him to call you."

"No. That'll take too long. Tell him Mary Stirling called. Take this down, please. It's important he knows all of this. Tell him Frank Fiske has made his move. He's lured Weldon Winslow and Heinrich Bauer to the Navy Yard. Tell him to meet me at Dry Dock 2."

She gasped. "You're not going there, are you?"

"If that's what it takes to bring in the FBI, then yes, I am. Right now I'm the only person who knows these men are in danger—or cares. If you care too, you'll call Agent Sheffield right this instant." She hung up.

What was she thinking? Her face looked pale in the mirror with twin red spots high on her cheeks. She wasn't a police officer or detective. She didn't own a weapon and wouldn't know how to use one.

If only Jim were here. Her eyes drifted shut for a moment.

Jim was no longer her undercover partner. He belonged to Quintessa.

She was alone, and she was the only one who could act right now. What if the dispatcher didn't call Agent Sheffield? What if the phone was busy or both men were out? Even if they did come, Mary could get to the dock faster.

The local police wouldn't be able to help on a military base, but there were guards at the gate. They could help. She wouldn't be dashing into danger alone like some silly movie heroine. She'd alert the authorities. It was the right thing to do.

Mary grabbed her red coat from the rack. Her old brown coat lay underneath, quiet and unassuming. She switched coats. Tonight invisibility might come in handy.

39

South of Iceland

Jim climbed into the gun director, where six men worked hard.

Lieutenant Reinhardt barked orders into his microphone. "Lay for star-shell spread to starboard."

Reinhardt acknowledged Jim with a nod. "Good to see you, Mr. Avery. No response from number one. Number two took casualties and damage, lost director control. Go check both guns."

"Aye aye, sir." Jim made his way back down to the deck.

The aft guns fired in a roar. Star shells soared high and hovered by their parachutes, showering light on the dark sea.

Toward the bow, the flames provided plenty of illumination, but a demonic orange sort. Jim pressed forward, careful not to interfere with the damage control party's work. Heat assaulted his face. Men trained fire hoses on the inferno and guided the wounded farther aft for first aid, black figures silhouetted by the flames, by the orange-gray smoke drifting to port.

Jim passed the number two gun mount and stopped

short. The bow was gone, and the number one gun tilted into the breach, mangled. His quarters were gone. Simply gone. Thank goodness Arch was amidships in the engine room.

He shook off his shock. Once they closed the watertight compartments, the destroyer could sail without her bow, although slower. But the number one gun? The seventeen sailors who manned the gun and its handling room? They'd been directly over the magazine that exploded.

And the sound room lay forward of the magazine. All the sonar operators . . . gone.

A stench rose, the sickly sweet smell of fuel oil and burning flesh.

Bile filled Jim's mouth, but he swallowed it. He had work to do.

Vince Banning shouted orders to the damage control party over the roar of fire, the hiss of water, the sizzle of water hitting flame.

Jim sidled past a pair of men guiding a fire hose. "Mr. Banning! Any word on the men in number one?"

An orange glow danced on the executive officer's features, and he pointed to a taut line stretching into the door to the gun mount, now at a precarious 45-degree angle. "We've got a man in there right now."

The line jerked, and two beefy sailors drew it up.

A man hauled himself out of the door and collapsed on the deck, coughing. Soot blackened his face. "All dead. All of 'em." Then he cussed the Nazis with words as black and orange as the smoke and flames.

"Oh, dear Lord." Jim's mind reeled. Seventeen men.

But nothing could be done for them. He had to think of the ship, of the number two gun.

A retort sounded to aft, a starboard K-gun firing. Jim grabbed a hanging tackle for support. A circle of light flashed on the surface of the sea, water gushed up, and the destroyer lifted from the water and pounded down again.

Jim set his feet beneath him and climbed the platform to the number two gun. He squeezed his way into the gun compartment. Homer Udell called out orders. His crew, ten Negro stewards, set a powder case and a projectile into the loading tray of the gun, slammed the breech shut, and rammed the projectile into firing position.

"How are things, Udell?" Jim asked.

The gun captain rubbed the stubble on his weathered cheek. "Bad but manageable, sir. We lost director control and power, so we converted to manual. But my men are ready. If that U-boat shows its ugly face, we'll blow it right off."

"Reinhardt said you took casualties."

"Three men injured in the handling room. They refuse first aid, want to stay at their stations."

"Good men, but let's get some replacements sent down." Jim borrowed Udell's headset, flipped the switch to talk to conn, and asked the bridge to send three replacements.

Udell put his headphones back on. "Any word on number one?" he asked in a low voice.

Jim glanced around at the men hard at work in the cramped compartment, men who knew the crew of that gun like brothers. He sucked his lips between his teeth and shook his head, sharp and short.

Udell squeezed his eyes shut, dipped his head, and swore under his breath.

"I see her!" Hank Gillis, the pointer, peered through his telescopic sight at the front of the compartment, and he cussed. "The U-boat. Coming right at us and mighty fast."

Udell cupped his hand over his headphone. "Captain says fire at will."

Hank cranked his hand wheels, depressing the gun barrel,

while the trainer turned his hand wheels, rotating the giant base of the gun on its ball-bearing ring.

"Range?" Jim shouted, stepping out of the way of the gun.

"Range?" Udell paused, listening. "Range five-double-oh and closing fast."

Jim grimaced. Five hundred yards. She probably meant to fire one more torpedo from her bow tube before turning the deck gun on the *Atwood*.

A muffled roar, and the ship shook. Numbers three and four guns must have opened fire.

"Both shots over," the pointer said.

"Adjust range to four-five-oh," Udell called.

"Aye aye." Hank cranked his hand wheels some more. "Range set."

"Bearing set," the trainer said.

Udell made a knifing motion with his hand. "Fire!"

Jim clapped his hands over his ears. The huge gun roared, blasted out its projectile, recoiled, snapped back into position.

The loading tray opened. The hot case man reached in with giant leather gloves, snatched out the spent powder case, and pitched it out the hatch in the back of the compartment. As soon as the old case was removed, the powder man loaded a new case and the projectile man loaded a new projectile.

"Shot fell short," the pointer said.

"Keep 'er at four-five-oh," Udell said. "And Mr. Avery, sir? Mr. Reinhardt wants you in the director."

"Tell him I'm coming." Jim clapped the man on the shoulder and squeezed out the tiny door.

To starboard, a sleek dark shape raced toward the *Atwood*, its bow wave white on either side, eerie in the light of the star shells.

An actual U-boat. His first sight of the enemy. Jim's breath locked in his chest. With the bow gone, the destroyer had lost much speed and maneuverability. What chance did they have?

The aft guns thumped out a greeting, followed by the rat-a-tat of the .50-caliber machine guns.

Jim continued on his way to the director. Three mess attendants approached at a fast pace. The replacements for the wounded men. "Head to number two handling room. Udell will tell you what to do."

"Aye aye, sir."

A shout rose, and Jim wheeled to starboard.

A torpedo track, a burning white spear, plunged toward the *Atwood*'s stern.

Lord, save us! Jim cried out and grabbed a ladder. "Brace yourselves!"

The destroyer jerked from the impact, bounced high, landed hard. Jim fell to his knees, one hand gripping the ladder, his shoulder wrenched.

How bad was the hit? He couldn't see that far aft, past the bridge and the funnels, but another orange fireball mirrored the earlier one at the bow.

The *Atwood* drifted to a stop. Swell, they must have lost the propellers. They'd be dead in the water. And above the propellers on the far end of the stern? The depth charge racks. The sailors who manned them. How many more had died?

"Lord, make it stop." He massaged his sore shoulder and climbed up to the director, but why? The ship settled lower, listed several degrees to starboard.

A new sound from the direction of the U-boat, a low thudding, popping sound. The deck gun?

Jim burst into the gun director. Commotion.

Reinhardt met his gaze, wild-eyed. "Number four's in bad shape. Three took damage."

The talker pressed his hand over his headphone. "Udell says number two took damage from the deck gun."

Jim couldn't move. Dead in the water. All four guns out of action. It was over.

Reinhardt swatted Jim's arm. "Check on two, see what can be done."

"Aye aye." A formality, but until the captain ordered them to abandon ship, he'd do what he could.

As he climbed out onto the signal deck, another star shell lit up the sky and gunfire sounded aft.

An American destroyer!

"Thank you, Lord!" Jim clung to the rail.

On the U-boat, black ants of men scrambled down the hatch. They'd submerge and flee and leave the *Atwood* to her fate.

The ship's alarm bell clanged, and the bugle sounded "abandon ship."

Jim's blood went as cold as the waters beneath him.

Durant's voice came over the loudspeaker. "All hands prepare to abandon ship. Another destroyer is on its way to aid in rescue. Do not enter the water until necessary. Repeat, do not enter the water until necessary."

He didn't need to tell Jim twice. Not only would the frigid water kill a man in less than twenty minutes, but the other destroyer would attack the U-boat with depth charges deadly to men in the water.

Sure enough, the second destroyer charged past, leaving a string of explosions in her wake.

But that destroyer couldn't rescue the men of the *Atwood*. Her primary job was to sink that sub. Same as when the *Atwood* had abandoned the men of that sunken Norwegian freighter.

Jim worked his way down to the deck. The ship settled lower and lower, listed to ten degrees.

"Ahoy!" a sailor shouted.

On the port side, a third destroyer dashed toward them in the strange bright light of the star shells.

"Thank you, Lord!" Jim headed toward the number two gun but found the deck too crowded to pass.

Men tossed lines and cargo nets over the side and lowered the life rafts. Sailors assembled at their embarkation stations, aft and forward, port and starboard.

The *Atwood* groaned, rolled slightly to stern.

"No time to waste!" Reinhardt jumped to the deck behind Jim. "Abandon ship."

Since the gunnery officer was in charge of embarkation on the port side, everyone sprang to action. Men climbed over the side and down the lines and nets.

Jim paused. His earlier order had been to check conditions in the number two gun mount, but his station at the abandon ship drill was to aid Mr. Reinhardt. That overrode the first order.

He peered through the thicket of men, straining for the sight of any of Udell's crew. "Lord, help them."

Jim pushed through to the lifeline and started helping sailors over the side. "One at a time, men. Leave plenty of room. Watch the fellow beneath you."

One by one, the men climbed down into life rafts and pushed away from the sinking destroyer.

About one hundred feet away, the third destroyer pulled alongside, heaving nets and lines and rafts over the side.

Jim helped a man down onto the net. "Make for the other ship as fast as you can, men. Get away from the *Atwood*."

He glanced around. His station was cleared.

"Mr. Avery!" Reinhardt climbed over the side. "Abandon ship."

"Aye aye." Jim prayed for strength, slipped under the lifeline, and nestled his feet in the ropes of the net. Since the ship listed to starboard, the drop to the water on the port side was greater now.

He glanced down at the black water, slick with fuel oil,

and found a life raft to aim for, half a dozen men inside beckoning to him.

Just aft, Reinhardt worked his way down the net, with Durant above him, the log book clamped in one arm.

"Help! Somebody help!"

Jim glanced up.

A dark face leaned over the lifeline, eyes frantic—Mack Gillis, one of the replacements Jim had sent to the number two gun mount. "Captain! Sir! Men is trapped in number two. Doors is jammed. Can't get out."

Jim's heart seized, and his hands contracted, pulling him up the net again to help.

"I'm sorry, son," Captain Durant said in a low, firm voice. "No time. Abandon ship. That's an order."

Mack twisted his head toward the gun, back to Durant. "Please, sir. They's my friends. My brother." His voice cracked.

"Abandon ship, Mack," Durant said. "That's an order."

Mack's brother Hank was the pointer. What would Jim do if Dan were trapped? Rob? His two little brothers?

Durant continued down the net. He was too fair a man to base his decision on the color of the men's skin. He'd made a difficult, strong decision based on the safety of the entire crew. Any men who formed a rescue party could also be lost.

"Mr. Avery?" Mack called down, his voice pleading.

Jim glanced away, to the dark water below, to the men filling the life rafts, paddling toward the rescue ship, bobbing in the water, climbing nets and lines on the other side, the sailors from the other ship dangling from the side to help them aboard.

He'd been ordered to abandon ship, to abandon Udell and Hank and the others to certain death. He could be bold and strong and ignore the tugging at his heart and follow Durant.

Or would the bold decision be to disobey the captain in

the slim chance he could save a few lives? Or would that be merely suicidal?

"Mr. Avery!" Durant shouted. "Don't even think about going back. You've been given a direct order too. Abandon ship!"

Jim squeezed his eyes shut. *Lord, help me decide. Which is the bold action? Which is floating?*

Maybe that was the wrong question to ask. Maybe it didn't matter whether he charged into action or floated into it. Maybe what mattered most was to do the right thing.

What was the right thing? Durant's list of questions ran through his mind. Yes, he could die if he went back. Yes, he might save a few men if he went back. But whichever way he went, the fate of the *Atwood* was sealed. And the war effort? It hardly depended on the life of one ensign.

Mary's sweet face flashed in his mind. If he went back, he might never see her again. But if he didn't go back, how could he face her again?

Mack leaned over the lifeline. "Please, Mr. Avery. Please."

"Mr. Avery!" Durant's voice sounded sharper than gunfire. "Get down here this instant."

Jim drew a deep icy breath and gazed down at the captain he respected. "I'm sorry, sir, but I have to go back. I have to try."

40

Boston

In the backseat of the taxi, Mary scribbled in her notepad, trying to piece together the puzzle. At 5:45, Mr. Winslow left home for the shipyard, and at 6:15, he called Mr. Bauer. Now at almost seven o'clock, Mr. Bauer would be at Dry Dock 2 as instructed.

Assuming Mr. Fiske was behind it all, what had he done? He'd told Mrs. Winslow to bring her husband's codeine to the shipyard, knowing his addiction would force the man to return for it. Mr. Winslow had sounded scared when he called Mr. Bauer—was he being forced to call at gunpoint?

Mary rubbed her temples. She couldn't let Nancy Drew plots invade her analysis. Only the cold hard facts, as Agent Sheffield would say. Plus an ample dose of intuition.

Why Dry Dock 2? What was the plan? Two destroyers were under construction, laid down side by side. Was he going to damage the ships?

His motive was clear—he wanted to keep the United States out of the war. The way events were going, he'd need something big and showy. Mr. Winslow wanted the United States to join the war effort, so he was a natural target for Fiske. And Mr. Bauer? A German for Winslow to supposedly frame?

Complicated and messy. Just like everything else Mr. Fiske had done.

The taxi turned onto Chelsea Street.

Mary tapped the driver on the shoulder. "At the gate, please."

"Are you sure, miss? It's dark, looks deserted."

"A guard's at the gate. Thank you." Why try to explain herself? She paid him and stepped out. A chilly breeze wrapped around her legs, and she tugged her coat tighter. The temperature was supposed to fall below freezing tonight.

Now to call in the Marines. She drew in a breath, approached the guard, and showed her photographic identification pass.

"Another one coming back after hours?" The young man shook his head. "You're the third in the last hour."

"The others? A small dark-haired man in a nice coat? And a tall blond man with a German accent?"

"Yeah." He narrowed his eyes at her. "How'd you know?"

Here was the opening she needed. Her sails puffed out. "Those two men are the reason I'm here. They're in danger."

"Danger?" His upper lip twisted.

"I'm sure you're aware of the sabotage case. The saboteur lured those men down here as part of his plot. They're at Dry Dock 2. He means to damage the two ships under construction and to harm those men."

The guard leaned closer and sniffed. "You been drinking, lady?"

Mary groaned. "Of course not. I've worked with the FBI agents on the case, and I know something horrible will happen if we don't stop him. Please send guards to the dry dock."

"Listen, lady. I don't know what movies you've been

watching. *The Maltese Falcon*? *Suspicion*? But there ain't nothing happening tonight." He raised his arm like a gate before her.

She had to act now. She had to force him to send guards. And quickly, before he decided she was crazy and arrested her.

Mary darted past him and jogged inside. "If you won't stop him, I will."

"Come on, lady! What do you think you're doing?"

"Call the guards. It's an emergency, you hear? An emergency! Two lives are at stake."

No, three lives. If he didn't call the Marines, her life could be at stake too.

She ran past the Muster House, past a storehouse, to the base of Dry Dock 2. Mary stopped, breathing hard, and she got her bearings. The street lamps that normally illuminated the dry dock were dark. The only light came from a half-moon and the little round pump house at the far end of the wharf.

Mary's breath seized. Were one or more of the men there?

What should she do now? The safe thing would be to wait for either the Marines or the FBI. But what if no calls had been made? Could she afford to wait?

Mary hugged herself against the night chill. "What should I do, Lord? Stay safely in harbor? Or sail into possible danger?"

A breeze came from behind her, lifting the hem of her coat and raising a wry smile. "All right, Lord. If anything happens, I'll say you pushed me."

She was no soldier, no detective with a weapon. She was a secretary, an observer. So she'd observe.

Mary slipped off her heels and set them by a bollard. She also set down her purse with her notepad inside, outlining her thoughts. If anything happened to her, perhaps Agent Sheffield could use her notes to arrest Mr. Fiske.

She padded down the wooden pier. A brand-new pair of stockings, about to be ruined.

Her eyes strained into the darkness, and her ears into the silence. The familiar shipyard sights and sounds seemed foreign and forbidding—the giant cranes looming black overhead, the lap of water against the caisson gate at the end of the dry dock, the faint city noises in the background.

No motion met her eyes, no voices entered her ears. As she neared the pump house at the end of the pier, her steps slowed and she held her breath.

Sounds, metallic sounds, but from the caisson. Thumps, scrapes. From inside the caisson.

Mary studied the huge bowed steel gate that held back the seawater, a structure with pumps inside to remove seawater from the dry dock. The caisson contained portholes with pipes to the harbor. When those pipes were opened, seawater would flood in to float the ships.

Her mouth went dry. Was that Mr. Fiske's plan? Was he inside the caisson, preparing to open the pipes and flood the dock? If the destroyers were floated now, without lines securing them to bollards on the pier, the ships would tip over and be damaged. And where were Mr. Winslow and Mr. Bauer? What part did they play in the plot?

Mary crept up to the pump house and peeked through the window in the door. No signs of life inside, but she didn't dare open the door.

Someone moaned behind her.

She whipped around. The moans came from deep inside the dry dock. Mary rushed to the edge and dropped to her knees. About four feet of space separated the steel hull from the granite dock, filled with wooden scaffolding. At the bottom next to the caisson, over thirty feet below her, lay a dark figure, rolling around.

"Hello?" Mary said in a stage whisper.

"Yes? Hello? Who's there? Help me." That was Mr. Winslow, his voice slurred. He groaned. "I'm tied up. My hand—I think he broke it."

"Who did this? Where is he?" Mary glanced around, eyes wide and searching.

"Mr. Fiske. He's going to flood—"

"Shh. I'm coming. Be quiet." The metallic sounds inside the caisson hadn't ceased, but she couldn't take a chance Fiske might hear her.

Mary found the stairs cut into the wall of the dry dock, angling toward the middle of the hull, and she made her way down.

The granite wall rose high on one side, the steel hull on the other. Almost no light penetrated the abyss.

Her breath ratcheted its way deep into her lungs. What if Mr. Fiske opened the pipes now, when she and Mr. Winslow were down here?

Mary climbed through the maze of vertical and horizontal beams supporting the hull, scraping her legs. Something jabbed the sole of her foot, and she bit back a cry. Silence was as vital as speed.

Her leg bumped into something soft and warm, and she gasped. A body? Mr. Bauer?

Mary fell to her knees. A man's body lay facedown, and she rolled him over. "Mr. Bauer?" she whispered.

No response. No movement. She pressed her fingers under his chin—a slow steady pulse met her fingertips. "Thank you, Lord."

But how could she drag an unconscious man up the stairs?

Mr. Winslow would have to help. "Lord, please send the FBI, the Marines, or both."

Leaving Mr. Bauer, Mary worked her way down to Mr. Winslow.

"Miss Stirling? What are you doing here?"

"Shh. Keep your voice down. How can I help?"

The man pushed himself up to sitting and leaned back against the caisson. "My feet. He tangled them up in electrical wire. I can't get free. That's the story he plans to tell, that I tangled my feet in the wire and plunged to my death. After I sabotaged the gate and made it look like Bauer did it."

Mary found his feet and felt around. A mess of wires wound around both feet, but she couldn't see worth beans. "Come on, we have to hurry. You have to help."

He hunched over. "I—I can't. After he knocked me out, he broke my hand, my right hand. I can't move it, and it hurts like—like the dickens." The pain in his voice confirmed his words.

Mary slipped her fingers into a loop of wire and tried to loosen it. She stared up at the caisson hovering over her. The sounds inside continued. Perhaps Fiske hadn't heard them.

"Why are you here?" Mr. Winslow asked.

She didn't have time. "Never mind that for now. I know why you came—I talked to your wife—but what happened after you arrived?"

"Fiske was in my office. He said he'd found my . . . my . . ."

"Your codeine?"

A heavy sigh. "He said he found it here in the pump house with an odd assortment of tools. He wanted to show me before he called the FBI. Like a fool, I agreed. As soon as we stepped inside, he put a gun to my head."

Mary's fingers stilled. He had a gun. "He forced you to call Mr. Bauer."

"Yes. How did you know?"

"I'll tell you later." She worked one loop over his foot and felt for another one. "What happened next?"

"He—he had a script for me to read to Bauer. He told me to say anything necessary to convince the man to come here. If I failed, he'd shoot me. Well, I succeeded, so instead of shooting me, he brought me into the bowels of this dry dock and knocked me out cold."

That loop didn't loosen at all, so she tried another. "Mr. Bauer's down here too. Unconscious but alive."

"Oh no. He drugged him with my codeine. That's how he's framing me. He ground up about a dozen tablets in a mug and filled it with coffee. After all, how else could a weakling like me overpower such a man?" He sounded as bitter as codeine-laced coffee.

Mary murmured her sympathy and pried a loop over his foot.

"He's framing me." Pain and anger frayed his voice. "He forced me to apply my fingerprints to the medication vial, the coffee mug, the tools he's using—and his gun."

"Shh."

"Now he's in the caisson. He said he painted 'Heil Hitler' and swastikas everywhere. He wants it to look as if I did the damage, as if I wanted it to scream of Nazi sabotage. But everyone knows Bauer isn't a Nazi. Is Fiske that desperate? He honestly thinks the American public will attribute this to a crazy interventionist? That they'll rise up in furor and return to the false comfort of isolationism? That—"

"Shh. We have to make sure you and Mr. Bauer survive to testify against him." No doubt, Mr. Fiske had become unhinged as his plans collapsed, one after another, and the country spiraled down into war. "Can you wiggle your feet, help me out?"

A mighty gurgle overhead, and water gushed out of a pipe, arching over Mary's head.

Cold water splashed her, and she squealed before she could stop herself. "Come on. We have to hurry."

He wiggled, she pulled. Water splashed off the hull, drenched her back. Another loop, another. Mr. Winslow kicked and squirmed, loosening the ties. Mary fumbled at them with cold wet fingers.

"There!" She yanked the last one free. "Come on. I need your help with Mr. Bauer."

Water frothed around her feet, and she pulled Mr. Winslow to standing. He sagged back against the caisson and groaned. "My head. He hit me—he hit me hard." He doubled over and vomited.

Although her stomach turned, she couldn't afford to be queasy. Their lives were at stake. "Come on. We have to get to Bauer, get to the stairs."

The second pipe opened, baptizing the infant ship.

Mary headed toward the stairs, stepping over beams, ducking under scaffolding, each step plunging into icy water, her foot, her ankle. Her arms shook from the cold.

"Mr. Bauer!" Water lapped against his cheeks, and Mary lifted his shoulders. "Come on, Mr. Bauer. Wake up. Please wake up."

"He won't." Winslow's voice dipped lower than their chances of survival. "That much codeine will knock him out for hours. I should know."

"You have to help me. We have to work together."

"I—I'll try. My hand—"

"Use your good hand, here under his shoulder. I'll get his other side. The water's almost up to the lowest beam. We might be able to float him through."

She sloshed through the knee-high water, banging her shins against the horizontal beams, cradling Mr. Bauer's head with one hand while she and Mr. Winslow guided his shoulders over.

A loud rush signaled the opening of a third pipe.

Mary's teeth chattered, and the water rose to mid-thigh, swirling the hem of her coat. If that became water-logged, it would hold her down. "Here. Support his shoulders. I need to take off my coat. You should too when I'm done."

She shrugged off her coat and abandoned it. If she survived, she'd be happy she'd taken her old brown coat rather than her new red one.

After Mr. Winslow took off his coat, he helped her remove Mr. Bauer's. The less weight they had to drag, the better.

Above her, beams creaked.

"Oh no." If the water rose enough to float the ships, the scaffolding would fall free, and the hulls would tip over.

"Come on, hurry!" Water rose to her hips, making her skirt balloon around her, but she had no time to worry about modesty.

The stairs had to be close. The water was almost up to the next beam, forcing them to submerge Mr. Bauer to get him through the opening. The poor man.

A loud thunk, and Mr. Winslow cried out and cussed. "Clobbered my head."

"Shh! We still don't know where Mr. Fiske is."

"I'm right here."

41

South of Iceland

Jim clambered onto the deck and got to his feet. "Come on, Mack. Let's see what we can do."

He followed Mack Gillis down the slanting deck.

"Avery! Hey, Avery!" That was Mitch Hadley's voice.

Jim spun around.

Hadley was serving in communications tonight. He must have been destroying records in the radio room. He motioned with his thumb to the cargo net. "You're going the wrong way."

"Men are trapped in number two gun mount."

"Captain ordered abandon ship."

"Yes." Jim walked backward, intent on his goal. "He gave me a personal direct order to do so."

"You—you're disobeying a direct order?" A tone of awe entered Hadley's voice. "You're not floating?"

"Nope. Making waves." Most likely a wave that'd drown him. Despite the destruction all around, despite the crackle of flames and the shouts of men and the acrid stench of smoke, despite the almost-certain death facing him, a smile crept up. "You don't have to help me."

Hadley paused, then loped toward him. "Are you kidding? And let Floating Jim get all the medals and commendations?"

Jim turned and dashed to the gun mount. "Most likely posthumous medals, you know."

"The more of us working, the more likely some of us will live."

"Thanks." Jim shot him a grateful look. "Those are good men in there. They deserve a chance."

The door to the handling room stood open. Jim poked his head in. Empty, thank goodness. Seven men safe.

Up to the gun mount. The ladder to the platform had been ripped away, so the men used pipes and dangling lines to get to the top.

Mack plastered his hands to the mangled wall of the mount. "Hank! Udell! Freddie! Can you hear me?"

Jim yanked on the twisted door, but it wouldn't budge. "We need something to use as a crowbar."

"The ladder!" Hadley leapt back down to the deck and handed the ladder up to Jim.

"That might work." He jammed the end of the ladder into gaps in the door frame.

The ship creaked and tipped more to stern, to starboard. The fire heated the metal beneath Jim's feet. If the flames reached the ammunition in the handling room down there, it'd be over in a gruesome flash.

"Come on! Hurry!" Jim and Mack leaned hard on the ladder, and the door squealed in protest. "Hadley, get back up here!"

"Already here." He joined in.

The three men shoved with all their might, feet sliding on the deck. Jim didn't want to think what was making the deck slippery. Fuel oil. Had to be fuel oil.

"O God, strengthen my hands!" The door popped open, and Jim flopped to his knees. "Out, out! Everyone out."

But Mack climbed in. "Hank! You okay?"

"Come on! Come on!" Jim grabbed the first hand he reached.

The hot case man tumbled out the door. "Thank you, sir. Thank you."

"How bad is it?" Jim inspected the man for injuries, while Mack helped the powder man out.

"One man dead. Lots of men is hurt."

"You're in good shape. Start getting these men off the ship. Fast as you can." Jim leaned inside. "Everyone out. Come on!"

One by one, the men climbed out. Mack assisted his brother, who was bleeding badly from the head. "That's the last of 'em, sir. Except Udell."

"Stay with your brother." Jim motioned him to the cargo net. "Thanks for your help."

"Udell's in bad shape, sir." Mack looped his arm around Hank's waist. "Doesn't want to leave."

Jim groaned and glanced at Hadley. "Coming with me?"

"In for a penny, in for a pound, my mama always said."

"Let's hope we're not in for a pounding." Jim climbed through the door, fighting to keep his balance on the tilted deck.

"Mr. Avery?" Udell's voice came out strained in the darkness. "What are you doing? Get out of here."

"Not without you." He yanked his flashlight from his pocket and aimed it at the voice.

Udell shielded his eyes from the beam. "I ain't going. Look at my feet. Just look."

With his stomach in his throat, Jim angled the beam down, to the twisted, bloody remains of Homer Udell's feet. "Oh no."

"I ain't never walking again. I'm a sailor. My life is over."

Light-headed, dry mouthed, Jim couldn't stop staring. Just like Lillian. Only this wasn't Jim's fault. And didn't Lillian's life disprove Udell's statement?

Jim licked his lips. "Don't talk like that. We'll get you help."

"What am I supposed to do?" Udell's voice climbed and broke.

"I don't know," Hadley said, "but can we figure it out on the other ship?"

"Great idea." Jim slipped his flashlight into his pocket. "You're coming with us. Durant ordered everyone to abandon ship, and that includes you and me and Mr. Hadley."

"Yeah." Hadley climbed out the door, then reached in and beckoned. "Mr. Avery and I are already in trouble. Don't make it worse for us."

Jim squeezed beside Udell and shoved his shoulder and hip. "Come on. Your hands still work. Scoot to the door."

"If you weren't officers, I'd cuss you out."

"Go ahead." Hadley pulled the petty officer's arm. "I'll return the favor, you stubborn old sea salt."

When Jim grabbed the man around the knees to lift him through the door, Udell rewarded him with a couple dozen of the Navy's best swear words.

The ship shifted to starboard, at least thirty degrees. Jim sucked in a breath, half icy, half fiery. They had to get off the ship fast so they wouldn't get pulled under when it sank.

"Come on. Let's go." Jim anchored his hand under one shoulder.

Hadley grabbed the other, and they dragged Udell up to the edge of the gun platform and swung his legs over the side.

Jim slid down to the deck. Hadley lowered Udell, and Jim braced the wounded man's fall.

Then Jim and Hadley took Udell under the arms again

and made their way up the inclined deck. Jim ignored the petty officer's moans and cries. If he had to hurt the man to save his life, so be it.

Breathing hard, coughing from the smoke, Jim grasped one of the poles that held the lifelines and heaved himself forward, muscles screaming.

No cargo net on this section of the hull, but with the destroyer at such an angle, they could just slide into the water.

Water covered with burning fuel oil.

Jim groaned. He'd seen the training film on how to escape through burning oil, but he'd prayed he'd never have to use it.

A shout rang out across the gap. On the other destroyer, men pointed to the three men on the *Atwood*.

Jim waved. He needed their attention and help.

He and Hadley stuck their heads under the lifeline, straddled the tilted deck edge, and helped Udell into the same position. The gun captain looked pale, his eyes rolling, his posture slumped. He was going into shock from the blood loss. All the more reason to hurry.

"Burning oil," Hadley said with a growl.

"We know what to do." Jim unfastened his life vest. "Take off your life vests so we can stay submerged below the fire. I'll slide down first, clear a hole in the flames. You follow with Udell. Get to me right away so I can help. Swim low and fast. When we come up for air, thrash like crazy to beat off the flames."

Hadley tossed aside his vest. "That'd better be a big shiny medal."

Jim grinned at him. Live or die, he'd done his best, and he'd even gained a friend in the process.

Following the instructions in the training film, Jim tore off his coat, unbuttoned his shirt except for the top button, and flipped the tails up and over his head to protect his face from the oil and flames.

Cold bit at his chest, and darkness closed in. "Ready, Hadley? You've got to come right after me."

"Ready."

"Lord, you promised, 'When thou passest through the waters, I will be with thee.' Help us all." Jim pushed off, sliding fast down the steel hull, friction warming his back and bottom, feet held flat to clear the largest hole possible in the flames.

He plunged into the water, the cold slapping every square inch of his body, squeezing him. Every instinct told him to surface, but training kept him down, as low as he could go.

He kicked out, wrestled the shirt off his face, leveled off, pushed away from the ship.

A muffled set of splashes sounded right behind him. Jim slowed his stroke, waiting for the other men. A hand brushed his leg, and Jim fumbled for it, yanked it, grabbed under the shoulder.

He swam hard, his free arm sweeping wide, legs kicking fast and sharp.

Udell's shoulder jerked in his grasp. Hadley must be surfacing for a breath.

Jim aimed straight up, to the flickering yellow light of the flames on the water. Turn away from the wind. Away, so the flames wouldn't go down his throat. "When thou walkest through the fire, thou shalt not be burned; neither shall the flame kindle upon thee."

He thrashed with his free arm. Wildly. Came up in a black circle of water surrounded by taunting, mocking flames. Jim turned his head away from the wind and sucked in a hot, deep breath, nasty with the taste of burning fuel oil.

He forced Udell out of the water, but the man's head lolled back.

"Over here!" a man shouted, maybe twenty feet away. "Not much farther. You can do it."

Over the flames, Jim caught sight of a life raft with two men inside, reaching for them.

"Ready?" Jim asked Hadley.

The man nodded, slow and thick.

Cold was getting to him, getting to Jim. They had to hurry. "One, two, three!"

Jim thrashed with his arm, then dove, kicking hard, his face and hands and legs numb. Swimming was harder now, more weight behind him. With each stroke, the weight increased, pulling him lower.

Please, Lord, keep Hadley conscious. I can't drag both of them. I can't. He kicked with all his might but felt like he was going nowhere.

His arms, his legs felt solid, immobile. His lungs burned for air. He needed to breathe. He kicked upward, like using tree trunks to stir a giant vat of syrup. Slow. So slow.

Jim broke the surface, drew in a breath. The flames. They were gone. He'd passed them.

"Over here! Over here!" So close, the voice. So close, yet miles away.

Splashing, splashing. A hand grasped his elbow and pulled.

Jim cried out, "Udell! Hadley!"

"Here." Hadley's voice came out weak beside him.

"This one first." Jim shrugged off the hand grabbing him and used his last ounce of strength to swing Udell to the life raft. "Get him."

The men on the raft hauled Udell up inside, then Hadley, then Jim. Like a flopping, dying fish, he lay on the netting, his back in the water, gulping giant frigid breaths.

He watched the scene from a distance, like a play on stage. The Negro sailors on the raft, paddling to the destroyer. A litter being lowered by a line, Homer Udell being rolled inside, strapped in place, and hauled to the destroyer's deck. The lines looped around Hadley's waist, around Jim's waist, the two flopping fish caught and cast onto the shore of the deck.

Men descended on him, tore off his clothes, all of them, scaling him like the dead fish he was. Somehow he felt warmer naked, then someone threw a blanket around him, and someone else tipped back his chin and forced a cup of rum down his throat, hot, burning, making him cough, making him vomit seawater and fuel oil. Then more rum came down, warm and woozy.

He liked the rum, liked the blanket, liked the warmth.

"These two are fine," a gravelly voice said, an unfamiliar voice. "Get 'em down to the wardroom to warm up."

Two men pulled him to standing. Jim's knees buckled, but he caught himself, forced his granite legs to walk, his naked legs.

How could he go to the wardroom? There was a protocol for how an officer dressed in the wardroom, and Jim found himself giggling like a girl, shaking, laughing at his hairy naked legs. "I'm not dressed for dinner."

"Told you. He's fine."

"Sounds loopy to me." The men helped Jim forward, down the hatch, down the passageway, and into the wardroom.

Half the room was set up like a medical ward. Homer Udell lay on a table with pharmacist's mates working on him, and other men lay on cots receiving first aid. The rest of the room was filled with men wrapped in blankets, familiar faces.

"Jim!" Arch grasped him in a bear hug. "Jim, old boy."

Thank God his friend made it. "You're not dressed for dinner either."

Arch burst out laughing. "Neither is Durant, so we're all right."

"I have to sit." Jim's legs gave way, and he sat on the deck and arranged the blanket around his legs.

Arch sat next to him, then Mitch Hadley.

"Hadley, my buddy." Jim reached his hand out of the blanket and shook the man's hand. "Glad you made it."

Hadley shook his head, his wet dark hair sticking up in all directions. "Blacked out at the last minute. Don't remember coming on board."

"But here we are."

"Yes, here we are."

"There you are." Lt. Cdr. Calvin Durant glowered down at Jim.

He would have looked more formidable if he weren't dressed in nothing but a blanket with his hair sticking out like angel wings on either side of his balding head.

Jim saluted with his free arm. "Ensign James Avery, reporting for my court-martial."

"I ought to, you know." Durant's glare didn't dim. "I ought to have you keelhauled, run up the yardarm, and flogged for good measure."

"I agree, sir." Jim tucked his shivering arm back inside the cozy blanket. "But first, tell me how many of the men survived. Udell? Is he going to make it?"

The captain gazed at the operating table. "They're amputating both feet, but he should survive."

"And the others?" Jim glanced around, saw Mack Gillis, Hank.

Durant turned back, his gaze firm. "Nine men survived from that gun mount. Only one didn't make it. I'm told he was already dead."

Jim sagged back in relief. They made it. Whatever punishment he received was worth it. Even if only one man had survived, it would have been worth it. For that matter, even if he and every man in that gun mount had perished, it still would have been worth the effort.

"Mr. Avery. Mr. Hadley." Durant lifted his chin and looked down his nose at them. "I have to write you up for disobeying my orders, but I'm also putting you in for medals. You were brave, bold, compassionate, and showed the strong independent thought I like to see in officers."

Jim gathered his blanket tighter and nodded his chattering chin. "Thank you, sir."

Durant walked away. "Fine officers, indeed."

42

Boston

Mary's heart jammed into her throat, choking off her breath and her hope. Above her, the dark scaffolding framed a figure on the wharf.

"Is that our Miss Stirling?" Mr. Fiske asked. "Didn't I warn you to stop poking your nose where it doesn't belong? Didn't I say I'd hate to see you hurt? It's a shame you walked in on Winslow as he was committing sabotage. A shame he had to shoot you before he fell to his death."

He stretched out his arm, his gun.

Mary pressed hard against the wall, pulling Bauer's body with her.

A shot cracked the air. A bullet blasted past, pinged off the hull beside her.

She screamed and hunkered against the wet granite, sheltering beneath a beam, raising Mr. Bauer's head out of the water. Next to her, Mr. Winslow's eyes were white and wild.

"Go ahead and hide," Mr. Fiske said. "I can wait. Eventually the water will bring you up to me. Or you'll drown."

"I can't swim," Mr. Winslow muttered.

Water soaked her to the chest, and fear and cold seized her

muscles. Why had she stuck her neck out and come down here? Why? Not only had she failed to save Mr. Winslow or Mr. Bauer, but now she'd die too.

A savage sensation knifed through her. Why not just stick her neck out all the way and get it blown off? At least this nightmare would end.

No one was coming to save her. No one even knew she was here.

Except God.

The tremors slowed, the knifing dulled. God knew she was here. God was with her. God could send the FBI or the Marines or a legion of angels. And if he didn't, she'd be home with him in heaven within the hour.

She closed her eyes. *Lord, be with me. Help me. Show me what to do. And if you'd like to send the FBI or the Marines, all three of us would appreciate it.*

The Marines . . .

Mary's eyes eased open. The gunshot. The Marines must have heard it, probably wondered what it was. But now in the silence, they'd return to their evening routine in the barracks, oblivious.

Another gunshot. Or two, or three. That might get their attention.

For once, Mary Stirling needed to put herself on display.

A sense of peace and certainty flooded her faster than the waters filling the dry dock. Waters that rose to her armpits.

"Mr. Winslow?" she said in her lowest voice. "Hold Mr. Bauer, keep his face above water. I'm going to draw his fire, alert the Marines."

"What? No. It should be me."

Mary shifted the unconscious man over. "No time for chivalry. Besides, I can swim."

Mr. Fiske laughed, a hard, mocking sound. "What are you plotting? You can't escape."

"That's what you think!" Mary yelled. She gulped air, dove beneath the stinging-cold water and swam, scrambling between scaffold beams.

Let Fiske think she was making a break for it, abandoning the two men.

A muffled roar. A flash of light zipped through the water ahead of her. Two bullets down. Four or fewer to go.

Her numb hands found a crossbeam. She tucked her legs beneath her and popped up for a breath.

Another shot. The wood exploded in front of her. She spun her face away. Splinters slashed her cheek.

If only she could make him waste the final three bullets without getting killed. A big breath, and down she went, bumping beams, her skirt sodden and heavy about her thighs.

A shot, and a bullet churned up water beside her.

She fumbled for a beam, but it was underwater now. She'd have to expose herself to breathe. Slowly, silently, she eased toward the wall and surfaced.

The wall edged away from her. The stairs.

What once had been her goal now could mean her death. Fiske could come down the stairs and shoot her point-blank. She plunged underwater and headed back the way she came, her lungs screaming.

Up for air. Her heart thudded in her ears, every muscle shook, her hair fell in clammy streams down her cheeks. Her hat—she'd lost it somewhere.

"Miss Stirling!" Mr. Winslow cried. "He's slipping. I—I can't hold him much longer."

"What do you care, Winnie?" Fiske called. "He's a Kraut. Thought you hated them."

"Who are you calling a Kraut?" Another voice rose, angry and male.

Who was that? Mary held her breath.

A shot, a thump, a cry, a thud.

"He's not a Kraut. He's a good man, unlike you. To think I trusted you, looked up to you."

"Ira Kaplan." A smile competed with the tremble in Mary's lips. He must have arrived at the Bauer home for dinner and grown as suspicious as Mary had.

Mr. Fiske cried out.

"Take that," Kaplan shouted. More thumps. "That's for framing Bauer. That's for putting me in jail. That's for the *Atwood* and all the sailors you could've killed. That's for—"

Whatever was happening, it sounded like Kaplan was winning.

Now to help Mr. Winslow. He hugged a beam with one arm and supported Bauer's head with another.

"Hurry, Miss Stirling."

She worked her way over, her arms and legs no longer feeling the bumps. Her feet couldn't touch the ground, but she propped them on a beam, grabbed another overhead, and lifted Mr. Bauer. Shouldn't the cold alone have awakened him?

"Hands up! Both of you! Now!"

Mary's lungs expanded with joy and hope, cool and fresh. "Agent Sheffield! The FBI's here. Thank you, God. Thank you."

"It's Fiske," Kaplan shouted. "He's the saboteur. Not me. He's the one."

"We know. Get off him so we can lock him up."

The beam beneath Mary's feet shifted and another groaned. "Agent Sheffield! We're down here."

"Miss Stirling?"

"Winslow's injured and can't swim, and Bauer's unconscious. We need help and now."

"You—cuff him. You two—can you swim? How about a rope? This is a stinking shipyard. Where on earth's a rope when you need one?"

Several men ran down the stairs and splashed their way over. Marines.

The FBI, the Marines, and Mr. Kaplan as well. Mary broke out in strange, shaking, loud laughter. She couldn't stop. When God answered a prayer, he answered it abundantly.

★ ★ ★

Tuesday, November 25, 1941

A podium. An audience. A clatter of photographers and journalists. Why did that frighten Mary more than a flooding dry dock?

In front of that dry dock, Mary sat on a chair to the side of the podium, waiting for the press conference. She clutched Quintessa's gloved hand. "Thank you for coming with me."

"It's the least I could do." Quintessa shuddered. "When you didn't come home last night, I panicked, and then the call from the hospital . . . oh, Mary, you could have died."

"I didn't. God was with us."

"You were willing to sacrifice your life for those men." Quintessa's voice dropped low.

"I couldn't let them die." She had to shake off the attention. "Speaking of sacrifice, you're the one who took a day off work so close to Christmas just to be with me."

"Mr. Garrett understood. I was overdue. It wasn't a sacrifice." She bit her lip, and her eyes looked dark, even in the frosty sunshine. "You'd sacrifice anything for me, wouldn't you?"

Mary already had. Although giving up a man who didn't love her hardly qualified as a sacrifice. "Why wouldn't I? You've been such a good friend to me, all my life. I'd do anything for you, but I know you'd do the same for me."

Quintessa glanced away, the same quiet distance she'd shown the past few weeks, so unlike her.

Mr. Pennington came to the microphone with Agents Sheffield and Hayes, and Rear Adm. William Tarrant, commandant of the Boston Navy Yard.

Mary gripped her purse in her lap. *Please, Lord. Don't let them call me to the stage.*

However, the prayer felt futile. Mary huddled inside her red coat and shivered as Mr. Pennington introduced Agent Sheffield.

The FBI agent went to the microphone, looking as small and pale and rumpled and un-agent-like as ever. "I am pleased to announce that the sabotage case here at Boston Navy Yard is closed. Last night we arrested Mr. Frank Fiske, a leadingman here."

Flashbulbs popped, and journalists scribbled notes.

"Mr. Fiske has pleaded guilty to multiple charges—placing gasoline in a champagne bottle at a launching ceremony, hiding a bomb on the destroyer USS *Atwood*, planting a crate of bomb-making equipment in the basement of Mr. Weldon Winslow, altering blueprints so as to sabotage ship construction, framing individuals, flooding this dry dock with the intent to destroy two ships under construction, and the attempted murders of Mr. Weldon Winslow, Mr. Heinrich Bauer, and Miss Mary Stirling."

Hands shot up among the journalists. "Agent Sheffield—"

"Our investigation was long and complex." The agent plowed ahead with his statement as he had with the investigation. "We are indebted to everyone at the Navy Yard, from the commandant on down, for their complete cooperation and access."

"What about—"

"We are especially indebted to Miss Mary Stirling." The agent motioned her up to the podium.

Prayer request denied, but how could she complain after the Lord sent the FBI, the Marines, and Mr. Kaplan too?

Mary stood, her legs still wobbly after last night's ordeal, and she coaxed her feet forward.

Good practice for the Christmas pageant, not even two weeks away. Then she'd be free to escape Boston and the attention and the humiliation of a broken heart. Rejoicing for Jim and Quintessa would be easier from a distance. Why should she torture herself watching them fall in love?

Agent Sheffield put his arm around Mary's shoulder and pulled her behind the podium. "Over the past few months, this little lady has made herself both indispensable and annoying."

The journalists laughed and snapped pictures.

Mary forced herself to smile. After all, she wasn't up there due to improper pride, putting herself above others. No, this was appropriate pride in a job well done with the Lord's guidance and help.

Agent Sheffield squeezed her shoulder. "Miss Stirling aided us with her keen sense of observation, attention to detail, and even a dose of womanly intuition. Her insight and analysis led her here last night, and her courageous deeds saved the lives of two men. We are indebted to her."

More applause, more flashbulbs, and as soon as Agent Sheffield released her shoulder to join the applause, Mary gave everyone a gracious nod and returned to her seat.

No nausea. No mortification. No fall. She'd survived.

Quintessa took her arm. "You were wonderful. Hard to believe you're the same girl who faked illness and stayed home from high school graduation so you wouldn't have to cross the stage."

Mary closed her eyes against the memory. How many good things in life had she missed due to fear?

She set her jaw and opened her eyes. "Never again."

43

Saturday, December 6, 1941

Jim strode up Monument Avenue, past dozens of people out for a Saturday stroll. The only outrage he'd heard in Boston was over the American League's Most Valuable Player vote. Joe DiMaggio of the New York Yankees with his 56-game hitting streak had been selected over Ted Williams of the Boston Red Sox with his .406 batting average, and it was wrong, all wrong.

Never mind that in the past two weeks the USS *Atwood* and two more American merchant ships had been sunk. Dozens of men killed in an undeclared war, and no one seemed to care.

He paused in front of Mary's apartment building. The survivors of the *Atwood* had been distributed among the destroyers escorting Convoy ON-39 to Halifax. Back in Boston this morning, they'd been granted thirty-day survivor's leaves while awaiting new assignments. Jim had accompanied Homer Udell to the hospital. The man was morose, but he was stubborn and smart and hardworking. In time, he'd flourish, same as Lillian had.

Lillian now had a job, thanks to Mary's tip. Starting in January, she'd work at Dixon's Drugs here in Charlestown. It would be good to have her here, even better to see her happy.

First things first. Jim had waves to make, first with Quintessa, then with Mary.

His feet thudded up the stairs, and his finger felt like lead on the doorbell.

The door opened. Mary stood there in a deep blue dress, her dark hair loose on her shoulders, her eyes like stars.

"Mary." Her name tumbled out of his mouth, perfect in its simplicity.

"Oh, Jim." She clapped her hand to her chest. "You're alive. I heard about the *Atwood*, heard—thank God, you're alive. Arch?"

"He's fine." All he wanted was to hold her. He needed her, needed her peace and gentleness, and he moved forward to claim her.

But she stepped back and called down the hallway, "Quintessa! He's here. Jim's here."

A bedroom door flew open, and a blonde bullet aimed for him, wrapped her arms around him. "Thank God, you're all right. I was sick with worry. When I heard . . . and then . . ." Sobs heaved Quintessa's shoulders.

He had no choice but to embrace her. "I'm all right."

But he wasn't, not with Mary walking away down the hallway. Not now. Not when he needed her most.

"I was beside myself," Quintessa said. "First what happened with Mary, and then your ship. Too much to bear."

"Mary?" Over Quintessa's head, he pinned his gaze on Mary. "What happened to you?"

She flapped her hand and stepped back. "It was nothing."

"Nothing?" Quintessa rolled halfway out of Jim's embrace and wiped her eyes. "You tracked down the saboteur, got him arrested, saved two men's lives, and were almost killed. I don't call that nothing."

"What?" Concern for Mary mixed with pride in whatever she'd done, plus a zing of satisfaction that he had an excuse to keep her in the room. "Come on. Like it or not, you're telling me the story. Let's sit down."

He shrugged off the overcoat over his new dress blues, marched into the living room, and plopped onto the couch. Quintessa snuggled beside him and clutched his arm.

Inside, he groaned. How could he have that long emotional talk when the girl was already a wreck? That would be cruel.

Mary hovered beside the couch, twisting her hands together. If only she were the one snuggled up to him.

Jim pointed to the armchair in the bay window. "You're not getting off the hook. Remember, I was there the day this whole case started. I've heard all about your investigation until recently. Don't you think I want to know how it ended?"

Mary sat, the afternoon sun lighting the edges of her hair. "Don't you think we want to hear how you survived the sinking?"

He chuckled. "Trying to deflect attention from yourself. I know your tricks, young lady. Besides, my father taught me manners. Ladies first."

Over the next half hour, Jim prodded her with questions, and she revealed the details, relaxing before him, returning to the easy camaraderie of their friendship. He leaned forward, his forearms on his knees, and Quintessa broke her hold on his arm.

All he noticed was Mary. Her feminine gestures, her sweet voice, and her measured words. Her modesty and intelligence and courage. Her care for others and her persistence in the face of opposition. She'd used her gifts as God intended, her sails hoisted and filled, the most beautiful thing he'd ever seen.

His love for her pressed against the bars of his rib cage, longing to escape, to reach her.

"There. My story is told." Mary sat back with a satisfied look. "Now it's your turn."

"Yes, your turn."

Jim glanced over his shoulder.

Quintessa leaned back against the couch cushion, her arms folded over her stomach, her gaze unswerving. Dissecting him.

She knew he loved Mary, didn't she? Would this make the big talk easier or harder?

"What *is* your story, Jim?" Quintessa's lips bent into a tight smile.

He shrugged. "I can't say much due to censorship. A U-boat torpedoed us. The ship was lost along with fifty-two good men. But Arch and I survived, and we're back."

"That's all you can say?" Blonde eyebrows lifted.

"And the water was cold. Really cold."

Mary gasped and sprang to her feet. "Oh goodness, the time. I have to get to the church."

Jim frowned. "On a Saturday afternoon?"

"The Christmas pageant."

"That's tonight?" He'd actually made it back in time, but not in a way he ever would have wished for. "I'd better let you ladies get ready."

"Yes, you'd better." Quintessa took his arm and hustled him out the door. "Are you coming?"

"Yes. Arch went home to Connecticut for a few days, but I'll see if any of the other men want to come."

"See you there." Quintessa shut the door on him.

Yep. She knew he loved Mary, all right.

★ ★ ★

While the choir sang "O Come, O Come, Emmanuel" from up in the gallery, Mary trudged down the aisle of Park Street Church, one hand supporting her pillow belly, the other clinging to Ed Fanarolli's arm, her Joseph.

Hundreds of eyes watched her, burning her like welders' torches.

Her gaze latched onto Jim. He sat on the aisle with Quintessa and several other men in navy blue. A dozen emotions whirled inside her, topped by the intense relief that he'd survived, the release of the burden of worry she'd carried for almost two weeks.

Jim grinned at her, meant to be encouraging, no doubt, but only a piercing reminder of their past friendship and a future that could never be.

Quintessa watched too, her eyes round and cool, as they'd been all afternoon. She was jealous and with good reason. She must have detected Mary's love for Jim. Mary had talked to him for over half an hour. How could she conceal her feelings that long? She'd failed, and now her best friend thought she wanted to steal her boyfriend.

This was why Mary had avoided spending time with the two of them. This was why Mary needed to leave Boston. Now.

"No room at the inn. No room at the inn. But please use my stable."

While the choir sang "O Little Town of Bethlehem," Mary disappeared into the stable, the curtain door dropped, and she wiggled the pillow out from under her robe.

She'd fulfilled her two weeks' notice at the Navy Yard. Mr. Pennington asked her to stay through the launching ceremonies on December 10, but she refused. She'd planned each detail and delegated each responsibility. Everything would run fine without her.

Tomorrow afternoon, she'd fly home. She still hadn't told anyone but Mr. Pennington about her departure. Quintessa and Yvette would ask too many questions. Mary needed to be honest, but for the sake of peace in the apartment, confessing her love for Jim and her decision to step out of Quintessa's way should wait for the last minute.

After church, she'd make her confession, and then she'd depart on her adventure. She'd decided to splurge on a cab and a ferry to Boston Airport, then her first airplane flight—land, sea, and air. After a few weeks at home for Christmas, she'd start her new life in Michigan. Not an escape, she kept telling herself, but a grand adventure.

The choir hushed, and a light shone above the stable. Ed drew back the curtain, revealing Mary by the manger, and she folded her hands over her heart and gazed adoringly at the baby doll in his swaddling clothes.

The eyes of the congregation ripped into her and sliced through her veneer of confidence.

Up in the gallery, Claudia, Bertha, and Edith sang "Angels We Have Heard on High." Despite Mrs. Gunderson's coaching, Claudia overpowered the older ladies, trilling and cascading and calling attention to herself.

Was Mary any less proud than Claudia? Her picture in the newspaper after the FBI's press conference? The caption that read "Miss Mary Stirling accepts the adulation of the crowd"? It made her ill.

And the way she'd been so friendly with Jim this afternoon, letting down her guard, telling every element of the story. Wasn't that a form of pride? She'd sought Jim's attention, and she'd taken twisted pleasure in stealing his gaze from Quintessa. Oh, she had. She most definitely had.

Pride, pride, pride.

The song ended, Claudia's voice lifting the last high note for all to admire.

Mary's cue.

Her throat tightened and her stomach roiled, but she scooped the doll from the manger and took slow steps forward on the narrow rickety platform before the entire congregation.

She'd been careful to use the restroom before the performance and to avoid drinking anything all day, but pressure built in her bladder, taunting her.

The musical introduction began.

Mary stood there in her blue robe, baby Jesus in her arms, and her throat clamped shut. She couldn't sing. Not one word.

Her head felt light, her stomach queasy. She swayed to the side and barely caught herself.

The piano paused, played a few chords, and began again. Mary had missed her cue.

Soft murmurs rose from the audience, and a soprano Claudia-like titter sounded from the gallery.

For the first time in her life, she longed for a spotlight, not to focus eyes on her, but to blind her to the faces, all the faces, so concerned and sympathetic and—

And Jim looked straight at her, his expression earnest, and he moved his hands up and down as if hauling on a rope, as if hoisting sails.

Could she? Should she?

Movement by Mrs. Gunderson's music stand caught her eye. The choir director looked pointedly at Mary and opened and shut her hand like a blinking light.

"Let your light so shine before men, that they may see your good works, and glorify your Father which is in heaven." Not so Mary would be glorified, but God.

She turned back to Jim's encouraging face. If she sang

well, God would be praised through the timeless beauty of the music and lyrics.

If she didn't sing, the pageant would be ruined, and what would people talk about? They'd talk about Mary Stirling! Refusing to sing would be the worst form of pride, choosing self over God, choosing fear over faith.

The musical chords built slowly, surely.

Mary drew a deep breath and a deeper prayer.

"Silent night! holy night!" Her voice came out weak and quavering.

"All is calm, all is bright." Hesitant, but stronger.

"Round yon virgin mother and Child." The quiver evened out, and her volume built.

"Holy Infant, so tender and mild." Mary gazed down at the doll's sweet painted features and stroked the porcelain cheek. "Sleep in heavenly peace. Sleep in heavenly peace."

Her voice soared to the high notes and caressed the low notes, with a waver that sounded right, poignant. A peasant girl feeling both the weight and the joy of her gift, her insufficiency to do God's will and her determination to do so despite her weakness, through her weakness.

Mary's vision blurred. She tipped her face to heaven and launched into the second verse, overcome by her own insufficiency, her own determination, the joy of accepting her own weakness and the Lord's strength.

Through her singing, maybe she could help others praise the Lord, and wouldn't that be glorious?

The final verse seemed too short and fleeting to convey the richness of who God was, but her role was complete, and others had songs to sing.

Mary returned to the stable while the shepherds came down the aisle, singing "While Shepherds Watched Their Flocks by Night."

She returned baby Jesus to his manger and arranged his

blanket, her smile heartfelt and genuine. In Michigan, she'd wear her red coat and join a new choir and do her very best on the job. Whatever else God asked her to do, she'd do it without flinching.

Ed gave her a concerned look and a handkerchief. Why?

Her cheeks tingled with happy tears. She hadn't even noticed. She laughed and dried her cheeks. "The joy of the Lord is my strength."

44

Sunday, December 7, 1941

Today was the day. No putting it off one moment longer. The church service seemed to last ten hours, and Jim fidgeted in the pew. How could he concentrate on the sermon with Quintessa beside him and Mary in the gallery behind him? How could he sit still when he needed to talk to Quintessa right now, end this charade, and declare his own path?

When the recessional played, Jim stifled a sigh of relief and led Quintessa outside onto the sidewalk.

"It's so cold today. I smell snow in the air." Quintessa chattered about the weather without a break long enough for Jim to ask her to lunch.

He shifted from one foot to the other, his gaze darting between the chatty blonde and the church door. Soon a quiet brunette emerged, wrapped in a red coat.

"Miss Stirling?" A middle-aged lady took Mary by the elbow. "You sang beautifully last night. So moving."

The woman's husband set his hand on his wife's shoulder. "That's all Nellie could talk about—how you made her cry."

Jim stood close, ready to rescue Mary if needed.

But Mary smiled and covered Nellie's hand with her own. "I'm glad you enjoyed the pageant. Everyone did a fine job."

"There she is." A woman in a very tall hat squeezed into the circle on Mary's other side. "Last night—that was the most beautiful thing. Don't you agree, Nellie?"

"Certainly. How you stumbled and hesitated—it reminded me that Mary was just a girl, like any of us. She must have been terrified, but she overcame her fears and obeyed the Lord."

Tall-hat Lady patted her chest and blinked. "You made me cry, young lady."

Jim had to smile. He'd heard an awful lot of feminine sniffles in the audience after Mary sang.

She smiled, both modest and confident. "I understand her. I stumbled and hesitated because of my own fears, but the Lord gave me the joy and strength to obey, to sing."

Jim's chest ached, he loved her so much. When would he finally have the chance to tell her?

"Well, it was simply lovely. Thank you, dear." Nellie squeezed Mary's arm, and the trio departed.

Mary turned to Jim and Quintessa and made a funny face. "Perhaps I should have worn Arch's curly blonde wig this morning."

Jim laughed. "Nonsense. You're doing great."

Then his breath hitched. He needed to talk to Quintessa alone. Now. That meant he needed to be rude to Mary.

Mary looked up at Jim, her eyebrows drawn together. "Um, Jim, I don't mean to be rude, but could I have Quintessa to myself for lunch? I need to talk to her about something."

Alarm jolted through him. "Actually, I was going to ask you the same thing." He faced Quintessa. "I really need to talk to you. Today."

Quintessa let out a nervous giggle. "Gracious, I've never been so popular."

"Please?" Mary asked.

"I'm sorry, sweetie, but you and I have all afternoon to chat at the apartment. Besides, I haven't had any time alone with Jim since he returned."

"Oh." Mary chewed on her lips. "I—I didn't mean to interfere."

"You never do, sweet Mary." Quintessa clutched her in a hug. "You never do."

Mary nodded on Quintessa's shoulder and glanced up to Jim. "Good-bye, Quintessa. Good-bye, Jim." Her tone sank low, as if wishing them farewell forever.

Then she headed for the subway, her chin tucked to her chest.

He'd probably hurt her feelings, but he'd deal with that later, along with everything else.

First, Quintessa. Jim motioned to a coffee shop across the street. "Will that do?"

"Sure," she said, her voice high and clipped.

At the coffee shop, Jim and Quintessa slipped into a booth. The waitress brought coffee and menus, and Jim took a sip of his coffee.

Quintessa didn't pick up her menu. "Let me guess. You don't love me anymore."

Jim choked on his coffee. At least she hadn't skirted the issue. He swallowed and wiped his lips with his napkin. "I never really did. I admit I was infatuated with you in high school, but it wasn't love."

Quintessa traced the edge of the menu with one finger. "You aren't even infatuated with me anymore, are you?"

"No." He kept his voice gentle but firm.

She blinked a few times. "Because you love Mary."

Jim exhaled a relaxing breeze of truth. "Yes, I do. Very much."

"Have you told her?"

"No. I planned to tell her when my ship came to port in November, but . . ."

"But I was there, throwing myself at you." She pressed her fingertips between her eyebrows, her head bowed.

Jim gave her a half smile. "I wouldn't call it that."

"I would. I was so blind, so selfish. Something was brewing between you two, and I came barreling in, full of plans to fulfill your dreams. How arrogant! I just assumed you'd still be interested in me, never thought you two might be interested in each other."

Something jumped in his chest. "Do you think she's interested in me?"

"I—I don't know. She's always guarded her emotions. But I never asked, never even gave her a chance to tell me whether she loved you. How could she when I proclaimed I'd come to Boston to make your dreams come true?" Quintessa groaned and rested her head in her hands.

Jim smashed his lips together. So that's what happened. "If she loved me, she would have told you."

"Would she?" Quintessa rummaged in her purse and pulled out a handkerchief. "Not Mary. She'd never interfere. That isn't like her. She always puts others first, puts me first. She—she helped me, insisted you and I have time alone together, insisted . . ." She held the handkerchief still on her cheek, the tears making her eyes even greener.

Jim frowned. "Insisted . . . ?"

She patted her eyes with the handkerchief. "I thought it was odd how she avoided us. After all, weren't you two great friends before I arrived? Then after I arrived, she fled whenever you came over."

"Do you think—"

"Oh, I don't know. I took her at her word, that she wanted to give us privacy. But what if seeing us together broke her heart?" She let out a low moan. "Oh goodness. Oh dear. She did that for me. She—she sacrificed for me."

Hope rose from his heart and threatened to fill his head, but he tamped it down. "We don't know that for sure."

"I got in the way. It's all my fault."

"Don't be so hard on yourself. I never told her how I feel, and if she's interested in me, she never told me either." Except with one luscious kiss.

"That's my fault too." She pressed her hand to her forehead, the handkerchief draped over her eyes. "When I was in Chicago, she talked about you so much in her letters, I asked if anything was happening between you. She said she didn't think so because you didn't act like you did around me in high school."

Jim's jaw clenched. "You mean, I didn't act like a fool."

Quintessa nodded. "I told her if you were interested, everyone in town would know because you wear your emotions on your sleeve."

"Not anymore, I don't." If only he had.

"Oh dear. There's more. You're going to hate me. You're both going to hate me." She slid the handkerchief over her eyes. "I lied to her. When you told me you'd kissed her, I was jealous and angry, and I acted like a spoiled brat. I wanted to test her. So I . . . I told her you'd kissed me too. I told myself it wasn't really a lie, because you'd kissed me on the forehead, but it was a lie, a peevish little lie."

Jim puffed air into his cheeks. Mary definitely thought he and Quintessa were an item.

"Oh, Jim, I'm so sorry. I made a mess of things."

"So did I. Believe me, the mess is all my fault."

"Ready to order?" The waitress stood next to the table.

"I'm not hungry." Quintessa looked at Jim, misery in her eyes. "And you need to find Mary and talk to her right now."

Jim gave the waitress a sheepish look. "Sorry. Just coffee."

She rolled her eyes and strode away. "Coffee don't pay the rent, pal."

Jim slipped out three dollars, more than he would have paid for lunch, then set his hand on Quintessa's arm. "Stay as long as you want, and—and thanks."

"Tell her I'm sorry. Please?"

"I will." But he had other things to say first.

Jim jogged down the street to the subway station. People clogged the stairwell, he couldn't find the right change, the ticket lady took her sweet time, and he missed the train.

The next train took even sweeter time. Then it stopped in North Station far longer than necessary, and the conductor apologized for the delay but wouldn't explain, and Jim seriously considered walking the rest of the way.

When the train inched into City Square Station, Jim couldn't find a cab, so he marched up the hill to Mary's apartment.

Now that he wanted to make waves, he didn't want to wait a minute longer. But what to tell her and how?

If only he could just kiss her and let his lips do the talking. But since she thought he was Quintessa's boyfriend, a kiss would make the situation even messier. No, he had to talk.

Floating had always seemed easiest, but this time he'd floated onto the rocks. Quintessa and Mary had charted his course, and he'd let them. No more of that.

Jim pounded on the apartment door, his breath white in front of him.

Yvette opened the door.

"May I speak to Mary?"

Yvette studied him. "You missed her. She left."

Jim groaned and glanced down the road. "When will she be back?"

"She won't. She's moving to Michigan."

"What?" Jim gaped at her. "Michigan?"

"She has a new job, and she left ten minutes ago."

350

"That can't be." He shook his head hard. "Quintessa didn't say anything."

"She doesn't know. I didn't know either." She stepped to the mail table and picked up an envelope. "When I came home from mass, Mary was packing her trunk. She wanted to tell Quintessa over lunch, but she couldn't, so she left a letter."

Jim reached for it.

Yvette drew back. "It is for Quintessa, not you."

The coffee churned in Jim's belly. "Why didn't she tell us? Why would she keep it a secret? That doesn't make sense."

Yvette held the envelope behind her back, her eyes dark. "If she will not tell you, neither will I."

"She left." Jim rubbed his hands down his thighs. "The train. Which station? Do you know?"

"She's flying. She wanted an adventure by land, sea, and air."

Jim blinked, but everything looked murky, sounded murky. "Land, sea, and air?"

"Yes. She took a cab to the airport, but she wanted to take the ferry also, to see the city from the water one last time."

"The ferry." Only one ferry ran on the harbor, between downtown Boston and East Boston, where the airport was.

"I know. It is ridiculous. So slow. But she insisted. The taxi driver will drop her off at one terminal, and she'll catch another taxi on the other side. She is wasting money and time."

But that bought Jim time. "Thanks."

He loped down the steps, searched for a cab, couldn't find one, and started walking. Finally, a cab. He hopped inside. "Eastern Avenue Ferry Terminal, please."

The driver nodded and drove away. Slowly. Of all the cab drivers in Boston, Jim had to find one who obeyed the traffic laws.

His foot tapped on the floor of the cab. Why would Mary leave without telling anyone? Only one thought came to mind, but was it just wishful thinking?

What if she did love him? What if seeing him with

Quintessa did break her heart? What if she was fleeing Boston so she wouldn't have to watch them?

What if he'd swallowed too much oil when the *Atwood* sank and he had brain damage?

The taxi drove south onto the Charlestown Bridge. Traffic slowed to a stop. Horns beeped. Jim cranked down his window and leaned his head outside. The El tracks ran down the center of the bridge on two decks, one heading south, the other heading north. Vehicular traffic ran on either side of the tracks.

Ahead of him, drivers stepped out of their cars.

Jim groaned. An accident or something. Swell. Maybe the Lord didn't want him to declare his love after all.

Yet he knew that wasn't true. It was time.

What could he do? Get out of the car, walk past the traffic jam, and hope he found another cab? How long would that take?

Down below on the Charles River, sailboats zipped along, racing sailboats with sleek lines, manned by Harvard boys in dark red sweaters. With a boat like one of those, he could catch any ferry in the world. But he didn't have a boat like that, didn't have any boat at all.

Jim opened the door and marched to the rail of the bridge, his fists balled in his coat pockets, his breath steaming from his nostrils. All this year, he'd worked so hard not to act like a fool. And all along, Mary thought he showed love by acting like a fool. In the end, Jim had made a fool of himself by *not* acting foolish.

"Biggest fool of all time, Avery."

Jim stopped in his tracks. An idea floated into his brain and lodged there, bold and crazy.

If he was a fool, he might as well act like one.

45

Mary leaned against the port rail of the ferry. Across the harbor before her, the Bunker Hill Monument lifted its farewell.

How she'd loved living in its shadow. And how she'd loved working at the Boston Navy Yard with dear Mr. Pennington. Even before the sabotage case, her work had satisfied her. Now she was leaving when everything was settling down, when everyone was beginning to work together again.

Too bad she'd miss having Lillian Avery for a roommate, but Quintessa and Yvette would make her feel welcome.

Mary faced away from Charlestown toward downtown Boston. The wind twirled a lock of hair in front of her face, and she held it back. So chilly today, just above freezing, but it would be far colder in Michigan.

There was the Custom House, and if she used her imagination, she could see Park Street Church. How she'd miss her friends, the choir, and Dr. Ockenga's inspired preaching. So much history in Boston, and she'd loved exploring every bit of it.

A heavy sensation squeezed her chest, but she drew a deep breath to rid herself of it. Yes, she'd loved her life in Boston, but a wonderful new life awaited her in Michigan.

If only this ferry would transport her toward that new life a mite faster. Although she had plenty of time to catch her three o'clock flight, she wanted to move faster, farther.

But the ferry plodded along, barely fluttering the water beneath her. Why, that sailboat would pass them in the blink of an eye. Trim and fast, she sliced through the harbor at a jaunty angle, men at work on sails and helm.

Pain coiled around her heart. Not so long ago, Jim had stood behind her at the helm, guiding her hands, showing her how to sail.

Mary pushed away from the rail and strolled around the stern of the ferry to the starboard side, away from that sleek boat and her bittersweet memories.

If only she could leave her memories behind in Boston. At least at home in Ohio and in her new job in Michigan, she'd form new memories and the old ones would lose their power and their sting.

Meanwhile, Jim and Quintessa could grow in their love without Mary's impedance. How long until she received a wedding invitation? Six months? A year? By then she'd be ready, surely she would. She would attend, she would rejoice with them, and she would wish them well.

Her departure today was a form of blessing on their relationship. Why shouldn't the two people she loved most find love with each other?

A low commotion rose on the port side of the ferry. Mary glanced over her shoulder behind the aft end of the cabin. People gathered at the rail, pointing down to the water, smiling, talking.

Hadn't Mary caught a glimpse of Harvard maroon on the men's sweaters? They were probably up to some college pranks.

She smiled and shook her head, glad to be away from antics and commotion as the frosty air nipped at her cheeks.

"Mother! You have to see." A girl of about fifteen dashed to the lady to Mary's right. "It's so romantic."

"Romantic?" her mother asked.

The girl clapped her hand on the green bow on top of her head and pointed to port. "There's a Navy officer on a sailboat, calling for his girl. I think I'll change my name to Mary."

Mary's heart went into a jitterbug, but it couldn't be Jim. He loved Quintessa and was with her this very moment. Besides, naval officers were a dime a dozen in Boston. As were women named Mary.

The girl dragged her mother to the other side, but Mary remained, studying the Inner Harbor and the waterfront.

The commotion built, and the crowd continued its migration.

Curiosity tugged on Mary. She did love a good romance even if she didn't have one herself. What would it be like to be that other Mary, to have a man chase after her in an extravagant gesture? She would melt, completely dissolve.

With a sigh, she followed the crowd. People lined the rail three or four deep, blocking her view. Through an opening, she glimpsed a bright white sail and a maroon sweater.

"Mary!" A man's voice climbed above the muttering of the crowd. "Mary Stirling!"

Her hand flew to her mouth. Jim? What was he doing? Calling her name? Why on earth?

"I need to find her. Mary! Mary Stirling!"

Oh dear. Maybe something awful had happened to Quintessa and he was trying to track her down. Mary found a slim opening and squeezed closer.

Between two ladies' hats, Mary spotted Jim.

He stood, holding onto the mast, leaning forward, his navy blue overcoat unbuttoned and flapping behind him. He cupped his hand over his mouth. "Mary!"

"What's the matter, sailor boy?" a man called down to him. "What'd you do to break her heart?"

The sailboat tacked away from the ferry, and Jim laughed, big and merry. "Never had the chance to break her heart. Never told her I love her. That's why I need to find her. I need to tell her I love her."

The deck, the whole world pitched beneath Mary's feet. She gasped and hid behind a large brown hat. It couldn't be. It didn't make sense.

"I love you, Mary! Are you there?"

No. No, she wasn't. How could he say he loved her? How could he do this to Quintessa? She'd never taken him for the type of man to dally with two women's hearts, but what else could she think?

Mary reached between the two ladies and gripped the rail for balance. A stew of emotions simmered inside her—anger, confusion, wonder, joy. But how could joy rear its head when this man was breaking her best friend's heart? Did Quintessa know what he was doing?

Oh, she had some questions for Ensign James Avery.

She wormed closer to the rail, then halted. If she answered Jim's call, everyone on the ferry would stare at her. And wasn't this a conversation to have in private? This time, avoiding the spotlight had nothing to do with fear, and everything to do with propriety.

"Mary! Has anyone seen Mary Stirling? About this tall. Dark brown hair and the most beautiful blue eyes you've ever seen, all silvery like moonlight on the ocean."

Mary ducked her chin, breathing hard. That couldn't be Jim. Couldn't be.

"Isn't that sweet?" the lady to Mary's right said.

"The poor lovesick boy," her companion said.

"Mary!" Jim yelled, his voice smaller, farther away. "I can't let you leave Boston without talking to you."

He knew she was leaving. How? Did Quintessa read him her letter, her pathetic letter detailing all her reasons for leaving? And what about Quintessa? What had he done to the poor thing? What had he said to her?

That was it. Attention or no attention, she needed some answers from that man in blue.

The sailboat tacked back toward the ferry.

Mary shouldered her way to the rail. "Excuse me. Excuse me, please. I'm Mary Stirling."

She couldn't believe she was calling attention to herself, but it worked. People fell back from the rail and cleared a path. Gaping at her.

Mary grasped the rail, her stomach wound into a knot tighter than any sailor could tie. "Jim Avery! What do you think you're doing?"

A grin spread over his face, wide and luminous. He took off his cover and held it over his heart. "My Mary."

A sight she'd longed to see and words she'd longed to hear, but how dare he? "I'm not your Mary. What on earth are you doing?"

"What I should have done months ago—telling you I love you."

All the tittering, the pointing, the staring. Mary put it behind her and focused on that adorable, infuriating man. "You shouldn't say such things. What about Quin—"

"No." He shook his head. "I never loved her. How could I when I was already in love with you?"

Mary's head spun, and she pressed her hand to her forehead, but the dizziness intensified. "How could you do this to her? Poor—"

"She's fine. She says to tell you she's sorry. She told me to find you and tell you I love you."

Just when things couldn't get more nonsensical. "I don't understand. I don't. This is crazy."

"I know." Jim swept his arm in a grand gesture. "Isn't it great?"

His exuberance, the glow on his face, the boldness of his actions—for her. Yes, it was great, and a smile sneaked up, but she wrestled it back down. "We need to talk."

His boisterous laugh bounced over the waves. "Yes, we do. Hold on a minute." He leaned over and conferred with the college boys, with much discussion and pointing.

The murmur of the crowd built, even as the space around her increased, everyone trying to get the best view of the woman on display.

Mary put on mental blinders, focusing on the man in the sailboat. So tall and handsome, so intelligent and strong, so thoughtful and enthusiastic. He was everything she ever wanted, everything she could ever want, but too many questions remained. She couldn't let herself get swept away.

Yet the thought of getting swept away into his arms . . . of feeling his kiss on her lips . . .

A tremble ran from her fingers straight to her heart, delightful and giddy and completely illogical.

No. She needed those cold hard facts. Why this sudden declaration when he'd never shown any interest in her?

Down below, Jim and the Harvard boys pointed to a spot, the sails luffing from inattention.

He said he'd never loved Quintessa? How could Mary have misunderstood? He'd been crazy about her in high school, confessed his love this spring, and when Quintessa arrived in Boston, he . . .

What had he done? He'd looked dazed. He'd asked Mary to come with them. He'd asked her about the kiss.

And what had she done? She'd told him the kiss meant nothing, told him his dreams had come true, and hustled them out the door.

Mary groaned. Oh dear. What had she done?

Jim straightened up, the same bright grin on his face, and he pointed toward East Boston. "See that wharf? Just north of where the ferry docks. Meet me there. Take however long you want. I'll wait."

Curiosity and regret would bring her, along with a sliver of residual anger for Quintessa's sake, and sheer, ecstatic hope. "I'll be there."

The boat tacked away, and Jim blew her a kiss.

Mary pressed her fingertips to her lips to blow one back, but stopped herself, her eyes wide.

Jim laughed, winked, snugged his cover back on his head, and sailed away.

She stood alone on the deck, surrounded by an applauding, smiling crowd. First the press conference, then the pageant, and now this. Her greatest fears, her greatest triumphs, and her greatest joys.

Her chin quivered. If she hadn't hoisted her sails, she never would have seen how the Lord could fill them and where he could take her.

No matter what Jim had to say, and no matter what she decided to do about him, she was a different woman, a better woman.

The crowd waited for her.

She turned, lifted a small smile, and headed toward the exit, determined to be first off the ferry. "Excuse me, but I have an officer to interrogate."

46

If she said she'd come, she'd come.

Jim paced on the sailboat to keep warm and to relieve tension. The two Harvard boys had left to see a movie. They'd be back in a couple of hours for their boat, but for now it was Jim's.

He spun and marched aft. Mary would keep her word. But what words would she have for him? Not only was she protective of Quintessa, but Jim had called down loads of attention on her. If Jim were in her shoes, he'd be furious.

But he'd do it again in an instant.

The pier creaked, and Jim wheeled around.

Mary approached, her arms crossed over her stomach, her eyes big, and her mouth small as a button.

Maybe the right gesture would dissolve the awkwardness and pull her straight into his arms. He stepped closer to the pier and held out his hand to her. "Come sail with me."

She stopped ten feet away. "I need answers."

He lowered his hand. "Where would you like me to start?"

"The beginning."

"Let's see. I'm the third of seven children, born in the small town of—"

"Jim!" At least she laughed. "You know what I mean."

He did. His foot nudged a tangled coil of line. Jim squatted and looped it properly, the Navy way. "This spring when I first came to Boston, I enjoyed your friendship, nothing more. I didn't even want a girlfriend, not when I was about to ship out."

"Mm-hmm." No emotion revealed at all. She wouldn't make this easy.

"After the shakedown cruise when we found the bomb, I started to notice how pretty you are, how much I like your company. I wanted to impress you, see if you might be interested. I didn't want to make a fool of myself, so I tried to act suave."

"Suave?"

He glanced at her, one eyebrow high. "As you can see, it was a highly effective campaign."

A glimmer of a smile, but then she drew her mouth in tight.

Jim moved to the next coil of line. For experienced yachtsmen, the Harvard boys were sloppy. "All summer I floated, waiting to see what would happen. I should have kissed you, should have told you I was falling in love. By the time I decided to act, it was too late. There we were on the pier, my shipmates hounding me to kiss you. Nothing I wanted more, but how could I when you can't stand public attention?"

No words, no movement from Mary.

Jim grabbed a rag on the deck and went to work on the brass. "Then you had to kiss me because I was too stupid to kiss you first. But I was determined. The night we returned I planned to march into your apartment and say, 'Ever since we said good-bye, I couldn't wait to say hello,' and then I'd kiss you and tell you I love you. If you weren't interested, I'd find out right then, but if you were—"

A soft gulping sound from Mary.

He looked up.

She pressed her fist to her mouth, and her eyes were red.

Jim needed to hold her. He stood and beckoned with his fingers. "Come here, sweetheart."

She shook her head. "Continue."

No more deck swabbing. He leaned his shoulder against the mast, flipped back his unbuttoned overcoat, and sank his hands into his trouser pockets. "But when I came back, Quintessa was there, gushing over me, and you told me the kiss meant nothing and you were so happy my dreams had come true. But they hadn't. You're my dream."

Another gulp. Mary ducked her chin and pressed her hand so hard over her mouth, her cheeks bulged out on either side. Somehow she looked more beautiful than ever. Her distress showed she cared, maybe cared a lot.

"I believed you." His voice came out too husky, and he cleared his throat. "But I didn't want to be with Quintessa. I wanted to be with you. Today after church, I told her."

Mary peeked at him over her hand, her eyes wary and worried.

He gave her a soft smile. "She'd already figured it out. She knows I love you. She feels awful that she got in the way, that she presumed to know what I wanted, what you wanted."

Mary closed her eyes and shook her head, but what did that mean?

Jim charged ahead. "We have her blessing. That is, if you're at all interested, if you want anything to do with me after the spectacle I made on this sailboat."

"Oh, Jim." Her voice came out muffled, and she lowered her hand. "That spectacle was the sweetest, most extravagant, most romantic thing I've ever seen."

If he didn't get her in his arms in the next five minutes, he'd explode. "Come here, sweetheart. Please, come here."

Mary stood up tall and coiled her fingers around her purse strap. "You need some answers too."

"Sure." He shrugged. "But can you come down here and give them to me?"

She chewed on the lips he wanted to kiss, her face competing with her coat for redness.

He held out his hand. He'd already laid down his heart. What more did he have to lose?

In a flash, she took his hand, hopped into the sailboat like an old sea salt, and threw her arms around his middle, her face burrowed into his shoulder.

Jim wrapped his arms around her as warm contentment wrapped around him.

"Oh, Jim, I love you so much. I have for so long, but I didn't think—I never thought—"

"Shh." He kissed her forehead. He didn't need to hear one more word from her.

"I never thought you were interested. You didn't act . . . didn't act . . ."

"Foolish."

She nodded against his shoulder. "So when Quintessa came—"

"You don't have to say anything more. We figured it out. You sacrificed for Quintessa's sake, for my sake—or what you thought I wanted anyway. I wish someone had asked my opinion."

Mary clutched at the back of his coat. "How can you ever forgive me?"

He brushed his lips down her forehead, nudging her face up. "What's to forgive? I'm at fault too. I never told you how I felt. But now you've told me you love me. That's the only thing I want to hear. That and the answer to my question."

She eased back and looked him in the eye. "Your question?"

Jim cocked his head toward the pier. "The one I asked earlier. Will you sail with me?"

Her eyes cleared, and her lips curved in a smile. "Aye aye, sir. Chart your course, and I'll be there."

Holding her in his arms wasn't enough. He leaned closer and tilted his head.

Her pupils widened, and her lips parted.

He knew the taste of her lips, and he longed for them, but first he had to attend to business. "For the record, I am about to kiss you, and it will not be just a friendly kiss. No, ma'am. In case there's any confusion, I intend to kiss you passionately because I love you and I—"

His words caught. How could he tell her he wanted to spend the rest of his life with her? Not yet. He swallowed hard. "And I—I never want you to doubt my love again. Are we clear?"

"Aye aye." Her voice was so breathy, so irresistibly close. "But that's an awful lot of talking for a man in the throes of passion."

His smile edged up, but he wouldn't take back one word. All year he'd failed to communicate, and so had she, and he didn't want to leave any room for doubt. "Too much talking, eh?"

"Uh-huh." She curled her hands up around his shoulder blades and drew him closer.

Jim brushed the backs of his fingers across her damp cheek, ran his hand into her night-dark hair, tipped up her face, and gazed into the silvery blue depths of her eyes. "Now I suppose you'll say I'm doing too much adoring and not enough kissing."

"You . . . are."

Well, if she insisted. Jim closed the gap and kissed her. He might have kissed her before, but not like this, open and honest, bold and gentle. Her body melted into his, and he gathered her even closer, savoring the vanilla sweetness of her lips, their warmth, their softness, and the message they spoke louder and clearer than any words. She did love him, and he did love her, and nothing could keep them apart.

She pulled back, her eyelids low, her lips full and smiling. "We sail well together."

He chuckled and kissed her red nose. "We do. I even promise to let you take the helm sometimes, as long as you wear that spotted blue swimsuit."

"Spotted?" She giggled. "They're called polka dots."

"I don't care what you call them as long as you wear them."

Mary dipped her head, then swept her dark eyelashes, beckoning him. "Once again, too much talking." She kissed him, long and fervent.

So she preferred kissing to talking. Falling in love with a quiet woman had its advantages.

"Found them!" A flash of light illuminated the boat, bright as star shells.

Mary whirled around in his arms, and Jim blinked away the spots in his eyes.

Two men stood on the pier, one with a camera, one with a notepad. For crying out loud. Reporters.

The journalist pointed at Jim with his pen. "So you're the fella who chased down a ferry in a sailboat."

Mary groaned and covered her face with her hand.

A giant protective impulse swelled inside, and he pulled her close under his arm. "Must have been someone else. Now, if you'll excuse us, my girlfriend and I were about to go for a sail."

"Ah, come on, Ensign. We know it was you. Got a great description from folks on the ferry. Dark-haired officer in blues, dame in a red coat. Why, you look like the Fourth of July, you two. Great story."

"It's all right, Jim." Mary gazed up at him. "I don't mind."

How he loved this woman. "You don't have to, sweet-heart."

Mary's face glowed. "People do love a happy ending."

"You admit it?" the reporter said.

Jim sighed in resignation. "That was me, all right."

"Swell. Betcha this will make the front page tomorrow. Roddy, get a shot of these two. Yeah, just like that with his arm around her, with the sail and the harbor in the back-ground."

Mary snuggled close to his side, and Jim embraced her slim shoulders.

The flashbulb popped—once, twice, three times.

"So, Ensign, give us the whole scoop." The reporter poised his pen over his notepad and licked his lips. "Start at the—"

"Roddy! Chuck!" Another man loped down the pier, brac-ing his hat, his black overcoat flying behind him. "Boss is looking for you two. Story of the century! We need every hand."

Chuck's shoulders slumped. "Story of the century. Yeah, I've heard that before. Least once a week."

"No, this is it." The newcomer stopped, rested his hands on his knees, and panted. "This is the big one. The Japa-nese—they bombed our naval base in Hawaii."

Jim went stiff. "Pearl Harbor?"

"Yeah, that's what they called it. Bunch of our ships have been sunk—battleships and cruisers. Hundreds of men killed, maybe thousands. This is it. This is war."

Roddy and Chuck let out the same expletive, then the three newsmen raced down the pier.

Jim's arm clamped around Mary's shoulder, and his mind reeled. Pearl Harbor? How many ships had been sunk? How many of his friends from the Academy had been killed? Injured?

"Oh, Jim." Mary rolled into his arms. "It can't be. It can't be."

He rubbed her slender back, determined to cheer her up. "On the positive side, now your picture won't be on the front page of the *Globe*."

She looked up, her expression saying she couldn't believe he was joking at a time like this, but she appreciated the effort. Then she buried her face in his coat. "We're at war now, aren't we?"

"Ask any man in the Atlantic Fleet. We've been at war for months."

"I know, but now it's official."

Jim gazed over her head at the buildings of the city. "Now maybe the nation will back us up. Maybe we'll be united. Maybe we'll put aside this stupid arguing once and for all."

"I'm sure we will. I've noticed things changing at the Navy Yard—" Her head jerked up, and her eyes grew big. "Oh no. My job."

He grimaced. "Michigan? Is it true?"

She moaned. "Yes, it's true. Oh dear. Now I don't want to leave Boston."

"Any chance Mr. Pennington would take you back?"

One corner of her mouth twitched. "He did say he'd hire me back in a heartbeat."

"Well, my heart's beating that you take him up on the offer."

"I'll talk to him first thing in the morning." She rested her cheek on his shoulder. "I'm glad I planned to purchase my airplane ticket at the airport. Oh, and I'll have to fetch my luggage from the ferry terminal."

"We'll do that. I have a thirty-day survivor's leave, and I want to spend every moment with you."

"Uh-oh." She cringed. "My parents are expecting me home for Christmas."

"Good." Jim kissed her forehead. "I told my parents Arch and I might come home for Christmas, but I didn't want to make any definite plans until I knew how you'd react."

"Do you think you'll still get leave now that we're at war?"

"I'll report in today, but we don't have our new assignments and the Navy is strict about offering survivor's leave."

"A whole month. And then . . ."

And then off to real declared war.

A sense of purpose solidified inside. The Navy would need good line officers who could make wise decisions, balancing the needs of the country, the ship, and the men. He settled a kiss on her nose. "Don't worry. I'm ready."

"I know." Her expression brimmed over with love for who he was and confidence in who he could be. "Don't worry about me either. You have a job to do, and I'll be right beside you."

"Not at sea you won't."

Mary laughed. "In my heart I will be. In my prayers."

"What more could I want?"

She brushed her lips over his chin. "How about a proper good-bye?"

"Only if I also get a proper hello." When she smiled her approval, he said hello, over and over.

Dear Reader,

Thank you for joining Jim and Mary on their journey. I want to assure you that there were no incidents of sabotage at the Boston Navy Yard or on board US warships during the war. However, this story reflects the extreme tension in the United States in 1941. The nation was divided, anger ran high on both sides, mob violence occurred, and fear and rumors ran rampant.

While the USS *Atwood* and the USS *Ettinger* are fictional ships, the situation in the Atlantic in 1941 is accurate, including the incident with the USS *Greer*, the torpedoing of the USS *Kearny*, the sinking of the USS *Reuben James*, and the sinkings of five American merchant ships—all *before* Pearl Harbor. Likewise, the United States occupied Iceland in July of 1941 and began escorting Allied North Atlantic convoys in September. This little-known aspect of American history intrigued me and inspired this novel.

Boston is one of my favorite cities due to the sheer mass of history, the color, and the Boston cream pie. But I had to be careful to use names from the 1940s—thus, the Boston Navy Yard instead of the current Charlestown Navy Yard, the "El" or the "subway" instead of the "T," and even the subway station names. Please don't use this novel as a map, or you'll get lost.

All characters are fictional other than Dr. Harold Ockenga,

pastor of Park Street Church, Rear Adm. William T. Tarrant, commandant of the Boston Navy Yard, and other historical figures.

If you're on Pinterest, please visit my board for *Through Waters Deep* (www.pinterest.com/sarahsundin) to see pictures of Boston, destroyers, and Mary's cute dresses.

Please join me for the second novel in the Waves of Freedom series, when Ens. Arch Vandenberg and pharmacist Lillian Avery find danger from U-boats and black market drug rings—and love!

Acknowledgments

Writing a new series made me alternate between "What*ever* made me think I could write about the Navy, and a mystery at that!" and "How thrilling to do something new!" Often within five minutes of each other.

Therefore, I have many people to thank, starting with my family, who has to listen to all of the above. Deepest thanks to our youngest son, Matthew, who stayed several extra days with me in Boston while I climbed inside 5-inch naval gun mounts, took photos of random doorways in Charlestown, and pored over documents at the National Archives. I felt much safer having a strapping teenager by my side. Thanks to my parents, Ronald and Nancy Stewart, for nautical information, and thanks also to my aunt, Ginny Siggia, who answers my Boston questions.

My brainstorming buddies, Marcy Weydemuller and Cathleen Armstrong, helped me flesh out this story, and I owe special thanks to Marcy for mentoring me on writing mysteries. And thank you to my critique partners, Marcy (once again!), Linda Clare, Judy Gann, Sherry Kyle, Bonnie Leon, and Ann Shorey.

Thank you to my writer friend Jennifer Zarifeh Major, and her botanist husband, John E. Major, for your help with tree identification and information (I told you I'd put you in here!). And thanks to Terry and Liliane Wasmund for alerting me to Battleship Cove, which I would have missed without you.

While researching this novel, I benefitted immensely from touring restored destroyer USS *Cassin Young* (Charlestown Navy Yard, Boston, MA), destroyer USS *Joseph P. Kennedy Jr.* and battleship USS *Massachusetts* (Battleship Cove, Fall River, MA), and battleship USS *Iowa* (Long Beach, CA). And deep thanks to the staff at the National Archives at Boston for the privilege of viewing primary documents and photographs.

Once again, thanks go to my agent, Rachel Kent at Books & Such Literary Management, for her keen insight and calm presence. And to my editor, Vicki Crumpton, for making the edits a fun learning experience. Really, they are! And thanks to Cheryl Van Andel and her team for the most gorgeous book cover ever.

And how I love my reader friends! You make it all worthwhile. Please visit me at www.sarahsundin.com to leave a message, sign up for my quarterly newsletter, or read about the history behind the story. I hope to hear from you.

Discussion Questions

1. Do you know anyone who served in the Navy during World War II? Do you have any stories to share? Have you ever been on board a WWII-era ship? What did you think?

2. Were you surprised at the divisiveness in America in 1941, given how united the nation was after the attack on Pearl Harbor? Do you see any parallels in today's world?

3. The involvement of the United States in the Battle of the Atlantic in 1941 was minor yet significant, given the country's neutrality. What did you find most interesting about this?

4. Mary suffers from a fear of attention. How does this hold her back? How has she sabotaged herself because of it? And how does she learn to overcome? Do you have past or present fears that have held you back? How can—or did—you overcome?

5. Mary tries to reconcile the godly principles of humility and letting your candle shine. How does she do so? Do you find yourself drawn more to the humble extreme or to the shining extreme? How can you find balance?

6. Jim has always floated with the current, and he struggles to be bold when necessary. How does he change throughout the story? Do you tend to be bold or "go with the flow"? Have you learned to temper your natural inclination? Do you want to?

7. What did you think of the various sabotage suspects? Who was highest on your list?

8. Mary loved reading Nancy Drew mysteries as a girl and is thrilled to have her own mystery to solve. Is there anything you've always longed to do because of a book or movie?

9. Both Mary and Jim are deeply affected by childhood events. How did those events shape their characters? Their fears? Why do childhood events seem to have a greater impact on us than similar events later in life?

10. Mary and Quintessa have been friends since childhood. What strengths do you see in their friendship? What weaknesses? How about with Jim and Arch?

11. Agent Sheffield wants the cold hard facts and scoffs at Mary's notebooks at first. Do you think the information she gathered would have been useful? What do you think about the role of intuition versus facts?

12. Jim has always been attracted to a certain type of woman and is surprised when he begins to fall for Mary. Have you ever been surprised by a friendship or romance with someone you never would have imagined?

13. Sailing is symbolic in this story. How do you see this?

14. The second novel in the Waves of Freedom series follows Ens. Arch Vandenberg and Lillian Avery, while the third novel will feature Lt. Dan Avery and Quintessa Beaumont. From what you've seen or heard of these characters, what might you expect?

Sarah Sundin is the author of *With Every Letter*, *On Distant Shores*, *A Distant Melody*, *A Memory Between Us*, and *Blue Skies Tomorrow*. In 2011, *A Memory Between Us* was a finalist in the Inspirational Reader's Choice Awards and Sarah received the Writer of the Year Award at the Mount Hermon Christian Writers Conference. A graduate of UC San Francisco School of Pharmacy, she works on-call as a hospital pharmacist. During WWII, her grandfather served as a pharmacist's mate (medic) in the Navy and her great-uncle flew with the US Eighth Air Force in England. Sarah lives in California with her husband and three children.

Look for Book Two of the

★ WAVES *of* FREEDOM ★

series

★ COMING **SUMMER 2016** ★

GET TO KNOW

SARAH
SUNDIN

★ ★ ★

To Learn More About Sarah,
Read Her Blog, or See
the Inspiration Behind the Stories
Visit

SARAHSUNDIN.COM

"Sarah Sundin seamlessly weaves together emotion, action, and sweet romance."

—*USA Today's* Happy Ever After blog